SWEET LOVE

"What's not to like?"   —*People*

"[A] tender look at lost loves and whether they were ever really lost."   —*Columbus Dispatch*

THE SECRET LIVES OF FORTUNATE WIVES

"[Strohmeyer] uses her observations to sharp comic effect."
                                    —*Boston Globe*

"The mordantly observant Strohmeyer skewers the lifestyles of the rich and fatuous with spot-on irony, painting her pretentious socialites with broad, sarcastic strokes in an uproarious, up-scale, tongue-in-cheek tour de force."   —*Booklist*

DO I KNOW YOU?

ALSO BY SARAH STROHMEYER

DO
I KNOW
YOU?

A NOVEL OF SUSPENSE

SARAH STROHMEYER

HARPER

An Imprint of HarperCollinsPublishers

DO I KNOW YOU? Copyright © 2021 by Sarah Strohmeyer. All rights reserved. Printed in the United States of America. No part of this book may be used or reproduced in any manner whatsoever without written permission except in the case of brief quotations embodied in critical articles and reviews. For information, address HarperCollins Publishers, 195 Broadway, New York, NY 10007.

HarperCollins books may be purchased for educational, business, or sales promotional use. For information, please email the Special Markets Department at SPsales@harpercollins.com.

FIRST EDITION

Designed by Jen Overstreet

Library of Congress Cataloging-in-Publication Data has been applied for.

ISBN 978-0-06-309129-0 (pbk.)
ISBN 978-0-06-314326-5 (library ed.)

21 22 23 24 25   LSC   10 9 8 7 6 5 4 3 2

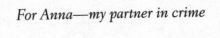

For Anna—my partner in crime

"The face is the mirror of the mind, and eyes without speaking confess the secrets of the heart."

—ST. JEROME (C. 342-347—SEPTEMBER 30, 420)

DO I KNOW YOU?

PROLOGUE

JANE

You don't see me, but I see you.

Two summers ago, you and your husband hurried past me, so absorbed in each other you had no clue I was framing and storing you in my mental database. Anniversary trip? Excellent idea. Marital relationships also need nurturing. Too often we neglect those we love the most.

Not your adorable children, though. Naturally, you dote on them, kneeling to tie their shoes and wipe their little noses, thereby providing me with an unobstructed view of the cherubs. Gotcha! Two more for my catalog, no upgrade required.

They may be six and four now, but I'll be able to recognize them when they're eighteen, twenty, thirty, sixty. (Something facial-recognition software can't do, I might add.) I don't envy you having to fly with them whining from here to Disney World, which would drive me up a wall. Still, you know what they say about parenthood: the minutes go by like years and the years like minutes. Treasure every moment.

Are you taking care of yourself? I'm a little concerned about the dark circles. Even with the new highlights (gorgeous!), you look drained. I suppose Christmas did you in, not to mention your job. Talk about stressful. Remember when you had to fly from Atlanta last spring and there were storms up and down the East Coast? You were as white as a sheet getting off that flight. I don't blame you. Turbulence. Is. The. Worst.

"Where the hell is Delta?" your husband bellows, squinting at the signs above the endless rows of airline counters, as if you'd know. As if you live at the airport. It's sweet how he trusts you.

Do you trust me?

You should.

I am what stands between you touching down in sunny Florida and ending in pieces scattered among floating fuselage. Those scanners? The metal detectors and pat-downs and X-rays you find so annoying? They're all useless. If we had to rely on them, we'd all be cooked. They're simply for show, to keep people like you flying and the stock market booming.

You knew that, right?

Because it's not what you see that'll save you, it's what you don't see.

Me.

Who am I? Well, yesterday, I was a mother like you, in yoga pants and a Red Sox cap, complaining on my cell about the never-ending construction at Logan. A classic. The week before, I was a gambler on my way to Las Vegas. Leather jacket. Tight jeans. Sparkly pink carry-on. That one's good, too.

Today, I am a sales rep waiting for a company car, my dark hair in a neat ponytail at the base of my neck. My makeup is a palette of understated natural hues. My suit is navy. One hand rests on the handle of my luggage that happens to be completely empty. The other flips through a phone that is not a phone.

If you notice me at all, you might feel pity for a pretty young woman traveling alone. No boyfriend. No husband. No children. How sad.

Don't be sad. Be grateful. Be glad that instead of cashing in on my unique talents by surveilling for a ruthless private military firm, I spend my days and nights roaming the bowels of Logan, identifying suspects merely by the shapes of their heads, collaring potential terrorists based on nothing more than a glimpse of their eyes.

Thanks to me, they don't even get a chance to fake their way through Security. I will alert my point person in the TSA, who will send an undercover agent to tap our unwanted traveler on the shoulder, politely directing him, or her, to what might seem like an expedited security check, but which will in actuality be a gateway to their final departure. Their DNA will be tested and matched, validating my identification. Because I retain ninety percent of the faces I see, not because I choose to, but because I have no choice.

After what I've seen, you would not want to be me.

ONE

JANE

"What're you getting Erik for Christmas?" Renee asks in my earpiece as I cut the interminable line at Customs, two passengers behind my target, a white supremacist nicknamed Radix.

Last week on BitChute, Radix transmitted a coded call to arms urging his followers to cause national havoc by "disrupting" air travel, whatever that meant. Clearly, he didn't blow up the plane that brought him here, but that doesn't mean he's given up. He remains in the midst of a very crowded airport packed with holiday travelers. Lots of potential for mayhem and death.

I flick a thumb to the US Customs and Border Protection agent monitoring camera #9. "A turkey."

"Doesn't sound like much of a present."

"Not just any turkey. It weighs twenty pounds and it's covered with a mat of woven, hickory-smoked bacon and filled with a sriracha-infused chestnut stuffing. I mail-ordered it from a gourmet restaurant in Kentucky and it drained my bank account. Erik and I are gonna be living on ramen for weeks."

She bursts out laughing. "That's if you don't end up in the ER. Hope it comes with a defibrillator."

"I think that's complimentary."

"By the way, your target is in the gray sweatshirt with the eagle. He's got his phone out and appears to be communicating. Might want to make your move."

I listen to Renee, who's an actual detective, holed up in a back office surveying passenger data on her computer. As a natural super recognizer with added training in forensic facial analysis, I'm a grunt in comparison. Any information I gather is likely to be struck down in a court of law as too subjective. Instead, my job is to avert an immediate disaster by identifying passengers I recognize as disguised high-value threats so they can be detained and questioned before entering the United States, or—if I'm working with the TSA on the domestic side—an outward-bound plane.

"Gotcha." Turning off the mic to save Renee's hearing, I yell in an exaggerated Boston accent, "Excuse me! This is my spot. I went to the ladies' and now I'm back so move!"

An older woman in front of my target purses her lips in disapproval. I know what she's thinking. My generation has no concept of decorum. We are *sooo* rude because of cell phones. Little does she know that her life might hang in the balance depending on what the guy next to her has up his sleeve—literally.

Unfortunately, the target is bobbing his head to a silent beat streaming from his AirPods, oblivious to my caterwauling.

"What are you looking at?" I bark at the poor woman. "How about getting off my case and minding your own damn business!" I punctuate this with an extended middle finger.

My flailing catches his attention. He turns and I get a clearer shot of his features, noting, with irony, that he happens to possess a disarmingly pink baby face with pinchable cheeks. And while he could be Radix's younger brother, he is not the infamous white supremacist attempting to pass himself off as another college student heading home for Christmas break. He simply *is* another college student heading home for Christmas break.

"Learn some respect," the woman hisses.

"I'm so sorry," I reply, because I am. Sort of.

Wheeling my bag out of line with apologies to the people behind me, I head for my usual post by the restroom. "That's an all clear on 15," I tell the CBP agent at Counter 5, where College Boy will be directed.

"Delta 405 from Paris," the CBP agent returns. "Alert on number 27 with the green backpack. Originated at BGW connected through CDG." Originating in Baghdad, the airport ranked number one on the Global Terrorism Index, is the kiss of death.

Who would leave Paris for Boston the week before Christmas? People smuggling in cheese, wine, and jewelry, that's who. Bless 'em. I pull out my iPad—just another sales rep checking the next day's calendar—and call up the twenty cameras zooming in on the maze of stanchions as the rear doors open and the passengers of Flight 405 trudge out. They look none too pleased to have to wait in these holiday lines. It's a long flight and they want to get out of the airport and home to sleep off the jet lag. Gosh, it's almost ten their time and a lot of them probably had connecting flights, like our number 27.

First class is, of course, first. Easy and familiar. While I wait for 27, I watch the parade entering ahead of him. There's the couple who fly to Paris monthly and then there's the businessman with the mole on his cheek. Haven't seen him in a while. (I bet she ended the affair.) Whoa, there's that supermodel who was on the cover of *Vogue* a while back. Man, she's tall. They head straight to Global Entry and the fast pass to freedom. No tedious questions for them.

In what is bound to be a futile effort, I conduct a quick sweep for Kit, checking each passenger for any one of the trifecta of quirks that can't be surgically altered—her swanlike neck, the unconscious hair flicking, the way she favors her left leg, the one she broke at sixteen. No match. As always, I feel a fresh pang of disappointment. I don't know why I put myself through this torture.

Because she might be out there somewhere, an inner voice whispers. Right. I take a deep breath and refocus on my duties. There will be another flight, another group of passengers, another remote possibility. I must never lose hope.

Now comes economy class. Families. Grandparents. Students. I enlarge number 27, my backpacked target from Iraq, and clear him right away. He's some sort of environmentalist, if I'm not mistaken. He was in a group from MIT on their way to the Arctic last spring.

"AC on 27," I tell CBP.

"You sure? He seems kind of sketchy."

I have to resist the temptation to inform CBP for the umpteenth time that just because a man has a beard and dark hair and dark skin and comes from the Middle East does not mean he has come to this country to detonate a car bomb during rush hour on Storrow Drive. "He's a scientist. Recently returned from an expedition in the Arctic to protect endangered ring seals or something."

"If you say so. He also visited Iran last year. Never heard of seals in a desert."

There are no deserts in Iran, a piece of geographic trivia that's not worth explaining to this numb nut. I sigh and text him all clear on Delta 405.

Five minutes later, the rear doors open again and passengers from JetBlue 924 enter, most of them in short-sleeved Hawaiian shirts, shorts, and sandals because it's eighty degrees in the Dominican Republic. Wait until they get outside and find the skies are raining ice water.

They dutifully weave through the maze. Only half of these faces are familiar to me. Many of them belong to children whom I haven't catalogued before. Even so, I have to study each one, hitting pause on my iPad, expanding, resuming play, and working down the line.

Wonder why Customs takes so long? This is why.

"How come you're working that side today, anyway?" Renee asks in my earpiece. "Don't tell me DHS understaffed the holiday rotation again. Honestly, they've got to get their shit together, budget cuts or no."

"Who knows?" I flick the screen and text CBP: All clear on 924. There are four hours left in my shift and I'm already counting the minutes until I can hop the Blue Line to the Orange Line and then hike the eleven blocks from the Sullivan Square stop to the top floor of our East Somerville triple-decker to feast on congealed leftovers from last night's Chinese takeout.

"Intel reports there's a Level 5 incoming from Bogotá," Renee says. "All I get from CBP is it's a potential high-security risk. No further details."

"That's helpful." I still have no idea if the Level 5 is a VIP or a drug lord. CBP can be sloppy that way. "Anything else?"

"Lemme check the manifest and see if I can find out more," Renee replies.

I can hear her artificial nails clicking on the keyboard. She lets out a whistle. "Definitely a VIP. I don't know why he didn't fly private, especially if there's a security concern. Not like he can't afford it."

"Politician?" I ask, standing on my tiptoes for a clearer view.

"More like a pretty-boy trust funder whose daddy made a fortune investing his millions as a hedge-fund manager into his wife's influencer empire. He is super cute, though, so maybe there's something to be said for the coffee enemas they're pushing on everyone."

"*Eww!*" Relaxing slightly, I slide onto a plastic seat and kick off my flats, grateful for the break for my feet. "Can't wait to see this Adonis."

"Yeah. He's definitely gorgeous."

"Copa 311 from BOG incoming," CBP interrupts. "This is our Level 5."

So much for the respite. Hopping up, I flex my knees, making a mental note to buy new insoles. "I don't know, Renee, sometimes I wonder what I'm doing here. It's not like I've ever helped catch a terrorist."

"You don't know that. Even *I* don't know that. We just have to do our jobs to the best of our abilities and hope our colleagues do likewise. Besides, you're getting a decent salary, nice bennies. Those are key until Erik lands a full-time job."

"*If* he gets a job."

When it comes to academic openings for MD/PhDs in psychiatry who want to do research instead of actually analyzing people, you'd have better luck winning Megabucks. And even if Erik did land one of these plum positions, research pay would barely cover his student loan debt. I just wish he'd join a practice and rake in the money shrinking depressed Back Bay socialites. But, no, he says that's not why he invested seven years in grad school. Meanwhile, here I am, keeping us both afloat by making sure bazillionaires like our VIP don't get harassed while dirtying themselves among the masses.

Speaking of which, the rear doors open and first class from Copa 311 enters. I call up the cameras on my iPad, flicking through the faces: a pair of doctors who fly to Colombia quite frequently. A few men in golf shirts and a handful of small businessmen who are not themselves particularly small. A beautiful couple straight from the pages of *Town & Country*. Two hikers in muddy boots.

Hold on. I go back to the power couple, numbers 6 and 7. These must be my VIPs. I zoom in on the trust funder Renee's so gaga about. He is definitely model material. Expensive haircut close on the sides, full on top, with natural sun-kissed highlighting. Square jaw peppered with stubble. Thirtyish, rich, confident, and . . .

. . . *disturbingly familiar.*

I'm supposed to be scrutinizing those around him for his safeguarding. But I can't stop staring. I'm riveted.

"What's the ID on our VIP?" I ask Renee, though I already know the answer.

"William Pease. Family owns Love & Pease lifestyle empire. Hot, right?"

Didn't you break up with him right before you went missing, Kit?
"I know this guy."

"You know everyone. It's your job."

"This has nothing to do with my job."

I close my eyes and let the memories rush in of warm summer evenings when Kit would sneak home past curfew, her blond hair slightly disheveled, her neck flushed with excitement. "We're just having fun," she'd said, perched at the end of my twin bed, jiggling her tanned bare foot. "I'm not like the others who go crazy for him. Some of those girls are psycho."

A week later, she'd be gone. My only sister, vanished from a deserted Cape Cod beach on a moonless night, leaving me with nothing but questions. The first one being, who was that girl with her when she disappeared?

I suddenly focus on Will Pease's female companion in the winter-white belted coat. She is slim with long black hair and cherry-red lips, her skin as pale as Snow White's. She barely resembles the frightened teenager who ordered me to run, hide, and never tell anyone what I saw.

It's her, I think, dizzy. *Can it be?*

"Who's number 7?" I ask Renee, shakily.

"Um. She's down as Isabella Valencia. Hey, you okay? You don't sound too good."

Isabella flashes a smile at Will and pivots on her heels. At that moment her dark eyes meet mine and we freeze. All movement around us slows. Distance and time cease to exist. For what could be seconds or hours, we explode in a silent burst of recognition.

You!

Then she swiftly gathers herself and matches her steps to Will's as they head toward Global Entry and out of my life. I want to shout, but I can't. My arms are heavier than concrete, my legs leaden, and when I open my mouth, I am mute.

Don't let her get away! my conscience cries. *Do something!*

"Stop 6 and 7!" I holler to CBP. "Fast!"

"What?" he replies.

"Numbers 6 and 7. At Global Entry. Detain."

"Are you out of your mind?" Renee says. "They're not the threat, they're the VIPs."

My fingers tremble as I enlarge Isabella Valencia on my iPad, assessing her image from all sides. The pointed chin. The heart-shaped face. The long, aquiline nose. Check. Check. Check. I have never been so certain of a hit in my entire career.

Slipping the iPad in the interior pocket of my blazer, I speed-walk toward the front counters, not caring that I'm blowing my cover.

"Agent Ellison . . . Jane!" Renee cries into my earpiece. "You are way out of bounds."

"Number 7 is a 1073. She needs to be detained ASAP."

"You've made a mistake. I told you, she's with the VIP."

"She's wanted for felony murder."

"Where are you getting that? It's not in my . . ."

I've stopped listening to Renee. My heart is thudding hard against my chest, pumping out adrenaline. I am an animal. I want to run and pounce, attack and capture.

Oh, no. You're not slipping from my fingers this time.

I am almost at Global Entry. CBP has pulled Will and Isabella aside. Will is angry, gesturing madly as CBP opens a side door and ushers both of them into the interrogation room before the scene gets any more chaotic. I'm not sure if he's sequestering them for their privacy or their safety, because Renee is right.

I *am* out of my mind.

"Stand down!" A massive hand materializes inches from my nose. It belongs to Kurt, a CBP officer, who has struck the pose, legs spread, right hand on his holster. He's treating me like a threat.

"Number 7 is a fugitive from justice," I blurt.

Kurt doesn't budge and I can't get around him.

"CBP claims she's the executive director of the Pease Foundation in Bogotá," Renee informs me. "Will Pease says she's his fiancée. Doesn't seem like the dossier of a criminal."

My gut cramps. "Can't we at least do a DNA test on her before she's released?" The blood sample from Kit's T-shirt. It could be a match.

"Unlikely. CBP says Pease is threatening to call the head of

DHS and, considering his family's profile, that's a very real possibility. He's going to have all our jobs unless you can come up with some solid evidence in the next thirty seconds of why you're accusing a fucking international aid worker engaged to a celebrity multimillionaire of being a 1073."

Of course, I can't. I have nothing—but nothing to lose.

"That woman murdered my sister!" I yell at the top of my lungs, a last-ditch attempt to catch her attention, to force Isabella Valencia to explain what happened eleven years ago.

In a flash, CBP officers flank me on either side, hoist me by the arms, and drag me toward Security, my flats slipping on the linoleum, just as the unmarked, solid, gray metal door to the interrogation area opens. An officer gushing apologies escorts Will and Isabella out of the room, past Global Entry, and down the hall.

She does not grace me with a parting look, though Will does. He flashes me a thin, triumphant smile before leading away the only person in the world who knows the truth of what happened to my sister.

TWO

EVE

"Meg, sweetie, after we're done, how about we order some lemon rasam and mushroom crepes from the café." Eve Pease rubs her sore triceps, the reward of extending this morning's *Chaturanga Dandasana* an extra two minutes. "This low-pressure system has totally blocked my energy."

Blocked energy is the culprit behind ninety-nine percent of all problems, from acne and neck creeping to poverty and climate change, in Eve's theory of the world. If people would just adopt a clean Ayurvedic diet based on their own *doshas*, everyone's skin would radiate from their inner calm. She is forever preaching her regimen's anti-aging benefits on her personal lifestyle site, The Eve of Love & Pease, and its linked social media accounts. Yet, even the most ardent of her 7.4 million followers continue to sabotage their physical and spiritual progress by falling off the wagon to gorge themselves at a poison palace like Bob Evans.

Bob Evans! What made her think of that?

Evelyn Lushbaugh Pease may have left Paragon, Indiana, way back in high school, but the Midwest has never left her. On a miserable day like this, when the icy December sleet is pelting the mullioned windows of her Weston, Massachusetts, estate, she craves her childhood comforts of salt and fat. Lots of fat. She would give anything for a bowl of thick cheddar potato soup with bacon bits, a plate of chicken fried steak with buttermilk biscuits, and a chaser of coffee with two creams.

Alas, a fermented turmeric and ginger tea will have to do.

"Let's shoot you with this." Megan, her daughter and assistant, places the saucer and cup of tea on the hand-tooled maple table where Eve's legs are propped while she steals a minute of downtime. "There." Megan stands back, assessing the tableau. "I don't know why, but odd numbers are so pleasing. Hang in there, Mom. We're almost done."

They've run themselves ragged shooting an Instagram video for the Love & Pease "Pause & Reflect" holiday campaign. It takes so much more effort than people realize to appear down-to-earth while wearing a $479 puff-sleeved, champagne-silk Henley top with Italian wide-legged wool trousers. For Eve, it requires heaps of quiet meditation on self-denial, like, for example, not being able to stuff your face with biscuits.

She takes a sip and, indeed, the tea is soothing, if not satisfying. "I wish we were visiting Queenie at her new apartment in Malibu. I can't take much more of this dreariness."

Eve never would have settled in a stuffy New England town if not for her late husband and his Boston-based financial services firm. But now that Chet's gone—God rest his soul—she dreams about trading the ten-thousand-square-foot brick Georgian mansion for a modern house half the size on a hilltop overlooking Zuma Beach. She can't sell Heron's Neck, the Cape Cod home, because she doesn't own it outright; Chet's three adult offspring were also bequeathed that gem and they are deeply attached to that private island. Plus, it's the ideal setting to show off her Love & Pease summer collections.

"Malibu is not Christmassy." Megan positions a whiteboard to reduce shadows from the brass-and-agate wall mirror on the gray wall. "People want traditional around the holidays. Horse-drawn carriages and sugar cookies and snow."

"What snow?"

"Don't complain. You look lovely in this setting."

Megan always says the perfect thing. She's a natural mother that way, Eve decides, studying her daughter in the golden glow from the antique iron Tuscan chandelier, which unfortunately exaggerates the baby fat under her soft chin. She is twenty-two, the result of a fling between Eve and a flash-in-the-pan musician who went by the name Jonny Walker Blak. Lord knows where he is these days, a DJ in some Swedish disco probably, or pumping gas in Jersey.

If only Megan would knuckle down on her core workouts and skip those decadent coffees and chocolate croissants, she would be stunning. Eve is sure that with a few minor lifestyle changes, her daughter would be worthy of gracing a Love & Pease online catalog. Instead, she's been relegated to working behind the scenes.

That's where Jake's been such a stinker. While her stepson has never said in so many words that Megan is not *on brand* for the Pease image, he has implied as much through the most devious form of rejection—obsequious flattery. *Meg is a genius at staging. Style? Lighting? Patterns? A natural. A rare talent. She'd be wasted in front of the camera! We can't afford to lose her there.*

"So?" Megan prompts, not looking up from her iPhone, her thumbs tapping away rapidly. "Ready to shoot?"

"I'm not sure about this." Eve frowns at the steaming Danish mug. "Tea's a bit too Canyon Ranch, don't you think?" Marketing has shown that the secret of Eve's success as an influencer is her artful melding of wellness with decadence, and this is a classic example. "Let's do our signature martini with small-batch Vermont gin and those Spanish Gordal olives stuffed with organic lemon peel. They haven't been moving like Jake anticipated. They could use a boost."

"We've done martinis to death," Megan says with a sigh, then lowers her phone and pushes her trendy tortoise-shell glasses back onto the bridge of her nose. "We could do hot herbal *Glühwein* in the vintage Meissen."

"No, it's been done." Eve taps her front teeth, thinking, thinking, thinking. And then it hits her. "The Virgin Vessels."

"Oh, my god, yes!" Megan says. "We have so many of those. We were going to mark them down after New Year's just to clear them out of inventory." In minutes, she's returned with a white enamel flask, plain aside from the interlocked silver Vs printed on one side.

After setting the scene, Megan returns to her position on the opposite side of the table and adjusts the camera on the tripod to catch the thin winter light streaming through the side window. In it, Eve could pass for a woman half her real age (forty-seven).

"Let's open with you sniffing that sprig of rosemary," Megan suggests. "Deep in thought, happy and tranquil. The presents are wrapped. The tree is decorated. The table set. Guests are about to arrive and you're taking a moment to . . . reflect."

Eve doesn't argue, snapping the rosemary from the table's centerpiece of eucalyptus, holly, and white roses. She knows better than to question the girl's judgment.

Megan has been taking candid videos of Eve ever since she was old enough to work a phone camera, about age twelve. Early on, she displayed proficiency for catching her mother performing ordinary tasks as the newest Mrs. Pease: stirring canned soup on the massive burners of her La Cornue range, applying a second coat of mascara at her vanity, and, later, celebrating the sunset with headstands on a back deck at Heron's Neck.

Proud of her child's sharp eye, Eve posted these shaky, grainy shots on YouTube, hoping an influencer would declare Megan a prodigy and suggest a collaboration. When none came forward, Eve decided to become an influencer herself because why not? She was used to risks. She excelled at them.

Eve has always been determined to spare her daughter the treacherous path she'd been forced to trod, clawing her way out of central Indiana by humiliating herself on local TV commercials and then submitting headshots and résumés to blasé casting directors in New York who rarely called her back. The process was so dispiriting she almost gave in to her parents' pleas to return home.

If not for a fluke snowstorm that stranded a dispensable actress, Eve never would have landed a bit role on a soap opera, never would have met and befriended the soap's star, Queenie Jarvis, and, better yet, Queenie's financier husband, Harrington. Harrington, even better, better yet, was a close friend of one Chet Pease, newly divorced with an AWOL ex-wife and three rowdy teenagers in dire need of supervision. Had the skies that day been merely cloudy, chances are that right now she'd be cutting out Christmas cookies in a modular split-level back in Paragon.

"*Love* the daydreaming gaze." Megan zooms in on her mother. "That's it . . . go!"

Eve touches the sprig to her nose and inhales deeply, sighing with satisfaction as she swivels to the lens. "Shhh! Can you hear?" Her glossed lips form the conspiratorial smile that has sold a million tubes of Pease Puckers. She cocks her head to indicate there is no noise, aside from the fire crackling in the grate of the room's marble fireplace. "Silence . . . time for us. You know who you are, the holiday magic makers."

In under a minute, Eve urges her devotees to remember to carve out moments for themselves during this hectic season. "Breathe. Be still. Hold yourself precious so you can hold those precious to you. And should the kids break an ornament and your mother-in-law quip that parental discipline is a lost art, there's always this." From nowhere, Eve holds up the Virgin Vessel flask and unscrews the top, delivering a generous pour into the mug. "You have my permission." With a wink, she takes a sip. "Because the holidays can be—"

"Shit!"

Eve blinks. "Geez. Really?"

Megan taps on her phone. "No. Sorry. It's a text from Will. He's been detained at Customs."

Eve warily sets down the flask. Will is adorable, but he definitely has his father's reckless streak. It'd be just like him to smuggle in a few illicit Colombian hug drugs, if only for the challenge.

Will is Chet's youngest son, whom the Fates blessed with his father's strong brow, his mother's Byronian wavy hair, and a gaze of captivating intensity. Family friend Ralph Lauren once begged him to model, though she and Chet nipped that in the bud, her being all too familiar with the cocaine- and Adderall-saturated atmosphere of the fashion industry. Will has never been the type to resist temptation—in any form.

Now that he's survived his treacherous twenties and is well on the way to becoming the mature, though still hip, online image of Love & Pease, Will definitely can't afford a scandal so déclassé as drug running. The men who plunk down $95 for 1.7 fluid ounces of PeasePower face cream are not aspiring to be aging addled frat boys.

Eve grips the underside of the table. "What did he do now?"

"He's saying it's no big deal." However, the girl's body is practically vibrating as she texts her stepbrother. "A simple misunderstanding."

"Let's hope." Relieved not to be dragged into whatever mess Will's gotten himself into this time, Eve sips the tea, now lukewarm, and drums her fingers on the crafted table. They need to get back to the shoot.

"He says he has a big surprise and he's reached out to Jake and Dani to make sure they're around when he gets here. ETA is six thirty." Megan abruptly looks up, her cheeks flushed pink as her mouth forms a silent O.

"What?" Eve asks, now on alert.

"Mom. He says he's stopping off on Newbury Street to pick up *an order from Cynthia Britt's.*"

A gasp catches in Eve's throat. There's only one thing a man like Will Pease would order from Cynthia Britt's jewelry store. Only one *very, very* special thing.

"Get the fuck out!" Eve leaps out of her chair and toward her daughter. "Oh, baby!"

Megan drops her phone with a clunk and begins to cry. Eve snaps up a napkin from beneath three shining forks and uses it to dab away the dark rivulets of mascara dripping down the girl's cheeks. "Sweetie, don't. You'll puff up."

Ice water, that's what they need, and lots of it, followed by a Love & Pease Totally Cool eye mask. And if that doesn't do the trick, Preparation H. "Come on. Go and take a therapeutic shower." She gives Megan a slight shove toward the stairs. "Use the exfoliating brush, too, and borrow my black slouchy turtleneck, the Yang. Casual but sexy. I'll call Yvonne for an emergency blow-out. Hurry!"

Giddy, Megan does as her mother instructs, lashes damp with joyful tears, while Eve grabs her own cell and, taking a deep, empowering breath, calls her stepson, Jake.

Jake has been dead set against Megan dating his brother Will ever since he caught them in bed last summer. He was horrified, and started going off on how their relationship basically amounted to incest, though it was no such thing, not at all. As CFO of the family company, he demanded Will "earn back his dignity" by working for the Pease Foundation in Colombia, Chet's pet project, which he founded with his former wife, Madeleine, after they adopted Bella.

Despite Megan's protests, Will complied with his domineering brother's command, angrily flying to Bogotá the next day to join his drip of an adopted sister, now all grown up and smug. That girl's so earnest she might as well be a nun, lurking on the sidelines of Eve's parties with her arms folded and lips pinched in disapproval at the elegant canapés passing by on silver trays. Eve doesn't have to be a mind reader to know that Bella silently judges her for throwing a dinner party that costs more than what the foundation would pay to feed ten orphans for a year. As if she should be serving friends and business associates thin gruel instead of organic duck breast with fresh Japanese yuzu.

Anyway, who cares? That proverbial water is under the proverbial bridge. Will's served his sentence at the foundation and paid his penance. Now, he's back to claim Megan with a fabulous ring and Jake will simply have to suck it up.

This will be the wedding of the century. Eve is already envisioning the months and months of buildup on the Pease website. Glowing Megan in soft lighting, flowers in her hair, her gauzy dress billowing in a summer breeze against a backdrop of luscious, luxurious, irresistible product. There'll be dress designers to promote and chefs and florists and tchotchkes galore!

"Eve?" Jake answers on the first ring.

"I have huge news," she blurts. "Will's back from Colombia and he—"

"I heard. This is a crisis. A fucking crisis!"

She flinches. Surely, he still can't be that furious at his brother, not after all these months. "I hardly think . . ."

"Just got off the phone with Dani. She's pissed, too. She's headed over to your house. If you have plans, cancel them. We need a family meeting. This needs to be nipped in the bud ASAP."

It crosses Eve's mind that Jake might attempt to intercept Will to prevent him from popping the question. That cannot happen. It would totally destroy Megan, and the pain of watching your baby's heart break in real time is too much to bear for any mother, to say nothing of a self-sacrificing mother like her.

"They're adults, Jake. You can't tell them what to do . . ."

"I don't give a shit what you think, frankly." Jake inhales and exhales, fuming audibly. "Arthur's on the other line and brainstorming about how we can get Will out of this without too much damage to the family. Meanwhile, please keep your mouth shut. Don't go blabbing to your seven million lemmings. This crisis needs to stay private."

He clicks off and Eve stands there, shaking.

From those early dark days, after Jonny Blak made it clear he would not contribute financially to his daughter's upbringing, Eve feels she has been constantly fighting some man to secure her daughter's welfare, including a dead husband when Chet's will revealed he'd cut out Megan entirely. Every morning she awakes prepared to go toe-to-toe with another male, whether that's Jake or the family lawyer Arthur Whitaker, or, once, a nosy cop whose investigation into her family threatened to unravel the entire Pease dynasty.

Now, with Will's proposal, all her hard work finally is paying off. Megan will be formally brought into the Pease fold with all the appurtenances, privileges, and wealth afforded by a legal marriage. This is nonnegotiable.

So, no. Eve will not stand by to watch Jake lay waste to her creation. She will do as she has done in the past to guarantee Megan rises to the top—which is to say, whatever it takes.

THREE

EVE

Less than an hour later, calmed by a sauna with mugwort steam and a medicinal elderberry martini, Eve decides she'll deactivate Jake's negative energy by holding the family powwow in her sacred space, a skylit room she uses for meditation due to its healing sunlight and ghostly inspiration.

Back in the 1920s, this brick-walled retreat was a studio for artists who painted and smoked and made lazy, passionate love underneath its eleven-foot beamed ceiling. Eve still senses their creative ectoplasm electrifying her neural pathways when she comes here, perhaps even inspiring quirky inventions of hers like the wildly popular Pease Yourself® sex toys.

Tonight, she hopes lightning will strike twice. Having set about several Pease Breathe In/Breathe Out/Repeat® scented candles ($72 a pop) in Mowed Himalayan Hay, Goddess Taleju Sandalwood, and Pendleton Lavender, she assumes the tree pose, resting the instep of her left foot above her right knee, hands brought together in prayer as she meditates on how to break through her stepson's thick skull.

What does Jake prioritize more than his family's reputation? Even more than upholding the impeccable Pease name, she knows, Jake relishes the prospect of one day controlling the entire Pease empire with Eve's support and, it goes without saying, her valuable shares.

Eve's totally on board with this. Before this disagreement, she and Jake shared a clear vision for Love & Pease. Yes, improving the lives of the brand's devotees through high-quality organic products and wellness awareness is all very well and good, but at the end of the day, the reason for their company's existence is the reason for any company's existence: pure profit.

The only one standing in their way of achieving that is Bella.

Bella, whom Chet granted disproportionate shares of Love & Pease in his will, would steer this company off a cliff if given free rein. She repeatedly dismisses Jake's practical proposals for cost-cutting by claiming they're "unethical." Only Miss Bleeding Heart would impoverish her own family by refusing to employ Chinese labor because she pretends to care *sooo* much about some Uighurs she's never even met. Why Chet allotted so much of the company to a young, inexperienced girl who wasn't even his own flesh and blood is something Eve will never understand.

She can only conclude that Chet must have identified in Bella qualities he found wanting in his biological offspring. She was an exceptionally bright child, eager to learn, and, on some level, achingly vulnerable. He often remarked to Eve that he pitied her, which made absolutely no sense. Bella was one of the fortunate ones, thanks to the whims of Chet's first wife.

The idea of adoption never would have occurred to Madeleine Pease if she hadn't watched a documentary about the widespread and appalling murder of children in Bogotáno ghettos by both nongovernmental and governmental entities who considered the atrocious acts to be a form of "social cleansing." She insisted Chet travel with her to the Colombian capital immediately to see how they could help put a stop to the horror.

The results of their admittedly virtuous efforts were two-fold: the Pease Foundation, which consisted of an orphanage and school for young girls impacted by the raging drug war, and a doe-eyed four-year-old named Isabella.

Madeleine was showered with praise for adopting an older child instead of a baby, though behind her back acquaintances questioned her true motives. After all, Jake, Dani, and Will were mostly raised by nannies and then shuttled off to boarding schools while their mother disappeared on shopping excursions and spa vacations at destinations unknown for weeks on end. Some of her cattier girlfriends mocked her for modeling herself after Madonna or Angelina Jolie.

At any rate, the naysayers proved to be at least partly correct. Once the excitement of bringing Bella home dimmed, Madeleine soon grew bored with all aspects of family life and declared herself emancipated from motherhood forever. Last anyone heard, she had relocated to a seven-mile island off Bali, where she keeps company with an elderly energy-drink magnate. At Christmas, she sends the kids a box of prickly pink rambutan as a reminder of her existence.

But this is not the time to muse on the tragedy of Madeleine and Bella. Eve must channel all her energy toward securing the happiness of her own daughter.

She releases a breath and lowers her left foot as she pivots her right foot frontward, spreading her arms and bending until the fingertips of her right hand brush against her right ankle in an expertly executed *Trikonasana*. If she can convince Jake that Will plus Megan plus her creates a unified front in the boardroom, then he might come around. It's not in Bella's nature to fight the five of them; she simply doesn't care that much about the family company or the Love & Pease mission. Perhaps, with time, they can buy her out and Bella can return permanently to Bogotá to pursue her passion, wiping the snotty noses of orphaned waifs.

But how best to pitch this plan to Jake? He'd been so bruised by Chet's practice of ridiculing his business proposals, he takes offense at the slightest hint of being overruled. It will require a soft touch to make him believe it was his idea to give in on Will and Megan and bless their union. She must treat him gently, as pink and soft as the inside of a viper's mouth—especially since he's never been deferential to any woman. He chose as his wife a compliant Catholic girl named Heather with a fondness for black headbands and biennial procreation, whom Eve has never once witnessed standing up to him.

"Hey! You here, Eve?"

Heavy footsteps clomp up the stairs. Before Eve has a chance to ease out of her yoga pose, Dani bursts into the salon, accompanied by a cloud of cold air and burnt *Cannabis sativa*. She has tipped the ends of her bleached-white cropped hair in brilliant purple and she is more emaciated than ever in skin-tight black jeans.

"Don't stop on my account." Chet's oldest child tosses her black leather jacket carelessly on the couch. "It takes for *fucking* ever to get to this place these days with the traffic. I hate coming out here."

Dani's hands are stained with blotches of red and green, indications she's been in one of her manic states, probably painting up a storm in the attic of her architecturally significant Jamaica Plain house she shares with her wife, Cecily. No doubt the two have had another argument.

When Dani is in one of these moods, Eve stays clear.

"Is any of Dad's booze still up here, or did you pour it all down the drain?" She places her hands on her hips and scans the room.

"I think there's some scotch in that cabinet." Eve smooths her fluffy cashmere sweater and gestures half-heartedly to an antique sideboard. She wishes Dani would ease off the toxins. It's not helping her domestic situation. "How's Cecily?"

Kneeling, Dani rustles through the bottles with a disturbing clanking. "She's pissed. I was supposed to attend her school's holiday concert this evening and now I can't. It'll be a whole thing when I get home."

"Oh, I'm sorry." Dani's wife is the principal of an alternative school for gifted children in JP. It seems to Eve as though there've been holiday concerts every weekend. Then again, all those Suzuki violins and, of course, the parents demanding solos. "Don't blame me for making you come out to Weston. Jake called the meeting and he made it sound like you were all in."

"Damn straight." Dani pulls out an old bottle of Glenlivet and squints. "Fifteen years. Not thirty, but it'll have to do." Removing a cut-glass tumbler, she asks, "What's the latest?"

"Megan got a text from Will about him being detained at Logan and broke into tears." Eve doesn't want to ruin her daughter's moment by divulging too many details. "That's all I know."

Dani stops mid-pour and holds the bottle aloft. "Aww. She's such a sweetie, that kid."

Except not so much of a kid. Eve was a new mother when she was Megan's age. She is about to make this point when she hears another set of footsteps thumping up the mahogany stairs and Jake arrives, AirPods in his ears, conducting a conversation with the ether.

"Exactly," he says, sliding down the zipper of his waxed Barbour, his gaze vacant. "No, no. You don't have to. I'll write a draft and then send it to you for a quick vetting. Uh-huh. Uh-huh. Yeah, don't worry. I'll avoid mentioning any legal action. Got it. Not directly. Okay, bye."

He ends the call and, as if just realizing where he is, says, "Sorry about that. Arthur."

"And how is the trusty old legal bulldog?" Dani takes a sip, straight, no ice or water.

"On top of it, per usual. He just got off the phone with his contact at Homeland." Unlike his sister, Jake gently lays his coat on the couch armrest. "He doesn't want us to do anything until Baby Bro gets here." Jake practically steps over Eve in his eagerness to get to the whisky. "Please tell me you didn't drink it all, Pinky."

"Not yet, J.D." Dani pours another glass and hands it to him. "How was the drive from Newton?"

"Hell." He downs it in one swallow. Eve makes a mental note to call the car service to take them home. "So many goddam SUVs clogging up these narrow country roads. They allow anyone out here now. Not like it was when we were growing up."

"You should try it from JP. I could have made it to New York in the time it took me to get here."

It's as though Eve isn't even present. When two or more of Chet's offspring are gathered, she is invisible. They even have a coded language among themselves, referring to each other by childhood nicknames—J.D. and Pinky and, for Will, Baby Bro. No affectionate monikers for her and Megan, however. Or, come to think of it, Bella.

Jake pushes back the sleeves of his gray pullover to reveal toned forearms and goes to the window overlooking the back forty. He has the jet-black hair and piercing blue eyes of his attractive mother, the discipline and nervous energy of his driven father. Tonight, he is even more antsy than usual, shifting his feet, checking his phone every two seconds, sniffing back a postnasal drip. His restlessness is rubbing off on Eve, who finds herself growing anxious, too.

"Your brother will be here soon, I'm sure," she says, wishing Jake would chill like Dani, who has her feet up on a divan and eyes closed, pinching her brow, sinking into her marijuana high. Okay, well maybe not exactly like Dani.

"It's so hot up here," he says, pulling off the sweater, exposing a maroon Amherst College T-shirt. "It's like we're in a yoga studio."

"Because it *is* a yoga studio," Dani says, and sits up. "Now, walk me through what actually happened. What's the big surprise, and what does it have to do with Baby Bro getting detained at Customs?"

"Jake, can I make a simple request before Will gets here?" Eve says. "Before you fly off the handle, please consider the positives."

A burst of laughter explodes from the other end of the room, and Dani brings a hand to her mouth, trying to stifle it. "What could possibly be the upside of being trapped in the seventh circle of hell otherwise known as Logan?"

"Shh! Keep your voice down!" Eve puts her finger to her lips. Megan is one room below them prepping for her big Cinderella moment and Eve will *not* have it ruined by a wicked stepsister. "Have you two even stopped to consider Will's feelings? Obviously, he's old enough to know his own mind."

Jake furrows his brow, as if she's just spoken gibberish. "Will's *feelings* have nothing to do with anything. I'm sorry, Eve, but this really doesn't involve you."

"It sure as hell does! This involves my—"

"Um, excuse me, but you still haven't filled in the blanks and we're running out of time." Dani taps her Apple watch.

Gently nudging Eve aside, Jake joins his sister on the divan. "Here's the deal. Will's going through Fast Pass at Customs when he hears someone screaming. There's a Homeland Security agent, some batshit woman, aiming her finger at Bella and calling her a murderer."

"Bella?" Eve says, the corner of her vision tunneling.

"Murderer?" Dani leaps to her feet, helping herself to more of the scotch. "Get out!"

"According to Arthur, the agent apparently suffered some sort of psychotic breakdown on the job. Turns out, this woman's sister was murdered or disappeared or whatever eleven years ago at the townie park across from Heron's Neck, and for some reason at that moment she starts hallucinating that Bella was the one who killed her."

A fog has descended over Eve. *Why would Bella be in the airport at the same time as Will?*

"Oh, man. That is so bizarre." Dani sits and swings her legs over the divan. "What happened to the agent?"

"If Arthur has his way, she'll never wear a badge again." Jake checks his phone. "What's taking them so long?"

Them? Eve scratches her neck under the suddenly itchy sweater. Jake's right. It is overly warm.

"You talk to Baby Bro?" Dani asks.

"Only briefly. He was pretty shook up."

"No doubt. I remember that missing waitress." Dani brings the glass to her lips and hesitates for a moment. "Hard to forget."

"Geesh. I don't remember that at all." Jake presses on his phone, thumbing in the password.

"You would if you saw a photo of her. She was kind of a stringy blonde. Pretty in a Kate Moss, heroinish kind of way. Used to hang out with Will. They might even have had a thing."

Jake doesn't look up from scrolling. "Nope. Not at all."

"Oh, come on. Yes, you do. She was all over Heron's Neck that summer, either with Will or working for one of Eve's caterers."

"Serena," Eve whispers, rousing from her reverie. "She still works for me sometimes."

"That's it," Dani says. "And didn't the girl actually work a party for you the night she went missing?"

Eve nods, feeling her head start to pound.

"No shit," Jake says, though his voice is a monotone as he remains transfixed by the screen. "How did I miss that?"

Dani rolls her eyes. "Because you see only those of your own class, J.D. The servants are out of sight."

Jake chuckles softly. "Oh, and I suppose you're one with the people?"

"At least I make half an effort."

Eve stiffens, memories of that disturbing night unrolling like a carpet. Bella frantically knocking on their door. Chet getting out of bed despite her urging him to stay. His absence stretching on for what felt like hours . . .

"Eve?"

She blinks back to reality to see Dani and Jake staring at her intently. "Hmm?"

"The name of the waitress who went missing," Dani prods. "It's on the tip of my tongue."

Eve recalls the willowy sprite, a delicate creature too ethereal for this plane of existence. As she'd warned Megan over and over, evil preys on girls who are careless. That's what happened to Kit Ellison.

"It was so long ago. I can't—" No. An outright denial is too obvious. "I think it was . . . Kate."

"*Kit*. Kit Ellison!" Dani snaps her fingers. "See? The kush hasn't fried my last brain cells after all."

Jake shrugs. "Still doesn't ring a bell. Maybe that was the summer I interned at Lazard."

"Nuh-uh. That was the summer after," Dani says. "You were definitely on Heron's Neck. You and Will had a competition going. Who could get laid the most."

At this, he finally drags his eyes away from the phone screen. "Obviously, I won. Not even a fair fight."

"Yeah, right."

Dani and Jake are so fixated on ribbing each other, they have failed to notice how Eve has balled into herself, ruminating. Wasn't Bella staying in Colombia for Christmas? Will said as much last week when they were finalizing holiday plans. Eve was certain he mentioned something about how she loved celebrating the holiday with the orphans, Three Kings Day or whatever. At any rate, nothing should detract from Megan. This is her moment to shine.

"Why is Bella coming home?" Eve pipes up.

Jake stops chattering and exchanges a guilty look with his sister, then says, "It was supposed to be a surprise."

The surprise? Hopefully, no, though the hairs on Eve's arms rise, a classic portent of doom. She deep-breathes and banishes all negative energy.

"I'll be pumped to see her," Dani says as she helps herself to the last of the bottle. "From what Will's been saying, she's been doing super-cool stuff down there. Lots of community outreach, connecting girls to local artists, holding showings of their work."

Jake is glued to his phone again, responding with a brief snort.

"Has it been three years since she's been in the States? At least since Dad's funeral."

"I'm pretty sure you mean the reading of Dad's will. She made sure not to miss that."

Dani wags a finger. "Now, now. Don't be bitter, J.D. You ended up just fine."

"It was a slap in the face to you, me, and Will and you know it. If Bella weren't such a saint, I'd hate her guts."

"But you don't because you can't." Dani rubs his shoulder playfully. "Look, I'm sorry I even mentioned Dad. Let it go for Will's sake, okay?"

"Wait!" Eve interrupts with a sudden thought. "Did Will mention anything to you about a ring?"

A flush rises up Jake's neck and for the first time in all the years Eve's known him, he gives her a sheepish smile. "Nah, I can't go there. He'd kill me."

Aha! Eve wants to shout. "Then it's true?"

"Can't say. I've been sworn to secrecy."

"I think I hear a car," Dani exclaims, getting off the couch.

"Helloooo!" Will's deep voice echoes from the foyer. "Come on down, everybody. We're home!"

Dani and Jake rush to the stairs, and Eve jumps up, too, not caring that she knocks over the lit Pendleton Lavender candle as she dashes out of the room or that she nearly breaks her neck on the polished mahogany stairs.

"Will!" Megan cries, her heels clicking across the slate hallway as she goes to greet her Prince Charming. She is photo ready, from her volumized hair, mink lashes, and bee-stung lips to her newly applied French manicure.

And then, silence. Reaching the landing, Eve watches helplessly as her daughter's joy deflates upon the realization that the man she loves has an arm looped possessively around another woman's waist as they enter the foyer. Under the light of the chandelier, Bella is positively radiant in her white coat, her cheeks rosy from the cold.

"Look what we did." Will removes the kid glove from Bella's left hand to reveal a glittering emerald flanked by two diamonds. Dani and Jake gasp, but Megan can only gape as she did when she was a child and her birthday balloon sailed from her hand into the clear blue sky, growing smaller and smaller until it popped.

Eve feels her daughter's crushing rejection with such pain, she has to resist the temptation to do something rash, to throttle Will or punch a wall or scream bloody murder. But she doesn't. Instead, she centers her laser focus on Bella, who regards her stepmother with a knowing twitch of her red lips that seem to whisper, "He's mine."

Not so fast, Eve thinks.

Bella may have conned her step-siblings into believing she's sweet and innocent, but they don't know what Eve knows—the truth.

FOUR

JANE

I can't sleep. My mind keeps replaying images from this after-noon: Isabella Valencia's stricken glance of recognition, the heat of Agent Troiano's meaty hands on my shoulders, Will Pease's dis-missive grin, the rush of anger and frustration pulsing in my veins as I was forcibly led away, realizing that my career as I knew it was over.

The shadows on the ceiling cast by the streetlights outside our bedroom window shift and blur into images of my sister collapsing on the beach the night she disappeared, gentle waves lapping over the tips of her alabaster white fingers. No matter how I twist or turn, they are there as reminders that I have failed her, yet again.

This can't be the end. I cannot let the only person who knows what happened to Kit disappear into her cocoon of wealth and privilege. I have to do something, now. So against my better judg-ment, I slip out of bed, go to the living room, and call my mother's old boyfriend Bob, chief of police in Shoreham, Massachusetts, my hometown.

"Durgan," he answers promptly, though it's after two a.m.

"Hey, Bob. Sorry to wake you." I speak softly so as not to disturb Erik, who's snoring on the other side of our tissue-paper wall. "It's me, Jane."

"Jane!" Naturally, he sounds alarmed. I haven't talked to Bob since June, when we met up to watch the Sox get slaughtered by Tampa Bay. "Well, at least you're not dead. That's the good news."

Having been in law enforcement for the better part of his sixty-five years, Bob assumes the absolute worst from any out-of-the-blue phone call, especially one arriving in the wee hours. Either I crashed my car or I'm in the hospital or, more likely, I've experienced another "episode," as he calls my occasional mood swings. But he's always said no mistake can't be corrected as long as you're alive.

That's the type of paternal aphorism I've been getting from Bob since I was in second grade, the year he started dating my mother. Mom was the Shoreham town clerk, a pretty single mother on the hunt for a stable man, whose office was one floor above the police HQ. When Kit and I visited her at work, we'd hit up the policemen's vending machine for Twix, usually with quarters Bob had doled out in an attempt to win our mother's affections. Besides providing us with candy, he courted her by pulling her car out of a snowbank. She thanked him with a dish of home-made baked mac and cheese. After that, they were inseparable.

Since our biological father had left Mom for a woman on the other side of the world, Bob stepped into his role, picking us up after school and, later, taking us to sports practices, teaching me the basics of baseball and Kit essential karate moves to fend off pushy boys. He used to treat me like his own daughter, which is why I don't feel too guilty waking him with a serious problem.

"I got fired from DHS this afternoon," I tell him right off. "There was an incident."

"Shit. What happened?"

"I broke cover."

Crickets from his end, which means he's disappointed. Bob used to brag to his colleagues that I'd followed in his footsteps by landing a sweet assignment with Homeland Security, even if my job conducting surveillance in an international airport bore no resemblance to his daily duties unlocking cars for tourists who'd lost their keys in the sand.

"I had to," I continue, doing my best to keep my voice steady. "I spotted the girl—now woman, I guess—who I saw with Kit on the beach that night."

Streetlights shine through the windows of our darkened apartment in East Somerville as I wait for his reaction. In the past eleven years, everyone and their mother with any connection to our small coastal village has contacted him to report sightings of her. They've brushed past her on the narrow streets of Province-town or spied her heading down the stairs for the outgoing train to Alewife at Park Street. As a result, Bob tends to treat these reports with caution, even—or, maybe, especially—when they come from me.

"You sure?" In his North Shore accent, it comes out as "shaw."

"I'm sure." I recount what happened in Logan, omitting the part where I loudly accused Bella of murder. Bob is not impressed by hysterics. "Same eyes, forehead, chin, posture, the whole pack-age. I'm one-hundred-percent positive."

I can hear the sheets rustle and imagine him sitting up with interest. "You get a name?"

"Isabella Valencia, though apparently she goes by Bella and, get this, she got off the flight with Will Pease. As in the Peases of Heron's Neck where Kit worked her last night."

"And?"

Ugh. Men can be so thick. "*Aaaaand*, Kit and Will were pretty hot and heavy that summer, right? Now, Will's with Bella."

"Big whoop. Will and Bella have known each other for years."

From the other room, Erik is turning over in bed, probably wondering why I'm not there. I get up from the couch and go to the window, confused and more than slightly unsettled. I don't like the turn this conversation has taken. "What are you talking about?"

"Listen, Jane, I gotta ask . . . you doing okay?"

The question immediately tightens the muscles in my back. I know where he's going with this line and I don't like it. I was fine when I identified Bella Valencia hours earlier. I was at the top of my game, razor-sharp and operating at full capacity.

"Come on, Bob. You should know better than to go there." I am no longer speaking quietly.

"Relax, kid. It's a reasonable concern. Here I haven't heard from you in six months, now you're calling me in the middle of the night with some story about running into a woman you may or may not have—"

"Did! I *did* see her."

"Okay, okay. I have no doubt that in your mind you believe she's the same person, but there are a few kinks in your theory. For starters, Bella Valencia was not on Heron's Neck on the night in question."

"Jane?" Erik inquires from the bedroom. "Everything all right?"

No, don't get up, I think, my fists balling as I begin to pace the eight feet that accounts for the entire length of our living room. Erik cannot find out what I'm up to.

"How do you know?" I ask, wearing a track in the faux Persian carpet from Pottery Barn, our first big purchase as a couple.

"I interviewed her. Twice."

Erik pops out of the bedroom, wearing nothing but his blue boxers, and flips on the hall light, squinting at me through his thick glasses. *Who?* he mouths.

Bob, I mouth.

He taps an invisible watch on his wrist. I wave him back to bed, but he ignores me and goes to our kitchen area, fussing.

"When did you do that?" I ask Bob. "The interview."

"Um, like within seventy-two hours into the investigation. It was over the phone 'cause she was in school out in California, but, geesh, I remember raking her over the coals pretty good. Unfortunately, Bella was in the air on her way to LA when you supposedly saw her with your sister. So, yeah."

No, this can't be. "I know what I saw and what I saw was definitely the grown-up version of the girl who was with Kit."

The girl who may have killed her.

Erik turns on the faucet, pretending like he's not eavesdropping. He has a certain sensitivity when it comes to the issue of Kit. In the beginning of our relationship, he was supportive of my hunt for the truth, and even took a road trip to the Cape once to retrace my steps in the hopes of dislodging a memory.

Lately, however, he gets uptight when I start going down what he calls a rabbit hole. He says my doggedness has become an unhealthy obsession that could lead to more serious mental illness. Then again, he's got an MD and a PhD in psychology. His kind thinks everyone's nuts.

"I'm sorry," Bob says. "I don't know what to say."

"I do. Tell me you'll drive up to the Peases' place in Weston and interrogate her again. You can use my sighting as an excuse to reopen the case."

Erik gulps a glass of water, studying me over the rim.

"I don't think so. Doesn't quite qualify as fresh evidence."

This is stupid. Bob has all but confirmed he briefly considered her enough of a potential suspect eleven years ago to give her the third degree. She produces a sketchy alibi and he calls off the dogs. Now, he doesn't think anything's changed, even with my testimony. What the what?

That's when I realize in retelling my story about this afternoon, I failed to impart a salient detail. "Wait. This might change your mind. According to Renee, my friend at DHS, Bella and Will are engaged."

"Bullshit," he says, not missing a beat. "They can't get married. They're brother and sister. She's adopted, but still."

My heart thumps. Is he serious? He must be half asleep or sleeping it off. "No, way. There were only three other kids in that family when Kit was dating Will—Jake, Dani, and a stepsister named Megan. Kit never mentioned a Bella."

"'Cause they kept her under wraps. Something about her being from a foreign country where her parents had been murdered and she had to be out of the limelight for her own safety is what I heard."

My head is spinning. Either Bob is totally confused or the Peases are way more messed up than I thought. If he's right, even if Bella is no blood relation to Will, marrying your adopted sibling is super skeevy. It feels off. "Why does she have a different last name, then?"

"I dunno. Don't ask me to explain rich people to you. All I know is that Bella Valencia was flying to California on Chet Pease's private plane that night, which is why there's just no way she's the same person you thought you saw on the beach. Chet showed me the logs himself. You either made an innocent mistake today, Jane, or . . . you know. You hallucinated. Saw what you wanted to see. It happens."

Erik slides next to me and gives my knee a squeeze, a signal he wants me to wrap it up. The spot above the bridge of his wire-framed glasses has creased into medical concern. I need to deescalate my conversation with Bob so he doesn't start imposing limits on Kit discussions "for my own good."

Shifting gears, I say brightly, "Well, then, I suppose you have a point, Bob. You certainly cleared up my misconceptions."

Bob, no dummy, says, "I gather the boyfriend has just appeared."

"Absolutely!" I wink at Erik. "We'd love to come down to the Cape and see you. It's been too long. Maybe this summer?"

"Oh, no. Don't go doing that, Jane," Bob says. "I know what you're like when you think you got a lead on Kit. You're like a dog after a T-bone. You're only gonna make things worse for yourself and the investigation."

What investigation? From where I'm sitting, it looks frozen shut. "Then I'll leave the matter in your capable hands."

Erik nods in approval.

"Listen to me, Jane," Bob says in his all-business cop voice. "Take it from me. You do not mess with the Peases unless you have all your ducks in a row. They've got enough money and lawyers to bankrupt you into misery."

"What do I care? I've got fifty bucks in my checking account. Can't get blood from a stone."

"Look, what I'm trying to say is, these types . . . well, they think they're too high and mighty to have to follow rules like us. They could walk out the front door of Tiffany with a hundred grand in diamonds and get nothing but a polite phone call from the manager asking them to return the jewels. They're untouchable, like."

And here, at last, we've come to the rub. Bob didn't aggressively investigate Bella Valencia because she had an airtight alibi.

He let her off because she was a member of a wealthy family. He was intimidated. I've seen him kowtow before to second-home owners in Shoreham. It's sickening.

"Promise me you won't come down here to play detective," he says, with a hint of desperation. "For your own well-being, please don't."

"You bet," I chirp. "Love you!" And then I end the call.

Erik plants a kiss on my cheek. "Good. I was really glad to hear you let this go. That's such great progress and I know that even if it was hard to do in the short run, in the long run walking away from Bella Valencia will be healthier for you and for us."

Then, I think, *we don't stand a chance because no way am I giving up.* Bella was on Heron's Neck that summer and she's engaged to the man who used to be the boy my sister was in love with. That kind of love triangle isn't a coincidence.

It's a motive.

FIVE

JANE

I will say one thing for Lisa Hayes: in addition to being obviously brilliant and extremely efficient, she has a really nice ass. I should know, since I've been staring at it every evening in what has to be the most luxurious yoga studio in Boston. Even the sweat here smells like jasmine.

Lisa is thirty-nine, about one hundred pounds, and partial to high-waisted gray yoga leggings. She is the number eight (possibly soon to be number three) top executive at CO2Glas, a high-tech company in Kendall Square whose prize invention is the Wunder-Windshield. The WunderWindshield is a specially coated windshield that acts as the battery for a zero-emission car, in part by absorbing and using atmospheric CO_2 created by its lesser counterparts. Elon Musk is interested. So is Ford. And Toyota.

Should Lisa get the all clear, she will go from being a decently paid scientist to a stock-holding billionaire overnight. Which is where I come in. My job is not to make sure Lisa is squeaky clean—she was more than thoroughly vetted when she was hired six years ago—but to guarantee that all those with whom she associates are equally pristine.

Following Lisa from morning to night is my daily routine now that I've exhausted all the appeals of my dismissal from DHS. No federal agency will touch me despite my eight years of stellar performance reviews. My once good name is dirt.

The day after I was fired from Homeland, still groggy from my early-morning phone call with Bob, a carrier came to my door with a certified envelope from the Peases' lawyer. It contained a letter on woven legal stationery stating I was not to come within fifty feet of any member of the Pease family and/or within a mile of their private property, nor was I to attend a Love & Pease event nor post a single comment on any form of social media regarding the Pease clan or brand.

Erik called bullshit because it was merely a stern letter, not an official judgment order. *Not yet.* As the final paragraph made clear, should I fail to abide by said restrictions, the Peases would have no other recourse than to seek an injunction, at which point my name and address would be listed in public documents, thereby all but eliminating my chances of landing a job with benefits.

"For now, the Peases have taken the magnanimous approach and decided to issue a preliminary statement to satisfy the media on the premise that in so doing, this maelstrom will lose energy and dissipate." The letter was signed, Arthur A. Whitaker III, Esq., Graves & Whitaker, The Prudential Tower, Boston, MA 02199.

Depressed and bedridden, I initially avoided the internet so I wouldn't come across the "preliminary statement," whatever that meant. Erik volunteered to read it for me, though, and reported with a shrug it didn't feel all that damning. But I knew it wasn't the statement that would freak me out; it would be the comments.

After tossing and turning and rationalizing about how know-ing would be better than not knowing, I finally bit the bullet and went on Twitter. And there it was: #prayforpease.

Seriously? Had they lost their entire family in a tornado? Was one of them about to go into open-heart surgery? Were they in a war zone? Flooded out of their homes?

I had to wade through hundreds of posts until, at last, I found the so-called preliminary statement:

Upon returning from Bogotá, Colombia, where she is Execu-tive Director of the Pease Foundation, Bella Valencia was verbally accosted by a Department of Homeland Security agent who is re-ported to have an unbalanced obsession with members of the Pease organization. The obviously disturbed agent was promptly termi-nated from DHS and hopefully is receiving appropriate psychiatric care. As this matter was swiftly resolved to our satisfaction, Love & Pease, Inc., feels no further comment is warranted. We wish to ex-tend our warmest regards to U.S. Customs and Border Patrol who put their lives on the line daily to keep our country safe. Peace and Love to all this holiday season, The Pease Family.

"Unbalanced obsession"? "Obviously disturbed"? A wave of nausea roiled my gut as I scrolled through the 6.7K likes and com-ments, some of which were so brutal, I actually ended up rushing to the bathroom to vomit. People I'd never met, total strangers, proclaimed me a deranged stalker.

luvisluv @luv54371 OMG! How frightening for you! Hope he's getting the help he needs. #prayforpease.

And then . . .

peasebw/u @noshameshamrok Too bad you had to run into one of the sickos. Crazy people everywhere. Stay safe! #prayforpease.

There were lots of remarks in this vein . . .

peasephan4EVR @girlgottadue1659 Bless you for rising above it all. Once again the Peases are about CLASS & DIGNITY. May he come to find the LORD and cast out Satan. Matthew 12:26. #prayforpease.

"Keep your head down and wait for this to blow over," Erik said. "Stay offline and it'll be forgotten after the next scandal. Be glad everyone thinks you're a dude."

That anonymity lasted for about a minute.

Despite the extreme measures I'd taken to protect my identity due to the classified nature of my (previous) job, the internet magicians managed to unearth my full name, that I was a woman in my late twenties who'd graduated from UMass Amherst, that I lived in East Somerville and even once owned a cat named MissFit. Somehow they also managed to confirm that I was a legit super recognizer, a detail that generated tons of sneering.

I figured this was the end of Jane Ellison. Clearly, the only solution was to move overseas, change my name to something unpronounceable, and ride out the rest of my days plucking chickens in a Mongolian open-air market.

Either that or I could accept an invitation from Stan, my biological dad, to visit him in New Zealand. Stan and I try to text each other on a semi-regular basis—more frequently after what happened at Logan, it seems. Ever since I lost my job, he's been begging me even more often to come to his sheep farm, where he's promised his wife will greet me with open arms and I can get to know my four (four!) half siblings and milk cows and eat muesli and take long beneficial walks through verdant valleys and up green hills.

I was this close to taking him up on the offer, despite the eye-popping twenty-hour flight, when I received a letter (in the mail—the most secure form of communication these days) from Allan Gennings, founder of CO2Glas.

"I was very intrigued to learn from a former classmate of mine at Harvard, who's now on faculty there, that you may be a rare natural super recognizer. I am writing to request a meeting to discuss how we may use your skills at our company," he wrote.

I enjoy Allan, even if conversing with him is as warm as interacting with my microwave. He's similarly cold and radioactive. But he does pay well, which I appreciate, since the assignment to track every person interacting with Lisa Hayes no matter how casual or random is about as exciting as manning a tollbooth.

I accepted because I desperately needed the paycheck and a reason to get out of bed. Erik gently suggested maybe a new job would distract me from my obsession with Bella Valencia, a growing source of tension between us. I told him it probably would.

I lied.

Once Bob made it clear that he wasn't going to be any help in pursuing this Bella lead, I researched all I could on this woman, which, oddly, considering she's a member of a famous family, isn't much. After Googling her name until my fingertips turned numb, I did manage to find a few gems that explained how Will and Bella are brother and sister and, yet, legally able to marry.

Through a bio on the Pease Foundation website, I learned that her parents were working as anti-drug activists in the Bogotá ghettos when they were gunned down on their way to work, leaving Bella an orphan while still a toddler, one of many during the early 1990s when Bogotá was subjected to massive drug violence.

Moved by the horror stories surfacing from that region, Chet Pease and his then-wife Madeleine chose to fund a Bogotá orphanage, where they met their future daughter. "Chet and Madeleine fell in love with four-year-old Bella at first sight," crowed a piece in the *Boston Globe's* society pages. "They couldn't wait to take her home."

Or, as a columnist in *Mother Jones* snarkily noted, "The arrogant Peases fancied themselves white saviors, yanking young Bella out of her native homeland and plopping her in their huge Massachusetts estate, where she was formally adopted and granted the privilege of the Pease surname."

From the bowels of Reddit, I read rumors that due to concerns that those connected to Colombian cartels might attempt to kidnap Bella and possibly hold her for ransom considering her new lucrative connections and the Pease Foundation's ongoing activism in Bogotá, Chet and Madeleine made every effort to keep her adoption secret. That's why she was never included in family photos or publicity shots, the commenters said.

Other Redditors, however, declared this story bogus. There was never any concern about Bella being kidnapped. The Pease parents were just jerks who treated their adopted daughter like a second-class citizen unworthy of being officially brought into the family fold.

At age eighteen, after several trips to her home country, where she immersed herself in her native culture while volunteering at the fledgling Pease Foundation, Bella legally reverted to her original surname, Valencia. She went on to graduate with honors from Pomona College and then returned to Boston to work for a philanthropic organization before returning to Bogotá. Under her leadership, the foundation expanded from an orphanage to a multifaceted education center focused on providing safe housing and quality education to at-risk local girls.

When Will Pease went to Bogotá to work for the foundation, he apparently saw Bella in a flattering new light, not as his adopted sister but as a beautiful, strong, successful, and principled woman with whom he fell instantly and madly in love, according to *Bustle*. Cinderella fantasy fulfilled. Their relationship, as *Go Fug Yourself* phrased it, was "vintage Austen," except, technically, in Jane Austen novels it's cousins who marry, rather than siblings.

On paper, Bella Valencia is without blemish. She is generous, self-sacrificing, intelligent, and moral.

I have one question: If Bella's so moral, why didn't she reach out to me directly about Kit after the Logan incident to ease my distress? Why did she have her lawyer write a threatening letter instead?

I find this disconnect between the saintly Bella Valencia heralded in *Buzzfeed* and the basic truth, that she is a potential witness withholding key evidence to a crime and that she herself might have harmed my sister, to be maddening, if not sinister. There are no two ways about it: I have to meet Bella Valencia in person and interrogate her myself.

But how? I'm not allowed to get within fifty feet of this woman. I can't even send her an email.

It'd help if I could lean on Erik for assistance, but I'd prefer to avoid the endless sessions on the psychoanalyst's couch that would ensue. He's even consulted his adviser, Dave, and his wife, Sheila, about my so-called fixation, fleeing one recent night to their house in Cambridge after we had a fight about how I had not actually "let it go." I assumed they passed the evening flipping through the latest volume of the *Diagnostic and Statistical Manual of Mental Disorders* in a haze of purple kush because the next morning he showed up with a bouquet of apologies and a little brown plastic bottle of hefty-strength Klonopin.

So I never mention Bella these days, just to keep the peace. Every morning, I wake up, take a shower, get dressed, grab a cup of coffee, give Erik a kiss, and begin my day stalking Lisa Hayes. I'm there when she steps out of her South End apartment at the ridiculous hour of five thirty a.m. to when she finally turns in, around ten. Through her thirty-six peppermint teas and twenty-seven Downward Dogs, I plot and plan a way to confront Bella face-to-face.

And then, while sitting across from Lisa on the Red Line to Cambridge, a Google alert pops up on my phone that changes everything. The Love & Pease website has just announced that the happy couple will wed August 22 on Heron's Neck, a "beloved family island retreat dear to their hearts, where they made many happy memories and hope to make many more."

This is my opportunity to corner Bella at last. All I need is to somehow wheedle my way into that event, whereupon I can confront her in person and in front of a huge audience; this time she won't be able to escape.

The thing is, I'll have to convince Erik we absolutely must vacation on the Cape over *that* weekend and that weekend only. But unless he's suddenly taken up reading *People* magazine in the checkout line, the man who claims celebrity culture has collectively lowered the national IQ won't have a clue.

So, while I wait for Lisa to finish teaching her Thursday bio-ethics class at MIT, I search for Shoreham rentals on Craigslist and VRBO. During her Zoom conference, I write to old high school friends, asking if they know of anything available the third week of August that's also affordable, so as not to alarm my frugal boyfriend. No replies. Seems I'm blacklisted everywhere, even in my hometown.

"Anything?" Allan asks at our standing Friday meeting in his windowed office overlooking Mass Ave.

For a minute, I mistakenly think he's asking about my summer plans and then I remember Lisa. "It's weird, but she seems to have absolutely no associations," I tell him. "Even the barista at Crisps Cookies where she orders a peppermint tea and egg-white breakfast sandwich every single day doesn't attempt small talk. She is either bent over her phone or a book when they call her name."

Allan rocks back in his chair, smiling with satisfaction, and I wonder if there's more to this assignment than concern for his company's security. Maybe he's a possessive ex-boyfriend who would lash out in a jealous rage if I reported Lisa has a new love interest. Maybe he's a potential killer, just like Bella.

As if reading my thoughts, something that's entirely possible considering he's most likely an alien in human form, Allan says, "My chief concern is infiltration. Lisa is very introverted, but she is also sheltered. I need to be assured her naïveté is not being taken advantage of by a bad actor."

Actually, there was a disturbing moment on the Red Line a few weeks ago when she happened to sit next to a guy I recognized as Christian Chong. Christian Chong is really Kolzak Jernov, a physicist and possible KGB spy born in Ukraine who entered the US from Seoul several years ago. He arrived at Logan not as the blond-haired, blue-eyed wrestler we'd known him as, but as a much slimmer Korean man wearing glasses and trendy sneakers, his dark hair flopping over one brown eye.

My colleagues in DHS couldn't believe it. No way were they the same guy, they told me. Christian was taller—a discrepancy I chalked up to lifts in his sneakers—and younger, a discrepancy I chalked up to fraudulent and flattering paperwork. Not until a sharp TSA agent managed to swipe a single strand of hair from Christian's head was I vindicated. The DNA results were irrefutable: Christian Chong *was* Kolzak Jernov.

Still, undergoing international facial reconstructive surgery isn't a crime, and we had no reason to detain Kolzak, who continued to travel back and forth between Moscow and Boston under his Christian Chong alias. We couldn't prove he was up to no good at MIT, where he was supposedly a graduate student in computing physics. But I did find it mildly interesting that he chose a spot next to Lisa on a ten-minute T ride from Park Street to Kendall.

Coincidence? Maybe no. But more likely, maybe yes. Lisa Hayes is an earnest, diligent nerd, exactly what Allan wants for a member of his inner sanctum. Divulging that she sat next to Kolzak might unnecessarily alarm him and punish Lisa, who's worked so hard for this huge promotion. So I decide to keep it to myself.

"I've done my due diligence," I say. "From my tracking, her associates are very few and squeaky clean."

Satisfied that I'd thoroughly examined Lisa's even remotest associates, Allan thanks me for a job well done, hands me a huge check, and grants Lisa her well-earned promotion. End of story, right?

Wrong.

Flash forward to a few months later. I'm riding the Green Line back from a therapy session in Brookline, when Lisa gets on at Boylston in a silky pink tank top and her trademark high-waisted leggings. It's July and super muggy the way Boston is during a heat wave. I don't know how she can stand the leggings since the air in the subway car is about a hundred degrees and stinks of BO. I'm almost tempted to wave since I feel as though we know each other, when a text from Erik pops up on my phone.

Someone named Zara Bevins just called my office, said she knew you from high school and was trying to reach you. Lost your cell but remembered you'd mentioned I worked at Harvard. Said she had a last-minute cottage cancellation the week of August 15th in

Shoreham. Wanted to know if we'd like to rent it for $300! Needs an answer ASAP.

I hold my breath, watching as Lisa places her pristine white yoga bag on the cruddy floor. Odd. Usually, she clutches it in her lap.

What do you think? I reply, my thumbs shaking, gobsmacked that Kit's old high-school gymnastics teammate, Zara, came through, especially since she didn't sound optimistic when I contacted her at Starlight Realty back in March. It's a lot of money.

Are you serious? It's a steal!

I can't get over my luck. A place for three hundred dollars is unheard of—and during a peak week, too, when every house, hotel room, Airbnb, and campsite in that area is full. This will put me smack in the middle of Pease territory and with all those days at my disposal, I'll have time to dig into Bella's whereabouts that night, maybe check in with Serena, Kit's old boss, to jog her memory.

At the realization that we're actually going, I'm near tears. All I need is ten minutes with Bella Valencia one-on-one. Ten minutes for her to answer the question: What happened to my sister?

Up to you, I text. I don't want to appear too eager and have Erik suspect my true intent. Your call.

K. Calling her back to say we're going for it!

Out of the corner of my eye, I catch a foot in a trendy sneaker, jiggling nervously. I recognize the brand—the same one Kolzak Jernov favors. Glancing up, I see it's him again, sitting right next to Lisa, who is totally focused on her phone as usual. Then it hits me: why would a woman with many millions in stock options choose to be in a cramped, stifling Boston streetcar during an epic heat wave?

The train screeches to a halt, and Kolzak gets up and quickly exits not with *his* bag, but with hers. Lisa does nothing, simply kicks his bag between her feet and continues texting, as it slowly dawns on me with a cold panic that I messed up huge. Lisa is not an oblivious nerd. Nor is she as naive as Allan fears. She is savvy, calculating, and a traitor to the United States of America.

I was devastated, not only because I'd let down Allan, but because I hadn't trusted my valuable instincts, and I won't make that mistake again. Because just like Lisa Hayes sitting next to Christian Chong wasn't by happenstance, neither is Bella Valencia's relationship with my sister's former boyfriend. Despite Bob's assertions, there are no coincidences—just hidden truths that have yet to be uncovered.

SIX

BELLA

Will Pease lifts his strong jaw to the late summer sunset and lets the salty breeze blow back his umber-colored curls. He's been growing them out at the urging of his stepmother, who's convinced flowing hair will add the perfect romantic touch to the regal cream silk sherwani he'll be wearing at his nuptials.

Though neither Will nor Bella has a drop of Eastern blood in their veins, their chief wedding planner, Eve, is charging full steam ahead with an Indian-themed ceremony that will be featured prominently on the Love & Pease site. The couple of honor will be draped in garlands of pink jasmine and red roses as they recite their vows barefoot on a sandy bluff overlooking Cape Cod Bay against the backdrop of a setting sun.

Afterward, the chosen guests will enjoy a sit-down, six-course dinner of French/Indian fusion cuisine. Eve thinks it's likely the Punjabi wedding attire will cause an outcry on social media about her audacious cultural appropriation. She is equally confident that by this time next year, every bride will be hennaed and donned in embroidered scarlet silk. One simply cannot buy the kind of publicity that's generated by righteous outrage.

"Want some?" From the pocket of his Tommy Bahama silk short-sleeve shirt, Will produces a neatly rolled joint for Bella's inspection.

She holds up her hand. "I'm good."

"You sure? It's kind of the ideal moment." He gestures to the unspoiled beauty before them, the gray seabirds diving for their dinner in tide pools tucked among the undulating marsh grass. "It'll enhance the experience."

"When have I ever said yes?"

"Whatever. It's cool." He flicks a lighter and then hesitates, his expression inscrutable thanks to the classic aviators that he wears constantly to hide his eyes. They've been a squinty red, it seems, ever since he and Bella returned to the States from Bogotá last month. "Is this how it's gonna be?"

"Is how what's gonna be?" she asks, poking a clump of knotted green seaweed with her toe.

"For the rest of our married life, you giving me that look."

She bends to remove a small starfish caught in the seaweed's tendrils. "I'm not giving you a look."

"Yes, you are. Even behind your sunglasses, I can tell. You disapprove."

He's right about that. Pot makes Will stupid and slow and lazy. It does him no favors, not with his addictive personality. She's counting the days until this summer of festivities ends and he'll be out from under the influence of his former frat bros and their vapid girlfriends. In Bogotá, Bella can get him back on the schedule they used to follow. Work. Running. Healthy food. Books. He flourished in those conditions.

"You know I can't stand the smell," she says, flipping the tiny starfish over to marvel at its spiny white underbelly. "Like body odor."

"Sometimes, I don't get it, Bella." He cups his hands and puts the tip of the joint to the flame, inhaling and holding his breath, exhaling with expert slowness. "Why the hell did you agree to marry a stoner?"

That's a question she's been asking more and more lately, she thinks, tossing the starfish into the gentle waves. She's thrilled to be engaged to a man who can trigger ripples up her inner thighs by merely grazing his fingertips across her wrist. But that's basic lust, hardly the basis for a lifetime commitment.

She tells herself she loves him, except she doesn't—not *this* version of Will. She loves the Will from her childhood buried beneath the buffed and polished celebrity persona, the Will she sees glimpses of more and more in Colombia. With time and lots and lots of dedication, she believes she can peel back the cushioning of privilege and clear the haze of intoxication until she reaches the scarring layer left by his mother's abandonment. And once she removes that hardened barrier, there he'll be, the inventive and goofy boy who delighted her as a little girl.

Bella was a small, frightened child when Chet and Madeleine brought her to the frigid New England countryside populated by galumphing monsters who didn't speak her language or eat the same food. The house was so huge, it gave her nightmares, and her new siblings were so loud and boisterous, their voices made her ears ring.

Jake took scant notice of her existence, and Dani was so besieged by rage, her only focus was on which rule she would break next. It was only Will who paid her any attention.

Bella remembers watching in wonder as he transformed mounds of the unfathomable snow into an actual fort you could crawl into, safe and cozy from the chilling winter wind. He laid down a rug and opened a can with a candle that, when lit, produced surprising heat. In the spring, he climbed into a tree and, using planks of wood from the shed, constructed an actual house, complete with a trapdoor and rope swing.

Five years older, Will was her magic maker. His playful winks eased her fretting. His stupid jokes across the dinner table made her laugh. He taught her to play checkers and how to ride a bike and cut that first daunting turn on her skis. He was cute and funny and carefree and she adored every inch of him.

And then Madeleine abruptly left and he followed his older siblings to boarding school. The big house was even more empty, just Chet, the cook, a housekeeper, and the private tutor who taught four days a week, it having been decided that, for various reasons, Bella would learn better at home.

She passed the days by reading and her nights being further tutored by Chet, her only constant adult companion. He dismissed checkers as babyish and taught her chess. On weekends, he took her to Boston museums or to his fancy glass office downtown, where he explained the nuances of finance in such boring detail she had to pinch herself to keep awake. They forged a bond during those years together, before Eve pounced, curling up next to Chet on the couch like a hungry panther. She changed him. And not for the better, either.

When the others returned for school holidays or summer vacations, they also weren't the same. Jake immediately went off with friends and eventually his boring girlfriend Heather. Dani locked herself in the carriage house, where she smoked cigarettes and painted, the light from her studio window spilling out until morning. As for Will, he, too, was unfamiliar. Distant. Sophisticated. Sexual.

That's when the girls descended on Heron's Neck. Beautiful girls. Tanned and lithe with long, straight hair they flipped over their brown shoulders as they lowered themselves into the cool, blue pool, their bodies covered by the barest of bikinis. Will had eyes only for them, and treated Bella as if she were invisible. They sat on his lap while he sunned himself on the chaise lounge. They giggled as they raced him to the dock, sliding against him unnecessarily as he helped them into the boat, speeding off around the point, returning hours later looking flushed and sated.

Megan, Eve's daughter, longed to join his harem, despite being even younger than Bella. Though not quite an adolescent, she boasted about wanting a nose job and how she planned to surgically enhance her boobs. The space behind her crystal blue eyes wasn't empty so much as cluttered with useless noise, chatter about clothes, parties, and boys.

Eve expected Megan and Bella to become great friends, though the only common ground Bella could find was their mutual worship of Will, which didn't feel like a basis for a close tie. So each went her own way and Bella was grateful for the fall when Megan was packed off to school, too.

Several years passed without Will's and Bella's paths crossing until Chet died three years ago. Will was barely recognizable at his father's funeral, what with his rumpled suitcoat and cranky demeanor, reeking of stale bourbon and weed. Bella feared he was something of a lost cause, a loose cannon careening on the deck of a wayward ship. He lacked Jake's financial acumen and Dani's artistic passion. He squeaked through law school, the last bastion for the directionless, but couldn't seem to pass the Massachusetts Bar and eventually gave up.

All he was good for, it seemed, was gracing the Love & Pease websites. Though how long could that last? Modeling—even male modeling—had a depressingly short half-life, especially with Will's habits, which were beginning to leak into social media, much to Eve's distress.

If word got out that the face of Love & Peace was actually a dissipated, aging partier, the brand might never recover from the downgrade. Something had to be done to turn him around, Eve insisted, though nothing happened until Will crossed the ultimate line the summer before Bogotá. That's when Jake discovered Megan had finally managed to get her hooks into her stepbrother. Appalled, the older brother voted to disown Will from the family once and for all.

Bella suggested another option—sending Will to Bogotá to rehabilitate himself and his reputation by doing good works for the Pease Foundation. Jake objected, but Dani agreed. Besides, as a major stakeholder in Love & Pease, Bella usually got her way.

As she'd anticipated, the foundation eventually gave Will a purpose beyond grinning for photo shoots. Being particularly adept at seduction—no surprise there—he wooed Bogotá's social set, channeling hundreds of thousands to the foundation's coffers by holding fundraisers at student art installations and even a charity ball, where the mere appearance of him in a Saville Row tux was enough to add a zero on the checks dashed off by one or two *damas*.

Without his destructive habits, Will soon reverted to his breathtakingly handsome state, and much to her dismay Bella would find her pulse racing at the sight of his shoulder blades under a skintight Love & Pease cotton T-shirt or when he smoothed back his curls with his long fingers. She was weak, she decided, superficial.

She didn't care.

They'd been working long hours together on the foundation's

budget, meeting for morning runs or coffee almost daily and ending the evenings on the rooftop deck of her apartment overlooking the twinkling lights of Bogotá's capital district. Often their conversations went on for hours, with Will rambling and Bella mostly listening, occasionally falling asleep to the rhythm of his voice.

He first kissed her in the cab on their return from a silent auction. Subconsciously, she must have anticipated this step, else why would she have worn the faux-wrap Armani dress with the plunging neckline? The kiss broke the restraints that had been keeping them apart. It was as if a curse had been lifted and now Will was under her spell. He did whatever he could to please her, working harder, running longer, forsaking all drugs, including marijuana, which he'd been smoking daily since age fifteen. He even cut his hair, which she'd been nagging him to do for months. One night, while admiring the view from their table at Casa San Isidro on the majestic Monserrate, Will took her hand in his and floated the prospect of sealing their union permanently.

Marriage didn't fit her plans, yet here was the only man she'd ever truly loved offering himself to her forever. She bit her lip, debating. Her cynical side warned there could be a dastardly motive to his proposal. Except Will was so moral these days, so thoughtful. *Sober.* Married, they could achieve so much more as a couple.

And what would happen if she said no? He'd leave, that's what. He would latch on to some other woman who'd give him the stability he inwardly craved, which Madeleine stole when she left. Bella couldn't imagine having to attend future Christmases where Will appeared with wife and children in tow, having to smile and pretend she wasn't haunted by regret, as if she weren't tormented by what might have been.

So she said yes.

And now, as she watches him take another toke, she fights

a tickle of apprehension that maybe, just maybe, she'd been too hasty.

"Well?" He caresses her chin. The warmth of his touch momentarily erases her doubts.

"Well, I'm marrying you because I love you. Lame, but true," she says. As he leans down for a kiss, she spies over his shoulder a skeletal figure in a white shift at the water's edge, headed in their direction.

"Jesus," Bella murmers, stepping back. "Queenie."

To the rest of the Peases, Queenie is Eve's beloved mentor, a fun-loving, martini-swilling, Marlboro-inhaling former actor, a onetime fixture at Studio 54 and an Andy Warhol acquaintance whose addiction to cocaine destroyed her nasal septum that, fortunately, her addiction to plastic surgery repaired. She and Eve met when the latter had a short run on the soap opera *Hopes & Dreams*. Eve played a scheming debutante; Queenie played an eccentric socialite named Pippa Ellington who suffered from multiple personalities—perhaps not too far of a stretch for either.

"Hey, you two!" Queenie shouts and then immediately erupts into a fit of coughing. Though she can't be much past sixty, she has the dry skin and brittle bones of a woman in her eighties. Her thinning jet hair has been yanked into a severe bun, which only adds to her elfin vulnerability.

Queenie's mangled toes, twisted by decades of spike heels and pointy pumps, are barely able to negotiate the shifting sand, so Will offers her a hand and leads her to where Bella stands.

"I was looking for you everywhere." She breathes heavily, panting. "They said you were at the beach, but there's a helluva lot of beach around here. God, I'm thirsty." Reaching into the tiny bag slung across her body, she shakes out a cigarette. "Don't worry. I won't light it, Bella. I wouldn't dare."

Will gives his wife-to-be a conspiratorial wink. "Tell you what. You stay here and catch up while I get us some drinks. It's after five, right?"

"What's five got to do with it?" Queenie replies.

"Good to see you again," Will says. "It's been too long." Turning to Bella, he says, "What'll you have?"

"Water's fine."

Queenie says, "Ditto. Only make mine with gin. No ice. And, come to think of it, you can give my water to your bride. Wouldn't want it to go to waste."

"Totally." Will nods and jogs off, oblivious to the tension coursing through Bella as her buffer disappears around the bend.

"My, my, he's fine," Queenie says. "How'd you do it?"

A trap, Bella is aware, but cannot resist playing one round of Queenie's game. "Do what?"

"Get him. All those women, hundreds of them, out there dying to be Mrs. William Pease. Including," she adds, with a slight cough, "your own stepsister. Why you?"

Bella averts her gaze. "You should ask him."

"I did."

Of course she did. "And?"

"Oh, he said he saw you in a fresh light down in Bogotá. You with your *philanthropy*." Queenie doesn't attempt to hide her skepticism. "He waxed lovingly about your serene beauty and how you two got along so swimmingly, how you *saved* him, for chrissakes."

"And you think he's lying?"

Queenie glances up so Bella is reflected twice on the lenses of her oversized sunglasses. "Let's just say I was into branding back when it was done with hot iron pokers. I know PR copy when I hear it."

"Do you, now?"

Queenie sticks the unlit cigarette between her red-painted lips. "You know, Eve thinks Will's still in love with her daughter and that you simply took advantage of the situation while he was in exile. Now, with the wedding having become a massive Love & Pease event, it's too late for him to admit his mistake and back out."

Bella tries not to show that she's affronted, well aware the older woman's simply trying to get under her skin. As Megan's god-mother and protector, Queenie's always had her stepsister's back.

"That's not even close to the truth, you know."

"I couldn't agree more. Obviously, you marrying Will is fantastic for business and isn't that why he's marrying you—for money?"

Now she's good and irritated. "I'm sorry. What was that?"

Queenie peeks over the top of her glasses. "I'll boil it down for you: forty-five percent."

Bella does not take the bait. Yes, Chet bequeathed the lion's share of his ownership in Love & Pease to Bella, granting the other children an insulting pittance. Despite the advantage, Bella's tried to work cooperatively with Eve, though it hasn't been easy. Her stepmother is forever resentful at not having been placed in control. Love & Pease was her baby, after all, her birth of creation. But because Chet provided the seed capital, like any good, ruthless capitalist, he insisted on calling the shots.

"You think Will is marrying me for my shares?"

"He's not marrying you to forsake all others." The cigarette bobs up and down when Queenie speaks. "I've heard about his business trips this spring to New York and London for the foundation. The only deals he sealed were between the sheets, is my understanding."

Bella doesn't flinch. "I talked to Will about those rumors and he laughed."

"He wasn't laughing when he drafted that prenup, though,

was he?" Queenie removes the cigarette with one hand and flicks her gold lighter in the other, reneging on her prior promise. "My understanding is there's a clause buried somewhere stating that should your marriage end due to your infidelity or . . . *illicit* acts . . . Will gains your shares. *All* of them."

Hardly news to Bella, though hearing out loud someone else raising the red warning her rational side has been flashing is, admittedly, disconcerting. "Please," she says with an exaggerated sigh. "It's not like you've read the prenup."

"I don't have to. My sources are very, very reliable. It's the phrase *illicit acts* that had me intrigued."

Bella wishes Queenie would sink into the sand and be sucked into the underworld, where she could be among her people.

"Boilerplate prenup jargon," she counters, with a brave lift of her chin. "I don't plan on cheating on Will or breaking the law, so I feel pretty safe."

"Do you?" Queenie smiles. "I'm not so sure I would, in your position. You know, I went out for a cigarette that night and I saw everything."

Something hard lands in Bella's gut and she has to fight the impulse to gasp. Though she's long suspected Queenie was the figure she caught sight of in her long, flowing robe, to hear it confirmed from the woman herself is a shock to the system. It is all Bella can do to arch her eyebrows in feigned puzzlement.

"Oh, don't pretend to be bewildered," Queenie shoots back. "You know exactly what I'm talking about."

"I'm sorry," Bella manages. "I'm really not following."

"Yes, you are. That mortifying incident in Logan when the agent shouted those accusations was only a few months ago. How could you forget?" Queenie drags on her cigarette. "I know Arthur did what he could to make her go away, but lawyers can only do so much with what they're given. And the fact is, you took the rowboat out to the cove that night, right around the time that poor waitress went missing."

Shouldn't Will be back by now with their drinks? Bella cranes her neck to look for him when Queenie says, "Chief Durgan from the Shoreham Police called Arthur a while back, looking to talk to you. Did you know?"

Hearing the name Bob Durgan is another blow. After all these years, why would that crusty old cop be sniffing around now? It can't be because of the incident at Logan. The ravings of a delusional woman wouldn't be enough for him to reopen a closed case, would they?

God. She hopes not.

Queenie, as perceptive as a feral cat, notices Bella's alarm and gives the screw another twist. "Hmmm." She sucks on her cigarette again. "Arthur probably didn't want to ruin your special day. Do you know, I had no idea that Homeland Security agent was related to Chief Durgan. I think Arthur said she's—"

"Insane," Bella cuts in, ready to take off in a run if Will doesn't return pronto. "Mentally unwell. Seriously. She has a history of institutionalization. Look, maybe we should go back to the house. It's getting close to dinner."

Queenie turns to the bay, having laid down her inroad. "Give me a minute. Eve won't let me have cigarettes around Jake's kids."

They stand side by side, Queenie smoking deeply, Bella's mind racing madly, as the last rays of light disappear quickly behind the horizon, leaving the sky a dull, despairing gray.

SEVEN

JANE

No, he didn't leave her. She left him . . . after he snuck in a woman half his age from the psych ward!"

"Psych ward?" I hear the crackle of a potato chip bag followed by the *zip-pop* of a soda can opening. "Why was Chris in the psych ward?"

Yes, I wonder, spying on the group with one slitted eye, *why?*

Normally, I'm not one for eavesdropping, at least not in my spare time. But when you're lying on a towel on the outer Cape's most pristine public beach in late August with the ambient noise of crashing waves and squealing kids in the background, coconut-smelling sunscreen up your nose and sand in your swimsuit, it's like the conversations of nearby groups are being piped right into your ears.

From what I've been able to discern so far, Chris is some sort of hippie "wood-based" artist in Maine who married Janelle, a twice-divorced nurse, and mooched off her steady pay and platinum health plan, bonking female students in his rustic studio while Janelle—poor Janelle!—was changing bedpans and taking temperatures during her seventy-two-hour shifts.

I am ready to make the drive from Shoreham to Bangor just to give the dude an overdue kick in the nuts.

"He did mushrooms."

"What kind?"

"The silly . . . psychedelic. Apparently, he took some bad ones that he found under a log in the woods and Janelle came home from work to find him, literally, hanging from a beam in his studio—upside down, by his ankles. Some kinky sexual thing."

"Oh, my god. You're kidding. He even managed to mess that up?"

"I know, right?" This is followed by cackling and more crunching of chips.

I squint through my sunglasses at the guy between the two women. He's in purple octopus swim trunks his wife, who I believe is the one in the white lace cover-up, probably ordered off Amazon. So far, he's been pretending to be fascinated by the James Patterson hardcover clutched in his hands, but he hasn't turned a page and keeps shifting in his chair, which indicates he's distracted.

I'm trying to remember where I know him from. Logan, definitely. Flies at least every other week. He's in finance or maybe real estate. Serial lech. Hangs out in the American Airlines Admirals Club, which he exits with a *Wall Street Journal* under one arm and a traumatized employee under the other. Bet this stuff about Chris cheating on Janelle is hitting a little too close to home for Mr. Patterson.

"The thing is, Janelle's always had shitty taste in men," says the woman with gold-painted toenails, handing the chips back to her friend.

"Always," says White Lace Cover-up. "Her first husband pulled the same move. It's like, I don't know . . . sorta that she expects to be disrespected?"

"Low self-esteem," Golden Toes confirms.

Ah, yes, the familiar game of blame the female victim.

"Then again, like, what kind of idiot would hook up with a guy she met in the psych ward and then go back to his house while his wife's in the picture?"

"The needy kind, of which there are more than a few in this world." White Lace Cover-up crunches on a Lays. "You know how it is. Some women will do anything for a man. An-y-thing. Like, they would even go so far as to kill."

"Yup. Tons of those all over Investigation Discovery."

"Tons."

And, now, I'm the one squirming, this line having hit too close to *my* home.

Rolling away, I turn to Erik, whose pale Nordic skin has been slathered in a thick coat of sunblock that turns out to be no match for the blazing nuclear reaction ninety-four million miles away. His freckled back is dangerously pink. "You're getting burned."

"I know," he mumbles into his towel. "I can feel it. How about you?"

"Fine."

I never burn. Maybe it's because I grew up here and my mother's lectures about skin cancer so scared the crap out of me that even in the dead of winter I don't leave the house without a layer of SPF 50. Kit was blond and fair-skinned like Stan, our actual dad, and even though she heeded our mother's warnings, she was always red and peeling.

Me? I'm darker like our mother. Brunette, olive-toned, built for sunny climes. Erik says I'm a dead ringer for the woman pictured on the jar of pasta sauce, with my zaftig curves and full lips. The only traits Kit and I shared were our low laughs, bordering on snickers, and double joints, which enabled us to bend our elbows and fingers into distorted positions. Kit loved grossing friends out with that.

Reaching into our backpack, I pull out a spare T-shirt and gently lay it over Erik's raw shoulders. That burn will heat up when the sun goes down, which reminds me of dinner. The crew next to us was talking about going to Arnold's for lobster.

"Wanna go out tonight?"

"Too expensive." Erik keeps his eyes shut. "Sorry."

"Not your fault."

While we've never been exactly flush with cash, after I spent Allan's last check on our rental car and the cottage, we've been scraping the bottom. Zara, the Realtor and Kit's old friend from high school, wasn't joking when she said the house was tiny. It's basically an oversized garden shed with a galley kitchen and a tiny loft bedroom overlooking a postage-stamp living room. Good thing Erik and I are used to living in a place the size of a Chinese take-out container.

Luckily, I don't plan on spending much time inside. When we're not at the beach or biking, I'll be casing out the best way to make it onto Heron's Neck, which connects to the mainland by a small wooden bridge and miles of marsh. I have to figure out which of the plans I developed back home is most realistic. Posing as a florist? Or taking a kayak from Camp Pequabuck, across the inlet to the island at night? Both are risky.

Erik gets up and slips into his T-shirt, wincing. I make a mental note to buy some aloe vera at the general store on the way home. "Should we go?"

"Might as well," I say, gathering my towel and taking it to the water's edge to shake off the sand.

While I'm there, I scan the dwindling crowds for any sign of Kit. This is a fantasy I frequently enjoy, imagining that she escaped Bella Valencia's clutches and somewhere along the way suffered amnesia. She might be one of these mothers packing up her kids and their plastic toys, or among the women strolling along the surf hand in hand with a boyfriend or girlfriend. When she sees me, she'll snap out of her daze and we'll be rejoined in a reunion of tears and laughter and reminisces.

After all, the bloodstained T-shirt the cops found in the marsh a few days after she went missing had no trace of Kit's DNA. That's important to keep in mind. Really, *really* important.

"Just amazing." Erik joins me in gazing at the sea as it transforms to a gray-blue in the waning light. Seagulls swoop and dive for fish with artful choreography. The air smells bracingly of cleansing salt.

"The golden hour. My favorite time to be at the beach. Kit and I used to ride our bikes down here this time of day. No fees. Swam for free. That was before the Great Whites took over."

He slides his arm around my waist and pulls me to him. "We needed a break, you and I, after all the craziness this year. I'm glad we're doing this."

"Me, too," I say, though I have the feeling the real craziness has yet to begin.

The lifeguards have called it quits, their white wooden perches abandoned, and the few remaining beachgoers take advantage of their absence. There's a couple making out, a family bobbing in the waves, precariously far from shore. A skinny teen skimboards along the edge of the surf, nearly crashing into a casting fisherman, who gestures with a warning to be more careful.

A breeze picks up and the sun dips a little lower, blessing the white sand with a golden hue. It's magical and making me nostalgic for my childhood when life was so much less complicated, when Kit was just a know-it-all older sister. When Mom was alive.

Sensing my wistfulness, Erik says, "You know, I bet oysters wouldn't be too expensive if I shucked them myself."

I bend into him, loving how he cares about the small things that make a huge difference. "It's not that easy to do, shucking."

"What's so hard about it?"

"Those suckers are closed tight and the edges are super sharp. You'll need a special knife and mesh gloves."

"Peanuts."

"Much sharper than peanuts."

He chuckles and kisses my head.

The family that was way too far out are coming in. Father and tweenage daughter fight the riptide, a powerful current funneled through two invisible sandbars. The lifeguards would be blowing their whistles and directing the swimmers to move left or right, but they've gone. I tense, watching how this is going to play out.

The father frees himself and drags his daughter with him, finally lifting her over the rolling stones at the water's edge. They turn to the mother, bobbing out there alone, and wave. She waves back and, as if to show she's perfectly capable, stretches herself into a crawl, arm over arm, riding the waves.

I used to do that, too, swimming unsupervised in deep water. It was a job requirement when I worked as a lifeguard at Pequabuck, the crunchy nature camp we called Camp Pekky, just across the bay from Heron's Neck. We had to begin each morning logging fifty feet out and fifty feet back. First freestyle, then breaststroke. Even on that side of the Cape, the water was shockingly cold at seven a.m., especially after the mandatory three-mile run on the beach.

Kit made fun of my job that summer, the last summer we had together. As a waitress at Serendipity, she slept in past noon most days while I was freezing my butt off every morning. She told me I was out of my mind. "You're risking hypothermia for minimum wage," she'd say. "Why don't you come work for Serena? No one ever died from serving crab puffs."

I reassess the woman swimming alone. All I can make out is her wet head, still like a buoy bent at an odd angle.

Holy shit.

Erik elbows my ribs. "Wanna go? The fish market's gonna close soon, I bet."

Pushing him aside, I run to shore, shielding my eyes, cursing myself for leaving the bird binoculars behind. I could so use them right now.

This much I can tell: her skin is pale, eyes are closed, jaw is slack, as if she's deep in meditation. She's not. She is most definitely not, I realize, my heartbeat ratcheting.

"Hey, hey. What's up?" Erik asks, suddenly by my side.

"Get my towel," I order him as quietly I can, pulling off my own cover-up.

"What?"

"My towel. Hurry," I say quietly. I don't want to alert anyone or cause a scene, which could create total chaos and panic.

Erik tosses me my towel and I catch it, hesitating for a moment. It's been so long since I've attempted a rescue and my skills are rusty. Plus, all I have is this length of terrycloth, not a rope or raft or even a life preserver. That said, the hard truth is, there is no alternative.

She is not my sister.

But she is drowning and if I don't act fast, she'll be dead, too.

EIGHT

JANE

Stones cut into the baby-soft pads under my toes, the powerful breakers knocking large rocks against my ankle bones. I wish I could go back for my water shoes, but I can't. There's no time. I must reach the trench between the sandbars where the drowning woman is trapped before it sucks her under.

Plunging into the frigid surf, I rise, gasping at the cold, only to duck under the next pounding wave. I can't see her now; I have to estimate her location as I extend my arms in steady strokes, hoping I'm swimming in the right direction. The icy northern Atlantic is bracing and churning in the evening wind, pushing me back to shore. I have to fight its pull and dive under each swell.

Swimming freestyle while clutching this saturated towel, as heavy as a lead weight, is unsustainable. I don't have the arm strength to keep going like this for much longer. Already, I'm out of breath, although thankfully the exertion has warmed me up somewhat. Rolling onto my back, I slap the towel onto my chest and use the backstroke. People have begun to congregate on the beach. The water's too choppy for me to see if any of them are guards heading out to save her.

So I persist.

Though not the opportune moment to mentally catalog all the ways my rescue attempt could go south, I nevertheless run through the list. Most likely, she'll be gone before I get to her. Or, when I do, she'll be in a semiconscious flurry of panic, flailing and dangerous. What will I do then? Hope for the best. Pray that she doesn't pull me down with her or wrap her arms around my throat so tightly she cuts off my air.

Obviously, she got caught in a riptide, an invisible undercurrent that can swiftly carry even the strongest swimmer out to sea. The most effective way to extricate yourself from its grip is to swim parallel to the coastline and let the waves bring you in naturally. But most swimmers waste their precious energy by heading perpendicular to shore, discovering, too late, they've already lost the battle.

Confronted with imminent death, their bodies switch into survival mode, shutting off blood flow to the extremities to preserve the core organs. Fingers and toes go quickly numb. Senses power down and the brain, already the most untrustworthy part of our anatomy, misfires random messages urging the drowning victim to relax, give up or, even, go to sleep.

Suddenly, from behind me comes a strange sound, not part of the sea, a faint haphazard splashing. It's her. I turn and assess her state—eyes glassy and vacant staring up at the sky, her blue lips snapping mechanically, drawing in oxygen. She is half dead.

No, I think, kicking toward her, *she is half alive.*

"Take this," I cry, casting the water-logged towel in her direction.

She doesn't respond, possibly because her hearing has shut down, all her attention now directed toward keeping those air passages above surface. The towel sinks, rippling to the depth below. My life for a buoy. Or a boat.

Treading with all my might, I manage to snatch the towel and hold it above my head again, my arms screaming in protest.

"Hey!" I wheeze, flinging the soaked mess at her head, hoping it doesn't knock her underneath. "Grab it."

There is a whirl of activity, a sudden awakening, and she pivots to me, her eyes widening with terror. She's older than I'd estimated, closer to fifty than forty, and I don't recognize her, which could mean either she's a stranger or I'm so stressed, I can't process her identity.

Panting, I try once more. "Grab. The. Towel."

I feel a tug. Not just a tug. A hard jerk. She's clasping the towel and hugging it to her abdomen. "That's good!" I shout, accidentally gulping and spitting out seawater, my aching legs bicycling below. "Hang on. Help is coming."

Then it happens, my worst fear. Her hand reaches past the towel, crawling toward me. I try kicking her off but she manages to grab on to my right calf and now we really are in trouble. We are sinking.

There is no reasoning with her. There is no *her*. She is not a mother, a wife, a daughter, or whatever she is in her professional life. She is a collection of organisms determined to persevere at any cost. She cannot follow directions, not even a simple "Let go!"

Her fingers dig into the flesh of my upper arms, painfully, as she drags me under an incoming wave. Water pours into my ear canal, causing instant deafness. I can't breathe. I can't see. Despite my old lifeguard training, I can sense an uncontrollable surge of panic as my muscles begin cramping due to the release of lactic acid.

Wait! All of a sudden, something bright yellow pops up in my peripheral vision. I must be hallucinating because this is too good to be true. A rescue board being paddled by a guard is only a few feet away.

Surfacing, I point to him madly so she takes notice and watch as, all business, he hops into the water and expertly flips the board before climbing back on. Lying on his stomach, he moves closer, hooks his hands under each of her armpits, and keeps her head above water as another guard joins him in a red kayak. On the count of three, they hoist her onto the kayak, her body hitting the plastic with a thud, whereupon the guard immediately turns her to her side and begins CPR, pumping water out of her until she coughs.

Oh, my god. It's over. They got her. Only then does it dawn on me how cold and weak I am. In this condition, I'll never be able to make it back to shore.

"Here. Grab this," a man shouts from behind.

I flip around, assuming he's another guard, but something's off. His surfboard is gray, not regulation yellow or red. I turn back to the other guards, but they're busy transporting her to shore, where an ambulance is waiting, lights flashing.

"Come on!" he shouts again. "It's your only chance."

My eyelids are swollen shut from the irritating seawater so all I can make out is his beard and what he's holding toward me—a long, thin stick that might be a fishing rod.

With no other help nearby, I take a gamble and reach for it . . . and miss.

"Come closer." He extends one arm, lying prone on his gray

surfboard like the guard, but he's not a guard I realize as I swim nearer. He's the surf caster who moments ago was yelling at the kids to be careful. Instinctively, I recoil.

He's familiar. He wants to do me harm.

I *know* him.

But before I can escape, he attacks, turning his hand into a fist that he smashes against my temple with one massive blow. Excruciating pain bursts across my head in red pulsations. I sink fast, doubled over into a protective fetal position as the word *why* pinballs through my muddled thoughts. My jaw goes slack and water rushes into my mouth as I somersault. I must swim up, out, and away. I have to or else I'll die.

I'm not fast enough and he manages to snare my ankle so I'm hooked like a fish. The next thing I know, I'm being hauled against my will, thrashing to break free.

"It's okay," he says as we tussle, securing me in an iron clutch. "I gotcha. Calm down."

To my amazement, I feel the chill of fresh air and realize I'm on the red kayak. Gripping its slippery sides, I lean over and expel my lunch into the sea.

"Say something," orders the guard, his face close to mine. His hair is blond, skin baked brown. Not the fisherman.

"Speak!" The guard is pressing on my back. "Say anything."

I nod. I know from my training that demonstrating an unblocked airway is key. If I can't, he will pound on my chest to release the trapped water just like he did with the drowning victim. "Anything," I squeak, near tears I'm so grateful for him, for the entire National Seashore lifeguard team. Sixteen dollars an hour is not nearly enough for these heroes.

He lightly touches my temple and I wince. "Looks like you hit your head pretty bad. You're bleeding. We'd better get you looked at. What's your name?"

Still coughing, I manage a hoarse "Jane." I want to see if the surf caster on the gray board is nearby but I don't dare sit up.

"Well, Jane. That was a brave and stupid thing you did, but it turned out all right."

"The swimmer . . . ?"

"Gonna make it." He gives me a thumbs-up. "Take it easy." He grabs his paddle, motoring us to shore. My body is like jelly. My head is in agony. My nerves are pulsating along with my calves and biceps. All I want is a cool drink of water and a firm footing on land.

The crowd clustered at the water's edge has grown, watching the victim being loaded on a gurney into the rear of the ambulance. Erik has both arms up waving.

But there is no sign of the man who did his best to get me killed.

Jake Pease is gone.

NINE

JANE

"Y ou're a hero, you know that, right?" Erik says as we pull out
of the beach parking lot. "I mean, the lifeguard gets all the
credit for pulling her out of the water, but I saw what you did and
it was awesome."

He gets to the main road and looks both ways twice, super
cautious about everything, which is how Erik behaves when he's
had a fright. Assured of no incoming cars for at least a mile, he
turns the wheel extra slowly for a left. "The way you kept at it,
throwing her that towel and staying with her. Shit, I was worried."

Also, he rambles.

"Jane, say something."

I wish I could, but the pounding under my skull is wicked
intense and I can't stop shaking from the cold that's seeped into
my bones. Or, more likely, I'm coming down from the adrenaline
spike that the lifeguards predicted when they wrapped me in a
blanket and made me hang around for observation. They shined
a penlight into my pupils and gave me microwaved hot chocolate,
rubbing my arms and legs to keep the blood flowing as they as-

sured me the victim was absolutely fine. She'd been taken to the hospital only as a precaution.

In the meantime, Erik jogged to the far parking lot to get our rental car and drive it up to the lifeguard station. By the time he returned, I'd convinced myself I was almost back to normal, aside from the headache. But that was a lie.

I am *sooo* far from normal.

"You sure you don't want me to take you to the emergency room? Last chance." Erik grimaces at my temple, where I can only surmise a huge reddish-purple bruise is blooming.

Clearing my throat, still sore from the seawater, I assure him it looks worse than it is. "Nothing more than a bunch of broken capillaries. I'm fine."

Erik goes *hmm* and reluctantly turns right to head north on Route 6, away from Hyannis and the closest ER. He doesn't want to bring up "brain damage," but I know that's what he's thinking. As a psychiatrist, he knows lots of scary stuff about the hidden hazards of seemingly mild concussions.

I, on the other hand, keep replaying a loop of my attack: Jake's heavy closed fist coming down on me slo-mo, the radiating pain, the ringing in my ears, my stunned reaction, the dark water rushing into my nose. I can't make it stop.

Also, I don't understand why no one saw him hit me. Or why no one saw him at all.

Erik had been right on the shoreline, watching the scene like a hawk. But when I asked if he'd seen the guy on the surfboard, he shook his head and said as far as he could make out it'd been just me, the woman, and the guards.

"You sure there was someone else out there?" he said. "I mean, I did kind of have my hands full getting help and then holding back the husband from jumping in." He paused, inspecting the bruise again. "You've been through quite an ordeal. It wouldn't be out of the norm for your mind to be playing tricks on you."

My mind is not playing tricks. There were two lifeguards in the vicinity. After two saved the drowning woman, the other came back for me. Jake was right there. Though when I asked the lifeguard if he'd seen the man on the surfboard, he also thought I'd simply hallucinated and that my bruise was inflicted by the fists of the drowning woman.

"That's why we have rings and ropes and buoys because getting that close to a victim is suicide," he'd said, not unkindly.

Of course, I know that. Day one in lifeguard training is all about the rules of using the tools at our disposal, rather than ourselves. And I suppose it's theoretically possible that while frantically clawing at me, the drowning woman *might* have thrown a devastating punch that *might* have rattled my brain, causing me to temporarily imagine things that weren't there.

But when I surreptitiously check my phone, angled so Erik can't look over and see what I'm searching, the first image hit for "Jake Pease" verifies my so-called hallucination. Yup, that's the same guy, right down to the beard. The only difference between the surf caster and the doting father hugging his wife and children in a Love & Pease ad for nontoxic sunscreen ($60 for a four-ounce tube of PeaseProtection) is the glare of murderous intent.

"Whatcha looking at?" Erik asks, sliding his gaze right.

I can't tell him the truth, having sworn up and down that I won't even *think* about Bella Valencia or the Peases while we're here. "Head injury symptoms."

He groans. "Geesh, don't do that. Google will have you believing you have terminal brain cancer and are minutes from death. If you're so worried, seriously, it's no problem to turn around and take you to Hyannis."

"No. I'm actually feeling a lot better. Just curious is all."

I return to cyber-hunting Jake Pease, and land on his bio page, where I learn Jake—

known to close friends and family as J.D.—is the CFO of the Love & Pease empire, as well as the father of three children with Heather, his wife of the past five years.

Also of note is that two years ago Jake authored a *New York Times* bestseller entitled *The Tao of Pease* ($26.99 hardcover) about how he "upped his business game" by adopting the 30/30/30 method. Apparently, 30/30/30 requires waking at five a.m. to drink thirty ounces of filtered water before meditating on gratitude for thirty minutes and then doing thirty minutes of hot yoga. By seven a.m., you are at your computer, revitalized, calm, and, according to the Pease website, "ready to harness the yin and yang of the market for ultimate profit power."

So, yeah, the idea that a wealthy CFO of an exclusive self-care brand, a bestselling author, and attentive father of three would be on a public Cape Cod beach waiting for me to foolishly attempt a rescue of a drowning woman just so he could hop on a surfboard and punch me in the head is more than mildly delusional.

Except for one teensy little detail that comes to me now—a brief conversation I had with my sister about a week or so before she went missing. We were jostling for sink space in our common bathroom. Kit was nimbly plaiting her hair into a French braid for work and I was rummaging around for tampons in the vanity. She was giving herself a pep talk that sounded more like practicing a speech. Role playing was a technique she'd learned in rehab, a way of preparing for stressful situations.

This particular "rehearsal" concerned me, though.

Back then, Mom and I maintained constant vigilance about Kit's "condition," always on the lookout for signs she might be using again. We had valid reasons to be worried. Kit had been acting secretive that August, waking up late and stumbling to the bathroom, where, even behind closed doors, the unmistakable sound of retching could not be disguised. She was also especially pale, her skin practically translucent, and she barely ate.

When Mom or I would gently confront her, she'd claim to be nervous about the prospect of returning to UMass in a few weeks. She said she couldn't get to sleep thinking about how the other students would perceive her and whether she'd be up for the academics. She assured us that once she settled back into a school routine, her appetite would return and everything would be okay.

Having attended a smattering of Al-Anon meetings, I had my doubts. I'd heard plenty of stories about addicts secretly using while painting rosy pictures for families who didn't learn the truth until their loved one OD'd or died. Which is why her mumbling to her reflection about having a boyfriend (though she didn't, to my knowledge) raised enough alarms for me to pop up with the box of tampons and ask directly if she was having a problem.

"Probably not," she said, twisting the mascara tube closed.

It was an unsatisfactory answer. I remember being skeptical as Kit slowly removed the tan elastic from her wrist and wrapped the end of the braid with shaking hands. "Seriously. What's going on?"

She leaned into the mirror and checked her eyeliner. "Nothing major, Janie. I swear. There's a guy at work who's been hitting on me and I need to tell him to piss off. He's got a huge ego, so I have to let him down lightly. Helps to have my lines memorized."

After Kit disappeared, I mentioned this exchange to my mother's boyfriend, Bob the cop, who said he'd check it out, though his inquiries turned up nothing. There was no guy on Serena's waitstaff who'd been pestering Kit, none of the vendors, either. The only two male employees on Serena's payroll were the bartender and a sous-chef—and they were dating each other.

Above all, no one went by the nickname I overheard Kit say to the bathroom mirror—J.D.

Initials that had no relevance, until now.

TEN

JANE

"Tell you what," Erik says as we turn into the small shopping center off Route 6. "When we get home, I'll unload the car and you can get straight into the outdoor shower. I'll even bring you your robe and an iced tea. Then we can sit on the back porch, have some cheese and crackers, a few oysters, and then . . . who knows?" He runs his finger suggestively along my inner thigh.

"Aww, that is *sooo* sweet." I move his hand up a bit and kiss him lovingly on the cheek.

It's vital Erik believes nothing is amiss with me other than a bump on my head. As soon as he enters the fish market, I quickly erase any trace of the search from my phone. While he's not the kind of creep who checks my online activity, he's been so anxious about me since the airport incident, I wouldn't put it past him to be tempted.

He emerges with a foil container of a dozen Wellfleet oysters freshly shucked on the half shell with wedges of lemon and red blobs of cocktail sauce on a bed of frosty ice. "It's not much," he says, handing me the container. "But I figure that with the Brie from the gift basket, it's a fairly romantic feast."

"To celebrate our first real vacation as a couple." The oyster tray is so cold that I shift it to the car floor. When I sit up, I catch him studying my bruise.

"She really clocked you, huh?"

I have no idea what he's talking about and then I remember the lifeguard's theory. "Does it look that bad?" I ask, gently patting the sore spot.

"Hmm, a little. It'll probably be gone by morning. All you need is a good night's sleep."

He's right about that, I think, yawning. The sharp spike of adrenaline and the day under the sun have caught up with me. Suddenly, a shower, food, and a bed with crisp, clean sheets sound like heaven.

We turn onto our street and see a pricey late-model Volvo wagon parked on the crushed-shell driveway to our cottage.

"Shit," Erik says through a pasted grin. "Sheila and Dave."

"You sure? They're not supposed to arrive until Thursday."

"I'm sure. That's their car. Maybe they're just dropping stuff off." He gets out and snatches our beach bag. "Look, I know you're exhausted, but try to be civil. He's my adviser. All roads to post-graduate fellowships lead to him."

As I am often reminded.

To be honest, I wasn't thrilled when Erik invited him in a spirit of collegiality to visit for a day. Anyone else would have figured out that a couple who hadn't ever taken a trip together might like a week to themselves. The answer should have been thanks but no thanks, you guys have fun.

Instead, Dave said, Sure! He and Sheila would love to come

down and bring the kids for a couple of nights. Erik explained the house was only eight hundred square feet and that, per the rental agreement, it's allowed to sleep no more than four. To which Dave replied that as he and his wife "practice family sleeping" this wouldn't be a problem and, besides, two little kids don't count. They would all hunker down in the one king-size bed in the loft, leaving Erik and me the pullout couch in the main room.

Which I could handle later in the week. But this is Sunday, the first day of our stay. I've just suffered a near-death experience and, on a more mundane note, our clothes are still in our suitcases. I have an outdoor shower waiting. And these oysters.

"Hey, guys!" Dave throws open the rickety screen door, greeting us as if it's his house. He's a big man with a moon face and wispy, nearly transparent hair. "What a place, eh?"

I note his colorful Hawaiian shirt and khaki shorts and bare feet. He's obviously made himself at home.

A girl about seven appears, gaping up at us with big blue eyes shaded by a mass of coppery brown curls. She is wearing a rainbow tutu, of which I am instantly envious. "Who are they, Papa?" she asks.

"Erik and Jane, the people we're vacationing with," answers her father.

With implies you're chipping in for the rent, but whatever.

"Can you say hi to our friends, Mabel?"

"Hi. Thank you for coming." Mabel extends a hand, as if she's the chair of the board and we've arrived at her annual meeting. I get that she's only a kid, but I'm irked her father doesn't set the record straight.

"Caleb's inside," she informs us. "He's two years and three months. I usually do the talking for him."

Erik crouches down and asks her if she remembers him from back in Cambridge.

"You have the small office," she replies. "Papa's is much bigger."

"Oh, hey, Jane, let me take those." Dave reaches out and grabs the oysters from my grasp. "Yum. Yum." He runs his tongue around his large lips and finishes with a smack. "I could suck these all down in a snap!"

Inside our tiny cottage, Sheila, a physically fit woman wearing a sleeveless navy jumpsuit that shows off her toned biceps, greets me with a quick, firm hug. "So great to see you again," she says, adding sotto voce, "You didn't happen to pick up any groceries on your way over, did you?"

By groceries, I assume she means food for children. "Only raw oysters, I'm afraid."

"Darn. Traffic on the bridge was so clogged, I didn't want to swing by the Stop & Shop and get here even later, but it's an hour past their dinnertime and they're starving! *Oooh*, what happened to you?" She flinches at the bruise.

"Kinda had an incident in the water."

"That must have been some incident. You know what will take that right down? Arnica."

I brush my damp hair over the sensitive spot. "Do you have some?"

"No. I didn't think to pack it. When you go to the store, you should pick up a tube though."

When I go to the store. I paste on a plastic smile and turn to Erik. This is me being civil.

He winks an "atta girl."

"Look what Erik and Jane brought! Wasn't that nice of them?" Dave holds up the foil container before opening the fridge and placing it on the second shelf beneath a four-pack of fancy Vermont beer.

My smile remains, though I'm wondering what the hell is happening. Who are the guests here?

Sheila makes a face. "Oysters? There was an article in *The Guardian* last week claiming that thanks to climate change, the bacteria growth is so high in summer, oysters're no longer safe even on the Cape." She wags a finger. "You know what they say, only eat an oyster in the months with an R."

"Gotta love the month of Argust," cracks Dave as he hands Erik a beer. "Dude, our vacation starts now!" He pops the top to an explosion of white foam. "Want one, Sheel?"

Sheila nods to the chardonnay chilling in the door. "Think I'll wait for the wine."

What wine? *Erik's* wine?

Sheila might not have been able to stock up at the Stop & Shop, but she has come well prepared in the kiddie snacks department. Before Dave closes the refrigerator door, I sneak a peek at rows of organic applesauce and organic kiddie yogurt containers as well as organic juice boxes, further proof they're here for the duration. Oh, man.

"Have you two met before?" Erik asks, tipping his can to Sheila and me.

"I think so," she says vaguely. "Perhaps at the reception Dave threw for the department last spring?"

While Sheila may have only met me once, I realize now I have seen her on at least three occasions. The first was at Whole Foods years ago when she was out-to-there pregnant with Caleb, who is currently drooling over a wooden train he is running around the coffee table. The second time was on Memorial Drive on the Fourth of July, when Sheila was nursing him under the fireworks.

The third was last November at the Natick Mall, where she was buying Happy Meals for the kids and stuffing her own face with an extra-large order of fries from McDonald's.

Not that I will own up to any of this, having learned the hard way to keep such sightings to myself.

"We tried calling you." Dave leans against the counter, taking up almost all of the galley kitchen. "We were going to stay on the lower Cape with some friends but turns out their kids have measles and since our guys don't do shots . . ."

Anti-vaxxers. Naturally. Just then, I notice the wheel of Brie Erik brought is gone, a ripped wrapper and smattering of cracker crumbs revealing its demise. Fucking A. I need a break.

"Well, I'm going to wash off that sticky salt water." I head toward my suitcase, which, I see, has been buried under a pile of toys.

"Oh, there's no water," Sheila says. "The kids were super hot and we didn't have stickers to park at any of the ponds so I decided to let them play with the hose. You must have a pretty dinky well here. It's totally drained."

No. Way.

"You should ask for a discount on the rent." Dave takes another swig and gestures to my laptop that, at last recollection, hadn't left my suitcase. It's been opened, as though someone's been using it. "By the way, do you have the password for the Wi-Fi? I'll have to do some work here this week, unfortunately."

All. Week. Confirmed.

Erik is melting in polite Minnesotan mortification, I can tell by the redness around his collar. Serves him right. I shoot him a glare of resentment; he returns fire with a grin of helpless apology and then reaches into his back pocket for his wallet. "I'd better head over to the general store and get some—"

Not so fast. "No, no, sweetie. You stay here with your friends. Let me go."

"You can't, Jane. Your head!" he exclaims.

"It's fine. And I'd enjoy the bike ride."

"Definitely not! What if you black out?"

I wave this off. "For the millionth time, I'm—"

"Would you pick up some mac and cheese?" Sheila interrupts. "Preferably organic. Like Annie's. Also, cauliflower and kale for me."

"And more of that Brie," Dave adds. "I don't know where you got that, but it was terrific."

Part of a fruit basket from Erik's parents that we'd been saving for a special occasion, I want to say, but don't when my boyfriend, reading my mind, clears his throat. "Please, baby . . ."

"I insist!" I respond far too sharply than I'd intended, but it does the trick. Erik gets the message and hands me the wallet.

"We're low on IPA. I prefer double and a local brew if they stock that at the packy," Dave says, using the local euphemism for the liquor store that he must have picked up from a Ben Affleck movie, seeing as he hails from LA. "And you'd better get more oysters. That's not enough for all of us. Even Mabel likes them, the sophisticate." He gives his daughter's curls an affectionate rub.

There is no mention of a financial contribution to what is fast becoming a shopping trip that will consume our entire weekly food budget.

"Here. I'll make a list." Sheila rummages through a kitchen drawer and brings out a pen and pad. She must have cased this place head to toe earlier to be able to find them that fast. "I was searching for batteries," she says by way of explanation, seeming to notice my reaction. "I'll add them, too."

It's already seven thirty. Serena's place will be closing soon. "It's okay. I don't have time for a list."

Caleb lets out a wail for no reason and his sister begins to scold him on the etiquette of behaving in front of guests. Politeness, she informs him, is its own virtue. I'm impressed and simultaneously terrified by the Emily Post prodigy. I can't escape fast enough.

"I'll text you," Erik says.

"Don't bother. I got it. Organic mac and cheese, kale, cauliflower, oysters, arnica, Brie, and double IPA. Preferably local."

"Also kimchi!" Sheila calls from inside. "Though don't go to any trouble if they don't have it."

I'm in the driveway getting on my bike when Erik rushes out, waving my helmet. "You forgot this."

I take it, but I have no intention of putting it on. It'll hurt too much.

"Wear it. Your brain's important."

I perch it on my head and fasten the strap loosely. "Satisfied?"

"Not yet." He leans down and plants a soft kiss on my lips. "Sorry about all this. I'll find a moment alone with Dave and delicately broach the idea of them cutting their stay short."

"Whatever. Don't worry about it." The last thing Erik needs is to stress about pissing off his adviser, especially during a relaxing week in the sun.

Plus, now that I think of it, Dave and Sheila might provide much needed distraction for when I want to sneak over to Heron's Neck. If it's just Erik and me, I'll never find an opportunity to slip out, not with the way he hovers.

"I wasn't lying when I said I was looking forward to the ride," I tell him. "I'll take the rail trail like I used to when I was a kid."

His lips turn up in gratitude. "Be careful, okay? If you feel dizzy or anything, call me. No . . . call 9–1–1, then call me."

"I'm fine."

I'm actually more than fine, because if I can make Serendipity Seafood before it closes, then it'll be worth the trip to Wellfleet to check in with Serena, Kit's former boss, the woman she was working for the night she disappeared.

Maybe she has some insight into why Jake Pease just tried to give me a concussion, or worse.

ELEVEN

JANE

Now that I'm pedaling madly and the blood coursing through my veins is exacerbating a pounding headache, I'm not so sure the ride to Wellfleet was such a hot idea after all. I should have taken the car, even though I can't stand sitting in bumper-to-bumper traffic on Route 6, the main thoroughfare from Sandwich to Provincetown.

The Cape Cod Rail Trail, which runs through the preserved National Seashore, is a smooth, paved delight, a reminder of riding bikes with Kit when we were kids. We'd pick up the trail in Shoreham and head six miles to the Wellfleet General Store with its narrow, creaky wooden floorboards and stacks of newspapers held down by chunks of silver driftwood.

We'd gorge on candy (Twizzlers for her, Sour Patch gummies for me) while gawking at teenage pregnant moms in *US Weekly*, inevitably forgetting our own mother's request—the quart of milk, the stick of butter. Arnie, the store's owner, would give us a discount, seeing as how my mother was raising us on her piddly town clerk salary and couldn't afford the jacked-up prices he charged the tourists for their whole-wheat pasta and imported olives.

On the way back, Kit, far more athletic on land than I, would suggest a race, her long legs churning in a whir. She'd sit up—no hands!—while I, panting and grunting, gripped the handles until my thumbs ached, pumping to keep up. Never could. She'd get so far ahead, she'd have to circle back to check if I was okay.

"Oh, my god. You are *sooooo* slow. Put some muscle into it." She'd pause long enough to laugh and then off she'd go again, her bright blond ponytail flying behind her like a royal banner.

I used to envy that hair. I dreamed of snipping off that ponytail in her sleep. It wasn't fair she got all the best parts of our parents' DNA while I was stuck with a long-distance swimmer's body: big feet, broad shoulders, no breasts, and a padding of fat to keep me buoyant.

Mom said Kit's golden blond came from our father's Swedish genes, ones that in my more generous moments I've blamed for Stan's Viking wanderlust, a marked contrast to our homebody mother. Our parents met when he was in the Massachusetts Maritime Academy down in Buzzards Bay, where she manned the Howard Johnson's lunch counter. To hear Mom tell it, it was a whirlwind romance: three dates, each of which involved some form of fishing, capped off by a wedding at Town Hall, a ramshackle building that dates back to the 1700s.

Five years later, they had two little girls and Mom was working as an assistant town clerk in Shoreham, handling property taxes and land records and filing birth certificates, while Stan was an officer in the US Merchant Marine, bobbing along the seven seas. Their lives couldn't have diverged more starkly. After a few shore leaves, they found they had simply, er, drifted apart, with

Stan sailing all the way to New Zealand, where he formed his new family on a two-hundred-acre sheep farm.

We have a relationship, of sorts, in that Stan constantly sends me photos of the farm. More specifically, sheep on the farm. My phone is filled with shots of white sheep dotting green hills, of their dog, Roxie, herding sheep, of sheep eating grass or sheep taking a nap, sheep entering through the split-rail fence, sheep exiting. Sometimes he'll caption them with texts that make absolutely no sense. Like, "Here's a gimmer ready for crog!" During lambing season, he's totally out of control.

Lately, he's been off the sheep kick and onto Homeland Security. Ever since I was fired for breaking cover or, as he suggests, pissing off the Pease family, Stan's been emailing me iffy internet posts about how my former employer is a fascist organization I should be glad to be free from.

"Dodged a bullet, I'd say," was his most recent "secret" message—transmitted via WhatsApp, of course, because he doesn't trust the US government.

I can remember meeting him in person only once. The week after Kit went missing, he made the nineteen-hour flight to Boston for "support." I accompanied Mom to the airport, and even in my grief and worry I was bristling with anticipation, expecting to greet the handsome, trim sailor from the framed wedding photo our mother still kept tucked in her lingerie drawer. I was shocked when a beefy, wind-burned farmer in rubber muck boots and a grimy green rucksack appeared at the double doors instead. He was nothing like I'd imagined and, while I could vaguely see a resemblance to Kit, I was disappointed to find no hint of myself in his rugged features.

"You must be Jane," he said, extending a rough hand after attempting an awkward hug. I couldn't stop staring at the calluses on his palm and the long white scar running up his thumb, and thinking, *This isn't my father. This is a total stranger.*

I'd felt far more paternal affinity for Bob, who'd never missed one of my swim meets, who gripped the dashboard while teaching me how to drive stick, the confessor to whom I'd divulged my unforgivable sin. Bob was my actual father, not this guy . . . *Stan.*

"You don't have to be afraid of me, Bumble," Stan said that day at the airport, daring to call me by my baby nickname. "I'm not all that bad."

Though he was, especially when it came to his relationship with Bob. Looking back, I suppose it was understandably awkward to have Mom and Bob head up to bed together and leave Stan to sleep uncomfortably on the couch, his size-thirteen feet sticking over the armrest. But I could tell it was more than your typical machismo that fed their deep, smoldering, mutual hatred.

Back then, Bob was fit and disciplined, up at five a.m. to run his usual three miles before donning a starched uniform and heading off to the station, where his priority number one was finding my sister. Stan slept in and shuffled around the kitchen in ratty, handknit wool socks, making useless pots of tea while Mom and I organized search parties and phone trees, hunting down anyone who might have been on the cove that night with Kit.

Bob was a karate instructor with a black belt to boot. Stan watched professional wrestling on cable. Bob avoided red meat, nitrates, and eggs. Stan seemed to subsist on hamburgers alone.

Stan made quips about how police in New Zealand didn't carry guns because they were real men. Bob observed that real men didn't leave their families for other women halfway around the globe. Stan wondered out loud if Kit never would have succumbed to addiction if the man of the house hadn't been such a hard-ass. Bob cited statistics about the rates of teenage addiction in families where fathers had abandoned their parental duties. On and on. Back and forth for seven long, miserable days.

And the worst of it was, I couldn't compare notes with the only other person who would have commiserated: Kit.

"Come visit our farm whenever you want," Stan said, his last words to me when we dropped him off at the airport. "You're always welcome there, Bumble. You might be surprised how much you like it."

What else was he supposed to say? He's my father. Of course, he has to invite me to stay even if neither of us has any intention of taking the offer seriously. I told him sure, and he gave me a hug and that was essentially it for our physical reunion.

Since then, I've had enough therapy to come to terms with my conflicted feelings toward Stan. It's not simply that I resent him being out of the picture during our childhood, or that he has other children he may love more. I just don't think I'll get over how he blew into town to help us find Kit and left without doing jack squat, as though he was robotically going through the motions out of some vague fatherly obligation.

"You know she's gone, right?" he'd remarked almost as a casual aside, the way you talk about the Red Sox's chances for the pennant, one afternoon while we were combing the bay on our daily hunt for clues. "I mean it'd be a miracle if she survived, and we'd all jump for joy to see her. But your sister was fighting an uphill battle that by all indications she lost. It's not your fault. It's not even her fault. Addiction sucks, Jane, but eventually you'll have to accept what happened and move on, for your own sanity, for your own future."

As if I could envision a future without Kit.

I was so furious, I shouted at him to fuck off and ran back to the car, leaving him to hitch a ride home. Stan had no idea what

Mom and I had been through with Kit, or how much effort she'd put into fighting her brain's constant cravings. He didn't have an inkling of how lovely and normal our lives had been before the accident and how everything changed in the flip of a poorly executed move on the uneven bars during an otherwise routine practice.

Ironically, despite the pain and inevitable surgery, Kit wasn't particularly devastated by her broken leg at the time. Sure, the accident meant the end of high school competition—that was a bummer—but lots of sporty teenagers break bones. You could even say it's a rite of passage.

We were so, so naive.

Kit went into surgery a scholar-athlete with a straight-A average at Shoreham High and 1580 SATs. She took the dose of Oxy-Contin she was prescribed and two months later she was a junkie on academic probation. That's how fast it happened.

Kit said opioids helped "turn off her mind" so she could sleep, but the addiction counselors said, actually, it was the opposite. Now, the drugs were in control of her mind. That post-surgery dose had changed the receptors in her brain so she would have to work super hard on maintaining sobriety—with our help. From then on, nothing was normal. Mom, Kit, and I were consumed by one mission: keep her clean long enough for her brain to rewire itself so she could move forward to hopefully enjoy a healthy, rewarding life.

The battle was constant, as were the fights and tears. The lowest point came when Kit was busted for selling oxy in a sting set up by none other than Bob, an arrest that set in motion a chain reaction of one humiliation after another.

As an elected official dealing daily with the public, Mom had to keep her chin up when the local paper ran Kit's cheesy mug shot and people started to gossip about her bad parenting. Bob had to issue a public statement that despite all his law enforcement experience and alleged expertise, he'd been unwittingly harboring not only a user but a dealer.

And then there was me, the sibling who lost her sister—and closest ally—when Kit was drained by drugs and then by the justice system. Girls I'd considered to be good friends suddenly started coming up with lame excuses about not being able to sleep over on Friday nights because, I could only surmise, their own parents thought we lived in a crack house. Teachers treated me differently, pulled me aside after class to ask me sincerely whether I "felt safe at home."

Mom fretted. Bob glowered. I retreated to my room.

Kit was released from outpatient rehab in January, determined to stay clean. We told her we believed in her, but, privately, I had my doubts. I'd read so much depressing stuff online about how addicts aren't ever the people they were before. I desperately wanted to believe Kit would be the exception, that she would recover and be back to her old self.

The problem was, she didn't look like she was improving the summer she was nineteen, the summer she worked as a waitress for Serena, the summer she started sleeping with Will Pease, the summer that ended with her disappearance. In retrospect, she seemed tormented. By what, I've never been certain.

I've long suspected Serena was far more aware of the demons Kit was facing than she's ever let on. She must have overheard her staff gossiping about my sister. She must have noticed Kit's paleness and weight loss, her wan complexion and chewed nails. But because Serena's such a private person and, frankly, slightly intimidating, I've never had the courage to ask her outright if there are any secrets about my sister she's been hiding.

But that was before I recognized Bella Valencia in the airport, before I lost my job and the Peases' attorney threatened to ruin my life, before I was tarred and feathered on Twitter, and before Jake Pease pounded me in the skull. Now, my need to know what really happened that summer isn't just a matter of finding Kit, it's quite possibly a matter of my own survival.

TWELVE

JANE

A t the trail's end, I leave my bike in the rack, not bothering to lock it, then grab my backpack and head over the sandy berm to the parking lot. The sun is beneath the horizon, the sky over the marsh growing a dark gray blue, and the temps have dropped by several degrees. A few customers dawdle over red plastic baskets in the small, enclosed eating area behind Serendipity Seafood where a fan beats out the greasy, county-fair smells of an overworked fryer. My empty stomach rumbles at the thought of battered clam strips dipped in Serena's homemade tartar sauce.

The bright purple, yellow, and green paint on the once whimsical Serendipity Seafood sign has dulled to faded pastels and the screen door looks like it could use a new set of hinges. The summer humidity and brutal winter winds have rusted the springs, and I suspect a downturn in clients has delayed cosmetic maintenance.

Back in the nineties and aughts, Serena's establishment was the darling of Boston yuppies in Birkenstocks, their beards still damp from their dips in the freshwater kettle ponds, that week's *New Yorker* rolled under their arms as they waited in line for the catch of the day. Bob told me last summer that Serena had lost a lot of business to Wellfleet's gourmet seafood markets with their baked oysters Rockefeller, raw-bar party platters, smoked bluefish pâté, complete take-and-go lobster dinners, chilled French wines, and, for dessert, artfully frosted cupcakes.

Pretension never was Serena's style.

The shop is empty when I step onto its white concrete floor. Framed yellowing newspaper clips clutter the walls, along with photos of her past summer staff, the years noted at the bottom of each frame. I count back eleven and find Kit's group, all wearing that year's signature Serendipity Seafood T-shirt. I scan the faces of three smiling teenage girls and two grinning boys, and wonder why my sister's not in the shot. Then it hits me like a sucker punch. This was taken after she disappeared.

I step up to the counter and take a deep breath. The place looks and smells like any other fish market, simultaneously fresh and rotten. A cloudy lobster tank divided between halves and chickens gurgles in the corner. A few remaining steaks of swordfish harpooned in Chatham and bluefish caught off Billingsgate lie on melting crushed ice. This late in the day, the cases have been picked over, though there's a steel pan of unopened oysters left. I check out the price—twice what we locals used to pay.

The beaded curtains tinkle and Serena emerges, streaks of gray in her curly dark hair the only indication she's aged since I last saw her. I'd forgotten how tall she is—that Ethiopian heritage—and how curvy, the contribution of her Italian mother, owner of her own fish market in Boston's North End, who taught her how to cook *fruits de mer*. Kit told me Serena bragged that she knew how to hook, gut, and filet a fish while she was still in diapers. She could poach a sea bass with dill and arugula while other kids were playing with Legos.

Serena is about to rattle off the specials when she shuts her mouth and widens her eyes. I give her a big smile. I even consider dropping my pack and opening my arms for a hug, but my Yankee sense of restraint kicks in and I hang back.

"Jane?" She brings a hand to the white bib of her apron, splattered with fish blood. "Oh, baby. You're back!"

"Just for a week." Inexplicably, the warmth in her voice makes me choke up a bit and I have to fixate on the cracks in the floor for a minute to keep from getting emotional. "Erik—that's my boyfriend—he and I are renting down in Shoreham."

"How're you doing?" And then she waves her question away. "No, you don't have to explain. I read about what happened. Twitter."

This takes me for a loop, I'll admit. I've always thought of my hometown as a protected bubble immune to the invasion of social media. I don't know if that speaks more to my naïveté or how things have changed since I left. "Don't believe everything you read."

"*Pffff.* No worries. I don't trust anything anymore . . . Or anyone."

Ditto. Checking to make sure no one's coming from outside to interrupt us, I move closer. "Look, I'm here to pick up food—but can I also ask you a couple of questions?"

She glances at the clock behind her. "Yeah, of course, but I'm closing in a few minutes. I have people coming to the house. Dinner guests."

"Cool. What're you serving?"

"Fresh tuna with capers and olives, probably. I put aside a couple of steaks." She snaps her metal tongs, eager to move on to the business at hand. "Now, what can I get you?"

It's been a little over a decade since we've seen each other, when we shared the loss of my closest friend and someone she adored, and yet I get the sense Serena is rolling up the welcome mat. Whatever. I try not to take it personally.

"How about a dozen oysters?"

"Gladly." She pulls a plastic glove from a cardboard box on the wall and slides it over her long fingers. "What's on your mind?"

"So, thinking back to those parties you catered at Heron's Neck the summer Kit worked for you, do you remember running into one of the Pease kids, an adopted one? She may or may not have gone by the last name Valencia at the time."

Serena reaches into the oyster bin and grabs a handful of the gray shells. "Are you talking about the woman you accused—" She's about to add "of murder" and catches herself. ". . . At the airport?"

"Mm-hmm. Long black hair, big brown eyes. She would have stood out from the other Peases, as she's originally from Colombia."

"You're talking about Will's fiancée. His adopted sister, Bella."

"That's right." I stifle a bubble of hope that her quick answer means Serena's been thinking about Bella's connection to Kit, too. But either Serena didn't hear me or she's crafting her response because she slowly counts out three oysters—one, two, three—and goes back for more.

"Would she and Kit have known each other back then?" I prod.

"I don't know. I try not to get involved in my staff's social life." She doesn't make eye contact when she says this, still concentrating on counting out oysters—like she couldn't do that in her sleep. Okay, now I can't help but be hurt.

I move to the next topic on my mental list. "By the way, Jake Pease was surf casting down at Coast Guard Beach today. Is that unusual for him?"

"I have no idea." She tips the scale of oysters into the plastic bag, rolling open the edges so they can breathe. "He fishes all over the ocean side. Maybe the snappers are running."

"Are they? I'm not sure he even had bait on his hook."

Finally, she meets my gaze. "What're you getting at, hon?"

"This might sound nuts, but I think he tried to drown me this afternoon."

She doesn't show surprise—or concern. In the passing of a second, she reassembles her response and gives me a blasé laugh. "Jake? You've got to be kidding. He's a big ol' puppy dog."

"I am not. I saw him up close and personal. Or, to be more accurate, his fist."

Her hand is still clutching the bag. "This, I wanna hear."

"It was after hours. The guards had left and I saw a swimmer struggling way past the sandbar. So I kicked into action and went out with a towel. Once a lifeguard, always a lifeguard, right?"

Serena seems to have stopped breathing. She's not even moving. Just standing posed like a statue, one hand on her hip, one on the bag.

"Jake paddled out on a surfboard soon after. While the lifeguards were rescuing the drowning woman, he came over to me and offered a hand. Except, instead of pulling me out, he punched me down. Literally." I swipe back my hair and show her the bruise. "*This* is what he did to me."

She blinks, whether stunned or skeptical, I can't tell.

"Swear to God." I cross my chest. "On my mother's grave."

Her body shifts and, along with it, the atmosphere of the tiny shop, and I can't help but fear I've made a mistake.

"That's quite a story, but I don't think so." She places the oysters on the counter. "I know Jake well, very, very well. He and his family are excellent customers. If it weren't for them, I'd have gone under long ago."

I could kick myself for being so stupid. Of course, Serena, like a lot of small business owners, is in debt to the Peases. That family throws around cash like confetti, especially when it suits their interests. Apparently, it pays off, considering Serena's mild reproof of my allegation.

"And I can't imagine him actually hitting someone, not Jake," she continues. "He's such a stand-up guy, holding fundraisers for the fire department and police. They're all about creating community connections, those Peases. Exactly like you see on their website. I mean, I might not go for their New Age, tune-into-your-chakra mumbo jumbo, but from what I've seen, they really do try to walk the talk."

Well, this is disappointing. A person I once respected as a self-made, independent woman with a moral code is such a sell-out she is willing to put her allegiance to a bunch of zillionaires above the life of my sister. Time to cut my losses and move on.

"Oh, okay. Yeah, that's what I figured," I say, brushing off my prior gravity with a shrug. "I must have hallucinated him when I bumped my head."

"Uh-huh." But she doesn't seem that convinced. And now she's gone ice cold. "Is that all?" She shoots another glance at the clock, which reads eight fifteen p.m., way past closing time.

There's a clash of dishes in a sink coming from the back, and it occurs to me that perhaps Serena fears someone might be eavesdropping.

Snatching an order slip, I jot down my number with the pen attached to the counter by a piece of dirty string. "This is my cell. Text or call when you get a chance. It'd be really . . ." I search for a more meaningful word than *helpful* ". . . *therapeutic* if I could discuss that night with you. There's a lot I have to put to bed."

She slips the paper with my number into her apron pocket. "That'll be thirty-seven fifty-five with tax."

We cash out and she swipes my credit card, before passing over the bag of oysters. "Thank you for coming in," she says stiffly. Then, softening slightly, adds, "I loved Kit like one of my own, Jane. It's good to see you again. Come back soon."

I thank her and step outside to the parking lot, where I check the receipt in the dimming light as Serena switches the sign behind me from OPEN to CLOSED. Thirty-eight bucks for a dozen unshucked oysters. Tourist prices. Must not be that good to see me.

"Whoa!" a voice says and I nearly walk head-on into a middle-aged man wearing a Mets cap and a pair of Oakleys, though it's way too dark to be wearing sunglasses. "Didn't see you there."

You would have, I think, *if you took those off.* "Sorry," I say, stepping to the side. "I wasn't paying attention."

"Aww, shit. They're closed?" He scratches his head, gawping at the sign. "I thought she was open 'til nine."

"Me, too. She has guests coming for dinner. She seemed to be in some sort of a rush."

But I misjudged. For as soon as the words leave my lips, Serena undoes the lock and pushes open the screen. "Hey, you. Long time, no see," she coos, ushering him in. Then, catching sight of me, she smiles weakly before shutting the door and turning the lock.

And that's when I realize my other big mistake. I should have told Serena that if she runs into Bob, please, under no circumstances mention I'm in town. Because if there's one thing I know about Serena, she likes to talk.

Except, apparently, to me.

THIRTEEN

JANE

It's not like I'm trying to avoid Bob. Well, actually, I am. For now. I'd simply prefer to stay off his radar until I've had a chance to jostle the memories of those who knew Kit and what she might have been up to the days before she went missing. If I can find even a scintilla of evidence that Bella Valencia was in the area that night and not on a plane to LA as she claimed to be, then I can present that morsel to Bob on a silver platter and he'll have to reopen the case. He'll simply have no other choice.

The problem with Bob is he's way too protective, especially after what happened to Kit. If it gets back to him that I'm in his jurisdiction, he'll assign his lackeys to twenty-four-hour surveillance to make sure no hired Pease goon runs me off the road or whatever harm Bob in his cop paranoia imagines they can inflict. I often replay our last serious conversation about Bella and his line that the Peases could get away with walking out of Tiffany with a hundred grand in diamonds. What comes through is that Bob's chicken-shit scared of bringing them to justice, probably scared of how they might destroy his reputation, and, more important, scared of how they might come after me.

To all that I say, bring it.

———◆———

By the time I've loaded up my pack with locally brewed craft beer and cheeses, crackers, kale, cherry tomatoes and basil, frozen cauliflower (nonorganic, sorry, Sheila), batteries, coffee, half-and-half, and cocktail sauce—along with the oysters—it's pitch dark and a good hour after I should have returned to the cottage.

Erik has sent me a couple of texts: What's taking so long? and You're missing all the fun. We're really having a blast! followed by an update that the kids are in bed FYI.

Out of oysters in Shoreham so I had to go to Wellfleet, my thumbs lie. On my way!

Even though I have to get back ASAP, on impulse I decide to make a quick detour to the town graveyard. The historic cemetery is tucked behind the Shoreham Police Department on a slight hill surrounded by a locked wrought-iron fence thick with multiple coats of glossy black paint. If I'm going to visit, it's got to be now: Bob's office, in a new addition to the Town Hall, has a clear view of the graveyard, and if I go there during the day, he'll have a clear view of me.

Some of the graves go all the way back to the 1600s, when Miles Standish was running around the area stealing winter corn from the Wampanoag. Why the Standish family, the scions of Shoreham, seem so proud to share his homicidal DNA is beyond me. But, as they funded the graveyard I'm about to break into, who am I to object?

I lean my bike against the gate, drop my pack, and sneak in the way we used to in high school, through a bent pair of bars at the corner. At least that much hasn't changed.

The atmosphere is quiet and spooky, with the fog rolling in over the ancient stones marked with dulled indentations of skulls and crossbones. The boughs of stunted oaks could be ghouls in the encroaching darkness. I feel a growing sense of trepidation as my Tevas crunch across the yard to my destination.

The hardest thing about coming home is making this visit. Swallowing a lump of grief, I weave through the ancient headstones toward the newer section, fighting off the old waves of guilt. Mom isn't here because of what I didn't do or didn't say, I try to assure myself. But this is a lie.

The truth is, I could have saved my sister. I had a chance and I squandered it.

The night began with the ominous ping of a Facebook message.

I'd fallen asleep with my laptop open and was awakened by the notification of a message from Cobb Cooper, a guy I'd only exchanged a "hi" or "hey" with, whose parents, Barb and Harry, owned Camp Pekky.

The last session of camp had ended the day before and I was in total relaxation mode, staying up late texting with my lifeguard buddies, going online to watch stupid videos, and eating tons of junk food. When I saw Cobb's message, I sat up in alarm, checking the clock on my screen. It was fifteen minutes after midnight.

Right away, I knew there was trouble and I knew it involved Kit.

Hey, if this is Jane who guards at Pekky you should know your sister's partying with a bunch of townies at the cove. I heard my parents calling the cops and went down there to warn everyone. She's totally out of it and needs to get the fuck out before the cops arrive. She can't get busted again.

Even in the moment, it struck me that Cobb's message was hardly altruistic, since he had a personal interest in making sure Kit didn't get arrested. He'd been her dealer for everything from pot to coke to oxy and, while she'd refused to rat him out the first time she got arrested, there was no guarantee she'd do the same the next time.

On it, I wrote back. Then I pulled on a pair of sweats and zipped up my hoodie, sneaking downstairs to grab the car keys out of the bowl in the foyer, doing my best not to wake my mother as Cobb's message rolled around and around in my mind. She's totally out of it.

"Goddammit," I cursed as I started up my mother's Honda Civic and slowly backed out of the driveway. "You promised, Kit. *You promised!*"

In her plea bargain, the charge against Kit was downgraded to possession, but she had had to promise to complete an outpatient treatment program, perform five hundred hours of community service, and stay alcohol- and drug-free for two years. On top of that, the judge temporarily suspended her driver's license and imposed a ten p.m. curfew. However, he did allow her to keep her catering job, provided she headed straight home after her shift.

This meant I was often tasked with the duty of being her chauffeur, schlepping her back and forth to appointments with her probation officer/therapist/doctor. Usually, though, if Kit had to stay overtime to clean up after an event, Serena would drop her off.

At least, that was what she told our mother.

Toward the end of that summer, she started getting rides home from Will Pease, which was the long and short of what she'd tell me about their relationship. If I asked what was up with him, she'd reply with a bored shrug or "We're just friends," though, obviously, that was an understatement. Kit would stay out so late with Will some nights she had to hoist herself onto our outdoor shower and climb through my open window to avoid waking Mom. Once, I spotted her coming in with her shirt half unbuttoned, her hair a tangled mess, and her eye makeup smeared. She didn't offer one word of explanation on her way out my door except for a terse, "Don't start."

So, in a way, I was already programmed to rush to Kit's rescue. As I drove down a deserted Route 6 and turned toward the bay side, praying I'd beaten the cops, I kept thinking what a relief it would be to have Kit out of my hair the following week when she returned to UMass, because I was pissed. And rightly so.

She promised.

I parked the Honda in the public beach lot on the other side of the camp, where it wouldn't attract the attention of law enforcement, then hiked up the beach to the so-called party cove, a protected area near the marsh buffeted by tall grass and scrub pines.

Even in the pitch-black, I could make out the small bridge to Heron's Neck, where a mysterious black Suburban was permanently stationed by the wooden railings. There was a camp legend that during very low tide you could cross the mud flats to the marshy side of the Peases' private island, provided you could survive the sulfurous quicksand muck. Every summer, like clockwork, some cocky kid would attempt it on a dare and return slimed to his thighs with rich loam, stinking of rotten eggs and cursing the thousands of pinching fiddler crabs.

The bonfire was smoldering when I got to the cove and half-empty beer bottles had been tossed about, indicating a rushed exit. The stale funk of marijuana still hung heavy in the air and the sand was pocked with footprints. Perhaps the cops had come and gone. If so, had they nabbed Kit?

"You!" a man called from the darkness. "Stop!"

Instantly, I broke out in a sweat. *A cop*, I thought, preparing for my own dash into the woods. In my sneakers, dark jeans, and a navy hoodie, the odds were in my favor that I'd escape undetected. Cops didn't like to run if they didn't have to—another helpful tip from Bob.

No sooner did I pivot, however, when I tripped on a stray log and fell face forward into the sand. I rolled over, attempting to get up, and found a male figure looming over me.

"What are you doing here?" he demanded.

"My sister," I said, stumbling as I stood. "I came to pick her up."

"Sister, huh?" He switched on the flashlight of his phone. For a moment, I caught a brief glance of his tanned, leathery face crisscrossed with wrinkles and graying hair at the temples. Judging from his heavy platinum watch and pricey windbreaker, I figured he was one of the neighboring summer people.

"What's your sister's name?" he asked, rotating his phone so the light was trained on me. "She could be one of my daughter's friends."

I didn't know what to say. I didn't want to out Kit—or myself, to be honest—so I just shook my head. "Can you turn off that light? It's blinding."

He did as I asked and then grabbed my forearm, hard. "What's her name? It's important."

"Kit. Kit Ellison." I tried to twist out of his grip. "Can you . . . not?"

He let me go, perhaps because I'd confirmed Kit wasn't one of his daughter's friends. "You have no business being down on the beach at this hour, alone. It's not safe for a girl your age."

I wanted to spit back that he didn't know what he was talking about since he was from, like, Connecticut or some suburban hellhole, and didn't have a clue. "I'm fine," I said, rubbing the spot where his thumb had been bruising my bone.

"You won't be fine when the police arrive."

Awesome. That meant there was a chance Kit hadn't been rounded up, I thought with relief. But if what this guy said was true, I had to find her fast, because he wasn't the kind of person police ignored.

"Okay," I said, backing up. "Well, she's not here, so . . ."

"So go home," he growled. "This is my beach and I won't have my peace and quiet ruined by a bunch of rowdy partiers. I could have you arrested for trespassing, you know. Go. Go on!"

I didn't stick around to argue. I took off for my car as fast as I could.

FOURTEEN

JANE

My injury from earlier in the day must be playing tricks with my head because as I make my way through the cemetery, I swear the breeze through the pine trees sounds like it's whispering my sister's name. *Kiiiiit. Kiiiit.*

She was at the opposite end of the beach, near the public lot where I'd left the car. I'd just passed the boat landing, figuring she'd probably gotten a lift home, when I heard a cough. I turned and saw a strange figure on all fours like an animal, vomiting into the bay. I only recognized her by her favorite white shorts.

Kit!

Massively relieved that I'd found her and that she'd eluded the cops, I was also furious that she'd gotten so high she'd made herself sick. And I was panicked. How was I going to get her to the car in this state? How was I going to sneak her into the house without Mom and Bob hearing us?

If Bob had so much as an inkling Kit was using again, he'd have no choice but to call her probation officer, which would have scuttled Kit's plans to go back to school, which would have sent Mom over the edge.

"Jesus, Kit!" I cried, running toward her and stopping short a mere few yards away, recoiling in disgust.

In what would be the last time we'd ever make eye contact, Kit lifted her head and swiveled to glare at me over her shoulder. This wasn't the sister who taught me how to weave friendship brace-lets and set up a haunted house on Halloween for my friends and annoyed Mom by dyeing my hair red with beet juice. This wasn't the best friend who let me crawl into bed with her during thun-derstorms or when Mom and Bob were arguing in the kitchen. That sweet, kind person was gone and in her place was the shell of someone I'd once worshipped and adored. Someone I'd relied on to be my protector.

Unable to focus, this creature wobbled from side to side, moaning, a froth of white coming from the corner of her dry lips. In the dim light from the parking lot, I could make out a dark stain on the Serendipity Seafood T-shirt that hung off her emaciated frame. Worst of all, though, was the smell I could pick up even in the salty air—beer and puke and piss.

"Sorry, Jane," she whispered. "It's not what you think." Then she teetered and fell sideways, her head hitting the water with a splash.

I screamed and went to give her CPR, only to run smack into a girl who seemingly came out of nowhere. She was tall, raven-haired, with alabaster skin, and about my sister's age, though I couldn't ID her as a member of Serena's staff or one of Kit's AA friends who occasionally stopped by the house with her after meetings. She was dressed almost entirely in dark clothes like I was, as though she, too, was preparing to hide from the cops.

Wordlessly, she pulled Kit from the water and rolled her so

she was face down on the sand. I couldn't stop staring at my sister's rubbery figure, which reminded me of those dummies we'd used for practice in our Red Cross classes, even more so when the stranger self-assuredly pushed back the sleeves of her black sweatshirt and proceeded to pump the water out of Kit's lungs.

"Let me," I said. "I'm a lifeguard. I know how."

"So do I," she replied, pressing on Kit's back with a steady, firm rhythm.

My sister didn't move.

"Is she okay?" I asked, my teeth chattering. All I could think about was Mom, about the nightmare of having to tell her Kit had overdosed at my feet.

"She's breathing." She turned Kit onto her side and smoothed a strand of hair off her flaccid cheek. "I'll take care of her."

"I can. I'm her sister," I said with as much bravery as I could muster, though, in retrospect, not as forcefully as I should have. "My car's right over there." I waved to the lot, unable to stop staring at Kit's ashen complexion. She might have been breathing, but she looked dead.

The sad truth was that at age seventeen, alone on this beach without Mom or Bob to take charge, I was scared out of my wits for Kit and for myself. I didn't want this terrifying responsibility and was secretly glad someone else was stepping in.

"No. Not you," she said. Then, glancing up, she added resolutely, "You have to go, now."

Go? I couldn't go. "What, and just leave her?"

"I told you. I'll handle it."

I had no idea what she meant by *it*. "She has to go to the ER. We have to call 9–1–1!"

"That's the last thing your sister needs." She stood, put both hands on my shoulders and slowly and deliberately said, "Go home. Go to bed. If your mother asks where your sister is, tell her she called you to say she was staying over at a friend's. Got it?"

I couldn't speak. I was in some sort of shock. Hot tears rolled down my cheeks. I wanted Mom to be there and also not to be there. I wanted very, very much for this not to be happening. "Just tell me she's gonna live."

At that moment, Kit let out a groan. I am sure of it. I have re-played this scene over and over and over in my mind. She moaned and stretched, her arm splashing the water. This was not my imag-ination. I heard and saw what I heard and saw. Kit was alive, I know it.

Right then, there was a faint ding. The tall girl reached into her pocket and pulled out a flip phone, reading the screen before snapping it closed. "The cops are here," she said softly. "Run as fast as you can. Don't try making it to your car. Head for the woods in the camp and hunker down. Make yourself small. And remember, you never saw me."

I did what she instructed; I don't know why, something about the authority in her tone. Blindly, I made a beeline for Pekky until I found a tent platform, its canvas sides rolled down in prepara-tion for the off-season, and slid under one of the empty wooden bunk beds.

There I waited for an hour, maybe more, silently crying and trembling, praying that Kit would live, that the cops—whose ra-dios I could hear crackling over the water—wouldn't find her. Or maybe that they would, and call an ambulance. I just wanted her to survive. I wanted everything to be like it was before she broke her leg. I wanted to turn back the clock—if not years, then at least hours.

"Do you know where Kit is?" My mother's frantic question

catapulted me from a deep sleep, and I wondered groggily how she'd found me under the bed in the camp. Then I noticed the morning sun streaming through my windows over the familiar white coverlet and, with dizzy confusion, recognized my own bed.

To this day, I have no idea how I got there. The trauma of that evening erased my memory, I suppose.

Mom gave me a shake. "Where's your sister? She's not in her room. She said she'd go to church with me this morning."

"Oh, um." I sat up, squinting in the bright light. Church was part of Kit's recovery program. Higher power and all that. "Yeah, she called me last night and said she was staying at a friend's. Didn't want to wake you."

With that, my mother relaxed a bit, her shoulders slumping. "Oh, Kit." She shook her head, disappointed. "This is not a good sign. She knows how important it is to stick with the plans she makes. We'll have to talk about commitment when she gets home."

Mom left for the service and I stared at the wall, recounting the bizarre scene on the beach. My sheets were gritty with sand and there were pine needles in my hair. It hadn't been a bad dream, though how I wished it had.

Sunday morning turned into Sunday afternoon, anxiety in the house ratcheting with each unanswered text sent to Kit's cell phone, each call that went immediately to voice mail. Mom phoned Serena, apologizing profusely for contacting her at home, pacing back and forth when Serena said Kit hadn't mentioned which friend she was staying with, but assuring her everything was fine. I Facebook messaged Cobb to see if he knew anything, but he didn't reply. Then I figured out he'd blocked me, the jerk.

By evening, Bob had ordered his entire department to report to duty and spread out in a search. Even then, I kept my secret, clutching at the illusion that Kit would be furious if I told our family that I'd seen her drunk and/or high, that she'd accuse me of ruining her life over one stupid mistake.

I spun a fantasy in which Kit was safe with that girl, whoever she was. I told myself that at any moment she'd sashay through the door with her usual bullshit excuses. She'd lost her phone or had run down the battery and didn't have a charger. She might even go so far as to throw Will under the bus, knowing full well Bob wouldn't dare cross the Peases.

The next day, Kit's teal Serendipity Seafood T-shirt washed up in the marsh on an incoming tide.

It was splattered with blood.

That did it. I finally blurted out the truth to Bob. I told him about Cobb's Facebook message, about finding the bonfire fizzling and then about seeing Kit on all fours, sick, but stopped short of telling them about the stranger, who'd told me to pretend as though I'd never seen her. Bob told Mom, who sat on their bed, clutching her middle and rocking back and forth mumbling, "Why? Why? Why?"

There were so many whys. Why hadn't I woken Mom up when Cobb messaged me? Why hadn't I called her from the beach after finding Kit on the edge of consciousness? Why had I obeyed this stranger?

"Maybe she's okay," I said. "She wasn't alone when I found her."

Mom stopped rocking, her red-rimmed eyes blinking up at me with desperate hope. "Who else was there?"

I hesitated.

"Who?" Bob demanded, looking angrier than I'd ever seen him. "Jesus, Jane. This is a matter of life and death. Who the hell was with her?"

Between sobs, I described the dark-haired girl and said I'd never seen her before. "She said she'd take of everything."

Bob immediately proceeded to pepper me with questions. Was there anyone else there? Was there another car in the lot? A boat? According to him, the police breaking up the party that night hadn't seen another soul—and they'd conducted a thorough search. He took me down to the station, where I flipped through hundreds of mug shots, not one of which resembled the woman on the beach.

I didn't think to mention running into Chet Pease on the beach until the following day when Bob sat me down and forced me to detail the night step by step. Once I got to "grumpy old man" and "owning the cove," Bob hopped in his cruiser and drove right over to Heron's Neck.

Upon questioning, Chet Pease admitted he'd tried to shoo me off the beach while waiting impatiently for the police to respond. "Took them long enough," he told Bob. He confirmed that he'd urged me to go home, told me it was dangerous for a young girl to be out on her own. Then he said something along the lines of being right, since her sister was missing and wasn't it a pity parents didn't bother to control their kids. (I got that from Bob, who had enough sense not to pass it along to Mom.)

As for having seen Kit or the girl she was with, Chet was clueless. Sorry, he'd said, all teenagers looked the same to him these days.

"I only went there to put an end to that racket, since it was obvious you people weren't going to," he griped. This was followed by a lengthy complaint about the shoddy policing in these parts.

After Bob had explained the limited resources of a small town, though, Chet dashed off a huge check to the Shoreham

Police Department with strict instructions to put another officer on the force.

He never said a word about being down there to find his daughter. Or, maybe, considering Bob's deference to the wealthy, he was never pressed for details.

Days and months passed with no solid leads. After a year, we had to confront reality, however grim it was. Kit had last been seen in a critically ill state, possibly suffering from an overdose. The mystery woman "helping" her was most likely the one who'd dealt her the bad drugs, probably cheap and lethal fentanyl, according to Bob. Considering the circumstances, he said, there was no way she would ever come forward to face a heap of criminal charges.

Because Kit was dead.

Because I had trusted a stranger.

My mother never said this in so many words, but I could sense the questions she was longing to ask. Why had I abandoned my sister in her darkest hour? What kind of selfish person had she raised? From that moment on, it felt like we never spoke unless necessary, never smiled at all. Dinners were dour meetings over dry food and clattering silverware. When I was upstairs, she'd be downstairs. Christmas became another day. Kit's birthday was unbearable. No longer did we say good night or good morning. We were two raw wounds unable to heal in the acidic mix of grief and guilt.

A couple of months after graduation, I fled for college in the bucolic town of Amherst, Massachusetts, and though I was only a bus ride away, I never returned to Shoreham, managing to stay on campus and work over the holidays. When I was a junior, Bob called one bleak January morning with the grim news that Mom had slipped on a patch of ice on her way to work, hit her head on the sidewalk, and died of a subarachnoid hemorrhage.

According to the neighbor who saw her go down, Mom's last word was *Jane*.

I haven't been back to see my mother since we put her in the ground that spring. But I'm here now, standing alone in this damp cemetery looking for what? Forgiveness, I suppose. Always forgiveness. And to deliver some news, for once.

"I found her, Mom," I whisper in the dark as I approach her plot. "The girl with Kit. I know who she is now, finally, and I'm gonna get some answers."

Out of the mist, I catch a whiff of perfume, flowery and light. I follow the haunting fragrance of Versace, Mom's signature scent, to a cluster of fluffy white flowers that has been gently placed against a smooth slab of granite.

ROSE ANN JENKINS ELLISON
A MOTHER IS A MOTHER FOREVER.

Snatching the bouquet, I bury my nose in it, my tears flowing onto the delicate, soft petals. Peonies. Mom's favorite.

"Oh, Mom. I am so, so sorry." With that, I give in to a sudden urge to throw myself on the brittle grass, wishing I could reach through the earth for one last hug. I want her to come back and stroke my hair and assure me all is well. I want her to tell me she loves me and, most of all, that Kit is fine.

That's where I'm lying when my phone dings. It's Erik again. I blink back the tears and read his anxious texts. He's beyond worried, thinking I've collapsed from an undiagnosed concussion, and is about to call 9–1–1. I respond that I'm almost home. Then, wiping my face, I tuck the flowers into my shirt, blow a kiss to Mom, and return to my bike, my legs almost too weak to pedal.

Every light is on at the cottage when I pull into the driveway.

At the sound of my brakes squeaking, the front door flies open and there he is, hands fisted onto hips, right as my phone buzzes an incoming text, most likely from him.

"What the hell?" he cries.

I open my mouth to speak and can't, my whole body is trembling as I read the text from an unknown number sliding across the screen.

Hey, those are Mom's flowers, not yours.

Put them back!

FIFTEEN

EVE

Peonies!

Eve stands at the far corner of the Prow Room and indulges in a mini-round of applause. Lush pink bouquets sit in the middles of five circular tables—her preferred shape for successful dinner parties—which have been strategically placed to maximize the sunset views through the massive windows, the wraparound deck of sustainable Amazonian mahogany set low enough to ensure no obstructions. When the women raise their champagne glasses to toast Bella this evening, they will be illuminated by the fiery orange ball dipping into the watery horizon.

She cannot wait until those photos are posted to the Love & Pease site, though despite the shopping list of linens, utensils, florists, and caterers, readers will find it impossible to duplicate the scene in their own ordinary dining rooms. They will be left longing and frustrated, these loyal fans and consumers, and therefore perpetually hungering for more of Eve Pease in the way a new lover yearns for unattainable sexual satisfaction.

Exactly!

Chet designed and constructed this room so it would jut out over the bay like the prow of a ship in a dramatic angle of thermal glass he had custom-made by Lithuanian artisans. With its polished cherry vaulted ceiling reminiscent of a church nave, you couldn't help but feel as if you were on a Viking ship headed out to sea. Absolutely breathtaking.

When he was alive, the room's decor was very masculine and nautical—all mounted sextants and spyglasses on tripods and faded framed maps. Also, way too much dark wood, which Eve is not a fan of. She much prefers clean lines and white, white, white to project, rather than absorb, energy.

After waiting a respectable year after Chet's sudden death, she and Queenie brought in Dormier, their favorite designer, to create a feminine vibe, not so much Poseidon as Circe. He started with the ceiling, stripping and staining the narrow cherry slats to a dusty hue. The walls were then painted with a hint of rose. "Titty pink," he called it, much to Eve's delight—at the time, she was in the midst of trademarking her intimate Pease Pleasure products to "inspire the ultimate femstasy."

Femstasy: a hybrid of *feminine* and *ecstasy*. She'd come up with that one herself, having decided that *orgasm* sounded too much like a high school biology topic, like *amoeba* or *mitochondria*. Since then, she's embarked on a quest to redefine and rebrand feminine sexuality, starting with the lame Latin terms used to describe female anatomy, which sound like a bunch of inexperienced guys in lab coats came up with them. After she and Queenie brainstormed for weeks, a dildo became simply a "wand" and a vibrator a "pleasure wand." *Labia majora* became "petals"; *labia minora*, "petite petals." *Clitoris* was replaced by "bud," and she rebranded *vagina* as "velvet." *Tickle your bud with our unique Pease Pleasure*

Wand. Slip it across your petite petals, into your velvet, and enjoy a rocking femstasy!

This new lexicon sounded much better to her ears, but it had the added benefit of getting her Pease Pleasure products past the Google filters. Win-win.

And now she is embarking on a new mission, to reframe the traditional bridal shower, which despite several waves of feminism is still marked by cringe-worthy party games and silver-wrapped gifts tinged with stale whiffs of housewifery.

The trend in the last decade of adding men to the mix had been, in her professional opinion, a total fail. No man with a drop of testosterone wants to ooh and ahh over a Cuisinart, Eve feels, and her thousands of Instagram followers apparently agree, because they are one hundred percent on board with her all-female party for Bella, which she is calling—drumroll—a "blushing."

That's right, a blushing. The term came to her during a meditation session, and she just could not push it along, it was so delicious. A blushing encapsulates a woman on the verge of embarking on the mystery marital journey, supported by girlfriends and mothers and stepmothers, all bestowing tips for a rich sex life.

"A blushing celebrates a woman's sexual-life transition from finding to fulfilled," Eve wrote in the post announcing the event. "To sustain the passion in such a long and lustful voyage, our bride's going to need a whole new set of tools." (All of which happen to be available on the Love & Pease website, starting at $65.)

"Fantastic!" Queenie exclaims, entering the room holding a flute of orange liquid that Eve suspects is more vodka than citrus. "Love the virgin vibe." As if crossing the room has been a monumental effort, she collapses in one of the upholstered couches with a sigh, some of her drink spilling onto the $65,000 vintage Art Deco rug.

Eve fights the temptation to check her Apple Watch to confirm that her best friend did not rise until after noon. Queenie's pallor matches the color of the couch on which she sits, and she reeks of cigarettes. That was all fine in the nineties—everyone smoked back then and after a martini or two Eve sneaks one on the porch herself—but Queenie is trapped in a time warp.

Ever since her husband toppled off his yacht, Queenie has regressed to smoking and drinking like she's still hanging out with Debbie Harry. Also, hardly ever eating, besides an almond here, a spoonful of caviar there. Eve is all for graceful slimness, but Queenie's figure is pretty disturbing, honestly. Being somewhere in the range of fifty-eight to sixty-eight years old—no one's quite sure, including Queenie—she cannot afford to risk her health this way.

"Oh, stop giving me the stink eye," Queenie says as she places her nearly empty flute down on the coffee table and shakes out a Marlboro Light. "I was up all night working out the details of our plan. I deserve to sleep in."

The plan. Yes, the plan. Eve takes a seat, assuming the lotus pose. "And?"

Queenie brings the unlit cigarette to her lips, inhales air, and exhales. "And we're good to go. How's Megan holding up?"

To Eve's astonishment, Megan has been oddly upbeat. If Eve didn't know how madly her daughter adored Will, she'd go so far as to say she seems almost grateful. "Good. She's off getting a facial."

"Around here? Where in god's name?" Queenie is not a fan of Heron's Neck or the surrounding area. When she's on the East Coast, she much prefers East Hampton or the Vineyard, provided there's an open bar. This part of the Cape, with its shuffling therapists up in Truro, bush-league watercolorists in Wellfleet, and van-driving suburbanites in Eastham, is dull and pointless. She wishes Eve would sell the whole place and join her in Malibu, but she never will as long as the kids have a say, the sentimental fools.

"Megan went to Boston," Eve says. "She'll be back for the party."

"You mean the blushing." Queenie's lips twitch. She is far more amused by this term than Eve would like. "Well, when you see her, don't say too much, but let her know that all good things come to those who wait."

"They do?" Eve specifically recalls Queenie's admonition to jump fast on a newly divorced Chet before he became enamored with some ingenue.

"No. But it sounds like something a godmother should say, right?"

"Right."

And then the women, two dear old friends with messy pasts, exchange wide smiles, barely able to contain their shared glee as they erupt into a fit of cackling.

SIXTEEN

The blushing is not so much an engagement party as an over-due debutante ball. Having been sequestered through most of her adolescence by Chet and Madeleine and then by herself, Bella is an unknown commodity to the curious guests, some of whom once crushed hard on the irascible Will. Who is this hidden "sister"? And why did Will fall for her and not them? (Or not their daughters.)

For the more ambitious in the group, an alliance with the future Mrs. Pease could secure their professional advancement via much sought-after invitations. That is, if they can bend her to their will. Already they've cattily registered who among them was offered accommodations on Heron's Neck and who was forced to rent "off island." Were these crucial decisions made by Eve or Bella and, if the latter, what criteria did she use?

After all, Bella doesn't know any of them. She didn't attend the same camps or academies or colleges as the women here her age. Then again, no one attended school in California, not if they could help it.

In a side hallway, Bella braces herself for the grand entrance, checking her appearance in one of Eve's many oversized mirrors. She is well aware that the bold custom-made red silk qipao, tailored for elegance, authority, and her curves, asks not for acceptance, but respect. Closer inspection reveals the embossed gold pattern on the dress is not an innocent floral, as it first appears, but predatory cheetahs. That should send a message. She's even worn her hair in a glossy chignon, to display the Italian drop earrings, a present from Will.

Lifting her chin and straightening her shoulders, Bella strides toward the Prow Room with the elegance of an empress, her fire-red heels silent on the wool runner. Internally, however, she is a quivering mess.

Eve swallows hard. She'd chosen the dress specifically because she hoped it would make an impact, but this is more like a nuclear explosion.

Dani lets out a silent whistle, shoving a hand in her blousy pants and grinning in approval. "Didn't see that on the L&P site," she murmurs to her wife, Cecily, who has perfected the ultimate indulgent smile during her long tenure as a school principal attending to the needs of anxious parents.

"Because the dress isn't a numbing neutral," Cecily replies, herself in a beige linen pantsuit, her Heron's Neck camouflage.

Megan is the first to break ranks, touching Bella's back to gently steer her to the closest, and potentially most damaging, guests. "This is Ainsley Maxham, an old friend of my mother's from LA," Megan says, pushing her toward a creature in a beaded minidress.

"Watch who you're calling old," says Ainsley with a wink. She takes Bella's wrist in a tepid grip and drinks in her outfit. "You." Then she releases her clutch and walks off, leaving Bella blinking. *What did that mean?*

Now Bella understands why Will was so down on this event.

He warned her not to go, but she had to. Eve has been promoting this shower for weeks. The buildup has been intense. And, besides, Dani promised she'd be right there by her side.

But she's not. Instead, she's immersed in Cecily, leaving Bella to Megan, who foists her upon one guest after another, each interaction more awkward than the last. The smiles are manufactured, the nods stiff, their masks blurring into a collage of mockery. Whatever confidence Bella had felt while assessing herself in the mirror begins to ebb. She wishes to be anywhere else but in this massive pink room with these frigid witches. Once her back is turned, their eyes will roll ever so slightly, the corners of their mouths will twist in hidden amusement. She knows they will never accept her as one of their own.

Good. Because she is not one of them and never will be, not if she can help it. She is proudly Colombian, born to brave parents who championed the health and safety of the very workers these vapid ciphers wouldn't consider human, much less worthy of full rights. What would they say if they learned the famous Chet Pease, their own personal kingmaker, had pronounced her head and shoulders above even his own biological children? He had recognized her depth right off and wouldn't dream of subjecting young Bella to the superficial priorities and manufactured dramas of Megan's social set. He spared her, god bless him. And for that, she will be forever grateful.

Bella's cell phone vibrates for the umpteenth time that evening. Will, most likely, drunk dialing to see how it's going—again. Jake is throwing him a simultaneous bachelor party, which is actually just the two of them getting wasted on Jake's catamaran along with Dingo and Boomer who, apparently, are not beloved dogs, but Delta Upsilon frat brothers from Will's days at Tufts.

Will promised Bella he would stop at the second drink, but if he's calling this often, it means he's already exceeded his limit. She mutes her phone.

"That wasn't too bad, was it?" Megan asks rhetorically as she deposits Bella with Dani and Cecily. "She's all yours now, Pinky."

"You deserve this," Cecily says, handing Bella the evening's signature cocktail. Bella's so thirsty for fortitude she could down it, but she finds it clings to the back of her throat, making her gag.

"God, that's awful," she says, wincing.

"That's why I mix my own. Try mine." Dani holds out her glass, which, judging from the smell, appears to be pure gin.

Bella takes it from her and inhales a long, burning draught, then wipes her mouth on a paper napkin embossed with the date. "Thanks. I needed that."

"Can't blame you," Dani says. "Nice job tiptoeing through the lioness den. No visible scarring, which means you did well. Also, you look fantastic. Love the killer paw prints." Dani nods to the bartender. "This time with rocks. I need to pace myself."

He pours twin cocktails as instructed, and the three women clink glasses, Bella feeling as if she has been rescued from a tribe of bloodthirsty cannibals. She is about to say as much when Cecily mutters, "Don't look now, but incoming at one o'clock."

Queenie Jarvis is crossing the room from the balcony, her fluttering wave triggering a peal of chimes from her bracelets. With her yellow-and-black dress cinched tight at the waist, her black penciled eyebrows drawn in a pointed arch, she reminds Bella of a hornet about to sting.

"You're on your own, kid," Dani says. "Cecily and I are gonna peace out."

Bella puts out a foot to stop them. "Not so fast. I need you two. The other day, she basically told me she'd ruin me if I went through with the wedding."

Dani scowls, disbelieving. "What could she possibly have over you, Saint Bella?"

"What do you think?" Bella hisses low so not even Cecily can overhear. "She told me she saw me that night."

"Shit." Dani straightens her spine in alarm. "You think she's telling the truth?"

Bella has no time to respond because, suddenly, Queenie arrives in a cloud of Chanel. "What are you girls whispering about? Enquiring minds want to know."

"You're dating yourself, sweetie." Dani plants a perfunctory kiss on the older woman's powdered cheek. Giving Bella's hand a squeeze, she adds, "We're just about to announce dinner. Gotta keep on Eve's strict schedule you know. Can't let the chilled soup get cold."

Bella could hug Dani right now, but Queenie pouts. "Boo. Eve told me herself dinner's not until seven thirty. That gives me fifteen minutes with the belle of the ball. Now, you two be dears and go play in traffic."

Dani shrugs. "I tried."

As the two women saunter off, Bella feels like the weakling who's been left alone with the school bully, though this bully is too fragile to pummel a marshmallow.

Queenie links her skeletal arm in Bella's. "Do you mind accompanying me out to the terrace? I'd like one more ciggy before dinner." She inclines her head to the far end of the massive room, to the side porch facing the marsh and the mainland.

Bella's throat tightens as she unlatches the doors onto a cedar porch, already silver from two summers' worth of salt. Queenie steps ahead and takes a shallow breath. The tide has turned, the sulfurous stench of rotted organic matter rising from the fertile mud and grass. The air is stagnant, the sky menacing over the mainland across the channel.

"The sunset's on the other side. Wouldn't you like to go over there?" Bella asks.

"No, I wouldn't. I like the view here." Queenie places her drink on the railing, closes the doors behind them, and opens an exquisite black onyx beaded clutch with a white diamond clasp to remove a gold cigarette case, another museum piece. Her hand trembles as she attempts to activate the unresponsive lighter. "Would you mind?" she asks.

Bella takes the lighter and flicks it to Queenie's Marlboro, studying the woman's papery skin, the way her shoulder bones protrude from beneath her sleeveless dress. She looks like a living corpse, any healthy flesh having been slowly desiccated by tobacco and alcohol.

The cigarette lights and Queenie sucks on it deeply. "Better than sex. Guaranteed satisfaction." Tucking the purse under her elbow, she casually lays the case and lighter on the railing where they could easily fall into the water and be lost in the muck. Bella ballparks their value at six thousand dollars, roughly equal to the average annual salary for half the population of Bogotá.

Queenie sips her bourbon and turns to the marsh. "This spot brings back so many memories of my late husband. Did you ever meet Harry?"

Harry was the regular-guy nickname for Harrington, a pink puff of a man. Even as a young teenager, Bella could tell his superpower was not financial acumen, but an ability to imbue any males around him with a sense of superiority. Harry was the golfer in the sand pit, the buffoon who spilled his drinks on the country club bar. He was no threat and that was the secret to his success— along with Queenie's soap-opera money.

"He was very charming," Bella says. "When I was younger, he used to challenge me to thumb-wrestling matches."

"Really? How adorable."

Bella rubs her bare arms. The ice queen's presence chills her to the bone. "I really should head inside. Eve can't announce din-ner without me."

Queenie leans on the railing, her cigarette, smoked down to the filter, still pinched between her knuckles. "You *should* go. Now."

Bella backs toward the door, grateful to be dismissed. "Okay, well—"

"For good." Queenie twists to face her. Tears have pooled in her rheumy eyes, jeopardizing the integrity of her thick mascara. "Get out while you can. Just vanish. That's what Harry did. It was the only option, you know. Either off the side of the boat or off to prison. He made the right choice." She flicks the extinguished cigarette into the water. "You should, too."

"I'm so sorry." Bella's head is spinning at this apparent confes-sion. "I had no idea it was suicide."

"Hah! As if." Queenie picks up her case and lighter, dropping them in the clutch, then snaps it closed with a click before shov-ing it at Bella. "Go on. Take it. Take my offer."

Bella gawks at the glittering onyx clutch, its jet-black beads sparkling with a history of evil. What kind of offer is this? Queenie must be very, very intoxicated, even for her. Getting all misty over her dead husband, now trying to give Bella her old purse. "Thank you, but I couldn't. That's a collector's item."

"It's your ticket out of here," Queenie says, looking intently at Bella as she presses it into her hands. "It's *yours*."

The clutch is weighty, well crafted, and solid. It feels as portentous as this moment. "But—"

"Sewn into the lining is a cryptocurrency card linked to an account with fifty thousand dollars in Bitcoin to start you off. The password is written on the inside of the last cigarette. The ID will be texted to you once you're safely out of the country."

No longer is Queenie trembling or slurring. Her spine is straight and eyes dry. The actress has stepped out of character.

"The tide will be dead low at one fifteen a.m. There's a pair of muck boots in your closet. Use them to walk to the mainland. A Town Car will be waiting in the public lot to take you to Boston. You'll find one thousand dollars in unmarked bills stuffed in an envelope on the seat. Don't forget to tip the driver."

Queenie's laying out strategy with the efficiency of a three-star general, and Bella wonders if she really drinks as much as reputed or if the soused socialite role has always been a convenient charade. "On your way to Logan, you'll receive a text for a one-way ticket to Montenegro. Undiscovered gem, Montenegro. Have you been?"

Struck dumb, all Bella can do is blink and shake her head.

"You're in for a treat. Lovely land and people with swell investment opportunities to grow your Bitcoin. Here's a handy tip: buy a flat with cash. You won't regret it. Best of all, there's no extradition treaty and everyone minds their own business. He'll never be able to find you."

This is all happening so fast. The money. Bitcoin. Montenegro. Bella stares at the beautiful clutch. Would she ever accept such a life-changing offer? Just kiss goodbye the only family she's ever known, the man she's loved since childhood? No. Of course not.

Though, on the other hand, a fresh new identity in a foreign country could mean a clean slate. No more having to constantly look over her shoulder.

"Won't people think it's strange if I disappear right before what's supposed to be the happiest day of my life?"

"They'll probably think you were so distraught to learn of your betrothed's heartless infidelity you walked into the bay with stones in your pocket only to be swept over the shoals into oblivion."

"I can't do that. I don't want the world to believe I took my own life."

"I suppose you'd prefer to break your neck falling down the stairs."

It takes her a moment to absorb Queenie's implication, and she sputters for a second before responding. "Whatever issues Will and I are—or will—encounter, he wouldn't have me murdered."

"Who said anything about murder? I'm talking about an accident, a tragic, tragic accident. Like on a boat, perhaps, sailing on a summer Sunday under a clear blue sky when a gust of wind sends you leeward into the sea, *plop*, and you sink like a stone. Did you know that, statistically speaking, there are more deaths from sailing than downhill skiing?"

My god, Harry really is alive in Montenegro, Bella realizes stupidly. He's probably the one who advised Queenie about cryptocurrency and set up this crazy scheme. And it is definitely crazy.

"Look, just for argument's sake, even if I wanted to start fresh, I'd never be able to bring myself to give up my work at the foundation."

"You mean you'd never be able to give up your shares of Love & Pease, right?" Queenie winks. "At least, if you get out safely before you sign that prenup, your shares won't go to Will alone. According to Chet's wishes, in that sad case, they'll be divided equally among Jake, Dani, Megan, and Will. This won't be the case if you should divorce or, god forbid, meet a fatal end after the wedding. In that scenario, Will becomes the major shareholder of the corporation, and Lord knows what he'll do with the family business. Sell it out to the highest bidder probably, live out the rest of his days smoking hash in an Amazonian yurt."

Something clicks and Bella finally grasps Queenie's motivation. Or, rather, Eve's. If Bella is ruled legally dead *before* her marriage, then Megan, previously excluded by Chet's will, could at last inherit shares of Love & Pease. Eve will add those to hers, giving her total control of the company worth millions and millions of dollars.

There is no good option. Queenie is determined to ensure Will doesn't marry her, that much is obvious. If Bella ignores the offer, the old battle-ax will go straight to Chief Durgan and tell him exactly what she saw eleven years ago. And just like that, Jane Ellison's allegations in Logan last December will take on a whole new meaning.

"Not saying I would do this, but what if I simply call off the wedding?"

Queenie nods. "Whereupon, I would go to the authorities and tell them the Customs officer was right; you did kill the Ellison girl. I was on the dock that night. I saw you take out the boat and return with blood on your shirt."

"You would do that, ruin my life for no reason?"

"If I saw an opportunity to help my best friend and my goddaughter whom I love with all my heart? You bet."

The French doors fly open, causing them both to jump, and Dani and Cecily appear side by side on the deck. "There they are!" Cecily says, frowning at Queenie's empty glass.

Dani grabs Bella's hand, pulling her toward the hallway. "We've been looking all over for you. Eve's about to pop a clot."

Bella doesn't budge. She gives Queenie one last look, and Queenie meets her gaze without blinking.

"Come on, they're waiting!" Dani says.

Reluctantly, Bella complies, heading to the dining room with Dani, replaying the bizarre conversation in her head as they greet the applauding guests. Only then does she recall the reference Queenie dropped into the conversation so casually Bella barely noticed:

He'll never be able to find you.

Who does she mean?

SEVENTEEN

JANE

We have settled into a little routine this week. Every day, I wake up early, make the kids breakfast, pack them snacks and lunch and take them to the freshwater ponds to swim while Erik entertains his adviser and his wife with fun outdoor activities. Yesterday, it was birdwatching at the Audubon Sanctuary (the trails and horseflies deemed too much for Caleb). Today, it was kayaking in Truro. I believe that makes me what is called an au pair.

Also, chef. That's because, for the most part, Dave and Sheila don't cook. They eat out. And since Erik and I are going to be spending the next six months subsisting on oatmeal so we can pay off the Visa bill from this vacation, that means we need to shop and cook. And by we, I mean me.

It's after seven when I return from the Shoreham market with mussels, a can of chopped tomatoes, a bulb of garlic, a tin of anchovies, a fragrant bouquet of basil, and a bottle of chardonnay, which I must procure nightly for Sheila, though I don't drink.

A telltale odor is wafting from the backyard along with a peal of Sheila's laughter. I can't help but be amused that the organic mother of the year who also happens to hold an MD in psychiatry and a PhD in psychology is a closet pothead. No doubt she grows it herself in composted, locally sourced, hormone-free cow poop.

Retrieving the groceries, I trudge around the corner to where Erik and Sheila are sitting on the deck around the small glass table holding a plate of empty oyster shells. Erik can't even meet my glare, he's so swamped with regret. I haven't had an oyster yet this vacation and we're next door to Wellfleet, the oyster capital of the freaking East Coast.

"Where'd you get those?" I ask, my fingers curling around the grocery bag handles.

"We bought them on our way back from Truro," says Sheila, tan and glowing from her day on the water. "They forced me to try one. I downed five!"

Five? I silently curse them with ptomaine.

"We were going to save some for you, but you took too long at the store" is the aggravating explanation of my beloved, whose cannabinoid eyes have been reduced to red slits.

"Oh, too bad," I reply with false cheer. "I would have come home sooner but I had to pick up everything for dinner after you guys got back from kayaking."

"Thank God," says Sheila. "I'm starving." With the aggravating giggle of a naughty schoolgirl, she adds, unnecessarily, "Munchies."

She has changed from her shorts into a slinky sundress, though the temperature has dipped drastically. If I were the jealous type, I'd wonder if she's been flirting with my boyfriend. But as I'm not, I'll just grumble internally.

"Where's Dave?" I ask, making a big production of attempting to pick up the oyster tray while my arms are full.

"Let me get that for you." Erik jumps up and grabs the tray along with the bag of mussels.

"He's putting the children to bed." Sheila extends her feet on the chair opposite and stretches. "Oh, my arms are so sore from paddling. You know, you really should take two weeks next year. One is not enough. Did you remember wine, by the way?"

Feigning deafness, I step through the sliding door Erik has opened for me. He's acting more solicitous now that he knows he's in the doghouse. "Sorry," he whispers, removing the grocery bag from my arms and setting it on the counter. "She was the one who ate all the oysters. I had, like, I dunno, two. What was I supposed to do?"

"Gee, I have no idea. Wait—" I snap my fingers. "Could you have possibly . . . actually have told her you needed to *save* me some? Or have I been relegated to the position of summer au pair slash cook who eats the kids' leftover mac and cheese?"

Erik hangs his head like a puppy who's been bopped on the nose with a rolled-up newspaper. "Look, this is not what I had planned. I don't want to fight."

"Me, neither. I'm—"

"What are you two lovebirds chatting about?" Sheila appears, holding a couple of plates.

Erik and I step apart, busted. "It's nothing," I say, embarrassed she overheard us.

"It's okay. Dave and I fight all the time. It's perfectly normal, even beneficial." Sheila sets the dirty plates in the sink. "Listen, Jane, Erik shared some more details with us about what happened at Logan and I'm on your side, girlfriend. Seriously, I'd have done the same thing in your position. *Completely* understandable."

I round on him, tamping a burst of homicidal rage. "You *told*

them?" While I was letting Mabel cheat her way out of the Mo-
lasses Swamp, they were tooling around Truro's marshes decon-
structing my obsessive disorder?

He raises his hands in defense. "Hey, it's not like they hadn't
already read about it. All I did was provide context." With that, he
ducks into the lower cabinets to rummage around for whatever.
"I'd better get those mussels started. Where's the colander?"

"It's there." I point to the counter, where cold, gelatinous pasta
shells have glued themselves onto the white plastic strainer.

This would be Sheila's cue to clean up after her kids' dinner,
but she makes no such effort, instead peeking inside my shopping
bag and letting out a squeal of delight. "Yay, you remembered!
Where's the corkscrew?"

"Just to set the record straight, there's a lot more to the story
than what you probably read, okay?" I say.

"Uh-huh." Sheila finds the corkscrew and shuts the drawer
with her hip. "Erik explained how you're a natural recognizer
trained in forensic facial analysis. *Suuuuuper* fascinating. Just so
happens, I wrote my doctoral thesis on the reliability of crime victims' memories, to put it in layman's terms."

I'm stunned. Not only has Erik shared the details of how I got
myself fired, but he's blabbed about my super-recognition ability,
a trait I don't reveal to casual acquaintances. I wonder what else
he's shared. Which days of the month I have my heaviest flow?
How ice cream makes me flatulent? My irrational fear of stuffed
animals? I suppose when you're a psychiatrist no personal topic
is taboo. Especially when you're on vacation with fellow shrinks.

Sheila grinds down the corkscrew, seeming to have a bit of
trouble. "It all came up organically, Jane. I asked how you two met
and Erik told us about the study where you volunteered to be a test
subject. I found it very touching that because of your sister you'd

been trying to hone your innate abilities—or what you *perceive* to be your innate abilities."

Love how she tossed in that *perceive*, as grating as biting on grit in a steamer clam. "So, you don't think I actually am a super recognizer?"

"I'm sure you think you are. But as Erik's own research shows, the hard science in this subject area still isn't there."

I shoot an eye dart at my boyfriend, who is scrubbing the mussels with such diligence he might rip off their shells. I never did get the results of that study, which he claims are confidential. Now I understand that there might be another reason for his reticence.

Sheila abandons the corkscrew, lopsided at the top of the bottle. "I give up. Can you do it?"

I start by unwinding the foil wrapper. "If you think it's just a skill I perceive to have, how do you explain my ability to recognize strangers on the T?" *And you at the mall stuffing your face with fries*, I am *sooo* tempted to add.

She flashes a superior smirk at Erik, indicating they've anticipated this question. "Well, without undergoing a proper analysis, my hypothesis is that you are seeing what you want to see. In other words, consider the client of a Tarot reader. No matter what cards turn up, the client will interpret the symbols based on the primitive desires of her id, whether it's a love interest or a new job. The subconscious is in control of our active processing way more than we humans would like to accept. You *want* to see the woman who was last with your sister, so you do."

Jake Pease on the surfboard. I don't mention this, of course, because I haven't told Erik what happened out in the bay. Whether I really saw Jake or whether I might have experienced another psychotic episode or whether I was hallucinating due to hypoxia are issues I have yet to resolve.

Sheila continues to drill into my psyche. "By the way, I am so, so sorry about Kit." She slaps her chest. "I can only imagine, under the circumstances, how frustrated and helpless you must feel. To have lost your mother and your sister so close together and to have your father living all the way around the world in New Zealand. That's a lot to bear."

Pop! I pull out the cork and exhale a breath I hadn't realized I was holding. "Success."

"Have you been talking to a professional?"

If Erik's divulged everything else, she likely knows I haven't. He's long been annoyed that I won't go back for more counseling and since he, Sheila, and Dave are in the business, they're guaranteed to see his side.

"I don't need more therapy." I stop myself before delving into my psychiatric history, of which even my boyfriend is only vaguely aware. "I quit earlier this summer and what I learned was that no therapist, no matter how skilled, can help me find Kit or her killer."

Sheila nods. "Uh-huh. Interesting. You know, a bit of role playing might help. Can you tell me more about that woman and your sister that night?"

Feeling as if I've been pushed onto the psychiatrist couch, I take down two unbreakable plastic goblets from the shelf. I could change the subject or feign a sudden urge to run to the bathroom, any excuse to extricate myself from this interrogation. But I have the feeling Sheila's not about to let this go. If I don't tell her now, she'll be pestering me all week.

"Okay, so here's the story in a nutshell." I fill Sheila's glass and open the refrigerator to grab a Pellegrino for myself, placing the bottle of chardonnay in the door. "When I came across Kit on the beach, she was OD'ing. Vomiting, passing out, typical symptoms. I would have called 9-1-1, except Bella showed up, told me she'd handle everything, and urged me to get out of there because the cops were coming."

Sheila samples her wine, studying me over the rim of her glass.

I take a sip of water and continue. "But it turns out that Bella didn't even bother to come forward when the police issued an appeal for witnesses, most likely because she was the one who gave Kit the fatal dose of whatever. So, yeah, I blame her for my sister's death."

A V forms between Sheila's tweezed brows. "I'm hearing a lot of anger here."

There's a loud clatter as a hot pan Erik was attempting to pick up barehanded drops to the floor. "Sorry," he mumbles, reaching for a potholder. "You know, Sheila used to work in victim services in the Middlesex DA's office. This is right up her alley."

"For heaven's sake, I was a mere intern," she qualifies, rolling her eyes, "in grad school."

"Some pissant place called MIT," he gushes.

Oh, my god. He does have a thing for her, I think, as Sheila gives him a flirtatious punch. "Like you're some lightweight, professor."

"Not a professor yet. That's up to your husband."

"No worries. I'll let you in on a little secret." She leans in close. "You're his favorite."

Whereupon my thirty-two-year-old boyfriend beams like a kindergartner with a gold star. "Thanks, Sheel."

Sheel?

"I'm gonna go dump this pasta in the compost," he says, holding up the compost pail containing her children's mac and cheese shells. He practically blossoms when she gives him a thumbs-up, as if he is single-handedly saving the planet with this routine chore.

After he's gone, Sheila turns back to me, her unwilling patient. "Let me offer my professional assistance. You've been so kind to us, it's the least I can do. And who knows?" She shrugs. "You might dislodge a true suppressed memory that could lead to new evidence."

Now she's talking. "You could do that?"

"Happens all the time in victim services. Human memory is a vastly uncharted territory in neuroscience. There are many, many nuances to long-term recollection and our amygdala often fills in blank spaces with our own imaginations. Or, sometimes to protect us, our brains simply refuse to open locked files. Hence, your blacking out how you got home that evening."

"Erik told you that, too?"

Her eyelashes flutter. "He mentioned it in passing. What interests me is that it raises questions about whether there were other occurrences you suppressed or . . . continue to suppress."

I consider what Sheila's suggesting, that there may be more details from that night I could remember with, as she puts it, *professional assistance*. "So, how do I free these potentially suppressed memories?"

She takes another sip of chardonnay. "The most logical approach is to revisit the scene of the trauma with a trained professional to guide you. I'd be glad to do it, if you're willing."

This could work. I'd been eager to get over to Pekky anyway, and Sheila and her kids would provide the ideal cover. A mom and babysitter taking children to the bay beach. What could be more innocent?

"Okay, but let's just keep this between the two of us," I tell her quietly. "I'm not supposed to go anywhere near Heron's Neck. If their security sees me, I'm a goner and someone else will be ticked off, too." I nod my head to Erik, who has just reentered with the compost pail.

Sheila gives me a conspiratorial wink. "Gotcha."

Erik trots in and puts the bucket in the sink to wash it out dutifully.

"You didn't take the oyster shells," Sheila observes.

"You can compost them?"

"You must! They're loaded with valuable calcium."

He gapes at the slimy shells lying in the bottom of the garbage and, with a resigned sigh, begins to pick them out, one by one, an odious task he never would have done if the request had come from me.

"Mission accomplished. Passed out halfway between 'Goodnight room' and 'Goodnight moon.'" Dave comes down the stairs from the loft, yawning and scratching his craft-beer paunch. "They're out like lights, though you ladies should keep it down." He gestures above our heads where Mabel and Caleb are sleeping.

Sheila slinks an arm around his thick waist and whispers in his ear. Probably something about my agreeing to let her help because he smiles and gives me an approving nod. It's all going according to their plan. When they exit to the porch and leave me to my role of chef, I'm actually thankful.

Erik again returns with the newly emptied bucket and goes straight to the sink while I pour some of Sheila's wine into the pan, adding a dollop of olive oil and two smashed garlic cloves. We parallel-cook in silence. When the wine is hot, he adds the mussels and covers them with a lid for me because I hate watching anything die, even brainless mollusks.

"Thanks for being so cool," he finally says. "I know coming back to Shoreham has stirred up a lot of psychic dross for you.

And Sheila can be a trial sometimes, but I'm really impressed by how you've been handling it all, taking care of the kids, doing the shopping, letting me hang out with Dave so I can rack up brownie points. You're the best."

I appreciate him passing the peace pipe, even if doing so benefits him more than me. "You shouldn't have told them all that stuff, you know. That's between us."

"Hear that. But, man, you've been wicked unhappy lately and I've been so worried. I had to unload and who better than to them? Anyway, it's not like they're going to break their sworn oaths of confidentiality. They're professionals, Jane. They can help you, if you let them."

I'm more and more convinced Dave and Sheila's extended stay here has less to do with their thoughtlessness and might actually be an attempted intervention. I don't want to press the issue, however. I'm tired and we have zero privacy. Better to bury the hatchet and call it a day. "I do love you, nerd boy."

"Ditto times a thousand." He bends down, kissing me with his big scratchy mustache just as the mussels bubble over the pan's edge, hissing onto the stove. "Crap!" Turning off the heat, he ladles them out before they overcook, shaking his hands and hopping up and down because again he's forgotten to use oven mitts with the metal spoon. The scene is so comical, I let out a bona-fide belly laugh.

Twenty miraculous minutes later, the four of us are gathered in the cool evening around a protective assortment of citronella candles and a fragrant bowl of my mother's signature dish: linguine with mussels in an anchovy and tomato sauce. Satisfied, Dave pushes back his chair and takes a swig of beer. "That was delicious. Thank you."

"It was nothing," Sheila responds, patting her lips. "Super easy."

I fight the temptation to kick her under the table.

"Whoa, look at that!" She raises her empty wineglass to the clouds drifting over the moon. "What a magical night. The smell of the sea, the faint roar of the ocean in the distance. God, I love the Cape. I'm *soooo* glad we decided to stay the whole week."

Despite my bone-weary fatigue, I still do not sleep well. I keep playing over and over the conversation Sheila and I had in the kitchen.

Lurking in the nooks and crannies of my white matter is another fuzzy memory that does feel significant, though I can't pinpoint exactly why. It has something to do with what I saw on the beach that night, besides Kit and Bella. Was there another voice? No. Another figure? Not that, either. Something else.

You up?

The text alert illuminates the screen on the end table. Normally, I make it a practice to keep my phone in another room while I sleep but with Dave and Sheila and the kids occupying the entire loft, that's not an option.

Midnight. The witching hour. Even before I look, I know there's no number or name. The question simply appeared on my screen. Should I ignore it like spam or answer? Could be Serena.

Who's this? I respond.

You know.

Probably nothing but a phishing scam. I feel like a chump for falling for it and am pressing my thumb on the button to shut down my phone entirely when the screen lights up again.

You still haven't replaced the flowers.

I freeze, staring at the letters until they fade to white.

EIGHTEEN

BELLA

Bella sits by the window of her bedroom overlooking the bay, watching the sky with dread. She is fully outfitted for escape in black leggings and a matching Lycra long-sleeved shirt, with her hair tucked into a swimming cap covered by a black scarf she has tied behind her head, pirate style. For now, she's in soft black ballet shoes, quieter than the muck boots she'll don later. Queenie's clutch and cigarette case—her only possessions from tonight on—are secure in a dry bag she'd snagged from the boathouse.

The clouds part and a brilliant beam of moonlight shines through the mullioned window, illuminating each infinitesimal stitch in the Irish rose pattern of the hand-sewn quilt on the antique bed. What a disappointment. She was hoping for the cover of a stormy sky tonight, the only night before the wedding that Will won't be in their bed, staying on his brother's catamaran instead.

He'll be back by morning, to sleep off his hangover. This is her last chance.

Anyway, it's not like she can call off the plan now. Queenie has orchestrated every detail, from the password inside the cigarette to the waiting Town Car. All Bella has to do is cross the marsh and then wade through a sluggish channel to reach the mainland without being detected by security. She prays the gatehouse is more focused on intruders attempting to sneak onto the island than off, though she's not sure and it has her worried.

Then again, no option is reassuring. She is a prisoner locked in the most luxurious solitary confinement.

Driving herself is out of the question because Jake—the boss of applesauce—says it's unsafe for her to be in a car alone, exposed to the paparazzi who are rumored to be arriving in advance of the wedding. When she told him she'd run out of tampons, he assigned Carla, her maid/prison guard, to fetch a fresh box from the general store.

As for her social media postings, what a charade! All those gushing, happy Tweets of hers are written by committee. For example, the week before, Jake approved this posting on her Twitter account: They might call it "touch football" but if that's touching, then I dread to think how they play for real! GO, WILL, GO! #Sundayfunday #Feelingblessed.

It linked to a photo of Will bare-chested in a pair of $180 red "performance apparel" shorts from the "Play Like a Pease" collection, gaining air as he caught the pigskin, his extended family applauding in the background. The message was obvious: buy into the Love & Pease lifestyle and your mug ($52, handmade German glass) will overflow with the bounty of health and wealth.

Of course, the Twitter account did not post a photo of Will taken five minutes after that publicity shot, the moment when he collapsed onto the grass, drained by the mild exercise, a joint in one hand, a beer in the other.

She wonders what the fallout will be when the public learns that not even airbrushed Will or the Pease fortune or Heron's

Neck, with its blue infinity pools and teak meditation yurt, its Japanese spa and private, raked beaches, were enough to keep Cinderella from drowning herself? Bella can only assume the family business will take a massive hit when the celebrity media and Twitterati start to wonder if maybe Love & Pease isn't so loving and peaceful after all.

She doesn't dare ponder what will happen if she's caught tonight. Her fiancé will know she's onto him and watch her like a cat guarding a mousehole until the ink on the marriage license—and, before that, the prenup—is dry.

Which is why she has no choice but to escape tonight. If even a modicum of what Queenie says is true, her life depends on it.

Raising the window, she removes a screen and, gripping tightly with her thighs, inches down the drainpipe, the boots carabined to her small backpack. The act of descending is far more terrifying than movies have led her to believe. The pipe feels so flimsy it might snap in two, and her flats squeak so loudly against the painted metal that she lets her feet go and slides until her fingers hit the braces, their sharp edges cutting painfully into her skin.

At last she touches onto the soft, thick green grass and takes off, crouching as she runs along Eve's bank of rosebushes, fragrant from a second bloom. She squeezes through an opening to avoid the circular drive and jogs down the sandy path to the road off the island and the invading bay.

She's like an animal, all instinct, relying on muscle memory and sharpened senses. She feels every stone under her thin soles and the marsh has never smelled so putrid or so fecund. Her ears are tuned to the faintest sound, even the gentle lapping of the tide, the twitch of every blade of grass. The crushed weathered white shells glow.

At the marsh, she slips off her flats and slides her feet into the boots. Hitching up her backpack, she crunches across the sturdy roots of the marsh grass, crushing snails and fiddler crabs. Occasionally she steps into a hidden tide pool and is suddenly up to her knees, sinking fast. She drags herself out, empties the water out of her boots and proceeds.

Keep going, she tells herself. *Whatever you do, don't stop.*

She knows this marsh. Chet used to take her clamming, illegally, since she didn't have a license. Nor, for that matter, did he. A shellfish permit cost, what, twenty-five bucks? He could have bought one for every resident of Cape Cod without feeling the pinch. But there would have been no sport in that. Instead, they'd leave before dawn to avoid the helicopters overhead—game wardens on the lookout for poachers—and skulk through the salt bog, pretending to be scared of getting caught.

What Chet liked was cheating. Not big-time. He wouldn't skim from his clients or mess with the IRS. But stuff a few sugar packets from the gas station into his pants pocket? Sure. Avoid a ten-dollar ticket by sneaking into a movie theater despite his multimillion-dollar asset portfolio? You betcha.

He'd even mix himself a cocktail and slip it into the cupholder of his Land Rover if they were going out for dinner. A "traveler," he called it, taking a sip with naughty glee as he drove past a cop knowing full well local law enforcement wouldn't dare pull him over. Why would they when it was rumored he supplemented their department funding with personal checks?

So it was with clamming licenses.

At the water's edge, Bella notes the tide has turned and is flowing not out to the bay, but inward. The water will soon be over the tops of her boots, and will drag her down if she keeps them on. She decides to hold them over her head and go barefoot to cross the deep, dark channel teeming with slimy eels, jellyfish, and prehistoric horseshoe crabs. If she survives those lurking horrors, she'll then have to cover more marsh on the other side until she reaches the sandy beach and, finally, the waiting car.

This is impossible. She can't pull it off. She will get stuck in the muck and have to cry for help or drown.

Behind her, she hears a creaking hinge and turns to see a golden glow lighting up the balcony of a guesthouse, the one where Queenie usually stays. Someone is standing there looking out at her, the red tip of a lit cigarette like a beacon, an exact replay of that pivotal night eleven years ago.

Except this time, Queenie's in on the crime, making sure Bella is following through with the plan.

A blond woman steps out of the open door, her hair glowing in the moonlight. Megan? Too broad-shouldered to be Eve.

Bella ducks down and watches the pair windmill their arms in silence. Even from this distance, and even with only the moon as illumination, she can tell they're arguing. It sounds like Megan is trying to convince her godmother to quit drinking and call it a night. For a moment, Bella forgets about her arduous journey and the quickly rising tide and watches, listening.

"No!" one of them shouts. Sound carries quickly over water and so does alarm. The women hurry into the cabin. A door slams. A light inside flicks on, then off, followed by a radio crackling at the guard station on the bridge. A search beam swoops over the marsh and Bella falls face first, pressing herself into the soft beach straw, her nose inhaling the sulfurous muck, holding her breath as the light passes within mere inches of her fingertips.

There is no crossing to the mainland now. Security is on the prowl, searching for threats, and she'll be lucky if she can even make it back unseen.

The door to the guesthouse opens again and this time the

blond woman softly descends the stairs from the porch and tip-toes around the corner. Having put the drunken Queenie down to sleep it off, Megan must be returning to her digs. Bella has a vision of Queenie snoring loudly in her hornet dress, smudging the pillowcase with her crimson lipstick, her painted toes sticking out from the blanket her darling goddaughter has carefully tucked around her mangled feet.

Funny how everyone on Heron's Neck is so trusting of one another, no one locks their doors here, Bella thinks.

Funny how security is so preoccupied with the bridge and the surrounding marsh, they forget to patrol the other side of the compound, where anyone could let themselves in and out of Queenie's guesthouse completely undetected.

NINETEEN

JANE

The vibrations approach hard and swift, the footsteps of natives fleeing a spewing volcano.

Thump. Thump. Thump.

The shriek that follows is high-pitched and demanding, hoisting me from a deep, deep sleep and thrusting me into the day. I have no idea where I am, only that my back aches and the room is filled with light.

A fire?

No, not a fire. Erik wouldn't groan and slap a pillow over his head if we were on the verge of imminent immolation. Plus, there's no smoke. Or beeping smoke alarm.

I open my lids to find I am eyeball to tiny blue eyeball with a gremlin. Or a demented doll with auburn curls. "She's up!" the demon screams. "Now, we can have pancakes, Caleb!"

Something wet and gross plunges its teeth into my exposed foot and I react accordingly, jerking it away so fast I accidentally kick the toddler's tiny nose.

Before I can bounce up and gush my apologies lest his parents race to him in alarm, Caleb opens his mouth cavernously wide and for one amazing minute he is completely silent—until he emits a howl that would crack the earth's crust.

"Shhh," murmurs Sheila from above, in the bed where we should be sleeping. She sounds not the least concerned, perhaps still half-asleep. "There, there, baby. Jane will make you some pancakes."

Oh, that's rich. I flop back on the foldout as Mabel makes a big production of comforting her younger brother, kneeling to inspect his nostrils and asking him to rate his pain on a scale of one to ten.

"Ten," he says. This from a child who cannot count past one hand of fingers.

"We should seek medical treatment," Mabel advises in a spot-on imitation of her mother. "Do you have a number for the local homeopath, Jane?"

Who is this kid? Pulling back the covers—being extra mindful of precious's little snoozle—I gather up his small warm body and head into the kitchen. I am exhausted yet again, having tossed and turned since the midnight text. This weariness must be what a mother of two young children experiences, except these are not my children and I am not their mother.

Their mother, in fact, is sleeping off the chardonnay, a fact that irks me further when I catch sight of the digital numbers on the clock stove. Five a.m. This is the children's earliest rising to date. I pray it doesn't become a trend.

Mabel, who's actually pretty adorable in her pink cotton nightgown, gazes up at me with awe. "Pancakes, please. Mama said you'd make some. You make them so good."

"Well," corrects Sheila from the loft.

For the record, I have made pancakes every morning since their arrival.

"Pan-pape," echoes Caleb, whom I have plopped on the counter.

"Just once more," I tell them, opening the fridge on the off chance it holds two plates of piping hot pancakes with melted butter and syrup and I can go back to bed.

Erik and I rarely eat breakfast. When I was working at Homeland Security, our morning routine consisted of funneling massive amounts of coffee into our systems while scrolling through Instagram and Twitter with a cursory glance at the *Boston Globe* before battling it out for the shower. Since leaving CO2Glas, however, I usually lie in bed scrolling through job sites until Erik leaves and then I summon the energy to fill out yet more job applications.

Free-range eggs and organic milk, that's what's in the fridge. Sheila must have bought them yesterday after I came home from the general store with the regular kind. A check of our stores reveals we're out of flour and baking powder. But there is a fresh loaf of bread, organic French country butter (again, Sheila), and cinnamon. French toast it is, I decide, getting out a bowl and whipping ingredients.

As the toast cooks, I leave a voice mail for Renee, my former colleague at Homeland Security, crossing my fingers that she's in a forgiving mood. My Christmas meltdown in Logan didn't get just me fired; it resulted in a letter of demerit filed against her, too, for not doing more to control my outburst.

"Hey, Renee, it's me, Jane Ellison. Hope you're doing well!" I say, trying to sound upbeat and normal. "Sorry to bug you, but do you know anyone who might be able to tell me how someone can send an anonymous text message and, if so, how I can find that person's real number? I know that might sound weird. I can explain later when you call back. Talk to you soon!"

I hang up wondering if I should have apologized—again—for the Bella Valencia incident and decide there's no point in ripping off a scab.

"I see your underwear." Mabel giggles, pointing to a hint of beige lace under my Red Sox T-shirt.

"You see London, you see France," I joke, flipping the toast. "You see Aunt Jane's underpants."

This causes Mabel to erupt in a fit of laughter and repeat the rhyme over and over until her brother has it memorized, too. I picture them singing it repeatedly in the backseat of the Volvo on the three-hour trip back to Cambridge and smile in sweet revenge.

Miraculously, the children do not protest the substitution of French toast for pancakes, perhaps because I have dusted the slices with plenty of the confectioners' sugar Sheila attempted to hide in the freezer. I've even managed to figure out the old-fashioned Mr. Coffee maker and have brewed a small pot.

"I see you have everything under control." Erik comes into the kitchen, hair standing on end, his eyes huge behind the thick glasses he wears when he's not in contacts. And for a brief moment, I get the appeal of the whole young mom thing—the scene of two young children happily smacking their lips over plates of carbs, a husband kissing you on the cheek appreciatively, the comforting aroma of freshly brewed French roast.

And then it's gone and all I see are two sugar-fueled rascals who are about to tear apart the minuscule cottage and a boyfriend taking his coffee into the bathroom with his iPad for a nice long catch-up with last night's baseball scores.

"Clouds. Is it going to rain?" Mabel, traumatized from the inclement weather a few days earlier, points to the damp porch and

I fight a knot of dread. There is not enough Candy Land in the universe.

Though when I'm not with kids, I love the Cape when it rains. The air turns into a cocoon of seawater, fog, and dripping atmosphere, perfect for making a fire and curling up with an engrossing mystery novel or jigsaw puzzle. My favorite childhood memories are of reading in the bedroom of our historic wooden home, listening to the rhythmic pelting of rain on the standing-seam roof. There was nothing cozier than being cuddled up in a blanket with a bag of black licorice, working through the entire Baby-Sitters Club series while my mother worked in Town Hall down the street, safely near yet far enough away to protect me from her nagging to go outside and play or to work through her endless list of yard chores.

"That's not rain; it's dew. That sky is bright blue!" Sheila dances into the living room, where the kids have their faces pressed against the glass and hugs them both. She looks surprisingly together, her short wavy hair neatly styled, her legs slim and firm in yoga pants sticking out from under an oversized off-the-shoulder gray sweater. There are even diamond studs in her ears.

It's not fair for her to be so rested and cheerful while I am creaky and musty, though I suspect her resilience is rooted in her normal lifestyle of exercise, vegetables, and frequent massages.

"I think we should go fishing," she declares. "And it just so happens I saw an eel trap in the garage. I bet we can catch some crabs off the bridge at Heron's Neck."

I practically spill my coffee. The bridge at Heron's Neck is the gateway to Pease territory and is *waaaay* off-limits to me. "Camp Pekky is okay, but no closer," I say.

Sheila gives me one of her conspiratorial winks and instructs the children to go upstairs and wake Papa. They do as they're told, running and screaming unnecessarily, while their mother pours herself the last of the coffee, finishing it off with a dollop of cream and—oh, god, I might be sick—a heaping chunk of her fancy butter.

"Bulletproof," she says, taking a sip and closing her eyes in ecstasy. "The secret to success." She plugs in her phone for a recharge. "Can you do me a *huuuuge* favor?"

This is never a good question.

"Since I'll have to take the kids to the beach so we can reenact the night you last saw your sister, would you mind making them a snack? Only—" She holds up a finger. "No plastic, please. You should use the reusable cloth bags I rinsed out last night. And let's ixnay on the ugar-shay. I didn't want to say anything in front of the children, but that breakfast was way over the top."

TWENTY

The unmarked, extended black Lincoln Navigator turns left off Route 6 onto Heron's Neck Road and slowly, somberly rolls toward the gated island. The mammoth vehicle stops at the gatehouse and crosses the bridge with permission.

The bay to the left is sparkling. White sails dot the horizon. The beloved herons are true to their reputation, swooping into the marsh with big flapping blue-gray wings to feast on the tide pool offerings. Even the air feels purged of its usual sulfurous odor. It is cooler, cleaner, clearer here on the island. Better.

As the driver, Mr. Johnson, continues on his way toward the cluster of shingled buildings atop the small hill, he must pull off to the side of the one-lane road to allow the ambulance to pass. The ambulance, too, is in no hurry. The medic pulls up to the hearse and lowers the window.

"She's all yours," he says. "There was nothing we could do. DOA."

Mr. Johnson nods and gestures to the flock of gulls bombing the water. "Looks like the blues are running."

"That's what I hear. Can't wait to get out there. This is the end of my shift."

"Lucky stiff," says the mortician. And they both laugh. An oldie but a goodie.

At the service entrance, he is greeted by another member of the family's security staff in the trademark Pease-green windbreaker, wearing a frown under his dark sunglasses and baseball cap, silent as he leads him to where Will Pease and his famous jawline are waiting.

The local celebrity's hair, usually tamed in magazine photos, is curly and unruly. His shirt is damp with a V of sweat, and perspiration darkens his pits. His eyes could be puffy from tears, though, from lacrimal experience, the mortician suspects not. Will's pallor is unhealthy for a man of his youth and he reeks of something chemical, of what the mortician's not sure. He makes a point to register every flaw so he can relay them to his wife later. Because, as he's often explained to her, no one's as naturally beautiful as they appear in Love & Pease ads—or in the coffin.

"That's all, Rick," Will says to his bodyguard. "We're fine."

After the unsmiling man leaves, Will drops the stoic veneer and thrusts out a shaking hand, visibly upset. "Thank you so much for coming. My apologies about requesting the expedited service. I'm getting married in a few days and as you can imagine, this is . . . this is . . ." He seems to be searching for the right words. "Quite an unexpected blow."

The mortician spouts the scripted line, "Please accept my deepest condolences for your loss." The words roll off his tongue like melted butter on a hot corn cob. "I thought it best if I came alone. Didn't want to make a scene."

"Thank you, Mr. Johnson. Yes. That was very considerate." Like all Peases, Will is an expert at ferreting out names and committing them to memory. The mortician is impressed, since this is a trick of his trade, too. He steps to the back of the hearse and opens the doors.

Will follows, talking as they do. "We're all a bit stunned. She'd promised to meet my stepmother for *Surya Namaskara* on the eastern deck this morning and when she didn't show, Eve checked in on her and . . ."

The gurney clatters to the ground. The mortician has no clue what *Surya Namaskara* is, but guesses it might be a green tea. "How tragic."

"This way." Will opens the door to the concrete utility area. "The EMTs had the idea to bring her body here. We're trying to be discreet for as long as possible. Once word gets out, we'll be inundated." He gestures to the blue sky in front of them, where a helicopter skims the horizon.

Mr. Johnson nods. "Certainly."

The body of the deceased lies on what appears to be a folding table in the immaculate laundry room. The sheet covering it creates a familiar pattern of hills and valleys. Will hooks his hands behind his back and lowers his head, closing his eyes as if in prayer. The mortician keeps his peace. He's an expert at making himself invisible.

After Will is done with his moment of silence, he lifts his chin and says brightly, "Thank you again, Mr. Johnson. I need to check on Eve and inform my fiancée. I'll be in touch to make arrangements."

Will lingers outside Bella's door, waiting for a sound of movement within. When he hears her rustle, he knocks lightly and enters. She is sitting up in bed as still as marble under the Irish quilt, her long, dark hair accentuating her bare porcelain shoulders, her heart-shaped face free of makeup. In this fresh morning light, she could be in a Love & Pease ad for home decor, she's so flawless.

There she is, his salvation. To think how not that long ago he'd paid no more attention to her than he did to their maid. Well, in all fairness, that was before he had The Talk with Jake. Jake who is always two steps ahead, who executes his moves like a knight zigzagging across the chessboard.

"What's going on?" she whispers, motioning for him to close the door. "Did I see an ambulance just cross the bridge?"

He tiptoes to the bed and kisses her on the forehead. "We've had an event." He sits and runs his hand over her smooth leg. "Queenie didn't show up for morning yoga and when Eve went to check on her, she found her . . . unresponsive."

Despite having practiced these lines over and over, he can sense a crack forming. He's not sure how much longer he can go on without breaking down and blabbing everything.

Bella blinks, confused. "What do you mean, unresponsive? Is she going to be okay? That ambulance was taking its own sweet time. Don't tell me she was in it."

"She wasn't."

"Phew!" Bella slides under the covers. "That's a relief."

"Actually, Queenie is . . . gone."

"What do you mean, gone?"

"As in . . ." He struggles to swallow, his throat tight. "She passed."

Bella's jaw drops. "Queenie's dead? How? What happened?"

Here is the part where he's supposed to say he doesn't know. That most likely his beloved Dutch aunt succumbed to her deadly vices, that one can't expect to reach old age on a diet of cigarettes, booze, and cocaine. But he can't because he knows—or at least strongly suspects—that Queenie's demise was premature and, most horrifying, his doing.

He opens his mouth to speak and finds he can't spout the lie he's rehearsed, not to Bella, who is melting him with her wide-eyed innocence. She who holds the hands of the girls from the foundation when they come to her with their troubles, listening without ever judging. She who delicately transfers even the most frightening jungle spider outside rather than squish it with a broom. Bella Valencia has never once wished another human harm, could never even imagine violating her code of ethics. He is confident that her fidelity to him is iron tight, that she loves him with every fiber in her being.

She would never get drunk, much less blackout drunk, at a bachelor party and commit the unthinkable.

"Will?" Reaching out and stroking his stubbled cheek, she regards him with sincere concern. "Tell me."

He can't. She's too good.

"Please," she purrs.

He traces the stitching on the white coverlet, an antique blanket Madeleine bought in Ireland, he recalls. There's something about the memory of his long-gone mother that unleashes his thoughts, along with his tongue, and he knows, with trepidation, that once he starts this confession, he won't be able to stop.

"Since we decided not to sleep on the boat, we changed our plans and docked last night. I saw the light was off in our room and decided not to disturb you," he begins. "If only I'd come up."

But he didn't. Jake and Will's old college friends, Dingo and Boomer, demanded he join them for billiards in the basement of the main house, *basement* being an understated term for bar, wine cellar, and wood-paneled games room. He was already on the verge of passing out, but they insisted a shot of top-shelf whisky would get him back on his feet. Besides, a guy didn't get married every week, right?

As he sets the scene, he can sense Bella's growing disappointment. Surely, she knows what's coming. Or, rather, who. The woman doesn't live in a bubble.

"I was gonna crash in one of the empty guest rooms when Megan showed up. She wanted to talk privately."

Bella's long, thin fingers slowly curl around the sheets. "And?" she says, warily.

"That was my big mistake."

There is a sharp intake of breath from Bella, but he goes on. He must. "In fairness, Meg was pretty wasted, too. Said she'd just come from putting Queenie to bed and had found out something important that had to do with us."

"You and me?" Bella asks flatly. "Or you and her."

All three of us, he thinks. "You and me. She had some fucked-up story that Queenie had a plan to get rid of you."

Bella snorts. "How?"

"I don't know. Something about paying you off and sending you to Montenegro, of all places. Megan said you'd be gone by today. I know, I know." He can't even look at her, he's so humiliated that he took this idea seriously for even a moment. "It sounds crazy and if I hadn't had been so fucked up, I would have just written it off as more Megan bullshit, but that's not what I did, unfortunately."

There is an ominous pause and then Bella says, "Uh-oh. What did you do?"

This is not so easy a question to answer. "The thing is, I'm not sure. What I remember is being really, really angry. I was just so pissed at Queenie for sticking her big nose in our business. It's obvious she never liked you and had some sick idea that Megan and I belonged together. Megan, who's not even . . ."

No. He's not going to go down that road.

"Anyway, I left and went to Queenie's to have it out with her."

"What time was this?" Bella interrupts.

Beats him. "I don't know. After midnight. Megan tried to stop me, but I told her to fuck off. She started crying and, actually, that's the last I remember, her standing there, bawling her head off."

"Then what happened?"

When he looks up, he sees, to his deep regret, Bella staring at him in shock, her disgust evident in the way her lips are drawn back in horror.

"I woke up on Dani's couch. Apparently, she heard me stumbling outside her window, 'ranting and raving,' as she put it. She and Cecily got me inside and put me to bed."

Bella finally closes her mouth and nods. "Okay, so what does Dani have to say about all this?"

"We haven't had a chance to talk. We were both woken up when Eve banged on the door, wailing about Queenie. Eve said that when Megan put her to bed, Queenie was fine. A little tipsy, but Queenie's always a little tipsy. I'm just worried that in my anger and drunkenness I went in and did something stupid, strangled her or suffocated or—"

"Will!" Bella grabs his wrist, tight. "Stop. You did no such thing. You are *not* a murderer."

"I could be. You have no idea what I'm capable of."

"I have some idea what you're capable of and you killing Queenie is not even a remote possibility. Might you have wanted to? Sure. Queenie is—*was*—totally aggravating. But consider the facts." Bella inches closer, forcing him to face her. "The woman was addicted to everything. She was a ticking time bomb. It was only inevitable that her heart would give out, that she'd smoke or drink herself to death. Frankly, she's lucky it happened fast. She could have had a stroke and lingered incapacitated. She would have been miserable."

As rational as this explanation is, he's still not convinced. "What if I sped that along, though?"

"You didn't. I'm sure that Dani got to you first, thank god, before you could make a fool out of yourself storming into Queenie's room throwing around some wild, ridiculous allegation." Bella cocks her head, smiling. "I mean, honestly. Where did Megan come up with that fantasy?"

For the first time since waking, he gains perspective on the ridiculousness of this story. "Yeah, you're right," he says, running a hand through his greasy hair, feeling relieved. "I must still be drunk to think I could have done something that awful."

"Well, you don't smell that great and you look like death yourself. Go take a shower and get some clean clothes. Eve is expecting us to surround her and comfort her, I'm sure. The sooner we drop the bomb, the better."

Will drops his hand, puzzled. "What bomb?"

Sliding out of bed, Bella begins to undress, pulling her lace camisole over her head. "That we're cancelling the wedding, of course."

No. That can't happen. That would ruin everything. He stands so they're eye to eye, for once ignoring her naked body, her perfect breasts. "We can't do that!"

"We have to. Your mother's best friend just died, a woman who—"

"Who had a lot of health issues. You just said so yourself." He picks up the pink silk robe draped across the foot of the bed and hands it to her. "You're right. I'm sure the coroner will conclude she died of natural causes when he does his autopsy."

Bella slowly pulls on the robe. "There'll be an autopsy?"

"I think there has to be, don't you?"

Suddenly, she's strangely silent, her gaze vacant as if lost in thought. *The morning has been too much for her,* Will thinks.

"Everything's going to be fine." He brings her to him, pressing her head to his chest. "You said Queenie was excited for us to get married. Ask yourself, what would Queenie want?"

"What we all want," Bella says, muffled, into his shoulder. "To live."

TWENTY-ONE

EVE

Eve sits in the middle of her gigantic four-poster bed, which is so large that both the mattress and the sheets had to be custom-made. When she designed this bedroom suite as an addition to the house, she and Chet dreamed of creating a retreat that would serve dual purposes: a private sexual oasis in this sprawling compound and, later, a gathering spot for the fruit of their union.

The babies never arrived, despite numerous consultations with Boston's premier infertility experts and a regimen of black cohosh and false unicorn prescribed by a well-respected shaman out in Cochituate. Having already adopted one child, Chet didn't want to go down that route again, and Eve, for her part, wasn't too keen on the idea, either.

From then on, they focused not on expanding the family but on expanding the family business. Chet continued to pour capital into his wife's fledgling lifestyle brand while Eve expanded its reach, touting her favorite fashion designers and architects, chefs, menus, exercise routines, kooky herbal remedies, and mindfulness practices on the website. She began to feature Will as a model—an instant hit—and discovered the power of weddings as promotional events when Jake married Heather in a glittering extravaganza she orchestrated for them.

Everything was going swimmingly until Dani infuriated her father by smashing Will's $200,000 Lambo into a Jersey barrier, narrowly avoiding a DUI charge thanks only to Arthur Whitaker's swift intervention. Chet had already been stewing over Jake and Heather's purchase of a $7 million monstrosity in Waban they were renovating unnecessarily. Did they really need two gyms or an expanded wine cellar? Must (one of the) family rooms be lined with mahogany?

Meanwhile, there was Bella living on a modest salary she earned at an NGO devoted to international social justice for women in developing countries. She didn't even own a car, much less a Lamborghini, and her apartment in Bogotá—which, granted, she couldn't have afforded without Chet's help—had approximately the same square footage as Jake and Heather's bedroom suite.

That's when Chet decided to teach his biological children a lesson. Having threatened on numerous occasions to cut the spoiled brats out of his will, he took the next worst step by allocating forty-five percent of the company to Bella, a tad more than Eve's forty percent ownership, and reducing Dani, Jake, and Will's shares to five percent each. He must have realized cutting out Megan entirely would be a blow to her mother, both for symbolic reasons and because she'd long counted on her daughter's share to fortify her standing. But by then he wasn't that fond of his wife, either.

No one was more outraged by the snub than Megan's godmother, Queenie. Having mentored Eve when she arrived from Paragon, Indiana, as green as Midwestern June corn, the worldly actress was even more bonded to the product of Eve's one-night stand with Jonny Blak. Tiny, plump Megan with her big blue eyes and incurious nature demanded all the protection Queenie could arrange. Hooking up her mother with Chet Pease, she'd hoped, would be enough of a security blanket but apparently not. She'd always suspected Chet was a bastard from the way he belittled her husband, Harry, so she kept a secret weapon in her back pocket just in case he tried to pull off his trademark checkmates.

For "legal reasons," Queenie spared Eve the details of how she would stop Will from marrying Bella, though, after the incident at Logan, Eve wondered if it had something to do with the missing waitress. Would Bella have gone so far as to "eliminate the competition" by drowning Will's girlfriend? Anything was possible.

Bella was a survivor, and survivors, Eve knew from personal experience, did not beat the odds by being sweet. They succeeded by being ambitious and crafty, wily and ruthless. She'd learned that lesson from no less than Queenie herself.

"Come back, dear friend," she pleads into her 1,000-thread-count Egyptian cotton pillow. "Don't leave me."

Knock. Knock. Knock. "Eve?" Will gently inquires from the other side. "May I come in?"

Her skin crawls. She is not in the mood to play the benevolent stepmother. "I need a moment, if you don't mind."

There is a pause and then she hears, "The police are here."

Shit.

Eve pulls herself up and leans against the tufted backboard, silently cursing this development. Most likely, the cops have showed up because they're nosy busybodies eager for any excuse to poke around her lingerie drawer. They have no real reason to be turning up on her doorstep at nine in the morning. It's not as though Queenie's been murdered or anything.

"What do they want?" she yells.

Another pause. "Permission to do a search."

Eve slides out of bed, unnerved now. "Can't they do that later?"

"I can put them off if you want, since they don't have a warrant. I called Arthur, but he didn't answer. He might be off on one of his early-morning bird walks, which means he won't be back for hours. I can tell them we won't allow it until we consult with our attorney."

No. Trying to stall the police will only raise suspicions. Eve opens the door and regards Will in his button-down navy-striped shirt and classic summer linen trousers, freshly showered and looking nothing like the hungover idiot she encountered on his sister's divan mere hours ago. "Where are they?"

"Downstairs." Will steps aside to let her pass, which is when she sees Bella, also crisp and neat, in a sleeveless royal blue dress, her lips coated with Queenie's signature red, her dark hair pulled back in eerie imitation.

Bella meets her gaze with an icy stare. Eve had prayed never to see that defiant smirk ever again. "And you are here because . . . ?"

"Because she's my wife-to-be," Will answers for her. "And it's her wedding that's being ruined. Mine, too."

That response is so self-centered and typical of how Will views himself in this family, as if he's entitled to the same income and privileges as Jake and she are, even though he can't be bothered to contribute more than a few hours of posing for the camera.

Eve has to bite the inside of her mouth to keep from spitting back a stinging retort. "Excuse me," she says instead, brushing past the smug couple.

They follow her to the foyer, where they are immediately met by a shiny bald man wearing a slightly wrinkled navy suit coat and a red tie marred by a dark grease spot. Eve imagines him slumped over an Italian sandwich dripping with mayonnaise, casually patting off the smear with a paper napkin.

"Chief Bob Durgan from the Shoreham police." He pronounces his name *Dah-gun* as he flashes some sort of ID in a foggy plastic sleeve he quickly returns to his pocket. He's gained a few pounds since their last encounter, though, to be fair, that was over a decade ago.

"Why, Chief Durgan, I barely recognized you!" Eve's lids flutter as she extends a limp hand. "Have you lost weight?"

Momentarily jarred by the unexpected compliment, the local cop chuckles to himself and ignores the offer of a handshake. "It's been many years, ma'am. I regret we're meeting again under such unfortunate circumstances." *Saw-cumstances.*

Rebuffed, Eve brings her hand to her chest, her pinky extending to her cleavage, barely visible under the gauzy mauve tunic she'd chosen for the morning yoga session she'd planned to take with Queenie. The cop's glance flicks downward for a second, which is enough encouragement for her to continue.

"Not all circumstances have been unfortunate. There was the reception we had to commemorate the donation in Chet's name to your department, as I recall."

At the blunt reminder of Eve's late husband's five-hundred-thousand-dollar bequest to pay for new cruisers and an updated dispatch system, Chief Durgan shifts his feet awkwardly. "Yes, that's right. And how very lucky the department was to receive that."

A thin smile spreads across Eve's lips. "Now, you were saying?"

"I was saying . . ." He pauses to clear his throat, long enough for Jake to make himself known.

"What's going on here?" he demands from the other end of the hallway, which he crosses with his diminutive wife, two-stepping to keep up with her husband's long strides.

Will squares his shoulders. "It's okay, J.D. I've got this."

"Doesn't look like it. There are police cars all over the island. The optics are horrible," Jake says, practically out of breath with agitation. Turning to Durgan, he shifts into neutral. "Hey, there, Bob, good to see you again," he continues, as if the two are old friends. "The blues are running. We gotta get out there on your SeaVee."

"Of course," Bob says with a nod, but is soon back to business. "So, like I was telling your stepmother, my deepest apologies for the intrusion. Your sister suggested we get this out of the way before the press gets wind of it and, frankly, I thought she made a good point. I'll remove a few cruisers, if that helps."

"What would help, Bob, is no search at all," Jake responds crisply, in contrast to his earlier friendliness. "Queenie is—*was*—a dear family friend and we are all suffering a blow this morning. Some of the wedding guests haven't heard yet, and it'll be upsetting to them to wake up and see cops crawling all over the place."

"My expectation is that we'll be finished before the guests are done with their morning coffee," Durgan says. "We're just dotting the i's and crossing the t's. More privacy for all parties involved to get this done efficiently and without risking public exposure by seeking a bench order."

Eve turns to Will. "What do you think? You're a lawyer."

"Not practicing," Jake says, scoffing. "He failed the Massachusetts Bar, thrice!"

Will's complexion has gone crimson. "Well, like, you don't have to be a member of the bar to see nothing criminal occurred.

And Dani's right—better to get this out of the way now. Where is she, by the way?"

Jake shrugs. "Cecily took her for a long walk to calm her down. Supposedly she's a mess."

"Yeah," Will says. "I was in her cottage when we got the news. Had to catch her when she started to faint."

Eve makes note of the fascinating interchange of knowing looks between the two brothers. What's that about?

"I'm sure it must be a great shock to all of you," Durgan says. "With your permission, ma'am, we'd like the search to include Mrs. Jarvis's quarters as well as the outbuildings. As you can see, we have quite a crew with officers from other departments assisting for speed and, er, discretion."

"Of course," Eve says, and as she does, she catches sight of Bella squeezing Will's knuckles so hard they go white. Why would Bella be upset by a police search? Surely Durgan, a trained observer, must notice, too, especially given their history.

Chet was so damned determined to get Bella off Heron's Neck early that morning—long before there was any mention of the missing waitress—they were gone by the time Eve awoke. Later, she learned he'd hastily arranged for a private plane to rush his daughter to California, though the semester didn't officially start for weeks.

When Eve gently inquired about the rush, her husband had clearly lied, "I don't know what you're talking about. Bella always planned to leave first thing Sunday. If you weren't so wrapped up in throwing your little soirees, you would have remembered."

Now, witnessing the girl's panicked response to Durgan's presence, Eve wonders if there was another reason Chet was so eager to shield his favorite child from police scrutiny.

She decides to give the screw a turn. "I concur. Let's get this over with." She sneaks a glance at Bella, who, much to her satisfaction, is teetering.

"This is a *huuuuge* mistake," Jake roars. "I can't believe you're going to allow police to rifle through our personal space without Arthur here." He, too, checks Bella, whose skin has turned a sickly puce. "Some of us are already traumatized enough as it is."

"Don't lecture me about trauma," Eve retorts. "I knew Queenie far longer than any of you. She was my dearest and closest friend. And if I can deal with a search, then so can everyone else. Anyway, it's my house and what I say goes." Turning to the chief, she points to the clipboard tucked under his arm. "I assume you need a release."

Durgan nods and hands her the form. "All I need is your signature at the bottom and then we'll get to work."

"I hope you won't trash the place," Will says. "My brother's right in that regard. I don't want to find our belongings scattered about everywhere."

Durgan assures him they'll leave things as they found them and then ascends the staircase, not toward the scene of Queenie's death, but straight into Bella's room, where Queenie's purse and Bitcoin card are hidden under the loose floorboard, under the antique Persian carpet, and underneath the handcrafted maple bed where, just before dawn, she managed to grab a few minutes of precious sleep.

TWENTY-TWO

JANE

Mabel, Caleb, Sheila, and I are all stuffed into Sheila's Volvo XC, which we've outfitted with enough food and equipment to withstand an onslaught of invading aliens and/or the two p.m. grumpies. We are off to visit Camp Pequabuck, and hopefully to unleash suppressed memories of the night I last saw Kit and, if I can pull it off, sneak in a quicky surveillance of my route to Heron's Neck.

While Sheila straps Caleb into his car seat, I am assigned with implanting Mabel into a monstrosity that belongs in a NASA space shuttle. She sits limply, arms and legs dangling, perhaps in a sugar coma. Having seen her play chess with her father, I bet she could learn to work the snap-ins if her mother could relinquish a smidgen of control.

"Is that thing really necessary?" I ask, getting into the passenger seat. "I mean, she's in first grade. When I was that age, Mom stuck me in the back, snapped a buckle over my lap, and called it a day."

"I know! Our parents were like criminals in broad daylight."

Despite her supposed safety consciousness, Sheila turns out to be your typical Boston driver, handily zipping in and out of Route 6 traffic, pulling left-hand turns in front of oncoming cars, merrily traveling up the breakdown lane to bypass congestion, and, in response to rightfully indignant fellow motorists, lowering her window and flipping the bird.

"Tweet, tweet!" Mabel pipes up each time her mother does this.

Sheila smiles into the rearview. "Mama's special way of saying hello."

It's a little while into the drive when I begin to understand that in order to avoid traumatizing her precious offspring with the poetic vernacular of Massachusetts drivers, not only has Sheila redefined rude gestures, she has created a brand-new language based on vegetables.

"I couldn't find this in any of the archived articles I read this morning, but were there any signs of rutabaga on your sister's shirt discovered in the marsh? Any beet juice?"

Rutabaga, I deduce, is violence. Or bruising? Hard to say. *Beet juice* is easy. Blood. "Yes. Though it wasn't hers, according to the—"

Sheila heads me off at the pass with a warning glance. "Peace pals?"

"Are they the ones in cars with lights on top?" I ask.

She nods. "They are our helpful friends."

"Then yes. Peace pals determined the stain on her shirt was not her own beet juice, but they don't know whose it was. The peace pals also never found any, um, anatomy." There. Brava me.

"Anatomy is our body that we must take good care of because it's the only one we get!" Mabel shouts from the back.

"The Museum of Science," Sheila explains with pride. "Upstairs. Human biology. It is her absolute favorite, especially the diseased lungs."

"Cigarettes have sixty-nine known carcinogens," echoes her second grader.

We pass the TOWN OF SHOREHAM EST. 1670 sign right before the municipal complex. As we go by, the fire station doors are open and Caleb coos at the bright red engines inside. In the town clerk's space, there's a Honda parked that looks so much like Mom's, a lump rises in my throat.

"That's my old house," I say, pointing to the restored colonial at the end of a cross street. It's been repainted in a palette of classic New England colors: gray, cream, dark green, and red, and the windows have been replaced. The interiors have undergone a pricey remodel, I feel sure, and in the driveway there's a fancy new Tesla, ready to be corroded by the salt air.

"How quaint," says Sheila. "Do you want to go around the block for a closer look?"

I shake my head. "That's okay."

"Confronting the past can mean revisiting joyous moments, too, you know," she singsongs from behind the wheel.

"Maybe later. I can deal with only so many memories in a day."

She smiles and keeps zigzagging down Route 6, our lives in her hands. "Must have been fun growing up on the Cape."

I am grateful for the change in subject. "It was, actually. After the tourists left for the season, Mom would give us free rein to explore the woods and beaches, pretty much roam all over. Just as long as we were home at six p.m. sharp. She was strict about family dinner, but loosey-goosey about everything else."

"Loosey-goosey?" Mabel asks, giggling. "Loosey-goosey!"

I turn around in my seat and start telling her how I used to make jewelry from shells when I was her age, carefully carving out the purple inlay of quahogs and then sanding the pieces into beads, just like the Wampanoags did hundreds of years ago. The Wampanoags nurtured the Cape, grew corn, and lived off it and the oysters and lobsters they could reach down and pick up from the shore. I promise to show her how to walk heel to toe so as not to make a sound in the woods and how Kit and I used to find arrowheads in the garden and, once, a stone tool for sharpening those edges.

"Who's Kit?" Mabel asks. "Your kitty?"

"Kit is—*was*—my older sister. Her full name was Katherine, but when I was a baby, all I could say was Kit, so it stuck. She went away many years ago." I tense, anticipating more questions I'm unsure of how to answer.

Mabel turns to look out the window. "I am sorry about your sister. I hope she comes back." She says this with such innocent sincerity my eyes burn and I internally rescind all my criticism of Sheila and Dave's parenting style.

"Is this the place?" Sheila points to an understated wooden sign with the word INDIGO painted in a muted mauve that's so hard to read, I would have driven right past—even though I spent two summers working there.

"Yeah. If the oncoming traffic's too much, you can go up to the National Seashore where there's a light . . ."

Nope. Not old Sheila. She swings into the passing lane and hooks a left, narrowly missing an assault of southbound vehicles. The kids' NASA-issue safety seats are beginning to make a lot more sense.

Turning into Indigo hits me with a brief flutter of nervous excitement, as if we'll find Kit sitting in the parking lot waiting for a ride. Though it's no longer a summer camp, the entrance hasn't changed that much since I lifeguarded at its bay beach. The silver-sided gate shack may have been painted with purple trim instead of green, but I can still make out the faded CAMP PEQUABUCK on its front.

The last time I was here was the Monday after Kit disappeared, after I owned up to not having taken care of my sister, after Bob asked me to walk him through my steps that night. There is a sudden sour taste in my mouth, remembering, and I fight the urge to spit.

Sheila lowers the window to greet a young man in a deep blue shirt and PHOENIX burned into his bark name tag. "Welcome," he says dreamily. "Are you here for the Artful Space Creation or Mindfulness Walking retreat?"

She smiles at him. "My friend used to be a lifeguard here, before it was a retreat, and she wants to show me around for old times' sake. I hope that's okay. We'll only be a half an hour at most. We're just going to walk around."

I can tell Phoenix is slightly hesitant about this. Kooks come in all forms, even in $50,000 Volvos with precocious children in NASA seats. He makes a phone call and after a lot of head nodding and descriptions of us ("two moms with little kids") hangs up and says we are "cool to go." We are to be respectful of meditating guests and also birds, he adds, warning us that it's the migration season for short-billed dowitchers so best to stay out of the marsh.

Sheila flutters her fingers and the Volvo crunches across the gravel to the parking area, where the counselor and staff cabins used to be, and chooses a spot away from the pines and their damaging dripping sap. We unbuckle the kids, who are placated by wandering about and gathering pine cones, tiny testimonials to their screen time limits. The sun is bright, and judging from the dank air and rank smell, the tide is out. Perfect conditions for collecting shells and reconstructing crime scenes.

"Show me where you left the car that night," Sheila says, swooping up Caleb and bouncing him on her hip, holding Mabel's hand on her other side.

I lead them along a narrow path between the pines that opens onto what used to be a sandy lot. It was separated from the bay by a concrete boat landing, which has now been smashed into large concrete blocks. Winter storms must have taken their toll because not only is the dune gone, so is the entire public parking area, leaving a sandy cave dotted by black pieces of old asphalt.

"This is . . . nothing." Sheila sets Caleb down, and he toddles toward the expansive mud flats.

"This is the future of the Cape. We're being eaten away. Eleven years ago, you could have put twenty cars here, easily."

Several Indigo guests sit on the blocks or on the beach, reading and dozing. There are about ten middle-aged adults, only one of whom I vaguely recognize. He's a little over six feet and broad-shouldered, in green board shorts, lying on his stomach reading on a Kindle. A white smear of sunblock stripes his nose and a wisp of sandy blond hair peeks out from the back of his navy Yankees cap, a perilous style choice in these parts.

"How marvelous!" Sheila beams in maternal approval as she watches her babies run, arms outstretched, to the far-off water, the morning sun lighting up their wispy curls. A couple of seagulls hop out of their way as they dash across the flats.

I have to bite my lip to keep from ordering the kids to halt. "Should we tell them not to go out so far? You know, toddlers can drown in a foot of water."

"It's sweet of you to be concerned, but Mabel is very conscientious. She'll watch her brother. Now, where did you last see Kit?"

We reach the approximate location to the best of my memory, considering the tide was in that night. I note where the boat landing used to be, retreat ten paces, and mark the spot. "Right around here. She was kneeling on all fours and Bella was standing where you are."

"Was there any light coming from the parking lot?"

"A bit. Enough so I could make out her features."

"Where did they find the bloodied shirt?" Sheila's starting to sound more like a cop than a therapist.

"Way down there." I point to the dense marshland on the other side of the Heron's Neck bridge, which is cluttered with TV trucks topped with Martian-like satellite dishes. "Unfortunately, you can't make out the marsh with all that stuff blocking the view."

"Are they all there for the wedding already?" Sheila squints over my shoulder at the scene.

"No idea." Though I wouldn't be surprised, considering Love & Pease's following. "See that bridge? For a while, there was a theory floating around that Kit was high and jumped off of it, injured herself, and was swept out with the current. But the gatehouse is manned twenty-four seven, and anyway, their security tapes didn't show anyone in the vicinity."

"Uh-huh. Interesting." Sheila puts a fist to her hip. "So, what time was it when you saw her collapse?"

I have one eye on the kids. So far, so good: Mabel is demonstrating her responsible nature by grabbing Caleb's hand as the harmless waves lap their ankles. But disaster can happen in a flash. "I'm not sure. Midnight? Two maybe? I really didn't keep track."

"Uh-huh. Okay. Now take a deep breath and close your eyes," Sheila instructs, doing it herself too. "Transport yourself to that moment. You catch sight of your sister on the beach and you're frantic and worried about Kit getting in trouble. You want to get her home. You are desperate."

I try to follow her directions, but, frankly, I'm too worried about Caleb and Mabel to concentrate. "You sure we shouldn't go out to the kids?"

"They're fine. There are plenty of people around them. Now, inhale the smells around us. Take a moment to transport yourself into that place and tell me everything you see and hear."

This would be easier at night, when I wouldn't be distracted by the sounds of squawking gulls and laughing children. I inhale and exhale, doing my best to focus on the lapping waves to block out the other noise.

Gradually, details bubble up from my memory, though I can't tell if they're legitimate facts or invented images. I'm slipping into a type of trance and I can see Bella Valencia not stepping out of the shadows, but coming through the black water. There's splashing and when she takes me by the shoulders, her hands are wet and they dampen my shirt. She smells like the sea. Behind her, I make out the vaguest outline of a small motorboat, no bigger than a dinghy. I hear a ding coming from her flip phone. She opens it and holds it up to one ear. She *speaks*.

"Jane?" Sheila prods. "You're shaking. Tell me what's going on."

I open my eyes, blinking in the overly bright sunshine. "It's all wrong. I have this vision of Bella answering her phone. I always thought she checked her screen, like she was reading a text, but now I think maybe she was actually talking to somebody on the other end."

Sheila steps close. "What was she saying?"

I can see her full lips snapping. Just one word. "*Help.*"

"Like she was calling 9–1–1?"

"No. Because there's no record of anyone calling 9–1–1 that night. So maybe she was calling a friend?" This is totally freaking me out. "I'd told the cops she'd read something on her phone. I must have blacked out the part of her actually *talking* on it."

If this memory is true, that means Bella didn't act alone; she had an accomplice, and there's another person who knows what she did. Another person who knows what happened to Kit!

If I'd remembered this crucial fact when it counted, when the investigation was active, Bob could have issued subpoenas for CDRs—call detail records—tracking pings to local cell towers. That could have led to Bella's phone. Unfortunately, from what I remember from my training at DHS, since those records are kept for no more than five years, they are long gone.

My pulse is pounding. I feel as sick with guilt as when I saw Kolzak Jernov sit next to Lisa Hayes for the second time on the Boston T and I realized their rendezvous weren't coincidental, that I had messed up huge.

This isn't as bad, actually. It's worse.

"Okay, it seems like you might be hyperventilating slightly. Shallow breaths." Sheila pants and motions for me to follow suit. "You need to reduce the cortisol rushing through your system. What you're experiencing is repressed memory and it can be a physical shock to your system."

My tongue is bone dry and my armpits are suddenly damp. "If only I'd remembered earlier, though. It might have made the difference in finding Kit."

Sheila's lips form an O as she coaches me to exhale. "As I explained last night, the human brain abhors a vacuum and will color in the lines with the most random of images. Most of what we define as a memory is really a combination of events embellished by our creativity. The *Looney Tunes* roadrunner isn't really running. Our brains make his legs move in a whirlwind."

"That's a cartoon," I say, breathing out and in twice until I am light-headed. "This was the last time I ever saw my sister. Aren't your senses supposed to be sharper when you're in a crisis?"

Sheila shakes her head. "In the moment, but not afterward. It's exactly the opposite afterward. Witnesses of traumatic events crumble under cross-examination because what they saw and what they later *think* they saw can be totally different. That's why police like to interview them as soon as possible and why lawyers are able to squash their testimonies. Trust me. This issue came up repeatedly when I was interning at victim services."

I am beset by a million questions. What else did I screw up? Did Bella say my name or not? Did Kit really say sorry or not? When she collapsed, was she passed out—or already dead?

Please, not dead.

If I can't swear to these essential moments of the most pivotal night of my life, how can I trust myself to identify a disguised terrorist, for chrissakes? My identity as a super recognizer is enmeshed with my ability to remember noses, ears, and head curvatures perfectly. It is my unique superpower and, until this moment, it was never in doubt.

But now it seems I was totally off the mark about what Bella was up to that night. I didn't even remember her wading through the water or there even being a boat. And if I'm wrong about all of those things, then what if I'm wrong about . . . *her*?

Oh, god. Oh, god. This is terrible. I'd been so certain and now I'm anything but. The world is upside down. I have a sensation akin to vertigo, simultaneously dizzying and deafening.

Only when Sheila says, "Are you listening?" do I realize she's been asking me a question.

I shake out of my fog, blinking. "What?"

"I was asking," she continues, "if you recall who she might have been talking to?"

That's when the hairs on my arms suddenly go straight up, detecting danger before my ears catch the panicked cry. "She's yelling for help," I whisper.

"Who, Bella?"

"No, your daughter."

Sheila abruptly turns and dashes to the water's edge, where Mabel is screaming like mad. I do a rapid scan for Caleb on the horizon, past the mud flats and the sun-dappled bay. He is nowhere in sight.

He is gone.

TWENTY-THREE

JANE

All right, sweetie. It's okay," I hear Sheila say as we race to a red-faced and bawling Mabel, an angry blue crab dangling from her tiny thumb.

Without a second thought, her mother inserts a finger between the claws to loosen the nasty creature off her child's hand. It snaps madly as she holds it correctly, from the rear end, to show Mabel who's boss.

To my great relief, her little brother is both present and alive, having been hidden from sight by a clump of marsh. He is digging in the sand, oblivious to his sister's distress and the incoming tide, the hem of his white T-shirt skirting the water as he plays.

Holding out a colorful scallop shell, I entice him to a drier spot while his mother attends to a hysterical Mabel.

"Shall we let him free?" Sheila might be playing cool, but there's a definite tremble to her voice.

Mabel slits her eyes with murderous intent. "I want to kill it."

Atta girl, I want to say, taking a seat next to Caleb, surprised to discover that I am still physically shaking from the revelations in Sheila's recovered memory session.

"I . . . was . . . just . . . following . . . the bubbles!" Mabel explains between sobs. "It came up and bit me."

I don't blame her for being upset. Blue crab claws are strong enough to crack open starfish. Having been pinched myself once or twice, I make it a practice to wear water sandals when walking the flats.

"But you invaded his home," Sheila says, still grasping the mad crab. "What if you were little like him with only one—okay, two—defense mechanisms, and a great big girl dug up your house?"

It isn't working. Mabel is bent on crabicide. This kid's really beginning to grow on me.

"If we put him in a tidal pool, he'll burrow down deep and won't bother us ever again," I suggest.

Sheila gives me one of her winks and Mabel, clutching her injured thumb, nods reluctantly. "Bye, bye, Mr. Crab!" she shouts with nervous eagerness as her mother flings it toward the grass. It lands in the pool with a satisfactory plop.

"Everything okay?" a man shouts, jogging toward us.

He's about my age and wearing a blue Indigo shirt, shorts, and a surfer-grade pukka necklace. His brown hair comes to his shoulders and his skin is bronzed, a far cry from the stringy-haired, disgruntled teenager who used to be permanently attached to his water bong.

Cobb Cooper, pampered son of Pekky's former owners, the dude who alerted me that Kit was on the beach partying, and, most crucially, her former drug dealer, is currently blocking my sun.

I can't believe his nerve, the way he squats for a closer look at Mabel's red thumb and feigns concern.

"Lucky you," he says, frowning at her injury. "Not every girl gets kissed by a crab, just the pretty ones."

It is all I can do not to punch him in the gut. Get away from her, I want to growl. Don't you dare contaminate this innocent child.

"I was looking for a mermaid," Mabel says, brightening.

"A mermaid, eh?" Cobb scratches the stubble on his chin. "You know, we have one who swims by every now and then. Her name is Anemone."

"That's not a mermaid's name. That's the name of a sea urchin. We saw one at the aquarium."

"The big one in Boston?"

Mabel nods vigorously. "They have penguins."

"And seals. That's my favorite place!"

"Mine, too!" Mabel says, clapping.

I wave Sheila over to where I'm helping Caleb with a sandcastle. "I need to talk to you."

"Do you think I handled that okay?" she asks, wiping sweat from her brow. "The crab, I mean. It was all I could do to keep myself from flipping out. She was so brave, my poor baby. I tried to act like it was no big deal, but . . . the size of that thing!"

"You handled it perfectly. Listen, that guy talking to Mabel . . ."

Sheila checks over her shoulder. Cobb has placed a tiny hermit crab on his palm, showing Mabel how it can't pinch him when his hand is stretched out flat, like he's Mr. Rogers or something. "Yeah. What about him?"

"His parents owned this place when it was Pekky, and I'm guessing he's in charge of the retreat now."

Her eyes go wide. "Is he here to kick us out?"

"Don't worry about that. I knew him from when I used to lifeguard here. He's got a history in the area. A bad one."

She reassesses Cobb as he asks Mabel if she wants to take a selfie with the hermit crab. "He seems rather sweet. What'd he do?"

"Back in the day, he was my sister's . . ."

Sheila clears her throat and nods to Caleb, a warning to watch my language. Shit. Unable to settle on a vegetable code word, I cut to the basics. "He was my sister's dealer."

"Heavens," she gasps, turning to her daughter in alarm. Sheila hasn't put the hammer down on Barney and Oreos only to have her precious firstborn be lured into a life of drugs. "Sweetie!" she calls over to her daughter. "Thank the nice man and then come here. It's snack time."

"Snack time!" Caleb repeats, tossing his shell.

"Would you mind?" she asks, wrinkling her nose at me. "I'd fetch the apples and peanut butter, but they're in my pack all the way over there and I don't want to leave the children, not with the *horse* dealer so close by."

Serves me right for telling her. Getting up, I brush off my hands and trudge past a couple of Indigo guests in saffron pantaloons with their legs crossed, meditating, and a fully clothed woman under an umbrella on a chaise lounge, reading a book entitled *What Color Is Your Chakra?* Quite the difference from my era, when this beach was crawling with screaming kids, Bain de Soleil bottles, and flying Frisbees.

The guy I recognized has picked up his towel and Kindle and left. I must be slipping, since I still can't pinpoint where I know him from.

Reaching into Sheila's pack, I keep a vigilant eye on Cobb. He's brandishing a gleaming-white clown smile as I distribute the snacks and juice bottles while Sheila checks her phone, probably Googling a local therapist to help her process the trials of motherhood.

Just then, my own phone dings and a photo pops up of a tiny black lamb attempting to remain standing on four wobbly legs with the assistance of a small neighbor child who seems to always be underfoot in Stan's pictures. I think her name is Lily. Apparently, it takes a village to run a sheep farm.

"Awww. How cuuuuute!" Sheila exclaims, boldly reading over my shoulder. "Where is that?"

"New Zealand." The photo is one in a series, apparently. "It's from my father. He's a professional shepherd."

"The father who abandoned you as a child?" Sheila whispers. "Erik didn't tell us you'd reconciled."

Honestly, that's probably the only thing he didn't share about my personal life. "I don't know if you'd call it reconciliation, though we do keep in contact via text. Mostly he sends me photos of sheep."

Lambin'. Never gets old, Stan writes. Been up 24 hrs straight. Community effort.

Adorable, I text back.

There's a pause as the message transmits to the satellite that bounces it to the other side of the world. Then a reply.

You should join us next year! Get out of the hot city.

"Oh, but you're not in the hot city." Sheila apparently has no compunction about reading our private correspondence. "Here. Give me your phone. I'll take a picture of you with the children on the beach."

I clasp my phone to my chest. "That's okay."

"Really?" Sheila squints, her psychiatric spidey sense probably detecting another personality quirk worth plumbing. "Why not?"

Because my father did not want me going to the Cape under any circumstances, I should tell her. Because he shares Bob's opinion that the more I obsess about finding out what happened to Kit, the more I risk my own, at times tentative, mental health. Because if he finds out I came here anyway, Stan Ellison will flip his shit.

"Want me to take a group photo?" a voice offers from behind us.

Sheila and I spin around to face a grinning Cobb.

"Um, I'm gonna go clear up the snacks so we can get going," she says, hurrying back to the blanket.

"Thanks, but we're good," I tell him, curious as to why he's so interested in us. It can't be only because Sheila and I snuck in. "Just showing off your beautiful place to my friend. I used to lifeguard here, you know."

Don't you? Surely, you must.

His smile grows even wider, as if this is a surprise. "Oh? When was that?"

"Long ago. Back when this was Camp Pequabuck." This charade is ridiculous. I can tell he knows perfectly well who I am. "I'm Jane Ellison." I do not offer my hand. "Kit's sister. You remember her, don't you, Cobb?" I wait a beat and add, "One of your most *loyal* customers."

"Bhakta." The creep doesn't miss a beat, pointing to his name tag. "Means 'devotee' in Sanskrit." He places his hands prayerfully and bows his head. "Born anew."

"I wonder if we could get a moment alone, Bhakta," I murmur. "Away from the kids." There aren't enough varieties of vegetables to cover the swears I plan to employ.

Cobb seems glad to take a stroll slowly and carefully toward the camp, nodding to Indigo guests along the way. Once we reach a spot free of people, he says firmly, "I was in the office when I got a call you were here. I told Security I'd take care of it instead."

"Just like the night Kit went missing, when you called and told me to come down to the beach so the cops wouldn't bust her and, therefore, you."

Smiling no more, he leans into me and says, "I am now escorting you off the property." He waves to an invisible someone, a fretting guest or perhaps a guard. "Look, I don't know how to say this politely, so I won't even try. Go home. Leave. This is an oasis of peace and tranquility. The last thing I want is for our guests' meditations to be disrupted by an invasion of rent-a-cops from the island."

Ah, now I get it. "I'm sorry. I assumed you meant your own security when really you meant the security at Heron's Neck. Perhaps they don't know you used to be the Cape's biggest dealer. Wonder how tranquil your guests would feel about that?"

He lets go of my elbow and takes a step back, assessing me warily. "The Peases have every right to be concerned about you, especially with the wedding just days away. I read all about what you did, how you went after poor Bella Valencia at Logan. I don't blame them in the slightest for taking extra precautions."

"You were there that night." This is my chance for a real confrontation and I'm not about to let myself be distracted by his arrogant disapproval. "I bet you also saw Bella with Kit, didn't you?"

"No, you're completely, one hundred percent off base." Tiny beads of perspiration are dotting his upper lip. "I never saw Bella. After I messaged you, I passed out. I was fucking wasted, sad to say."

"Then how do you know I'm wrong about Bella?"

His eyes dart left and right, searching. "Because . . . this is my home. I hear things. You know, gossip around town."

Give me a break. "*What* things?"

He sets his jaw and purses his lips. "I don't, I don't know everything exactly, but it's not fair to go after her. She—actually all of the Peases are great people. Super generous. Hell, I owe them everything." He spreads his arms wide. "They saved my parents' camp from being sold and chopped up into a subdivision." He emits an annoying high-pitched giggle.

Yet again, the Peases play the role of benevolent landed gentry rescuing the local serfs. By bailing out the Coopers, of course, they also preserved their unspoiled view of the mainland.

"Okay," I say, retreating slightly, giving him room to breathe. "Then what's your theory about what happened to my sister?"

Wiping the sweat off his lip, he says, "I've never been entirely sure, but I think her disappearance might have had something to do with her getting hassled at work. She mentioned there was a guy there forcing her to buy for him 'cause he was too high-profile or some such shit and didn't know where else to go. That's why she was coming to me for junk, even after she got clean."

"She was clean?" Mom and I had hoped this was the case, but to hear it confirmed by her own dealer is like a gift. "I wanted to believe she was, but . . ."

"Trust me." He must realize how ridiculous that statement is, seeing as how he sold her drugs and then made himself scarce when she disappeared. "The only reason I had any contact with her was because she was being pressured to score."

Instantly, I flash back to that time in the bathroom when she was getting ready for work, rehearsing her lines in the mirror. Most of the events she catered that summer were on Heron's Neck. She was constantly around the Peases while they partied. She adored Will, but she never had a nice thing to say about his older brother, Jake.

If Jake was the one bullying Kit to buy him dope, that would go far toward explaining why he tried to drown me the other day. A drug user-turned-murderer does not exactly jibe with the Love & Pease brand.

"You have no idea who 'he' was, do you?" I put "he" in finger quotes.

"Nope, and I didn't ask. Your sister was scared shitless." Cobb shudders slightly, as if recalling his own fear. "I didn't need some angry mofo coming after me."

"And you didn't tell the cops any of this?"

"If you're asking if I informed law enforcement that I was in the business of selling a crapload of coke, yeah, my answer would be no." He's recovered enough to flash me a wiseass grin. "Hey, when I learned Kit was gone and the police were involved, I went underground. It's a miracle I never got busted. There but for the grace of God go I, you know?"

Not the grace of God, the grace of being born white and privileged, I think, steaming. As the offspring of a respectable family who owned and operated a venerated institution like Camp Pequabuck, Cobb Cooper was exempt from scrutiny, unlike my sister. No mercy for her, not in a small New England town where any hint of special treatment would have cost Bob his livelihood. After all, Shoreham was founded by a band of Puritans whose judgmental traits flourish to this day.

"I think I know who her customer might have been," I say, trying to keep calm. "Jake Pease, am I right?"

Cobb places his palms together. "Ahh, Jane, you suffer so by being shackled to your past. To quote Ajahn Chah, letting go a little brings a little peace. Letting go a lot brings a lot of peace. Letting go completely brings complete peace. Just let it go."

"Sage advice. Hey, you know what would give me peace?" I ask.

Cobb raises an eyebrow.

"Telling you to fuck yourself."

There's a rustle behind us. Sheila's suddenly there with the children, eyes like saucers at the outburst she just overheard. "We need to return to the car," she says, clipped. "Someone has a poo-poo diaper and a case of the crankies."

"I do not," grumbles Caleb from her hip.

"Yes, you do," Mabel says, reaching up to stroke his curls. "You'll feel much better after a change. I'll read you a story and you can nappy nap."

Cobb once again segues into the role of jovial camp leader. "You're free to use the pavilion where there's a nice breeze," he says, bending over to tickle Mabel under the chin.

She giggles, but Sheila, stricken, pulls her daughter closer. "Thank you. Changing him in the Volvo always gives me a sore back." She turns to me. "Are you coming?"

"The kids will love the pavilion," I say, forcing brightness into my voice. "Is the Ping-Pong table still there?"

"We call it Zen ball now," Cobb says. "Indigo rules mandate no competition."

Sheila warms a bit. "Lovely. We will enjoy that. Are you sure you don't want to come with us, Jane? I could use the assist."

I'm not sure if this is her attempt at a rescue or an assignment of diaper duty, but I give in. "Sure." I take Mabel's hand and we follow the signs to the Peaceful Pavilion, keeping my gaze on the sandy path ahead, without saying goodbye to Cobb.

He insists on having the last word, though. "What appears is not always what appears, Jane," he shouts after me. "Namaste."

The pavilion has been renovated since I last saw it, when it was a rough-and-tumble gathering spot for rainy-day camp activities. At the far end on a suitably neutral couch, Sheila is wrestling a pair of Pull-Ups over Caleb's tiny legs. "We use cloth diapers at home," she says defensively. "But on vacation, it didn't feel fair to burden the rest of you with diaper laundry."

Which she'd probably make me do, too. "I'm not judging." I'm not. I'm thinking about Kit and her relationship with the Pease brothers. If Cobb's telling the truth and Kit was clean, she would have valued her sobriety enough not to get involved with Will if he was doing the hard stuff. Still, Will did skip town after she went missing. What if Will and Jake *both* had dirt to hide, dirt known only to Kit? Maybe Bella was phoning one of them for help that night.

"Mabel wants to show you an old photo that I think you'll find interesting," Sheila says, yanking up Caleb's orange swim trunks. "Check it out."

She nods to a wall of photos, some of which date back to when the camp was first founded as a bird-watching retreat in the 1960s. Mabel is pointing to the center one, and as I get close, I see it's a staff picture from my second summer at Pekky. My hair is pulled into tight braids and I'm fit and content in the standard camp white shirt over my navy tank. My arms are flung around two staffers and we're grinning widely, free of worries. I am all of seventeen.

This would be the last week I would ever see my sister.

"Is that you, Jane?" Mabel asks.

"It is!" I answer brightly, batting away tears. "You have a sharp eye."

She delicately touches her eyeball. "No. It's round."

"Looks like you were having fun back then," Sheila says as Caleb races past us, glad to be out of his dirty diaper.

"A blast." Already, I've moved on to a few photos down, a collage made of the campers' photos from years before, looking to see if I can find Kit, who attended a summer day camp here when she was younger.

"We're going to the car, Mabel," Sheila says. "Do you want to come or are you going to stay a bit with Jane?"

Mabel cozies to my side. "I would prefer to stay with Jane."

"Okay, but let's not dillydally. We have a few errands to run."

I've found one of Kit. She's ten and in the camp T-shirt, which that year featured a tern flying over the Pekky motto: "All Good Things Are Wild & Free," the famous Henry David Thoreau quote. She, too, is smiling from ear to ear, her blond head touching that of an equally smiling Black girl with cornrows, whom I recognize as Ettie Watson.

Ettie and Kit were super tight all through middle school. Not sure exactly what happened to their friendship, but if I had to guess, I'd say straight-A student Ettie was one of the many who distanced themselves from my sister after she started using.

Once more I curse the scourge of addiction. Kit should have had tons of friends and gone on to become what she dreamed of, a prosecutor like on her favorite show, *Law & Order: SVU*. She might have had children of her own, and I could have been one of those naughty aunts who snuck them candy and let them stay up late to watch scary movies.

I have the sudden impulse to spoil Mabel rotten. "We should go for ice cream tonight after dinner," I say, taking her tiny, sweaty hand. "With M&Ms on top."

She hops up and down on her way to the door. "Oh, please, please, please!"

I put my finger to my lips. "But you can't tell your mother. It'll be our little secret."

"I have a secret, too." Mabel stops her dancing and motions

for me to stoop to her level. Then she presses her mouth to my ear. "Mama said I found the picture of you on the wall, but I didn't. *She* did."

Huh. "Why would your mother do that?"

"It's a surprise."

"What kind of surprise?"

"I don't know. But I'm not supposed to tell you that we came here when we went to the house with the big blue pool where we must never, ever swim alone and the *biiiiig* white swing that's indoors! It's not a lie, though. It's just a kind of true story we don't share." She frowns. "You won't tell Mama, will you?"

TWENTY-FOUR

BELLA

You've lost more weight!" Shruti cinches the waist of Bella's silk lehenga, which has been lavishly embroidered with the most famous flowers of Colombia—yellow roses, blue chrysanthemums, orange passionflowers, purple orchids, and red carnations—to pick up the crimson in her choli. "If you're not careful, the skirt might slip too low when you're walking down the aisle."

Bella cannot stop staring at her reflection. For all of Eve's political incorrectness in appropriating Indian wedding attire for this event, she couldn't have been more correct that this outfit would be a showstopper. The expertly tailored choli enhances Bella's cleavage before tapering to her flat waist and navel. The flowing lehenga picks up where the choli leaves off, the crimson muting to a light rose to a blush pink to white at the hem bordered by the intricate zardozi floral pattern that required a total of ten thousand hours from twenty of Shruti's seamstresses, according to a recent Love & Pease Instagram post.

It is stunning.

And so wrong for so many reasons.

"Don't move," Shruti orders as she carefully inserts a pin into the waistband. "You keep fidgeting. Are you nervous?"

Nervous? She wishes. Nervous is the natural state of every bride, but most of them are not being discreetly investigated for murder. The moment right before Durgan bounded up the stairs to make a beeline for the room she shares with Will, the way the side of his mouth curved ever so slightly in smug success, haunts her. *I gotcha*, that smirk said. *Took me eleven years, but you're mine.*

"Are you cold?" asks Shruti. "You just shivered."

"Did I?" Bella manages a smile, her stomach filled with butterflies. "I don't know. Maybe I *am* slightly nervous."

"You shouldn't be. You're flawless." The famed designer makes one more mark with her dressmaking pencil and stands. "Wait. Before you get undressed, let's try the necklace."

The necklace is a heavy gold choker dripping with polki diamonds, emeralds, and rubies worth a small fortune. It's a wedding gift from Will, who must have had artistic assistance from Megan, since only Megan could have designed a piece so over the top. Shruti lifts it from its velvet case and gently places it around Bella's throat, its sheer weight almost suffocating as she fastens the clasp.

"Oh!" Shruti takes a step back and claps her hands together, genuinely in awe of the ensemble. "Absolutely amazing. With the light from the candles and the setting sun and the jewels bouncing off the walkway? I mean . . . talk about wow!"

Bella sighed inwardly. Eve had insisted that mirrored tiles set into the sand bordered by hurricane lamps interspersed with huge bouquets of native white hydrangeas in glass vases would do the most justice to Will's embroidered red-and-gold sherwani, not to mention Bella's royal regalia.

Weighed down by the jewels and the dupatta Shruti is draping over her head, Bella senses her freedom being snuffed out like a melted candle. Even if Durgan hadn't found Queenie's purse under the floorboards, he is watching her every move, she's sure of it. If she attempts to cross the bridge or the channel to the mainland, he will be there, waiting. He won't let her slip through his meaty fingers, not this time.

It's not as though Eve will help her extricate herself from this mess, either. Initially, she may have wanted Megan to marry Will, both to fulfill her daughter's silly crush and to gain his measly five percent share, but now, with Durgan on the hunt, Eve's clearly savvied a more lucrative scheme. Bella could see Eve taking in Durgan's smirk, his fixation on her. She'll just throw Bella to the wolves when Durgan makes his arrest, provided he does so after the ink on the marriage license is dry.

Then Megan and Will can finally enter into a legal union in which they'll own fifty percent of the company, per the prenup Bella is about to sign.

That is if she signs.

And if she doesn't?

As she steps out of the lehenga and hands it to Shruti's assistant, Bella again regards her reflection. Only this time she's not bedecked in lush embroidered silk and precious gems.

She is naked. Vulnerable.

And, most frightening of all, very much alone.

———— ◆◆ ————

Will's pacing anxiously in the Prow Room when Bella joins him to meet the lawyer. Outside the massive windows, a gray sky looms, bending to a dark bay.

"You're late," Will says, taking long strides toward her and planting a kiss on her hollow cheek, his cologne almost masking the odor of a recent bong hit. "I almost went to get you."

"Then you would have seen me in my dress before the wedding and that would have been bad luck." She gives him a coquettish smile.

"A little late for that," he says, referring to the staged ceremony he and Bella already shot for the new Love & Pease wedding campaign entitled "The Love & Pease Revelation," a play on *revel*, i.e., "party," and *elation*, i.e., "joy." Eve was extremely proud of herself for coming up with that. Minutes after their real vows are exchanged, the new Love & Pease Revelation site will go live with these photos accompanying gushing copy and shopping links.

Will takes Bella's hand in his, leading her down the wide hall to Chet's old office. Jake and Heather have been summoned to serve as witnesses, and Dani has promised to attend because she can't resist a car crash.

"I just love executions, don't you?" she said that morning while sipping a cup of pu-erh tea at the breakfast table.

"She means a document," Cecily explained to Bella. "Executing a document."

Dani smiled at her wife. "Did I?"

At the closed door to the office, she hesitates. "Wait."

"What's wrong?" Will asks.

"I don't know. It's nothing to do with signing the agreement. I'm okay with that. I don't even care about the money. It's just . . . what does this say about our relationship?"

Will shrugs. "Not much. That where there's money, there are lawyers with contracts. I didn't want to do it, but Jake insisted."

This, she knows, is a lie. While Jake and Bella have often butted heads when it comes to the philanthropic direction of Love & Pease, she is well aware he respects her level head and prudence.

Whereas Will, in his brother's opinion, is a slacker who shouldn't be allowed the responsibility of watering the houseplants, much less controlling the family business.

"Anyway," he adds, twirling a strand of her loose hair, "it's not like you'd ever give me grounds to divorce you, right?"

Is that a threat? "Maybe I'll die first, in which case you'll get everything," she says, testing his reaction. "With my forty-five percent and your five, you'd have exactly half of Love & Pease, far more than Jake and Dani. More than Eve, too." Funny how they've never openly discussed this until now.

"Jesus. I don't want your pile of dirt. I want you." And he ends the conversation with a long, slow, dizzying kiss. Bella tastes a faint hint of whisky on his lips, though it's not yet noon.

When they enter the office, Heather and Jake are seated side by side in upholstered armchairs, she in a peach top and white golf skirt, and he in a nearly identical salmon top with white pants, having clearly dragged themselves off the links. They do a grand job of smiling warmly, Jake standing to shake Will's hand and Heather giving Bella a quick, efficient hug. Only Dani remains sitting, one leg over the chair arm, an unlit cigarette between two fingers.

"You know Arthur," Will says to Bella, introducing the lawyer who, of course, she's met before, occasionally without the family's knowledge.

Arthur gives Bella's hand a squeeze that transports her back in time to a dark night, a furtive escape. His piercing gaze under bushy gray eyebrows and cautious "Congratulations" indicate he hasn't forgotten, either.

"I assume you've had a chance to read over the documents," he begins, cutting to the chase after they take their seats. "Bella, since I didn't hear from your attorney, I—"

She holds up a finger. "I didn't show it to another lawyer. I didn't see the point."

There is a creak in the armchair to her left: Jake leaning forward in keen interest.

Arthur clears his throat. "Naturally, you're free to do as you wish, and I understand that with the wedding right around the corner we are facing a crunch. That said, I would strongly advise you to have this vetted by your own counsel if only for your own peace of mind."

"In other words, sweetie," Dani interjects, "pay someone not half as clever as Artie here to explain exactly how you're being screwed."

Will grips her knee. "Bella's read it over. She understands the details. She knows her own mind."

Clearing her throat, she says, "Keep the prenup as is. I don't care about money. I've already donated my inheritance to the foundation, so I have nothing left to give."

"Ho, ho!" Jake chortles. "Not quite true."

"It is. And I want you all to listen because I'm not going to say it again." Turning to Will, Bella continues, "If you leave me or I leave you, it will be after something awful happens, something heartbreaking. Maybe you'll invent a way to blame me for the ruination of our marriage so you can get hold of my shares of Love & Pease, but I hope not. If that was your goal in proposing, then let's call off the wedding this minute and I'll give you my forty-five percent right now."

"Shit. Don't make that offer," Dani says. "He might take it."

A hush descends and the other Peases are at a loss for words, an unusual occurrence. Jake's neck has colored and Will rests his forearms on his knees, head bowed. Heather whispers, "Good thing Eve's not here," and even Arthur anxiously spins a pen.

"Look, Bella's noble speech aside," Jake says, "Will stands to get half of Love & Pease because of this prenup. That's hardly fair to me and Dani. If anything, the contract should be rewritten so that, should the marriage end due to Bella's sleeping around or whatever, her shares will be allocated equally among the three of us."

"Why should Bella have to give up anything because of a divorce?" Dani asks. "We all know Will's the untrustworthy one here, not her. That's why Dad gave her almost half the company."

Now it's Bella's turn to blush, her cheeks instantly turning hot.

"Dad gave her half the company because you cracked up a two-hundred-thousand-dollar car," Jake shoots back.

"And you were showing up the neighbors with your god-awful Taj Mahal in Newton," Dani says, sitting up.

"Some of my family money was invested in that house, too," Heather pipes up.

Dani rolls her eyes. "Please. Your so-called family money couldn't even pay for the hedges to be pruned around that palace, princess."

"Enough!" Bella holds out her hand for the papers. "This is why I hate, hate, hate money. It brings out the worst in people. Arthur, give me that fucking pen."

The lawyer indicates where she should apply her signature and which pages she must initial. She works through the three copies with methodical assurance, her penmanship schoolgirl-perfect on the thick legal stationery. After she dots B.V. in the final corner, Heather and Jake take turns signing and dating their own signatures as witnesses.

Then it's Will's turn.

Jake hands him the archival pen and checks his watch, as if he's hoping to sneak in a few more holes. Looking grave, Will signs where he's directed.

Dani leans into Bella. "It's been nice knowing ya, sist-ah."

Bella waves her away. "Stop it, you."

As soon as he's finished, all of them rise from their seats, relieved to be done. Normal color has returned to Heather's cheeks and Jake takes Arthur aside to recount a dull blow-by-blow putt on the ninth hole.

No one notices Will reach for the stack of documents until they hear the sound of paper ripping.

"What are you doing?" Heather practically screams.

"Holy hell!" Jake thunders while Dani slaps her thigh and doubles over in laughter.

Bella gawks, amazed. It's not enough for him to tear the pages in half; he's ripping them into tiny pieces until a pile of ecru covers the desk. The lawyer simply rocks back on his heels, regarding his shredded work product. Satisfied with his creation, Will gathers the pieces and pats them into a little hill.

He did it. He actually did it. Bella's heart swells with pride and relief. Queenie was wrong; he isn't simply marrying her for her shares. He loves her, fully and completely and forever, just like he promised on that glorious evening in Bogotá. Will might have his demons, he might be a work in progress, but deep down, the magical, delightful, principled boy from her childhood lives still.

Bella throws her arms around his neck and hugs him tightly.

"I love you, you know," he says softly into her ear.

She does, finally.

TWENTY-FIVE

JANE

You won't tell Dave about the Pull-Ups, will you?" Sheila says, low so the children in the back won't hear, as we leave Indigo. "I'm not trying to hide anything from him, exactly, but, honestly, if he had to change Caleb's diapers as often as I do, he'd break down every once in a while, too."

"No problem," I say, though after Mabel's little bomb back there in the pavilion that, in fact, Sheila and her kids have been to Indigo, I'm wondering what other white lies she's told. As for the house with the pool and the indoor swing, where's that?

"How'd you like Indigo?" I ask, to test her reaction.

"Pretty." She barrels into the Orleans rotary, totally ignoring a car entering on the right. "We should swing by the grocery store. We're low on supplies." Taking a righthand turn into the Stop & Shop parking lot from the left lane, she asks, "Do you mind going in? I'm going to stay and nurse Caleb to soothe him."

We park and Sheila gets out, unsnapping him from his car seat. "We had to hang around on the beach *soooo* long while you and that"—she drops her voice—"*dealer* chatted, my baby's schedule is all catawampus and so is he."

Mabel lowers her backseat window, which has been programmed to stop midway for safety. "I'll stay here, too. Me, tired." This grammatical error is meant to be whimsical, I'm sure, as I've overheard her correct her highly educated father on his misplacement of a direct object.

Dazed, I mumble, "What are we getting?"

"My full list isn't ready. I'll text you some more ideas." Sheila shoves a collection of cloth bags into my arms. "But can we stick to veggies tonight? We've had *so* much seafood. I could do with a few greens. A kale, almond, apple, and cheddar salad might be nice." She unbuttons her shirt, stuffing Caleb against her breast. "Thanks. You're so sweet."

Slightly disoriented, I dutifully get out of the car holding the cloth bags and head to the store. Actually, I'm grateful for a few minutes to myself. There's so much I need to unpack.

First off, although I've been trying to avoid running into Bob, he needs to know what Cobb said about Kit being scared shitless and being pressured to buy drugs for—most likely—Jake Pease.

At the double doors, my phone dings and Sheila's text pops up: ORGANIC kale, apples, cheddar, almonds, olive oil, grass-fed buffalo (if avail.), mac & cheese, milk, clementines, Josh chardonnay, water (Cape is yuck!), yogurt, and Seventh Generation Free & Clear training pants.

Ugh.

I enter to a whoosh of chilled air. Grabbing a cart, I throw in the bags and plow ahead to the crowded produce section. Stacked oranges, apples, grapefruit, and kiwi fill the aisles, along with a cornucopia of additional fresh fruit and vegetables. To the left, the deli line stretches all the way to baked goods, with beachgoers ordering to-go sandwiches, since there are no vendors allowed along the National Seashore. The entire store is geared to this one consumer dynamic: the well-off tourist in a rush, willing to blow the budget.

"Nothing worse than being in this hellhole when everyone else is out on the water, am I right?"

It takes a second to realize this question has been addressed to me by a man in a peach Vineyard Vines shirt and a Mets cap who is way too old to be wearing Oakleys indoors.

I grip the cart handles, frozen in place. He's the dude from the beach, only he was wearing a Yankees cap earlier, right? Also, don't I know him from somewhere else?

"And how come these never open?" Frustrated, he licks his fingers and plies apart the thin plastic vegetable bag. "Great. I probably just picked up the flu and now I'm going to spend the next three days flat on my back. So much for a vacation!"

Where else do I know him from? This is killing me. *Think*, Jane, *think*. He's staring at me, expecting a reply to his innocuous observations.

"I try to get through this place as fast as possible," I say. "That's my strategy."

"Good luck. This store is a zoo." He tosses a bag of carrots into the cart. "See ya."

He heads off to the fancy cheeses and I backpedal to the apples, my brain churning. Did I see him on Coast Guard Beach? At Long Pond with Caleb and Mabel? Did we pass on the bike path? At Ben & Jerry's? He wasn't in a Yankees cap, though. Mets, that was it.

And now I remember exactly where I saw him before: Serena's. He was coming into her seafood market while I was going out. Serena knows him. She treated him like a favorite customer.

At the meat counter, my phone dings again. Another order from Sheila. Better get 2 bottles of Josh since there's 4 of us. Three drinkers, actually, I think.

"Surf and turf." It's Vineyard Vines again, picking through shrink-wrapped packages of rib eye. "Ka-ching!"

Smiling weakly, I look for grass-fed buffalo. In my peripheral vision, I sense him trying to catch my eye. He's not here by accident, I have the feeling.

My instincts now on red alert, I turn down the organic staples aisle, picking out boxes of acceptable mac and cheese, a bag of almonds, and a bottle of olive oil. He's nowhere in sight for the rest of my excursion, which is a relief, until I enter the wine aisle and see him holding up a bottle of white. "If my wife were here, she'd buy this crap by the barrel," he says, his cart horizontal so I can't pass.

He meets my gaze and raises his eyebrows, like he knows I know. He *wants* me to know I'm being stalked.

Ding! Crap. Another message. Not now, Sheila! But it's not from her; it's from Stan.

My fellow Viking tells me you're on the Cape. You and I talked about this. Not a wise idea, Bumble.

Why did Erik tell him that? My boyfriend might be book smart, but he has zero discretion.

Don't worry, I text back. I won't go near the wedding. Had a great deal on a rental too sweet to resist. When I look up, Vineyard Vines is gone.

Until I get to the checkout area, where he cuts in front of me and into the shortest line. "Beat ya!" he declares, pumping his fist.

If he weren't a New York sports fan, I'd definitely classify him as a certified Masshole.

I redirect to self-checkout, where I quickly swipe, pay, and get out of there, my cloth bags straining at the seams.

Outside, I find a place in the shade and sit, breathing deeply to calm my jitters. Then I Google the number for Serendipity Seafood. I want to know who Serena's customer is and why he's on my ass.

"Serendipity Seafood," a perky young voice answers.

I watch Vineyard Vines cross the lot to a big black Lexus SUV, the plate too far away to read. He pops the back, shoves in the groceries, closes the hatch, and gives me a little salute before getting into the driver's seat and taking off.

"Hi, I'm looking for Serena," I say, glad he's out of my hair.

She tells me she's just finishing up with a customer if I don't mind waiting. I tell her no problem and am put on hold.

Two seconds later, the perky woman's back on, her tone having shifted straight to curt. "I'm sorry, but Serena had to run out and won't be back for the rest of the day. You can leave a message if you want."

Huh. I'd take this as a personal insult except I didn't identify myself. . . . Oh, wait. Chances are my name showed up on Serena's caller ID.

"Could you tell her Kit's sister called?" There. Let that sink in. "You have my number."

"Jane Ellison, right?"

Confirmed. "Got it."

"She's super busy so it might not be until tomorrow."

"Thanks," I say, and hang up, feeling even more unsettled.

A milk- and sun-sated Caleb is sleeping in his seat and next to him Mabel is reading a book, possibly a Russian novel, when I return. Sheila leans out the driver's side window, fanning herself with a copy of *The New Yorker*. "Geesh, you were gone a long time. I almost turned on the air."

I'm too frazzled by my Stop & Shop stalker and Serena's brush-off to let this barb sink in. "The lines were intolerable," I lie, loading the bags in the rear next to the colorful, sandy beach clutter.

"Guess what." Sheila turns the key in the ignition as I click my seat belt. "All those TV news trucks we saw on the bridge weren't there for a wedding. They were there because some woman died."

"A Pease?"

"Don't think so." Sheila swings around the rotary, cutting off one car and nearly sideswiping another to get ahead of traffic. "Apparently, she was a friend of Eve Pease from her soap-opera days. Queenie something."

I rack my memory for a Queenie on a soap and draw a blank. Soaps never were my thing.

"CNN said she had a heart attack yesterday morning. It's awful, though, to have something like that happen in the midst of a celebration. You think they'll cancel the wedding?"

Gripping the dash as Sheila bounces over the curb of the rotary, I scoff. "Are you kidding? They've invested millions in this event, from what I've read. It has to go on. What will they do with fifty-two roast ducklings and a planeload of imported Colombian carnations?" I sit back and try to relax, employing the calming techniques I learned when I was hospitalized.

My whole universe feels like it's fraying at the edges and I have to make sure I don't unravel with it.

TWENTY-SIX

JANE

At last, we pull into the driveway of our little cottage, safe and sound. Sheila gets out, unstraps the kids, and goes to the house while I'm left to unload the car of the towels, diaper bag, beach toys, and groceries. Her cell phone's unlocked on the front seat and, in a questionably ethical move, I grab it and rapidly punch in a number.

Serendipity Seafood picks up in two rings. Same perky voice, same singsong greeting.

"Is Serena there?" I ask in a Southern drawl.

"Um, yeah. Hey, boss. Call on line two." With a thud, the phone drops.

"Hello?" Now that the name popping up on Serendipity's caller ID is Sheila McAllister, she's ready to chat. There is no doubt now I'm being shunned. What I want to know is why.

I pause to gather my wits, but before I can figure out what to say, I hear a shout from the house.

"Jane! Come here. Quick!" Sheila's at the open door, Caleb

on her hip, Mabel dancing on the stoop because she desperately needs to pee.

"Are you there?" Serena inquires.

I quickly press a button to end the call and grab the groceries and Sheila's phone. "You forgot this," I say, handing it to her. "What's going on?"

Sheila snatches the phone and begins texting madly. "Stay outside!" she commands when Mabel tries to inch past her. "You didn't leave the house unlocked, did you?" she asks, not looking up from the screen.

The back of my neck tingles as I trace my steps through this morning's exit procedure. It was a whirlwind of bagging snacks and gathering beach toys and packing kids into car seats, but I did not forget to lock up. Our rental agreement requires it and Erik is a stickler for contracts.

"I did not forget. Why?"

The door is ajar, and Sheila gives it a slight kick. "Because it's wide open."

Okay, there has to be an explanation for this, I think, having maxed out my paranoia quotient for the day. "Maybe the guys came back early to pick up something and—"

"Nope. Dave just wrote back. They've been down at Chatham and are biking back. Thank god they're almost here." Covering Caleb's head with her hand, she whispers, "Someone's watching."

I snap my head around, ready to pounce on Vineyard Vines, only to find Mabel gaping up at us, tiny antennae extended at full attention. "I have to use the lavatory, Mama, bad."

Sheila flashes me an anxious grimace. I'd suggest the kid pee in the bushes, but maybe there's another family rule about it.

"Hold on, Mabel. There's a funny odor in the house." I pinch my nose. "We want to make sure the gas wasn't left on. How about you three stay out here while I check really quickly."

"Good idea." Sheila nods vigorously, placing her hand between my shoulder blades and propelling me inside.

Wielding the heavy grocery bag containing the wine bottles as a makeshift bludgeon, I inch down the hallway. The house is immaculate, perhaps even tidier than when we left it. I'm reminded of a story Bob once shared at the dinner table about a local cleaning lady who broke into her clients' homes when they weren't around. She'd done such a professional job of dusting off her fingerprints, the cops immediately IDed her as the suspect.

Honestly, though, it actually is kind of disconcerting how together the place is. The wooden floor is swept, the counters wiped down. All the breakfast dishes have been cleaned and put away. Even Sheila and Dave's bed in the loft is made, the corners neatly folded. The air smells faintly of orange oil. So, yeah, someone was definitely on the premises. But it doesn't seem like it was a thief. Maybe there's maid service on Wednesdays along with trash pickup.

The good news is, all the valuables appear to be present and accounted for. Sheila's jewelry is lined up on the dresser. Her laptop is on the bed, charging. Dave's and Erik's are on the table downstairs. My grandmother's heart locket with tiny photos of Mom and Kit, my most precious possession, is dangling from the knob on the cabinet where I left it.

"All clear!" I call, dumping my bag on the counter. "Take off your sandals, though. We need to keep it like this."

Sheila and the children tiptoe in, like they're afraid of waking a sleeping intruder. "Wow," she says gaping at the kitchen. "It's spotless."

"Realtor, I'm assuming." I begin unloading the bag. "Or maybe a maid service. Good thing my undies weren't on full display."

"What about the P-O-T?" Sheila spells this out, which is stupid since it's a three-letter word and Mabel's not an idiot. Fortunately, the child genius has made a beeline for the bathroom.

And then I notice something. Sheila, Dave, and Erik's laptops are here.

But mine, normally by my side of the pullout bed/couch, isn't, though its charging cord is neatly wrapped on the counter. "Do you see my computer anywhere?"

"Isn't it on the end table?"

"No, it's not." The flutter of panic I'd experienced at the open door slowly returns. Getting down on my knees, I check under the couch and then under the cushions while Sheila goes outside to make sure it's not on the deck. When Mabel emerges from the bathroom much more relieved, we even look there. It's not in the car, either.

It's gone.

I run through the potentially sensitive material it holds: bank account info, an Excel spreadsheet of our household bills, photos of our passports, stuff from work including the CO2Glas case, and, yes, pages upon pages of articles I've saved regarding Kit's disappearance, Bella Valencia, and the Pease family. "Crap!"

"You mean carp?" Sheila slides her gaze toward the ever-vigilant Mabel.

"No, I mean crap." She should count herself lucky that I'm not using my favorite expletives. "My whole life is on that laptop."

"Don't you have it backed up to the cloud?"

"Yes, but that's not the point." I push the couch away from the wall on the off chance it's slipped down there, but no luck. "I don't want anyone else snooping around in my personal stuff."

Sheila starts pulling books from the built-in shelves. "You have it password-protected, though, right?"

I place a hand on my chest to slow my racing heart. "I forgot about that. It's a solid password, too."

She gives me a thumbs-up. "An ounce of prevention . . ."

"Is worth a pound of cure," singsongs her mini-me.

"If the Realtor was stopping by, maybe she took it by accident," Sheila says. "You know, all Macs look the same."

This is true and this is logical and I am supremely grateful her head can be so level when mine is exploding. "I should call them. I think they close by five." The stove clock reads 3:55. That gives me about an hour.

Sheila removes the Starlight Realty magnet from the refrigerator, where it was tacked along with a list of takeout restaurants. "Let me call. You should go look for it outside. When I was interning as a victims advocate, I learned that if thieves can't immediately get into a laptop, they toss it ASAP because they don't want to be caught with stolen goods. If I were you, I'd check the bike path in the woods behind the cottage. You'll want to find it before it rains."

That's actually an inspired idea, especially since the sky has turned a menacing gray. "You okay to be here on your own?"

"Go," she orders with a flap of her hand. "We'll be fine. The boys are almost back and they can make dinner. I'm sure even Erik can handle boxed mac and cheese."

The path Sheila means is not the paved rail trail, but a well-worn, sandy rut through the wooded outback of the National Seashore. Over the years, teenagers and mountain bikers have violated Park Service prohibitions by zigzagging through its fragile undergrowth.

For the stoners at Nauset High, it led to isolated spots where they could get high without running across a ranger or local cop, since neither had the time, staffing, or inclination to patrol hundreds of wild acres, sniffing for weed.

Apparently, not much has changed. On my thirteen-mile ride over roots and under tree branches, I encounter no one. I do pass plenty of rusted beer cans and also a discarded first-generation iPod, though no sight of a shiny MacBook Air, to my dismay. Adding to my misery, a faint misty drizzle has begun to fall, turning my hair damp and frizzy.

I'm lost in thought, stuck on why Serena would befriend a guy who turns out to be a stalker—not to mention, a New York sports fan—when I hear the sound of someone crashing through the underbrush. I resist the temptation to turn and check, willing my legs to pedal faster as I clench the handlebars. This would be easier on the paved trail, but here in the rough wilderness, I have to be careful I don't spin out on soft sand or puncture my tire on a thorn.

It's probably just a kid, I tell myself, the rain falling harder now. Still, I'm far in the woods, so deep I can't hear Route 6 or the roar of the ocean. I think I know the way out, but what if I don't? The National Seashore is a huge, wild territory. I could get lost, no problem, and no one would find me for days.

"On your left!" someone shouts and I careen right, almost into an oak, as—sure enough—a cocky teenager blows past me, legs pumping. He looks about sixteen, a local like I once was, annoyed by a tourist invading his territory. Been there, felt that. "The bike path is over there, lady." He inclines his head. "Take that next time."

I'm so relieved, I'm not even irked by his obnoxiousness, and call out, "Thank you!" Then I stop and catch my breath, cocking my ears to hear the faint *zip-zip-zip* of cars on wet pavement. The road can't be too far. Thank god.

I pull out my phone and call Sheila, but it goes straight to voice mail. She's probably taken to her bed to recover from the stress of coming home to a clean house.

"Just checking to see if Starlight has my laptop," I say, then I try Erik, who also doesn't answer, probably because he's biking home from Chatham.

With no luck reaching them, I decide to head over to Starlight Realty and ask myself. For all I know, Sheila got caught up with the kids and forgot to call, though I hope that's all. For a fleeting second, I envision her being held up by a band of clean-freak burglars, before dismissing that thought. There's an underlying steeliness to Sheila, especially when it comes to her children. She would fight back.

Wouldn't she?

Starlight is at the corner of Route 6 and a quiet residential side road. There's only one car in the lot today, a purple Honda Fit, and I bet its owner is ready to knock off for the day. The drizzle has stopped, giving me a chance to shake the dampness out of my hair. Resting my bike in the rack, I head inside.

The interior is your standard vacation realty office. Lots of fliers advertising trips to watch whales and posters of multi-generational families reconnecting at their second—and quite expensive—beachside home. Thick beige carpeting is wall-to-wall, which I find strange for a Cape business.

I was hoping to see Zara, Kit's friend from high school who got us this sweet deal, but no one's at the counter. After I tap the bell to indicate I'm here, I study the listings posted to the wall and nearly faint from sticker shock. Simple cottages on postage-stamp lots far from the beach, ones that might have been considered working class or even run-down when I was growing up, have been rehabbed and are on the market for $700,000. Basic saltboxes with a cookie-cutter floor plan: en-suite main bedroom downstairs, two tiny bedrooms and a bathroom upstairs, cathedral ceiling open to a combined kitchen/dining/living room, small deck, and outdoor shower? Those are almost a million if they're within walking distance of a pond or the bay.

As for a water view, forget it. There are a few on the bay side on the aptly named Harmes Way, which would be cute if it weren't so prophetic. A few more years of a changing climate, a couple of winter storms, and those $1.52 million two-bedroom shacks will be piles of very expensive soggy firewood.

Mom rented our house by the Shoreham Town Hall because she never had the cash or credit score to buy. Bob offered to go in with her to buy a place, but she liked where we lived and, besides, I suspected she wanted to maintain at least the illusion of independence. As a single woman, I'd be priced out, too, if I ever wanted to move back to my hometown. Where do normal people live around here? They must have to commute across the bridge from Plymouth, though it's not exactly reasonable over there, either.

"That just came on the market last week." A bouncy woman about my age with unnaturally red hair bounds across the carpeted foyer. "I'm Terri. Looking for a single family?" Her blue-lined eyes brighten at the possibility.

"Oh, geesh. I'm not buying. I couldn't even afford a down payment on a garden shed around here."

She looks disappointed, but not that surprised. Hedge fund managers with millions to burn on seaside estates don't usually show up on ratty bikes with frizzy hair. "Totally understandable.

My parents bought their house in Wellfleet back in the eighties for something like a hundred grand. It'd go for eight times that now and, trust me, it's nothing special. That said, there are some bargains along the highway down by Orleans."

"If you grew up here like I did," I say, "you probably know how crazy prices have gotten."

"No, no. I'm from Connecticut. Hey, this shouldn't be up here. It sold." She unpins a posting for a waterfront lot and folds it in half. "My parents rented out our Wellfleet house in the summers until my dad retired a few years ago and they relocated here. The irony is, I hate the beach. I get a burn if I so much as go out for the mail without sunblock. But now I'm stuck here because I have to look after them. They've had, um, a few setbacks. They need me around."

I nod. "How good of you and how nice for them."

"Yeah. You're right." She flashes a beaming smile, returning to her prior upbeat attitude. "So what town are you from?"

"Just down the road, actually. I moved away a long time ago, though." I'm keeping the details vague out of an excess of caution. "Actually, that's why I'm here. We're renting a cottage through Starlight and we came home this afternoon to find it unlocked."

"Oh, no!" she says, her eyes widening. "Was anything taken?"

"Everything seemed to be in place aside from my laptop. Here's the thing. All the beds were made and the floors swept. Either we have maid service we didn't know about or maybe someone from your office came in to show it?" I pose it like a question. "And if that's the case, I'm wondering if they could have mistakenly walked off with my computer?"

"Oooh. I hope not. Let me check the lost and found." Tossing the paper from the bulletin board into the recycling, she slips behind the counter and ducks down, inspecting a hidden shelf. When she pops up, she's wearing an exaggerated frown. "Nope. No laptop here. Now, where did you say you're staying?"

I give her the address, which she types into her computer. "That cottage is so cozy, isn't it? I just love it. Normally it's one of my properties, but Zara's handling it because it was on the list for a major event we have coming up. She's in charge of all the event rentals."

"You mean the Pease wedding?"

Terri cranes her neck, checking this way and that to guarantee no one's listening, though obviously we're the only ones in the building. "I'm not supposed to say."

"It's trending on Twitter. It's hardly a secret."

"Yeah, but . . ." Her bright-pink mouth opens wide at the results of her search. "Wait. Are you on their guest list?"

"Oh, god, no."

"Well, that's not what it says here." She points to the screen. "Zara has it asterisked, which means you're part of the wedding block. If the cleaners came in, that's why. All those rentals get complimentary maid service midweek."

Shoot. I don't want to get Zara in trouble for putting me in a cottage reserved for the wedding. "Can you check under Jane Ellison?"

A flicker crosses her face at the mention of my name. Zara's probably told her about Kit, if she didn't already know. She clears her throat, focusing—or pretending to focus—on her screen. "Hmm. Okay, that might be the problem. The house is definitely part of the reserved block of properties, but Ellison's not the name on the lease."

"Because we're subleasing."

Terri winces. "Hope not. Starlight doesn't allow subleasing."

Terri's nails click across the keyboard. "Anyway, according to my records, the renters picked up their keys right on schedule at three p.m. on Saturday."

This has to be a mistake. "Our rental is from Sunday to Sunday. My boyfriend checked in around noon."

"Is his name Dave?"

My blood turns cold. "No. It's Erik."

"Well, I don't know what to say." She looks me up and down, as if reassessing her earlier impression. This once-over is accompanied by a discernible cooling in friendliness. "I worked last weekend and personally handed them the keys and the bucket. Super-cute family with a totally adorable little girl in a princess tutu."

The ground tilts. *Not princess, rainbow.* "Are you positive?"

"You know, this is weird. I need to call Zara and find out what's up." She reaches for the office phone.

My throat tightens as she presses a number. Alerting Zara might tip off Dave and Sheila and I don't want to do that until I've got a clearer picture of what's really going on. "Was the girl's name Mabel?"

"Then you do know them."

I think of Dave throwing open the screen door when we returned from the beach, the way his large mass claimed possession of our cottage like he was the renter and we were the guests. I think of how they helped themselves to the loft, how their food was already in the fridge, how Mabel was confused to see us arrive. Maybe Erik had told them they could get there before us.

But then, why would they have pretended they didn't? And, more important, why wouldn't Erik have told me?

Previously insignificant details like how Eric insisted on going to Starlight even though I protested that I should since I was the connection to Zara take on new relevance. "No, no," he'd said, unhooking his bike from the back of our car. "I need the exercise, my legs are so stiff. You relax. Take a walk around."

So I did, checking out the backyard, the porch, pressing my face to the windows to see inside. As soon as he returned, unlocked the door, and dumped our stuff, he insisted we go straight to the beach. I didn't even have a moment to brush my teeth. I laughed at what a kid he was and agreed because, sure, I wanted to make the most of the sunny day, too.

Terri's nails tap the counter in expectation of an answer. She's running out of patience. "I am such a ditz," I confess with an embarrassed laugh. "Of course, Dave and Sheila checked in on Saturday." Flicking a dismissive wave to the phone, I add, "Don't bother Zara. This is all my bad."

She hangs up and exhales with relief. "Phew! Good thing we got that resolved. For a minute there, I thought I was going to have to call our contact with the wedding and tell them we accidentally rented one of their reserved cottages to someone not on the guest list. That would have been a big whoopsie."

That would have been the least of it.

"Just to make sure," I say, "the name on the lease is Dave McAllister, right?"

Terri gives me a guarded glance and I can tell I've crossed a line with this question. She's now asking herself what's really going on and I don't blame her. I have only one choice and that is to lie and lie convincingly.

I sigh. "The truth is, there is no missing laptop."

She steps back from the keyboard, folds her arms, and leans against the wall, like she knew it all along. "Oh?"

"Yeah, the thing is, my boyfriend disappeared for a few hours on Sunday afternoon. We were on the beach when he checked his phone and suddenly said he forgot to sign the lease. Needed to go to the Realtor's before they closed. He got up and just left me there all by my lonesome." Blinking back imaginary tears, I add, "I figured it was bullshit. But I had to come here and see for myself."

She sucks in a breath. "I'm sorry. But I was here on Sunday and no one like that came in. Also we close at noon and the leases are signed when the deposit is sent. There's no paperwork when you pick up the key."

I give the counter a tiny pound. "Goddamn him."

"Maybe he meant he had to go sign something else?" Terri suggests. "Like to a locker? Or did he have to go get a pond sticker or one for the dump?"

"No, he's just a jerk," I say, adding an eye roll. "He said this thing with her was over, that he wasn't going to text her, that he was gonna cut off all contact, but"—I shrug—"Guess not! Apparently, they can't stand to be one minute apart from one another."

A low simmer of rage is rising to a boil inside me. I need to get out of here before I go ballistic. Painting him as a scheming, disloyal liar is easy, given what he's done.

Ever since my conversation with Sheila in the kitchen, the possibility that Erik invited his two shrink friends to the Cape so they could stealthily assess my mental state has been lurking in the back of my mind. But never would I have suspected that the three of them had planned this for months, going all the way back to Erik's story about Zara's cancellation and, later, pretending he couldn't confront Dave about overstaying his welcome because he didn't want to piss off his adviser.

Also, hold up. What did she say about them being on the Pease guest list? That definitely requires an explanation. "All that aside," I say, "I had no idea Sheila and Dave were going to the wedding. How exciting!"

"I know, right?" Terri grins conspiratorially. "Please don't say anything. I could lose my job if it got out that I let it slip your hosts were guests. We had to sign NDAs along with all the other vendors and I don't want to get my bosses sued."

This just can't be correct. There's no way the McAllisters even know the Peases, and from everything I've read, the guest list is super exclusive. More likely there really was a cancellation and Dave is subleasing, though, why would his name have been on the lease? A pain in my temple is spreading over the right hemisphere of my skull.

"I swear I won't say a word," I mumble.

"Look," she says, pinching one of her business cards from the holder and handing it to me, "if you need a place to stay tonight, here's my number. Call me and I'm sure I can make a last-minute arrangement."

It's a very sweet offer coming from someone who should be wary about a person with a cockamamie story about a missing laptop and a cheating boyfriend.

"I really appreciate all your help," I tell her and it's true. I am beyond grateful.

"Jane Ellison, right?" she says. "I gotta ask. Are you . . . ?"

I prepare for the inevitable ". . . *the one who was stalking Bella Valencia?*"

". . . Kit Ellison's sister?"

Huh. Not what I expected. "Yeah. Did you"—I have to pause because I despise using the past tense in reference to Kit—"Know her?"

"I didn't, but my next-door neighbor Ettie was in the same grade as your sister at Nauset."

There was only one Ettie Kit ever mentioned and that was Ettie Watson, the girl in the Camp Pekky photo I just saw. That's some Jungian synchronicity for you. Here I haven't thought of Ettie in years, and now her name pops up twice in the same afternoon.

"Man, that high school class has had some bad luck," Terri continues. "First Kit goes missing, then Ettie dies in a freak accident."

The hairs on my arm rise. "Ettie died?"

"Yeah, that horrible plane crash in P-town three years ago." She leans on the counter, whispering, though we're the only ones in the office as far as I can tell. "She was Chet Pease's 'assistant.'" Terri fingers air quotes. "But the talk around town is that they were way more than that. Rumor was, he couldn't keep his hands off any woman half his age. Guy was a total perv."

I'm reminded of Chet on the beach that night. What was this grown man really doing at that bonfire with a bunch of teenagers? Waiting for the cops? Telling the kids to go home?

No. I don't think so. I think he was up to something else. Because two young local women with ties to him are either dead or missing. And, like I keep saying, there is no such thing as a coincidence—just hidden truths that have yet to be exposed.

TWENTY-SEVEN

JANE

I do not go home.

I should go home, back to East Somerville. I should take an Uber to Provincetown, hop a ferry to Boston, and slog my way through the T to our tiny apartment. I should ask our downstairs neighbor for the spare and let myself in. I should toss all of Erik's belongings—including his precious Klipsch speakers—out the window, where they will smash onto the hard alleyway below. Then I should call a locksmith, change the locks, and inform Erik by singing telegram that we're through.

Instead, I bike down to the ocean and, like a pathetic character from a sappy Lifetime movie, sit on the barren dune, hugging my knees as the drizzle picks up and turns to rain, the wind whipping my skin raw red. I want to boldly recalibrate where I am right now—at the end of the earth, confronting the maw of a great and fearsome, unforgiving ocean.

I want a good, racking cry.

Erik is—was—my best friend, who I believed in my heart truly loved me for me. He's the only one I get to call my own. My mother's dead and my sister's been gone so long I barely remember her laugh. Erik is all I have of a family. Without him, I am cut adrift, bobbing on the sea of life like a fragile piece of driftwood.

"Hey there, snuggle bunny. Time to rise and shine!" That's Erik's dorky and lovable morning greeting. How can a man who calls you snuggle bunny drive a knife into your back? I never imagined he'd be capable of such deceit.

Our initial encounter in the fluorescent-lit basement of Whipley Hall eons ago was anything but romantic. Erik's windowless office reeked of raw garlic and anchovies thanks to his unwise lunch choice of a Caesar salad with extra dressing. He was furiously wrapping up the remains when I entered, taking a step back for a breath of fresh air. Erik was big and bearded with glasses that were so thick they reminded me of my grandmother's coasters.

But he was nice. Really nice.

"Thank you, so, so much for volunteering," he said, bumping his head on an overhead pipe when he stood from his desk too quickly. "You did it to me again!" He scolded the pipe with a wag of his finger. Later, he would confess that, taken aback by my beauty, he'd forgotten to duck.

I sat opposite him while he administered a baseline test, and then every two weeks I returned to his office glad to find it had been improved with a few green plants and a hidden air freshener. Mostly, Erik had me studying pictures of crowds and a photo series of similar individuals within those crowds to determine if the forensic analysis course I was simultaneously taking had enhanced my rare abilities. Whenever I matched pairs of the same people who appeared on the surface to be very different, Erik would respond with an automatic "Hmm, good." And then he'd flip to the next set.

I liked how he greeted me with a friendly smile tucked in

his golden-red beard. I liked how he was painfully polite, offering me coffee with cream and, once, chocolate chip cookies he'd baked using his Minnesotan mother's recipe. I even liked his style—a worn flannel shirt over a gray, white, or navy tee—and how, despite the orchid and lavender room spray, he still smelled of smoked fish and garlic. I was sad when the research study was over and he shook my hand and said it'd been a pleasure. I thought about asking him out and decided that was probably inappropriate.

A year and a half later we ran into each other on Mass Ave. At first, he couldn't place me. I'd let my hair grow to shoulder length and had lost about thirty pounds due to a new diet and exercise program I'd undertaken to limit my anxiety and keep me out of the hospital. Of course, I recognized him and made a crack about how nice it was to see that he didn't wear flannel in the summer, a joke that went right over his head.

He'd gotten into biking and had also toned up since our Whipley Hall days. He wondered if I had a bike and, if so, if I'd like to go out to Mystic Lakes that following Sunday. He moved into my apartment at the end of the month and we've been together ever since. Occasionally, when he's feeling particularly sentimental, he mentions marriage and kids. Not lately though. Not since the incident at Logan, and now I know why.

He thinks I'm insane.

And maybe I am. Because right here, right now, I am seriously debating ending it all. I could walk into that frigid water and power against the waves until the vast ocean swallows me whole. It'd be scary, terrifying, and my body would struggle with all its might to survive, but then it'd give in. My conscious brain would shut down, taking the autonomous system with it. There'd be a cold dark peace. A forever silence.

Erik would feel guilty he hadn't had me admitted sooner on

a Section 12, the Massachusetts law that allows for a three-day involuntary committal of someone who is considered to be a danger "to themselves or others." As a psychiatrist who's consulted on several such cases, he's convinced involuntary committal, while difficult, has saved distraught and depressed patients from tragic suicide. So, I know that if he—or Dave or Sheila—thought I was at risk, that's the route they'd take.

But I wonder if, deep down inside, he'd be relieved if I killed myself. No paranoid, obsessed girlfriend to console. No more embarrassing social media rumors or raised eyebrows among his priggish Ivy colleagues judging in their ivory towers. No more worries that I might tarnish his stellar academic reputation.

Yes, that'd be best for all.

I get up and pad down to the cold water's edge, the waves crashing and beckoning. Small stones roll over my bare toes. The fog from the rain is so dense it blankets the dunes. Just the sea and me—if I want it. If I have the courage. The guts.

And that's when I feel a buzzing in the pocket of my raincoat. The number on my phone's screen is absurdly long and I stare at it, debating what to do. Normally, we talk by text, so an actual call is alarming.

"Stan?"

He sputters a bit, obviously astonished that I've answered. "B-B . . . Bumble! Finally. What a delight to speak to my little girl at last."

I have to smile, though I feel a bit weepy. Maybe there's something to the old saw that blood harkens to blood because right now, cold and wet and alone and abandoned, it occurs to me that I'm not entirely without family. I do have a father, even if he's a world away.

"What time is it there?" I ask, starting off with the safe option.

"Oh, it's . . . well, I just had my breakfast. It's tomorrow!" He lets out a hearty chuckle. "What're you up to?"

"Hanging at the beach." I turn away from the water, toward the stairs, my bare feet sinking into the damp sand. "How are the lambs?"

"Getting bigger every day. Listen, I just want to know, why are you there, darling? Why'd you really go back to the Cape?"

He sounds so distressed, I can't possibly tell him the truth. "Like I said, we got a good deal on a rental." Hah! "And I was feeling a bit homesick. Needed to get my fix of the ocean. I feel bad I didn't tell you sooner."

"Ah, I figured that was the case, missing your mum and all. Don't be too hard on yourself. You always are."

He's being solicitous, but he's not calling to talk about the weather or breakfast. "Hey, Stan, lemme ask you something." I get to the top of the wooden stairs and lean over the railing, sticking my finger in my right ear to mute the roar of the ocean. "Has Erik been calling you?"

There's a long pause that has nothing to do with him being in New Zealand. "He hasn't been calling me," my father says. "I've been calling him."

He doesn't have to explain why. I know. Ever since the incident at Logan, Stan's been afraid that I haven't been taking my meds. That I'm unwell again. I push back a strand of soaked hair. "You don't have to worry. Really, I'm okay."

"Are you, Bumble? You've gone through a helluva lot alone. If your mother were alive, that'd be one thing, but you don't have any close family around to support you. I don't like it."

"I have Erik," I say, half-heartedly.

Another pause. "Erik isn't family. Not yet. I wish you'd let me buy you a ticket to Christchurch. You can stay as long as you want.

We have plenty of room and Delilah is dying to meet you. We have all these lovely newborn lambs to play with."

Delilah is Stan's new wife and by "new" I mean for the past quarter century. "I dunno, there's work and . . ."

"Please let me take care of you. I owe you that much."

There is a choke in my throat. I'm on the verge of sobbing. How did he know these were the words I so needed to hear? *Come home.* Even if this place where he lives is something I've only seen in *Lord of the Rings* movies and in those tons of photos he's constantly sending, home is not where you grew up, but where those who love you live.

Sniffing back tears, I say, "I'll think about it."

"Truly? Oh, that's awesome, Jane. My heart is soaring. Pick a date and I'll make the reservation. When?"

"Soon. First, I have to tie up some loose ends here."

"All right," he replies, hesitantly. "But you have to promise. And you can't go back on a promise you make to your old man."

It goes unsaid that he's gone back on plenty of promises he made to my mother, Kit, and me. But that's all water under the bridge. Anyone who pledges a new start out of love deserves a second chance. That's what Kit would say.

"I promise."

"Atta girl."

"Oh, and St—" I stop and correct myself, "Dad?"

"Yeah?"

"I love you."

"Back atcha, Bumble, times a million."

I click off and wipe away the tears, inhaling and exhaling a deep cleansing breath of moist sea air. The next day, the next hours, are going to be tough, far harder than I anticipated when I assumed Erik had my back. But I'm strong and I'm determined and I have a plan. When I get on that plane to New Zealand I will know, once and for all, what happened to my sister.

Even if it means burning every last bridge in my wake. Even if it means burning everything to ashes.

———— ◆ ————

"Jane!" Mabel screams, melting and breaking my heart as I let myself in the front door. "We were about to call the peace pals."

She wraps her arms around my legs tightly as her mother rounds the corner from the kitchen. "Oh, my goodness, you're soaked. Let me get you a towel."

I look beyond her to Erik standing in the living room, the cell pasted to his ear, my blood turning to ice at the sight of his feigned joy. "She just walked in," he says. "False alarm."

If they were about to call the police, as Mabel said, then who's he talking to? Skip it. It's all a sham.

Erik hangs up, tosses the cell on the couch, and opens his arms. "Oh, man. You had us so worried." He comes toward me and I let myself fall into him, fighting my knee-jerk craving to forgive.

"Sorry," I say. "My phone died and believe it or not, I actually got lost out there in the woods."

He kisses my forehead. Chaste. Platonic. "That's exactly what I figured though, shit, you were gone for hours, Janie."

Hours?

"Is it late?" I take the towel from Sheila and beam at her gratefully, really laying it on. "I had no idea. When your watch is your phone and your phone doesn't even come on, you're kind of clueless." I pray none of them will ask to charge it because, before I turned it off, the battery was at fifty percent.

Dave saunters in, saying nothing. A look passes between us and I can tell he's skeptical, jotting down mental notes for his psychiatrist's report.

"I rode all over the place looking for my laptop, in dumpsters, ditches, garbage cans. No luck." I rub the towel over my hair with such fury it tangles in twists. Then I stick out my tongue at Mabel and go, "Boo!"

She lets out a screech. "Don't! You look scary."

"That's because I'm a Gorgon." I pull on the strands until they stand up on end, thick with sticky seawater. "Do you know about Medusa? She had snakes on her head and turned men to stone."

Sheila gently brings her daughter to her, the alarm in her taut jaw confirming my hunch that, truth be told, she does think I'm slightly dangerous. "Oh, sweetie, are you okay?"

"Exhausted and famished. That's all." A quick, nonchalant shrug. "What'd the Realtor say when you called?"

Dave points to the table. "Saved some oysters for you."

"The Realtor saved me oysters?" I laugh and secretly delight in the way each fink reveals his or her tell. Erik scratches the right side of his beard. Sheila tugs one of Mabel's curls. Dave clears his throat.

"We saved you oysters. I didn't want to hear you complain again." Erik pulls out a chair for me. "Want some cranberry juice?"

"Ice water would be fine. I'm way thirsty after that ride." I shake out a napkin and help myself.

Sheila refills her glass with wine and sits opposite, watching me, her eyes fiery, like she's solving a mystery. "You'll be happy to know Mabel found your laptop."

Naturally. The child's a genius.

"No! You little rock star!" I pat cocktail sauce from my lips and wave over Mabel, who happily crawls into my wet lap. She grins up at me much the same way she did at Pekky earlier in the day when she confessed about playing along with her mother's fib.

That fib has a whole new meaning in light of Sheila and Dave's potential relationship to Will Pease and Bella Valencia. I have yet to fully process Sheila's role in this charade, but I have deduced this much: she lured me into a sense of trust and sucked out the details of my memory of Kit's last night like a spiny starfish wrapping its legs around an oyster and then drilling through its shell for a precious pearl. She is so good at mental manipulation, she even managed to turn my recollections topsy-turvy, twisting and distorting them until I was convinced I'd misremembered the order of events, that Bella was calling for help because Kit was overdosing.

Lies. All lies.

"We let Mabel stay up late to tell you," Sheila says, mouthing, *She was so excited!*

"Right. So where was it?" I ask Mabel, running my fingers through her soft ringlets.

"Under the back porch. I peeked down and there it was."

"Fortunately, it was under the grill so it didn't get any water damage," Sheila rushes to explain.

Uh-huh. I bounce Mabel on my knee, ignoring her conniving mother. "What a silly place for it to be. What was it doing there?"

Mabel throws up her arms. "I dunno! Maybe a bunny took it."

"You know. I bet a bunny did take it." I bop her on her button nose. "Maybe the bunny wanted to watch Bugs Bunny."

Mabel squirms, basking in the attention. Putting her lips to my ear, she whispers, "What about the ice cream?"

"Shhh." I give her a wink. "When the rain stops."

"When the rain stops," she repeats solemnly, the logic of ice cream being suitable only on dry evenings acceptable to her child brain.

"All right, time for bed." Dave lifts her off my lap. "We're gonna need to change your PJs. Aunt Jane got you wet, too." He throws her over his shoulder and carries her up the stairs to the loft. In any other situation, the scene would be painfully lovable.

"You should have kids. You're a natural," says Sheila. "What about it, Erik?"

"Has to get tenure first," I answer for him, snatching the last oyster. I avoid his gaze because I'm afraid if I see simpering love pooling in those baby blues I might drive this fork into his pupils. "Or maybe we should just go for it."

Erik blushes as red as his beard. "I'm game if you are."

Sheila wiggles her brows. "Good thing we're on our way out, then, so you two can get busy."

A flash of horror. Despite days of counting the minutes until they can leave us in peace, I now need them to stay. They have to. My plan depends upon it. "Oh, no. You're leaving? When?"

"Saturday morning." She makes a pouty face.

So it's true. They're going to the wedding after all. "That's too bad. How come?"

"Our friends whose kids had measles were just given the all clear by their doctor so we'll spend the weekend with them. Mabel and their girl are besties."

"What's her name?" I take a sip of water.

Sheila falters for a nanosecond and then rallies. "Oh, uhh, Amelia. By the way, your laptop's over there on the end table, charging. We got it inside before it really started raining. Dave thinks maybe you left it on the deck table and it fell between the cracks."

I go over to my laptop, unplug it, and bring it back to the

table, typing in the password 0330, Kit's birthday. Boots up right away. "Or maybe someone broke into it and downloaded all my searches." I giggle as if this is ridiculous.

For the briefest of seconds, Sheila and Erik exchange glances, validating their conspiracy. "I don't know," she says with a faltering lilt. "We didn't try."

"To log in," Erik clarifies.

"I don't care," I say, closing the cover and sliding it across the table. "Who needs a computer on vacation anyway? After this storm blows over, I'm doing nothing but biking, swimming, and sunning. There's been too much reliving the past. From now on, I'm having fun!"

To prove it, I reach over, grab Sheila's wine bottle, and pour some chardonnay into my water glass. Unthinkable. I never drink.

"Atta girl." Erik lifts his chin in approval. He'd probably like it if I went on a three-day bender and woke up after the nuptials were over. How would Bella and Will reward him then? A nicely funded chair at Harvard might do.

"We were thinking of doing a whale watch tomorrow. Our treat," Sheila says. "We need to pay you back. You guys have been *soooooo* gracious sharing your vacation house with us."

Correction. *Your* vacation house. I turn to Erik, who is flicking sand off his toenail. If I needed any confirmation of his role in this scam, there it is.

"How lovely," I say. "What a great idea!" To put me on a boat where they can keep me under total guard. As if. I hoist my glass. "A toast to friendship."

"To friendship!" they concur, glass clinking against glass. We each take our sips, Erik and Sheila frowning as I begin to grimace in discomfort.

"Oooh," I say, clutching my middle. "Maybe that oyster wasn't such a bright idea."

Sheila shoots a look at her husband. "See? I told you we shouldn't be eating these at the height of summer."

She's right. If I know food poisoning, I'll be puking up those "Argust" oysters by morning, praying for the bliss of death.

TWENTY-EIGHT

MEGAN

Megan stares at the shadowed grooves in the dove-white shiplap ceiling over her bed in her tiny Heron's Neck guest house, bummed that she missed another chance to see the dawn breaking on the ocean side. She just didn't have the energy to get up for it, now that Queenie's gone.

Her own mother is no substitute. Despite Eve's numerous blog posts about the spiritual value of waking at four a.m. to greet the sun rising from the Atlantic horizon as its "brilliant orange and yellow rays kiss the clouds" while in *Anjaneyasana*, Megan could not recall one time her mother had actually done this.

Megan's companion on these early morning excursions had most often been her godmother, who regarded their chilly trips not so much as ways to greet the day, but to close down the night. Queenie would bring a carafe of coffee, black, and sit on the dunes wrapped in a massive cape, her bloodshot eyes buffered by oversized Gucci sunglasses as she watched Megan at the water's edge. When the sun appeared, she'd erupt in an energetic applause, the cigarette clenched between her red lips. That was

Megan's cue to put her to bed, where she would stay until at least early afternoon.

Those days were over now. Never again would she inhale her godmother's unique elixir of Marlboro Lights and Joy perfume or feel her protruding vertebrae in a hug. Queenie might not have been the ideal role model, but she always found time for Megan when no one else, not even her mother, could be bothered.

Yesterday, the medical examiner preliminarily confirmed she'd died of a massive heart attack, most likely caused by years of abusing her slight frame with cocaine, booze, and cigarettes. So unfair.

"Is there life after death?" she whispers aloud.

"Dubious" is the mumbled response from the male form beside her.

Yes, that's what she thought. Having not been raised with any religion besides Eve's pop fads and her stepfather's devoted capitalism, Megan feels unmoored. If only Queenie would send a sign, like a delicate sparrow trilling on her windowsill. She'd heard of ghosts manifesting that way. Would that be cool? Or scary?

Scooching under the covers, she pulls the soft cotton sheet to her chin and watches the changing colors in the morning sky outside the plate-glass window. In the thin new light, she can just make out the turrets of the white tents on the manicured back lawn, which have been built between the turquoise swimming pool and the grass tennis court. Contractors have been working all month, sawing and hammering, constructing bars and decks architecturally designed to maximize privacy.

Yesterday, florists arrived to wind vines of jasmine over the pergola under which Will and Bella will exchange vows. The scent was intoxicating and romantic. After they finished the lush arrangement, the altar was hidden by a makeshift fence and protective covering so the reveal wouldn't be ruined for the family and close friends attending tonight's rehearsal dinner down on the beach.

Dress will be informal—lots of salmon-colored shorts and Prada florals—and the food will be rustic elegant: whole lobsters, mussels, and littlenecks steamed in seaweed buried deep in the sand. Raw oysters and Dom galore, too, of course.

A hot tear trickles down her cheek. Megan can't tell if it belongs in the ocean she's already shed for Queenie or if this is a fresh cloudburst brought on by the torturous reminder that she has to stand next to the bride when the man she loves pledges his undying love to another.

"It should have been me," she whispers into the silence broken only by her bedmate's soft snoring. "Why not me?"

Queenie drawled that Will really did love her, Megan. And he would marry her, too, except he thinks he needs Bella's shares to have any standing in the family company. Hence, the wedding.

"But *donne* you worry," she'd slurred. "I *haveasecretplan* so Bella will go away and her shares will be divided among all of you. He'll never marry her, not *ash* long as I'm alive."

Megan took her godmother's inebriated monologue with a grain of salt, more concerned with getting some food into her—Queenie refused, as usual—than her delusions about a ploy to rid them of Bella, if not her shares.

Queenie was bitter on Megan's behalf, that was no secret. She was appalled when Will put the ring that rightly belonged to her on Bella's finger. "That's rightfully yours!" Queenie told her. "Yours. He doesn't love her; he loves you!"

"You okay?" The bedsprings squeak as the lump rolls to his side. "Can't sleep?"

She uses a corner of the sheet to pat her cheeks dry. "Thinking about god monster, that's all."

"Yeah." He touches the delicate skin of her inner arm. "I'm sorry."

"Thanks." She means it.

"Can I do anything to help?"

"I don't think so. It's going to take time."

"And even then . . ."

He would know. Sometimes she forgets how much Will's been through and how, despite his moods, he can be so sensitive and caring. That's what she loves about him, that sweet inner core. She wishes she could confess what's really going on, how what he's doing is breaking her heart. But that would make her appear needy and he needs her to be strong. They have a big, big task ahead.

"Hey, come here." He slides his arm under her neck and pulls her toward his bare chest, where Megan rests her head, her fingers tracing the ab lines she knows by heart.

"Do you really have to go through with this?" She can't resist.

He sighs. "Like I said, it's just a transaction. I could be signing a lease or putting my signature on a contract. Hell, I was more excited about taking the bar exam for the third time. More emotionally involved, too."

Will lifts his head to check and places a finger at the corner of her mouth, forcing it into a half-smile. "There you go. Much better."

She raises up on her elbow, pausing to take in how gorgeous he is. Like a Roman god. David in marble, only tan and with better pecs. "You say that, but you ripped up your prenup so she can take you for all you're worth if you leave her."

"Did I?"

"Did you what?"

"Rip up the prenup."

"That's what Dani told me, and Jake and Heather, too. They couldn't believe it."

"I ripped up some paper. Don't think it was the actual contract."

Megan sits up all the way, puzzled. "Say what?"

"While everyone was patting themselves on the back, they
didn't notice that Arthur had slipped the signed contracts into his
folder, leaving me with a worthless copy, unsigned. That's what I
tore to pieces."

Her jaw drops. Will closes it for her. "Don't worry. One signed
set is safe and sound in Eve's vault. The other has been FedExed
to Arthur's office in Boston. We're good."

"And Arthur went along with that?"

"He wasn't exactly keen on it, but he works for me, right?"
He taps her on the nose. "You just have to be patient. You can be
patient, right?"

Hasn't she proven that already? "I can."

"Good girl." He stands and pulls on his jeans.

"Where are you going?" she asks. It's not even five yet. "It's so
early."

"I'm up. Might as well start the day. How about you?"

Megan lies back and wiggles her toes, suddenly tired. "I might
see if I can go back to sleep."

"My, my, Miss Lazy." He snatches his keys, leans over the bed,
and plants a parting kiss. "Everything will work out. You'll see."

"I hope so," she says with a yawn, before rolling over and closing her eyes, thanking her lucky stars that Queenie hadn't been
able to execute her plan, whatever it was.

TWENTY-NINE

JANE

I am running out of time.

The wedding is less than forty-eight hours away and the three of them are circling like sharks, not letting me out of their sight for a minute.

I woke this morning to Erik leaning over me, watching as I squirmed and fought the waves of nausea. He immediately sent Dave to the general store to fetch medicine to quell my stomach.

Though it's only seven a.m., Sheila is out of bed and serving breakfast, slicing up bananas and stirring blueberries into unsweetened yogurt with a sprinkling of unsweetened granola, which she sets into bowls before her children. "We need to use our inside voices," she whispers to Caleb. "Jane isn't feeling well."

"Should we call the homeopath?" inquires Mabel from her stool at the counter.

"I want pampakes," pipes up Caleb, banging his spoon.

Sheila places a quieting hand on his spoon. "No pancakes today and no, I don't think we need to call a homeopath. Jane has food poisoning. Bad oysters."

"What they do?" Caleb asks.

"They were filled with nasty bacteria that upset Jane's tummy," Sheila explains.

I am counting the minutes until they're satisfied it's safe to leave me alone. In the meantime, I watch them through slitted eyes, occasionally stirring on the foldout and moaning for effect.

The front door opens and Dave enters with a pink bottle of Pepto Bismol. "Had to go all the way to Orleans to get this," he complains, setting it on the end table. "Huge price markup. They really gouge you on the Cape, don't they?"

"Shh." Sheila stabs a finger in my direction. "The patient's trying to sleep."

Dave ignores her. "The clouds are burning off and it's turning out to be a beautiful day, the best all week, probably. We can't stay cooped up with her. It's not fair."

This is my cue. With a loud groan, I lean over the side of the thin bed, bring the empty bowl to my face, and cough violently. I think I'm convincing, though feigning illness was easier at three a.m. when all I had to do was make horrific retching noises from the other side of the bathroom door.

"Ugh." Dave clutches his middle. "I'm sorry, but I can't hang around this. You know how I get, Sheel."

She *tsk-tsks* in understanding. "Sympathetic puking. Like with the kids. Poor baby."

This is going swimmingly, even better than I'd anticipated.

"Any improvement?" asks my so-called significant other as he emerges from the bathroom that he's spent the past twenty minutes disinfecting.

"Afraid not," Sheila answers, pinching her nose. "Oh, wow. Did you use Clorox?"

Erik tosses the used paper towels into the garbage pail. "It's bleach. In case she has a virus."

"Did you dilute it though?"

"No. Should I have?"

"Holy jalapeño!" Sheila throws open the sliding glass door and ushers the children out to the deck, where their father's been enjoying thirty seconds of peace. "We definitely can't stay here. We have to leave."

Erik comes over and rubs my back, each stroke as welcome as nails on Styrofoam. If anything is making me nauseous right now, it's the smell of his aftershave, the spicy woodsy scent that used to make me swoon. Lying next to him all night was an exercise in discipline as I resisted the urge to prod him awake so I could rattle off his offenses. Does he assume that because I don't have a PhD like the rest of them I'm too dumb to have figured out what they're up to?

"Hey, babe. I don't want to leave you alone," he says with syrupy sweetness. "I'll stay and look after you."

I roll over and blink. "Please, go, hon. I just have to ride this out. Honestly, all I want is silence and sleep."

"Are you sure?" He can barely suppress his glee, the traitor.

"Positive. I'll probably be in the same spot when you get back. It helps not to move. All I need is quiet."

It seems like hours later that they finally leave for Provincetown and the whale watch Sheila's been so excited about. I track Erik's phone on my phone through an app I set up while he was sleeping. When they pass Truro, the coast is clear and I jump in the shower.

A half hour later, my clean hair is pulled into a tidy ponytail and I'm in white jeans and a yellow cotton blouse, appropriately dressed for a visit to the Town Clerk's Office, Mom's old haunt. I plan to search the land records and find who, exactly, owns this cottage Dave and Sheila are renting to see if there's a personal connection.

While I'm there, I'll use the public computer to Google Ettie Watson. I'd do it on my laptop or phone, but I don't trust my three prison guards not to have tampered with those—especially after my MacBook Air miraculously reappeared.

But when I step outside, I find two men in cheap suits and drugstore sunglasses leaning against an unmarked Chevy that happens to have my bike poking out of its trunk.

"Good morning, Ms. Ellison," says the taller one, waving me toward an opened rear door. "The chief would like to see you."

At least they're not Pease security, I think with a modicum of relief, though Bob's plainclothes cops are not much of an improvement.

———◆———

The tiny Shoreham Police Department consists of a sparkling lobby with a dispatcher behind Plexiglas, a short hallway leading to offices, a holding area, locker room, and jail cell. It was under construction the summer Kit disappeared and I remember Mom grumbling about the voters approving an $11 million bond for a police department that basically did nothing but hand out speeding tickets. Meanwhile, she was stuck in a rickety firetrap of a building with no more than four electrical outlets and a records vault the size of a refrigerator all because the Historical Society objected to any interior renovations on the historic Town Hall.

Tweedledee and Tweedledum, otherwise known as Officers Raleigh and Gillette, or so I was informed on the drive over, are painfully polite as they perp-walk me through the front entrance and down the hall. There is a back door we could have used but, knowing Bob, this touch of humiliation is either intentional or his idea of a prank.

"Princess!" he declares, popping up from his desk as I'm deposited inside his office, the door closed firmly behind me. "How lovely of you to find the time to pay me a visit." The sarcasm clings to every word of his greeting, which he knows full well will only add to my already simmering annoyance.

Bob hasn't changed much since we met up last summer to watch the Sox lose. His paunch is slightly rounder, the few remaining wisps of hair circling his bald head a tad grayer. Otherwise, there's the old bulbous nose above a bushy mustache, shirtsleeves rolled up to expose forearms tanned from days on the water. His one "work" blazer hangs on a hook and is draped by a red polyester tie, which, unless I'm mistaken, is the same one he wore when I was a kid. No doubt it's pocked with all sorts of stains he hasn't bothered to pretreat.

"Was that really necessary?" I ask, pulling out a plastic chair guaranteed to be uncomfortable.

"You didn't appreciate the door-to-door service?" He goes over to the crusted coffee maker, puts in a new filter, and starts scooping in grounds from a tin of Chock full o' Nuts, Keurigs, apparently, not having made it to the Outer Cape.

"You could have called." I sit. Yup. Hard as rock.

"*I* could have called. What about *you*?" He pours in water from a carafe and presses the button. "You've been here all week and didn't once give your old man a ring."

"You knew?"

"Of course, I knew. What kind of cop would I be if I didn't know you were traipsing through town to see everyone but me.

Serena. Cobb Cooper. You know how hurt I was?" He sticks out his lower lip in an exaggerated pout.

Oh, please, I want to say. He knows exactly why I didn't stop by and it had nothing to do with our relationship. It has to do with his dictate that I not interfere. "You're right. I was avoiding you."

"No shit, Sherlock. I told you in no uncertain terms to stay clear of Bella Valencia and them Peases but here you are for the week of the big wedding. Gee. What a coincidence." The coffee maker spits its finale. Bob grabs two semi-washed mugs and begins to pour. He hands me a cup along with a jar of Coffee mate, two sugar packets ripped off from one of his favorite diners, and a spoon.

"I was just about to call you," I say, spooning in the powdered creamer, bypassing the sugar. "You were on my list for today, actually."

"I'm honored." He blows on his coffee, but doesn't drink. He's watching, judging, gauging. Just like the rest. "Lemme guess. While on vacation with the shrink boyfriend you happened by accident—no snooping, not your fault—to dig up more evidence about Kit. Kind of fell into your lap."

I take a sip. "You done?"

"Maybe. Whatcha got?"

I rest my coffee cup on his desk. "Okay, so—*by happenstance*—I ran into Cobb Cooper."

"By happenstance. Sure." *Shaw.*

I relay what Cobb said about Kit being scared right before she went missing, about her being forced to buy drugs from him even though she was clean, because she was being pressured by someone at work and how I was pretty sure it was Jake Pease. Throughout this story, which I'd figured would have knocked off his socks, Bob says nothing. He doesn't even seem particularly interested.

"Jake, huh?" is Bob's only reply. "He's got a nice boat."

My jaw drops. "Excuse me. But are you not surprised by any of this?" I'm tempted to counter that, actually, Jake with the nice boat tried to kill the girl he thinks of as a daughter, but I'll save that for later. "Were you aware Cobb was selling drugs to Kit?"

"Not at the time, but during the course of the investigation, yeah, it came to our attention." He places his cup on his warped paper calendar blotter and dabs at a brown drip on his shirt. "Cobb cleaned up his act long ago. He hasn't dealt in years."

Bob is totally missing the point. "Okay, forget that. What about Kit being pressured by Jake?"

"How do you know it was Jake? Could have been someone else she worked for."

"Like Bella Valencia?"

At that, he snaps up his head, his gaze suddenly sharp. "What makes you say that?"

Intriguing that this is what finally caught his interest. "Nothing. A random hunch."

He balls the paper napkin and hook-shoots it into the wastepaper basket. "Look, without going into too much detail, there've been some developments on that front."

I keep my expression neutral, though internally I'm bursting with excitement.

"It has nothing to do with what or who you may or may not have seen at Logan," he says, holding up his hands. "Lemme be clear on that. This is a completely separate incident."

"Though it might have some connection to Kit's disappearance?" Under my seat, my fingers are crossed.

He rocks back and forth in his swivel chair. "I'll put it this way. Recent events have prompted me to reopen her case."

I make a fist. "Yes!"

"Don't get too excited, you." Rocking forward, he clasps his hands and leans into me. "Listen to me, Jane, and listen to me good. I want you to stay the hell away from Heron's Neck."

I open my mouth to explain, but he cuts me off.

"No. I mean it. I'm not fooling around. Those people, they eat their own."

"What?"

"They already know you went to Indigo. That's why Cobb called me. Said he had to talk down their security, call off the dogs, so to speak. And that's why I had the boys pick you up this morning and bring you here, so I could drive it into your stubborn, thick, Ellison skull that these people mean business. They will take you out."

I think of Jake pushing me down into that water, merciless, and feel a chill. For the first time, Bob's words of warning have relevance.

"Something happened the other day," I begin cautiously, twisting my coffee cup. "If I tell you, you have to believe me."

Bob shrugs. "Shoot."

I launch into the whole tale—the surf caster at the National Seashore beach, the riptide, the flailing swimmer, my rescue attempt, Jake. How no one saw him. How, because of that, I didn't tell Erik for fear he'd think I was having an episode. How I did tell Serena and she blew me off. Then I sit back and wait for his reaction.

"Holy shit," he says, rubbing his wrinkled forehead. "I wish you'd come to me with this sooner. I might have been able to round up witnesses. You said there was a crowd on the shoreline."

I nod.

"Damn. We'll never find those people now."

My heart does a dance. "So, you don't think I'm crazy."

"Oh, I think you're crazy. Don't get me wrong," he jokes. "But not about that. Like I said, them Peases will take you out. Just, doing it so publicly . . . wow. That takes a lot of chutzpah."

"I was thinking more like privilege. Probably, Jake's been getting away with this kind of bullying his whole life." Including shutting up my sister, possibly.

"That's more than bullying. That's attempted murder. I don't know, man. I've been out fishing with him once or twice. Seemed like a nice-enough guy. And he and the rest of them have made some very generous contributions to the department that, believe you me, they don't let you forget for a minute. But, shit, Jane, see this is what I'm talking about. You have got to steer clear of these people. You have no idea what they're capable of. Also . . ."

He tents his fingers, which is how I know what's coming. Bob always tents his fingers when he broaches my sanity.

"Don't get offended, but I gotta ask. You been taking your meds?"

"Because I was the only one who saw Jake Pease that day?" He's right. I'm offended.

"No. Because you're dealing with a lot of heavy shit these days and I know from past experience that when you get into one of your Kit spirals, it can take you down way fast."

Kit spirals? Honestly, what a phrase. Good thing I didn't tell him about the flowers on Mom's grave and the mysteriously disappearing texts. He'd have me hauled off to the loony bin by lunch.

Crossing my legs defensively, I respond with a bold-faced lie. "Yup. I'm on my meds."

"Good. That's all I care about. You gotta take care of your mental health, just like your physical health."

Preaches the man who is about fifty pounds overweight,

boasts a cholesterol reading around 160, and downs three vodka tonics nightly.

"No need to worry about me."

In an effort to change the subject, I point to a framed photo of Bob and Mom on a weathered dock holding a huge sea bass. It's between one of him proudly wearing his karate black belt and another of him with his pride and joy, the SeaVee. He got the luxe boat for a steal at a federal auction after the DEA confiscated it from a drug runner.

Those three photos sum up the highlights of Bob's life: the black belt, the boat, the babe, and, he would add, the bass.

"That picture of Mom is nice."

He swivels around and regards it like he forgot it was there. "Yeah. That was a great day. Your mom, she wasn't much for fishing, but when she went out, she always managed to haul in the biggest catch."

"Beginner's luck." I note his abrupt melancholy. "You seeing anyone these days?"

"Nah. That ship has sailed, so to speak. I'm just glad to wake up every morning in my bed instead of the grave. Another day in paradise." He clears his throat of emotion. "So, do we have an agreement?"

Bob wants me to promise that I'll spend the rest of my vacation on the oceanside, far away from Heron's Neck. Instead, I say, "If you keep me posted about Bella and what's going on with the investigation, I'll try to stay out of your hair."

"That's the best you can do?" He stands, hitching up his pants. "How about this. You avoid anything having to do with the Peases until this wedding's over. After that, you and I will reconnoiter and I'll fill you in on what we got on Bella Valencia—or Bella Pease by then. That way I can rest easy that you'll be safe while you're on the Cape. They'll leave you alone if you leave them alone."

This approach seems very logical and, from a personal perspective, absolutely impossible.

"Agreed." Rising, I put out my hand.

Bob takes it, shakes, and then covers my hand with both of his, his eyes watering. "I don't say it very often, but the years I spent with your mom and you guys were the happiest years of my life. I'd never forgive myself if you got hurt, kid."

"Knock it off. I'll be fine." And, pulling my hand away, I give him a comforting hug, closing my nose to the industrial strength Old Spice aftershave. No wonder he can't find a new girlfriend. He'd have better luck sprinkling on lighter fluid.

"Your bike's outside in the rack," he says, sniffing back tears as we break apart. "Made sure the boys brought your helmet."

There is something bizarre about a man who basically has you kidnapped but also ensures you have the proper safety equipment for your trip home. "Thoughtful," I say.

He shrugs. "We got an ordinance."

I smile and give him a pinky wave before showing myself out, leaving the building, and heading straight to the Town Clerk's Office. One minute in, and I'm already breaking our deal.

THIRTY

JANE

The Town Clerk's Office hasn't changed much since my mother's era. The wooden floors still creak. The steel bank vault holding the land records is still the same, and probably opened by the same allegedly secret lock combination passed down orally from one clerk to the next. It still smells of old paper and ink.

The woman at the desk even resembles Mom a bit, with a navy cotton cardigan draped across her shoulders and a sensible bob. I recognize her as Darla Harchek, a member of the Al-Anon group I attended briefly while Kit was in recovery.

As I recall, Darla had a son named Rex, who, like Kit, developed a codeine dependency while in college after being prescribed Tylenol #3 for shingles. Also like Kit, he went from being a student athlete on a full scholarship to a suicidal addict. I don't dare ask how he's doing.

"May I help you?" Darla asks, screwing up her eyes as if trying to place me.

"Jane Ellison," I say from the other side of the counter. "Your predecessor's daughter."

She rises from her desk and comes over. "I thought you looked familiar. I've heard so many wonderful stories about your mother. What brings you home?"

We chat a bit about my vacation and how the office has changed from card indexes to a searchable database on a public computer. I learn that some disease is hitting the lobster harvest and that second-home owners are having a fit about the new rental taxes. Inevitably, our conversation turns where any local conversation does—to ongoing issues with the dump.

At last I mention the reason for my visit—that I'm researching a piece of real estate up for sale. Darla shows me over to the computer, gives me the basics, and then goes back to her side of the office.

It takes all of three minutes to find out our rental cottage was purchased by AMW Properties, LLC, about ten years before, and another five minutes on the Massachusetts Secretary of State's website to learn that one of three principals in AMW is Arthur Whitaker, the Love & Pease lawyer who sent me the C&D letter.

His name appears in a number of Pease-related articles, which I look up and scan rapidly on the town computer. Whitaker, according to Google images, is slightly stooped and aged, exactly what you'd expect from a Boston attorney for a Brahmin clan. In older photos, he's young and dapper, eyebrows creased in concentration. I scroll through the pictures, searching for anything that stands out, but nothing does.

Next, I Google Ettie Watson and Chet Pease. Sure enough, the first photo is from a *Boston Globe* article. There are Chet and a much younger Black woman in a smart royal-blue suit walking side by side down a marble hallway.

The caption reads: "Boston financier Chet Pease and his assistant Amorette Watson were the only passengers on board the

Piper PA-28 that crashed in heavy fog shortly after taking off from Provincetown last night." Huh. I never put two and two together.

Wait. I've seen her someplace else recently. Enlarging the photo to the best of my ability, I analyze Ettie's most immutable features—her cheekbones and jaw, long neck, the space between her eyes.

Ettie Watson wasn't just in the Camp Pekky photo with Kit; she was in the annual Serendipity Seafood staff photo I saw on the wall the other night. That was the photo where Kit was missing because by then she'd disappeared. They must have worked together for Serena. Either I forgot that or Kit never brought it up.

Fumbling in my bag, I pull out the Starlight Realty business card for Terri D'Angelo, Sales & Rentals. She said her parents owned their place in Wellfleet, which means they should be on the town's tax assessor's list. I go to the Town of Wellfleet home page, scroll over to the assessor's page, and am pleased to discover a handy-dandy, searchable database. One of the benefits of growing up in a town clerk's office—you learn how to find all sorts of dirt about your neighbors.

I plug in D'Angelo and hit an address: 120 Periwinkle Circle. Assessed house value: $807,000. Yowza. Just like Terri said, it had increased in value eightfold from their original purchase price.

Typing in Watson, I'm rewarded with 122 Periwinkle Circle. Charles and Anita Watson. Assessed at $850,000. Next-door neighbors, still.

"Any luck?"

I flinch. Darla is suddenly behind me, nosily reading what's on my screen. "The Watsons have their house on the market? They've been talking about it for years, ever since their daughter . . ." She freezes.

So do I.

Darla has just fitted the pieces of the puzzle and now she has a complete picture. Ettie Watson died with Chet Pease. I have been accused by the jury of the internet of stalking Chet Pease's adopted daughter. And here I am on her computer indulging in my dangerous obsession.

"I just remembered where we've met before," she says, taking a step back like I'm contagious. "You were in my Al-Anon group. They said that after you stopped coming to meetings, you went through a rough patch."

"Rough patch" is code in a language she and I understand all too well.

"Better now," I say, clicking out of the webpage. "I hope Rex is okay."

She sighs. "It's a miracle, but he is. Thankfully, not everyone who's an addict . . ." She stops herself, her face blanching at the faux pas she was about to commit.

"Dies," I finish for her. "Good to hear. Gives the rest of us hope."

———◆———

It's true I did a stint in the psych ward.

In hindsight, it wasn't that big of a deal. Lots of kids have breakdowns toward the end of college, especially these days, what with all the stress of finding a job and fears of inadequacy thanks to the infinite middle-school cafeteria that is social media. On top of that, you really don't know who you are or what you want to do with your life, though everyone expects you to be TOTALLY EXCITED about becoming a full-fledged adult. Add the false perception your fellow students are doing better than you (see: social media) and it can be life-threatening.

My case of depression was sneaky sinister. I spent the final semester of senior year holed up in my room, skipping classes, sleeping, not eating, not showering, and watching *Gossip Girl* on repeat. I managed to finish a thesis for my poli-sci major, barely, but that was about it for productive endeavors.

I couldn't bear to be around "happy" people, like one of my housemates who was off to grad school or another friend who had secured an internship with a production studio in California. My best friend didn't have a job or further degree in the wings, but she did have a hot boyfriend and as soon as they got their diplomas, they were off to backpack across Europe.

Me? I had Blair Waldorf and *Gossip Girl*.

My symptoms worsened during the months leading up to graduation, which I approached with dread knowing my mom and sister wouldn't be there to cheer me on. Stan had said he wanted to come, had even booked a flight, but a freak snowstorm at the end of May trapped him on his hillside farm. Typical.

It all came to a head senior week when I lashed out at my roommates for making too much noise after returning from a graduation party. I remember none of this, but I apparently burst out of my room wearing nothing but a T-shirt and underwear screaming that they were going to set the house on fire. That I was holding a Venus razor dripping with blood from my freshly sliced wrists only supported their conclusion I was, as the saying goes, "a danger to myself and others."

Student health services sent a crisis counselor to our house at one in the morning, and the next I knew, I was being transported by campus security to a local emergency room and by ambulance to the psych ward for suicide watch and depression counseling. I was under lock and key for the first time in my life and it was terrifying.

On the upside, that's when I discovered I possessed a rare, amazing superpower.

Dr. Pearson gets the credit for that. She was my psych doc, as peppy as a cheerleader and smarter than her bright pink lip gloss and bouncy ponytail might indicate to a judgmental college student like myself. We were halfway through our third session, and I was in the process of listing everyone on campus who either hated me, didn't know I existed, or didn't care, when she lifted her pen from her notebook, wrinkled her adorable Barbie nose, and asked, "Have you ever been tested?"

"Tested?" I said, my anxiety spiking.

"For super recognition." Dr. Pearson went on to explain that she'd been noting my ability to list encounters with random students at UMass Amherst, which, with twenty-eight thousand kids, is larger than most New England small towns. "The average person retains a facial memory of approximately five thousand individuals over a lifetime at the max. That sounds like a lot, but super recognizers can recall *hundreds* of thousands. And I suspect you may be one."

That blew my mind because I'd never considered myself as special in any way. Okay, so maybe not everyone was able to ID Kirsten Dunst as the girl in *Jumanji*, but surely most people remembered passing each other on Mass Ave three years earlier. Or knew that the guy in the plaid shirt and headphones and black knitted cap sitting across from them on the subway had also been in the Asian wing of the Gardner Museum and then at Punjabi Dhaba in Inman Square a few months later. And the woman next to him with the intricate knitted scarf had been featured in a front-page *Globe* photo sunbathing along the Charles a few summers before.

"Doesn't everyone remember that stuff?"

"Uh, no." Dr. Pearson tapped her pencil on the metal table expectantly. Meanwhile, I was thinking, *How could you forget?*

We started with the Cambridge Face Memory Test, which is most often given to those who suffer from prosopagnosia, the *inability* to remember a face. I aced it, along with the Glasgow Face Matching Test. Then we did the UNSW test, which differs from the previous two in that it's designed to diagnose super recognizers by tasking them with identifying faces hidden by shadows, poor lighting, and other obstructions.

I scored a ninety-eight percent, and Dr. Pearson referred me to Chris Hawkins, a Harvard PhD candidate who was running a study on whether memory training, like the kind conducted by the FBI, could enhance the natural abilities of super recognizers. The study was funded by the US Department of Homeland Security, which was researching ways to expand its undercover surveillance methods.

Actually, Chris was more interested in the correlation between super recognition and depression, which is why Dr. Pearson referred me to him. Unfortunately, funding to study depression pales in comparison to funding for national security, so I ended up taking FBI courses just to meet the criteria. Which brings me to Chris's colleague, Erik, who ran the study I participated in at Harvard, where we fell in love. Or at least I thought we did.

My diagnosis changed my life by giving me a purpose. When Homeland Security analyzed my results and offered me a job at any international airport I wished, I picked Logan on the statistical odds that Kit would be more likely to come through Boston's hub than any other.

For five years, I scrutinized thousands and thousands of travelers, managing to identify a number of domestic and international terrorists in disguise bent on harming our country. But when it came to finding Kit, I struck out standing—until I recognized Bella Valencia and she recognized me.

And now I find that Kit catered for Serena with Ettie Watson, who ended up working for—and dying with—Chet Pease. So what more can Ettie tell me from beyond the grave?

That's what I'm about to find out.

THIRTY-ONE

JANE

The Watson family home is your classic Cape with antique gray siding and red trim in the middle of a quiet cul-de-sac adorably named Periwinkle Circle. It's in immaculate condition. The grass is a healthy green and the *de rigueur* blue and pink hydrangeas are generously mulched in cedar bark. I press the bell and hold my breath, waiting for the door to open. On the bike ride over, I practiced my opening lines repeatedly, trying to sound natural.

Hello, my name's Jane Ellison, the sister of Kit Ellison who I think might have been a friend of your late daughter's. And I am so, so sorry about Ettie's death. I, too, have been dealing with grief. My mother died after my sister went missing over ten years ago, which is why I'm here. Can we talk inside? I'm hoping you might have some memories of Kit you can share.

Once we get comfortable, my goal is to ask if any of the Pease men was hitting on Ettie when she worked as Chet's assistant, if she felt scared and intimidated like Kit had. I hope the Watsons don't immediately order me off the premises.

I ring the bell again. When there's no answer, I trot to the garage and peek inside. Only one car. It doesn't seem like the Watsons are around this afternoon, though they might be back soon, since I don't get the sense they rent the house. The furniture inside is upholstered and there's wall-to-wall carpeting along with tons of family photos on a table I can make out through the front plate-glass window—all hallmarks of a permanent residence. Going around to the back, I try the sliding door. Almost by accident, my hand slips to the handle. I give it a tug and it slides open with ease, presenting me with a gap of six inches and a huge moral dilemma.

If I follow my urges and step inside, I will officially be committing an act of criminal trespassing, a misdemeanor in the Commonwealth of Massachusetts, and if I'm caught, I can kiss goodbye any chance of working for the Department of Homeland Security ever again. On the other hand, if I close the door and bike home, I can kiss goodbye ever discovering what secret about the Pease men Ettie might have been hiding.

It's a no-brainer. After stashing my bike in the woods behind the house, I head inside, sandals off, door closed. Homeland Security would never put me on the payroll again, anyway.

The Watsons' home is as nice inside as it is outside. Neat as a pin. The interior has obviously been recently redone. Solid, polished wide-pine flooring runs throughout the kitchen, which has more granite than a Roman cemetery. The cupboards are custom made in a creamy beige that meshes well with the slightly darker walls and paler coffered ceiling. Sub-Zero fridge, Wolf stove, and huge windows looking out to the garden.

I tiptoe across the living room toward the center stairway that leads upstairs. If this house follows typical Cape style, the main bedroom will be on the ground floor and the other bedrooms upstairs. At the mantel over the brick fireplace, I take a detour to study the framed photos flanking an antique nautical clock. I scan past Mr. and Mrs. Watson's wedding photo and baby pictures of Ettie to a larger one of her all grown up.

It's a college commencement photo in which she's between her mother and father, who are beaming with pride at their daughter proudly wearing a kente cloth stole in black, yellow, maroon, and green. Her robe is bright red, the color of Boston University. The image of happy Ettie with her parents brings a lump to my throat. All that bright potential snuffed out by the hubris of Chet Pease who insisted on flying in thick fog like it was simply an annoying inconvenience. That his foolishness was his ending, too, is no consolation. I just hope the Watsons were compensated financially for their loss, even though money would provide little comfort in the wake of such grief.

As I predicted, upstairs there is a bedroom at either end joined by a common bathroom and a linen closet. The open door to the left reveals a pair of twin beds in matching seashell coverlets in what I bet is a guest room. The door to the other is closed.

Well aware I am committing an unforgivable violation of not only the Watsons' personal space but also Ettie's sacred memory, I turn the knob and step back in time. The Watsons haven't changed a thing. It looks like the room of a daughter who's simply away at college and might be home for Thanksgiving.

Stuffed animals are tucked in alongside the pillows of her double bed. Athletic ribbons hang from the wall—soccer and spring track—along with a framed Honors Society certificate. Ettie's earrings are arranged in an orderly fashion with hanging necklaces and bracelets on a jewelry tree. On the top of her wooden dresser is a digital watch, undone as if it had been slipped off her wrist moments before. The room even smells faintly of a teenage girl's cologne—Abercrombie.

My mother kept Kit's room the same way after she went missing. Of course, we never knew when she might roll in the front door with some excuse or another. This is different, yet there remains the same sense of disbelief. I know exactly what the Watsons are thinking—she can't be gone, not their baby, not their sweet sunshine. I say a short prayer asking for forgiveness and begin my hunt.

There is no laptop on her desk, which has been dusted clean, though the drawers are stuffed with junk: spiral-bound notebooks, old math tests, English papers, and homework sheets. I flip through a diary, but Ettie gave that only a half-hearted effort. Nothing about the Peases jumps out. I do find a couple of foil-covered condoms, so there's that.

No computer under the bed, on the bedside table, or in one of the zippered cases in the closet, either. I even check the bookshelf, where I find Octavia Butler, Sarah Dessen, Sharon G. Flake, Jenny Han, and Rainbow Rowell, some of my favorite authors. I have a feeling Ettie and I could have been friends.

Finally, I try the bedside table drawer. This is cringeworthy personal, right up there with rifling through a dead woman's underwear, but as it turns out, worthwhile. For underneath a box of tampons and a half-eaten lollipop are two Polaroid photos stuck together by the sugar of the melted candy.

It's so rare to come across Polaroids these days that I figure they're super old. And they are, sort of. As I carefully peel the photos apart, my heartbeat quickens. The background is dark, night, and in one corner it's possible to make out sand. The flash washes out the fire from the pit, but not the six bare legs of three girls captured sitting on logs. There are beer bottles in hands and cigarettes between fingers and when at last I have the photos separated, staring back at me are two ghosts.

Her hair in twisty braids, wearing a white tank top, Ettie Watson is putting up a hand in mock protest as she buries her face in the shoulder of the girl next to her.

I quit breathing.

From underneath her brunette bangs, Bella Valencia stares straight at the camera while leaning playfully against a blond girl in a Serendipity Seafood T-shirt that, days later, would be found washed up in the marsh flotsam and jetsam, stained dark red with blood.

Kit.

This photo must be from the farewell party on the cove, the last night she was seen alive. This right here could be proof that Bella and Kit knew each other well enough to hang out at a party. That they were not only acquaintances but possibly friends.

My chest tightens as I take the Polaroid to the window where the light is better. Kit looks good, I'm pleased to see. She looks actually really happy and, most of all, sober. Oh, how I wish Ettie were alive so I could ask her all the questions racing through my mind at this moment.

Did Bob interview her about Kit? How well did she know Bella? Were the three of them friends, or had they just met at the party? Who took the photo? What happened to each of them after it was taken? How did Kit go from looking so healthy to crawling across the beach on her belly, sick from drugs, a few hours later?

I'm so lost in thought I don't register the crunch of a car pulling up until I hear a door slam. Peeking through a slit in the Venetian blinds, I can make out the same Chevy that picked me up this morning. It's parked at the curb and the same plainclothes cops are walking up the Watsons' driveway.

Shit!

With such a pristine place, the Watsons must have one of those hidden security cameras to guard it. Why didn't I think of that? Stuffing the photos in my bra, I consider my options. Not hiding under the bed, that's too easy. Can't go into the hall. The window faces the driveway and, besides, I'm on the second story of the house.

If I'm caught—*when* I'm caught—the Watsons will be horrified, and rightly so. Bob will be livid and have to arrest me for trespassing, as well as burglary for stealing the photos. That's a felony.

If I'm lucky, I'll be sent back to the psych ward.

If I'm unlucky, I'll be sent back to the psych ward.

With no other choice, I slip into the closet, shut the louvered doors and secrete myself behind stored, bagged winter clothes. The doorbell rings. Once. Twice. My heart is thumping so hard, I can't hear my own thoughts. Then I remember I left my sandals inside the sliding doors.

Double shit!

I brace myself for the inevitable tread of footsteps, for Raleigh and Gillette to call out, for them to inspect each room until they get to Ettie's. I am crouched in this position for so long, my back pressed into a corner, hemmed in by the zip-locked plastic bags whose mothball fumes are making me dizzy, that my toes go numb.

And, yet, nothing. Only the *tick, tick, tick* of the mantel clock one floor below.

Finally, after what feels like an eternity, I open the doors an inch and cock my ear. Not a peep except for that clock. Then I emerge entirely and tiptoe, crouching, to check the window.

The unmarked car is gone.

That's impossible. Did I . . . *dream* it?

Closing the closet door, I dash into the hallway and fly down the stairs, snatching my sandals and exiting through the back door, unable to believe my good fortune. All I can figure is police aren't allowed to enter a house without a warrant. Chances are, those two cops are at the corner of the cul-de-sac, waiting to bust me as I pass by.

Fortunately, I don't have to take the streets back to the cottage. Brushing the clippings from the greasy gear, I hop on my bike and head through the serpentine trails so familiar from my childhood until the stunted oaks give way to houses. Zigzagging through residential neighborhoods, I cut through backyards that connect to shortcuts only the locals know. Ettie's photos are safe in the pocket of my white jeans.

When I finally reach our cottage, panting, I nearly collapse from relief that I made it back before Dave, Sheila, and Erik did. The house is dark and as tight as a drum. The car Erik and I rented sits in the driveway, dusted with dead, brown pine needles that also blanket the front step. Mission accomplished.

Parking my bike in its usual spot, I go around the rear deck and enter that way. I need a shower and a change of clothes so I can be sitting on the couch when they return, looking a little weaker, but much better since this morning. I remove the photos from my jeans and take another look.

Ettie and Kit are both dead and their one connection is Bella. I try that concept on for size.

Buzzzzzz.

The couch cushion is vibrating and I remember I left my

phone under the pillow. When I pull it out, I find the screen exploding with texts.

PICK UP PICK UP PICK UP.

CALL ME AS SOON AS YOU WAKE UP.

GODDAMMIT JANE - I NEED YOUR HELP, PLEASE!

And then the last one that catches my breath . . .

MABEL IS MISSING!!

THIRTY-TWO

JANE

Provincetown is the end of the earth. Literally.

A tiny, funky community of colorful clapboard-sided New England homes, galleries, quaint shops, and seafood markets clustered at the tip of the Cape, it's historically attracted artists and outsiders. Eugene O'Neill debuted his first play here. Back in the day, gay men and lesbians found refuge in the town's bars and cabarets, attending drag shows or making out on the traditional nearby "nude" beach at a time when public displays of same-sex affection were met elsewhere with scorn or even imprisonment for being "wicked."

Now though, it is mostly just wicked crowded. A thicket of gawking tourists, parents with strollers, and sightseers pack the narrow streets. Compounding this, it's Thursday evening and hordes of young professionals have taken the day off from their lucrative jobs in Boston's finance district to ferry across the bay to start the weekend early.

Erik meets me in the parking lot down by the wharf, where I manage to find a space for our car. I assume he's been following me on his phone as I crept up Route 6, congestion adding a half hour to what should have been a twenty-minute trip.

When I get out of the car, he hugs me with such force I can barely breathe. "This is awful," he murmurs into the top of my head. "Awful."

"It'll be okay. We'll find her. Don't worry."

"I hope you're right. Thank god you're here. You sure you're up to this in your condition?"

"Of course." I squeeze him back. "Must have been a mild case."

I gave myself a good talking to on the drive to P-town and resolved to press pause on my anger. No matter how Erik, Sheila, and Dave have conspired behind my back, I have to put my resentment aside for now. They need me. When I was at Homeland, we worked closely with the FBI Child Exploitation and Human Trafficking Task Forces, so my experience in this area is not insignificant. Mabel is just a little girl, an innocent victim, and the frightening fact is that her chances of being recovered alive and relatively unscarred diminish proportionally as each minute passes. After twenty-four hours, the odds drop dramatically.

"Tell me what happened," I say, when he finally lets go.

"It was so fast." He knuckles tears off his cheeks. "After lunch, we were walking down Commercial Street. Caleb was in the stroller, napping, and Mabel was skipping up ahead. It was all normal. They're this way . . ." He points past the parking attendant to Ryder Street and we head in that direction, Erik holding on to my hand like he himself is a lost kid. "We got to this one gallery, I don't know what it's called, and Sheila and Dave wanted to go inside and have a look. So we did."

"Mabel, too?"

"That's what we thought. We were flipping through some prints and then Dave asked where Mabel was. She was gone."

To be honest, I'm only half listening. I'm laser-focused on every passing face. There are a lot of sick individuals out there and most of the known suspects are already in the database inside my brain.

Erik says something I can't hear as we inch our way through the swath of humanity, tourists with shopping bags and ice cream cones packing the narrow alley. This is worse than Terminal E during spring break.

"Here's the gallery." He crosses Ryder, nearly getting creamed by a Prius. I follow and we step inside.

Sheila and Dave aren't there, but an earnest clerk is clearly aware of the situation. "No sign of her yet," she says, twisting a ring on her middle finger. "I'm so sorry."

A large divider containing art for sale separates one half of the gallery from the other. It is a lovely, well-lit space designed for perusing pastels and oils of tide pools and old boats, brilliant sunsets and weathered fishing huts. Closing my eyes, I can envision Dave, Erik, and Sheila mulling over these pieces, discussing how a photo of a full moon over the water might look in their hallway back in Cambridge while Caleb sleeps peacefully. I can imagine precocious Mabel disappearing on the other side of the divider and out the door.

"The candy store." I spot SALT WATER TAFFY in humongous letters across a glass window catty-corner to the gallery. A line is out the door. "I bet that's where she went."

"We've already been there. That was the first place we thought of," Erik says as we walk out of the gallery.

My fault. I was the one who told her about the gigantic bins of root-beer barrels, Pop Rocks, and more taffy flavors than she knew existed. She didn't even know what taffy was, thanks to Sheila's no-sugar rule. But even if she was tempted by it, she's no longer there.

"Dave's combing the beach," Erik tells me. "He's worried Mabel might have decided to go swimming like she'd been begging to earlier. Sheila's stationed herself at the intersection figuring that's where she'll be most visible."

Sure enough, despite the shoulder-to-shoulder crowd, it's easy to spot Sheila, phone pressed to her ear. She's sweeping her gaze from side to side while rocking Caleb's stroller back and forth. At the sight of me she stiffens, confirming my instincts that I am somehow to blame.

"How are you feeling?" she inquires without a drop of warmth when Erik and I catch up to her. "We tried texting and calling you all afternoon but you were out. Or ignoring us."

Having witnessed parental meltdowns under similar situations in Logan, I get how it's easy to direct your anger toward an unrelated individual. Sheila has devoted herself to providing Caleb and Mabel with magical childhoods, and that her daughter went missing because she and her husband lowered their guards for just a moment is too much to shoulder for a conscientious mother like her.

"I'm sorry. I was sleeping," I lie, and somehow I think she knows I'm lying. "What's important is finding Mabel. Provincetown is very safe. I'm sure she's fine."

"You don't know that. This is a place of itinerants and strangers and"—she shakes her head as a half-dressed man passes in silver body paint and a crown à la the Statue of Liberty—"Weirdos."

That's an unprofessional adjective for a doctor of psychiatry to use, but we'll let it slide. "Have you tried an Amber Alert?"

"She doesn't want to go there," Erik answers for her. "Not yet, at any rate."

Sheila gently covers Caleb's ears. "He cannot know his sister is l-o-s-t," she whispers. "He was asleep when she wandered off and he'll be inconsolable if he thinks she's not coming back. For now, we are waiting for her and Papa to return."

Oh, for heaven's sakes. Time is of the essence here! I do another sweep of the area, scouring faces and conducting a mental inventory of the interesting shops and gingerbread alleys that would appeal to Mabel's curiosity. "Let me search."

"Thank you," she says. "We need every eyeball." Sheila reminds me what Mabel's wearing: a pink leotard and her rainbow tutu, her go-to outfit.

Erik drops my hand. "I'll head in this direction, toward the beach. See if I can find Dave."

"I'll try Commercial Street," I tell him. "She might have gone to the toy store. Call me as soon as you get any word on Mabel."

"Mabel?" asks Caleb, trying to climb out.

"She'll be here any minute," Sheila singsongs, wheeling him back and forth.

Erik gives me a kiss that's full of gratitude and something sad and bitter that tastes like regret.

❦

I start with the toy store, which is cluttered with huge displays of Legos and puzzles, stuffed animals and kites, an endless supply of beach paraphernalia and art kits for rainy days. There's hardly space to move so I have to shove my way in, boldly shouting, "Mabel! Where are you, Mabel?"

The parents here need no explanation. They back themselves against the displays, clutching their own children, creating a space for a stage. "Hey, everyone," I shout, unabashed. "I'm looking for a little girl with reddish-brown curls in a rainbow tutu. Has anyone seen her?"

"How old?" asks a man, eyeing his own daughter playing with a wooden puzzle.

"About her age." I nod to the child. "Seven."

He shakes his head and the parents murmur to one another. "Do you have a photo?" a mom asks.

At the ready. I show them a picture on my phone of Mabel at the beach, squinting in the sun. She's even in the same skirt.

"Adorable," says a woman, clutching her heart. "Yours?"

"My friend's. They were at the gallery down the street and she slipped away. If you see her, could you call 9–1–1?"

They swear up and down that they will. A few rush out to the sidewalk to conduct their own hunts. I'm not a mother, but I know how devastating it is to lose a child, even for a moment.

Or a decade.

I make similar requests in other shops that might have fascinated Mabel—a different candy store, an ice cream parlor, and a puzzle emporium, with no luck. I even stop to check with a Tarot reader because her storefront is purple, Mabel's favorite color.

Provincetown Town Hall is surrounded by a park, so I try that, looking under benches and behind shrubs, just in case she's engaged in an elaborate game of hide and seek. I check the trees to see if she climbed up, not down. I ask every single person in the immediate area. Each peers at the photo on my phone and frowns with sympathy. Yes, they will look. They will call 9–1–1. Have we issued an Amber Alert? Ah. Well, we might want to consider that. It's very effective.

The howl of a female voice pierces the air, setting my nerves on edge until I realize it's only a few teenagers messing around. Still, I can't help remembering the primal scream Mom let out when Bob broke the news fishermen had found Kit's T-shirt in the marsh. This is what PTSD does to you, sneaks up and grabs you when you're most vulnerable.

The crowds are beginning to thin. It's time for dinner and people are either heading to restaurants or going home.

This is bad. It's almost six p.m. and Mabel was last seen three hours ago. Surely, if she'd simply wandered off, someone would have noticed a child alone, crying for her mother. The police would have been notified. This is a community of families who care about kids, who would raise questions if a second grader were darting down a street by herself.

Something is wrong. Really, really wrong. And I am growing increasingly afraid.

"Find her?" Erik says when I call to ask the same.

"No. And I've been seriously spreading the word." I list the places I've been, my breathing heavy as I ascend a gentle incline, away from the cacophony of Commercial Street. This is a residential area marked by picket fences and creative doorways. Fewer tourists here. "I'm headed toward the school now. She might be on the playground, if there is one."

"She's trying the school playground," I hear him say.

"Who are you talking to?" I ask, passing a street sign that says, ironically, WATCH FOR CHILDREN.

"Sheila."

"Is she still on the corner?"

"Yeah. It's the most logical place for us to wait."

Us? "Where's Dave? I thought you were going down to the beach to find him."

"He stopped by to take Caleb so he can run around."

"So, it's just you and Sheila?"

"I can't leave her alone."

"Absolutely, I hear you." I am being good. I am not letting myself be distracted by evil thoughts about how he and Sheila cooked up a plan to trap me, how they might be more than friends. That would be unproductive and do nothing to bring Mabel home.

Turns out the school doesn't have a playground so my trip up here's been a waste.

"She's not around the school," I tell Erik. "The gate is locked."

"Bummer. Got any other bright ideas?"

I look up and realize I've reached the Pilgrim Monument, a twenty-five-story tower and famous Provincetown landmark commemorating the Pilgrims' landing back in 1600 or something. Kit and I used to love to climb to the top on clear days, when you could see as far as Boston. Later, when she worked for Serena, she catered a wedding there and returned home raving about the magical setting, the twinkling boat lights on the water, the full moon hanging low in the sky. She said if she ever got married, that's exactly where she'd hold her reception.

Damn, these memories—they're everywhere. Inhaling deeply, I refocus on the task at hand. "You don't think she could have gone into the Pilgrim Monument, do you?" I ask Erik.

There is a pause while he discusses this with Sheila. When he gets back on, he sounds urgent. "That's a distinct possibility. Can you check?"

Naturally, he can't leave Sheila, I think, hanging up with a terse goodbye. At the bottom of the tower is a museum where a docent waits to collect admission fees. I don't have time to screw around so I rush up and cut in line, ignoring the outcry from those who've been waiting in the hot sun.

"Have you seen a little girl with auburn curls and a rainbow tutu in the past few hours?" I blurt.

"Here?" She flicks her gaze to a monitor on her desk with

several camera angles. "Don't think so. Who was she with? I might remember."

I nod to the images on her screen. "Is that recorded? Can you play it back?"

"I *thiiiink* so. Not sure since I don't handle that. Anyway, we're about to close." She pulls the belt from a stanchion to show she means business. "After these people behind you are admitted, I'm cutting off visitors. We're not supposed to allow anyone up at this hour."

"You've got to let me go. This is a seven-year-old who's missing. Her mother is hysterical." I'm half hysterical myself and no doubt I look it. Even those in line are clucking in sympathy.

She nods rapidly. "Okay, okay. I'll keep a watch here just in case. What's her name?"

"Mabel," I say over my shoulder, heading to the short flight of steps. "If you find her, tell her to wait right here for Jane."

Heading to the top of the tower would be impossible if this were all stairs. Fortunately, ADA rules required the installation of long, continuous, spiral ramps which, *unfortunately*, are major attractions for kids. A herd of them nearly stampede into me on the way down. *I need to get into better shape*, I think, breathing heavily as I attempt a near run, my sights set on a small, curly head.

Due to the hour of the day, I seem to be the only one heading in this direction, a fish swimming upstream against a current of humans, many of whom rudely don't bother to even turn around when I ask, "Have you seen a small . . ." It's as though I'm invisible.

A cluster of laughing women pass by and once they clear, there she is.

She is walking stiffly, almost marching, knees up, her eyes downcast like she knows she's in trouble. She's headed toward me and I'm so ecstatic I don't know whether to call Sheila or grab Mabel or what.

"Mabel!" I shout.

She doesn't react and that's when I notice something's off. She's not in her tutu. She's in a nondescript blue seersucker dress under a white cotton hoodie that covers most of her copper curls. I have never seen her in this outfit before.

Wait. Is this Mabel . . . *or another girl?* I'm reminded of what Sheila said the other night, about how my super recognition ability is not a reliable *real* ability but perhaps the manifestation of a wish. According to her theory, I wanted to see the woman Kit was with that night, so last December in Logan Airport I did. And now I want to see Mabel. But is it really her?

Or am I hallucinating?

Anxiously, I watch the tiny figure circle downward, disappearing behind a group of kids leaning over the railing. I'm antsy with the same urgency I felt my last day in Logan, only now I'm suddenly unsure of myself. If I go after Mabel and it turns out not to be her, there'll be a valid reason for Erik to request a Section 12 admission into a psychiatric hospital based on my unstable current mental health. If she really is Mabel and I let her slip through my fingers, I will never forgive myself.

There's no choice. There never will be. My gut tells me to act now.

"Mabel!" I cry as loud as I can. "It's me, Jane!"

She pauses in her march and slowly pivots, gazing up. Her expression is a mask of confusion, as if she's never seen me before. But it's definitely her. *Definitely.* Even if I told the docent and everyone I ran into she's in a rainbow tutu, this is Mabel.

"Stay right there. I'm coming to get you."

But instead of waving or even crying, she opens her mouth and lets out a blood-curdling scream, louder even than when she was being bitten by the crab. Then she turns and runs pell-mell to the lobby, as fast as her short legs can carry her.

"Come back!" I yell, ignoring the horrified expressions on those around me.

As I move forward, my ankle is blocked by something and I go down face first, the carpeted concrete floor rushing up to greet me. On the way down, I glimpse a familiar smirk. Though his eyes are hidden behind sunglasses, his black jacket is zipped up to his jaw, and his blondish hair is tucked under a Mets cap, I recognize him immediately.

Throwing out my arms, I brace for impact, just barely sparing myself a bloody nose. *Goddamn him,* I think, wincing as pain radiates up my knees, my entire body suddenly incapacitated. *Who is he?*

"Are you okay?"

The question comes from a man who's with a young boy. My stalker has disappeared into the crowd.

I try to reply and can't. The wind's been knocked out of my lungs. All I can do is nod.

"Let me give you a hand."

I take his hand and stand, leaning down to rub my swelling knee. "Thanks. I think . . ." My breath is coming back. ". . . I think I was tripped."

"Yeah, definitely," he says. "I saw that jackass stick his foot right in front of you. I was gonna go after him, but I figured I'd better check you out first. I don't know what's wrong with society these days."

Not society, I think, the Peases. *They're somehow involved in this. But why would they steal a child?*

He asks again if I'm fine and I assure him I am as they leave me be. The lobby a few feet below is empty and a CLOSED sign is on the counter. The docent is nowhere in sight.

I hobble past the front desk and into the fresh air, dejected, scanning the fenced yard on the off chance Mabel has hung around. Nope. Nor is she on the walkway leading to the street. No stalker, either. I pray he's only after me and not her.

"Is this yours?" A maintenance man in coveralls comes toward me, an object displayed on his palm. It's my phone. The screen is a glass spiderweb. It must have flown out of my pocket when I fell. "Found it near the lobby floor. Hope it still works."

Miraculously, it does. Collapsing on a wooden bench outside the tower, I call Erik to deliver the bad news and am almost grateful when I'm sent immediately to voice mail.

There are no words for my frustration. I was so close, close enough to reach her if I'd only hustled. But why did she scream? Mabel and I are buddies. She *trusts* me. And why was she in that getup? It's all so bizarre.

I have no idea how I'll explain this to Sheila and Dave. I wish they'd gone to the police, Caleb's separation anxiety be damned. If this isn't an emergency, I don't know what is.

With heavy dread, I force myself to get off the bench and limp over to Commercial Street, where Sheila is waiting for hopeful word. My eyes ache and my nose begins to swell. If she sees me crying, she'll know right off something bad happened. I have to get it together.

"Jane!"

Erik's on the corner across the street at Ryder, waving his arms madly. "We found her. She's okay!"

Thank god, I think, my bruised knees suddenly wobbly with relief.

He jogs toward me, dodging an oncoming car. "I just tried to call you. The police contacted Sheila. Mabel's safe and sound at the station."

What? That's impossible. "But that can't be. I saw her in the monument no more than fifteen minutes ago. I ran after her and tripped and when I got up she was gone."

He frowns. "That's funny. She wasn't anywhere near the tower. She was way on the other side of town."

"I'm telling you what I saw." I feel like I'm being gaslighted here. I'm near panic. "Look, I hurt my right knee running after her. This guy tripped me. See for yourself."

He bends down and examines my kneecap. "Doesn't seem too swollen. You sure you weren't imagining things?"

Uh-oh. I know what "imagining" means. "No, I'm not *imagining* things. So where was she?"

"Turns out she went to a drag show. How's that for spunk?" He laughs, back to being jolly. "For three hours, she was at a bar and apparently that was cool with management. They made her Shirley Temples and spun her on a stool. Figured her parents were in the audience, too, I guess. After the show ended, and the place emptied out, the club owners contacted the police. Sheila and Dave were actually in the station filling out a report when the call came in."

None of that happened. Mabel McAllister, age seven, did not walk into a cabaret alone and hang out in the dark for three hours watching a bunch of drag queens singing "We Are Family." That is a lie, and beyond that, one a second grader couldn't possibly have invented on her own.

So did Sheila lie to Erik or is he lying to me? Or both? "What a blast," I say with false cheer. "I can just picture her bopping along in her tutu."

"I know, right? You should have seen her in the police station sitting on the counter licking an ice cream cone in that crazy skirt of hers."

More lies. She was in a white hoodie and a fancy little dress when I saw her. "So, where are they now? I'm dying to get all the details. You know . . . the ones you haven't embellished."

He takes a step back, wary, probably not sure he heard me correctly. "Um, they said they're going back to get their stuff and go back to Cambridge. Sheila's pretty thoroughly rattled."

"She's not the only one."

He chucks me under the chin, a normally loving gesture that I now detest. "*Heeeey* there, why the 'tude? You should be happy. Mabel's okay and we finally have the place to ourselves. I say we celebrate."

"I'm not really in the mood," I snap. "Let's go back and call it a night."

"Yeah?"

"Yes."

We walk in silence to the car. I can tell Erik is bewildered by my iciness. He doesn't know that I know they set me up. It's now becoming clear to me that Dave and Sheila, for reasons I can't possibly begin to understand, put their own young child at risk so I might cause a scene in the monument like I did at Logan. They probably coached Mabel to scream at the sight of me, which is simply unforgivable. No doubt they assured themselves that doing so would be for my own good because by pushing me over the edge, I'd finally break and see a psychiatrist to address what Erik claims are my "unresolved issues."

I am so furious with him, I can't look him in the eyes. How could he turn on me like that?

"Do you have the keys?" He's on the driver's side. The car

seems like a weighty and solid barrier between us. We are over. We are so, so over. I can't even be sad. Frankly, all I am is numb.

Reaching in my pocket, I pull the keys out and toss them over the roof. That's when I notice the white envelope under the windshield wiper. It's sealed and addressed to me.

"What's that, a ticket?" Eric asks, slipping behind the wheel as I retrieve the envelope.

Doesn't look like a ticket, considering there's a note on it written in purple crayon.

Dear Jane—my profuse apology for what I put you through today. Do not blame Erik—or Dave. It was all my (misguided) idea. Will explain later. For now, I thought you might find a use for this. S.

I open the envelope and pull out a thick white card etched with a gray heron.

PLEASE JOIN US AS WE JOYOUSLY CELEBRATE
BELLA & WILL
ON THE EVE OF THEIR NUPTIALS.
LOBSTERS. CHAMPAGNE. SUNSET.
PEASE
&
LOVE.
HERON'S NECK.
7 PM
AUGUST 20TH
REGRETS ONLY, PLEASE.

THIRTY-THREE

JANE

"Name?" asks the security guard in the trademark Pease green shirt at the gate on the wooden bridge to Heron's Neck as he examines a list on his tablet.

My throat closes. I hope this is the only checkpoint I have to pass. Knowing what the Peases are like, I wouldn't put it past them to have their guests submit fingerprints in advance. "Sheila McAllister," I say with false confidence, adjusting my sunglasses so he doesn't catch a glimpse of my eyes, just in case. No doubt, my face is pasted on a Wanted poster in the guardhouse.

Fortunately, he's more interested in scrutinizing the list on his iPad. "Mc or Mac?"

"Mc!"

He makes a tick mark with his electronic pencil and goes, "Yup. Got it. Head down the road and take a left past the next gate and up the hill to the right." With a double tap on the hood of my car, he sends me on my way.

I am in.

I am also late. I don't care, though, because I've fulfilled the mission I set for myself months ago. By hook or by crook—but mostly by Sheila's guilt-induced invite—I am on Heron's Neck and have evidence to confront Bella with. After tonight, no one—not the Peases' powerful lawyer, not Bob, not Erik, not Sheila and Dave—will be able to accuse me of being delusional. On the last night she was seen alive, Kit was partying with Bella. I've got the photo to prove it.

At the next gate, I hold my breath, but another staff member waves me right through and directs me up the hill. This is almost too easy. The valet who awaits blinks at my rented Kia, but is well mannered enough not to scoff when he gets in and parks it between a red Tesla and a silver Maserati convertible.

Erik returned to Boston last night with the McAllisters. On the drive back to the rental from Provincetown, I finally let him have it. I told him I'd discovered that Dave and Sheila were the true renters. I didn't ask him to explain why he'd lied about the cottage. I didn't want to hear how worried he was about me and how desperate he was to get me into psychiatric care. Didn't want a lecture about how I should go back on medication or have to listen to his sob story about how he was standing by me, despite my mental illness.

What I said was this: "We are not going to talk. You are going to drop me off at the beach so I don't have to see the rest of you." I couldn't even conceive of Mabel's emotional state and how confused she must be after her mother's manipulations. "I'll give you guys the evening to pack up and you can leave me the rental car. You have forty-eight hours to clean your crap out of *my* apartment. When I come home Sunday night, I don't want to see or smell or detect any trace of you."

To give Erik his due, he didn't try to turn the tables and accuse me of forcing him to take action for the benefit of my mental health. He simply nodded and wiped away a tear.

Someday I'll figure out whether he loved me as a person or if I was a merely a fascinating lab rat. When I was Homeland's super-recognizing wunderkind, he was in my thrall. But he insisted on trying to turn me into a so-called normal person, wanted me to abandon what he downplayed as my "obsession" with Kit. He should have known that like many humans whose genius is concentrated in one particular area—painting, music, math—I am not, and will not, ever be "normal." I am a freak.

But that's for another day. For now, I'm here at Ground Zero about to take a wild leap into the unknown. If I'm successful, I will do what a slew of detectives, including Bob, have been unable to achieve. I'll find out once and for all what happened to my sister. If I fail, well, I'll probably be spending the night in jail, in Bob's custody.

Deep breath.

Before heading to the party, I smooth out the wrinkles in my understated floral dress, which is definitely not my usual style. Also not my usual style is my hair, which I clipped short in the bathroom mirror, à la Sheila, and dyed black with an application of Nice 'n Easy, about all I could find at the Stop & Shop. As for the sunglasses, I'm wearing those until the sun sets and I'm assured of more cover. Hopefully, that'll help me evade Pease security, which probably has committed my face to memory.

Unlit torches stand ready to light the way from the parking area around the house to the beach, a path marked with fresh seashells and lined with rows of planters bursting with blue, white, and pink hydrangeas, tiny candles tucked among the blooms.

Dogs run about, silky Irish setters, and handmade signs

meant to be kitschy direct guests toward the secluded cove. Wood smoke and merry chatter rise from the beach as I crest the dune. In the dimming light, I study each celebrity and high-profile guest, most of whom I gather are friends of Eve instead of the bride and groom.

The aging British pop star and his husband are easy to pick out in their matching seersucker suits. So are the multi-Oscar-winning actor with her trademark blond updo and her daughter, the Yale student-turned-runway model. There are at least two or maybe three designers, a couple of young influencers with seventy-thousand-dollar handbags slung over their arms. Also, there's the bestselling self-help author whose fine features and long legs earned her a modeling contract, too.

Less familiar are the hedge-fund managers—billionaire friends of Chet, I'm guessing. I find it predictable, yet no less disconcerting, that they're in deep discussions with the governor of a nearby state and a few members of the DC elite, including a US senator and a member of the diplomatic corps. Or, rather, the politicians are in deep discussions with them.

Finally, I focus on the family. Heather, the socialite wife of Jake, looks ridiculous in madras shorts and an untucked pink button-down from the Love & Pease site. An attempt to be casual that's failing miserably. Dani, in silk pantaloons and a plum silk halter that accentuates her bony shoulders, is standing off to the side nursing a drink and a cigarette with her wife, who I've read is the principal of an alternative school in Jamaica Plain. In her beige linen suit, she practically blends into the sandy scenery. Wonder if that's intentional.

There's no sign of Madeleine, the groom's mother. Too bad. I was looking forward to meeting the woman who abandoned her kids for a man who made a killing in energy drinks and owns a private island off Bali.

"Champagne?" A waiter, instantly by my side, displays a bubbling flute on a silver tray.

I decline just as the wedding party arrives from the rehearsal, the guests erupting in cheers.

First there is Eve Pease herself, much taller (and even thinner) than I'd expected. She is in a flowing gown in an exotic print, her hair loose and as wavy as a mermaid's, her feet bare. She looks just a few years older than the blond woman by her side, who I'm guessing is Megan, her daughter from a prior relationship. You hardly ever see her on the Love & Pease site. They pause at the top of the cedar stairs and wave to the crowd.

"Hey, who invited all of you?" Eve shouts to ripples of laughter. "You'd think we were throwing a wedding or something."

More laughter and more cheers. I have to say, I can see why Eve is known for putting on a helluva shindig.

She checks over her shoulder. "Whoops. Here they come. Let's give it up for the couple of the century!"

Just then, my phone dings. Shit. Pulling it out of my pocket to put it on silent, I see a text from Stan:

Erik called. We have to talk. ASAP. Don't do anything or go anywhere. CALL ME!!!!

Goddamn Erik. My father is *my* father, not his. Ugh. It's just like him to run to my dad saying I've lost it and am unstable. I waver about replying and decide I'll deal with him later. Then I put it on vibrate so there'll be no more distractions.

A hidden string quartet begins playing "Another One Bites the Dust" as Eve and Megan part for the bride and groom. Will is in a white shirt, open at the neck with the sleeves rolled up, and loose tan pants, as if this just another Friday night on Heron's Neck. I fight a swell of disgust, thinking about how he and Jake might have badgered Kit and turn my attention to his wife-to-be.

Bella leisurely descends the stairs with the grace of an elegant queen, each long, toned, tanned leg an execution in seduction. Her dress is a simple white strapless number, just in case it wasn't clear who the bride is. Her thick dark hair is tied casually to one side over a shoulder shimmering with what I have no doubt is Love & Pease body luminizer.

Concealed in the cocoon of the dunes, I watch the glowing couple welcome each guest with warm hugs and kisses on proffered cheeks. Will keeps his hand on the small of Bella's back and glances at her often as he leads her around the party, all the way to the dock and then back to where guests cluster at one of the bars gazing at the setting sun, a ball of fire at the water's edge sinking, sinking, sinking.

I find safety by insinuating myself into a cluster of chatting guests, nodding and smiling as if I'm part of their group.

Waiters light torches and from somewhere a band starts to play mellow jazz, just enough to add atmosphere until Will holds up his glass and the music stops. This is the part when he delivers his speech, thanking us all for making the effort to come to their intimate wedding, so grateful for the very, very special friends and family members in Eve's, I mean, *their* lives.

There is the requisite self-deprecating joke about how this is Bella's last chance to escape.

She turns her back to Will and pretends to tiptoe off.

"You're not getting away that easy." He hooks her waist and throws her back for a long dramatic kiss. More applause as she kicks up a playful heel.

We toast to Heron's Neck, where he and Bella along with,

awkwardly, *their* brothers and sister created so many wonderful memories setting sail or simply tossing the old pigskin. Guests shift their feet uncomfortably in the sand as Will leads a sentimental memorial to Chet, and then to Queenie Jarvis.

"To Chet! To Queenie!" we chime in unison, glad the sad part's over.

Waiters illuminate candles at tables situated on fresh bamboo decking under a series of connected pink-and-white-striped tents. Women reach for their shawls as Will says, "Before we enjoy this fabulous food, I want to express not only my gratitude for you all, but for my beautiful bride."

Bella tilts her head toward her future husband and smiles.

"You know, I hate to admit this publicly, but I thought she was such an annoying little kid when she came to live with us," he begins, flashing a devilish grin. "Always following me around, asking questions, getting me to build her sled runs and fix her bike, take her waterskiing. Total pain in the ass."

The crowd is hushed, pretending they're not sure where he's going with this.

"Then, years later, when I was at my lowest, I happened to visit Bella in Bogotá and saw that the nerdy bookworm duckling had morphed into a beautiful swan." He sniffs and blinks. "Sorry. I tend to get kind of emotional when I think of how this gorgeous woman saved me. God, I used to be *soooo* cocky."

"Used to be?" Jake teases. The guests roar at this comic relief.

Will raises a hand. "Fair enough. All I want to say is, Bella, I'm awed that you've agreed to be my wife." With that, he goes down on one knee and presses his lips to her fingers. "Don't ever give up on me, please."

I fight the urge to gag, but there's an *aww* from the crowd as

Bella rolls her eyes and motions for him to get up. Another kiss. More clapping and someone yells, "That's true love, folks!"

While the bride and groom split up to personally welcome each guest, I catch a glance of Megan and am intrigued by her tight frown and sad eyes. Hmm.

And then I freeze. Hovering by the rear entrance to the main tent, supervising her employees with quiet authority, in a tailored pantsuit of champagne crepe, her braids piled high in a sweeping bun, there's Serena.

Shit. Shit. Shit!

I am such a fool, such a naïve, stupid idiot, I think, ducking behind a tent pole. Here I was worried about being recognized by Will and Bella. It never occurred to me Serena would be the caterer. No wonder she was tightlipped about dishing on Jake; this dinner could make or break her business for the entire year. I remember Kit telling me once that Serena was so loyal to Eve because she cleared on average a ten percent profit on her functions.

Each custom-designed plate—Limoges porcelain hand-painted in Italy with whimsical patterns—cost a hundred dollars. (I've seen them on the L&P website.) And that's before you add so much as a dollop of Beluga caviar. Figure in the extensive raw bar, whole Maine lobsters, oysters *en croute,* and slices of delicate Napoleon tortes for dessert, not to mention bottomless glasses of Dom Pérignon, and this rehearsal dinner easily tops two hundred thousand.

So, yeah, if the same formula from eleven years ago applies, that's at least twenty grand in Serena's pocket—before tips. Repeat: *rehearsal dinner.*

"What's Austin up to these days?"

Suddenly, I hear Bella's voice right next to me and I have to resist the temptation to crane my neck around the pole and verify.

"Is he still out west?" She continues. "What everyone in their twenties should be doing, right? Such freedom."

At the sound of her voice, I'm transported eleven years back down a time warp. She's so close, I can get a whiff of her expensive-smelling perfume. The bangles on her wrist tinkle as she shakes hands, the chimes rattling my nerves.

This. Is. It.

How many nights have I lain awake fantasizing about this moment, imagining Bella's shock as I strip off her facade to reveal that she is far from being the gracious Cinderella known far and wide for uplifting the lives of young women. She's nothing but an envious killer.

This is when I finally get justice for Kit.

This is when I get answers.

Stepping forward, I wedge my way between a posh elderly couple congratulating Bella and thrust out the Polaroid. "Recognize anyone?"

Bella barely gives me a passing glance before focusing on the damaged photo of her, Ettie, and Kit and as reality sinks in, her megawatt smile flickers and dims. "Where did you get this?" she asks, not looking up.

"It's from a party at the cove you went to eleven years ago." I am shaking uncontrollably, despite having rehearsed this speech over and over in my head. "The night you told me you swore to take care of my sister—and didn't."

With that, Bella's head snaps up and she narrows her eyes, obviously stripping away my disguise. "Jane?"

"You could have at least told me what happened to her, what you did to her." To my horror and embarrassment, I find I'm sobbing, unable to control my emotions. I am a blubbering mess. "Instead, your fucking lawyer told me to stay clear of you or I'd be arrested. How could you? How could you leave me in the dark all this time? You killed my mother, you know. She died not knowing what happened to her daughter because of you!"

The elderly couple mutters and steps away, leaving me face-to-face with Bella. Over her shoulder, I can make out the profile of two beefy men in matching Pease green shirts, security guards.

"I wanted to tell you." Bella says this in a declarative sentence, steady, betraying not a hint of jitters. "But not here. You've got to go."

My heart starts pounding with a deafening thrum, and I feel as if I've jumped out of an airplane with a dysfunctional parachute.

"I'm not going anywhere," I manage to reply, wiping snot from my nose with the back of my hand. "Not before you tell me if she's dead or alive. I deserve that much." Then, from nowhere, my knees buckle and I realize I can't stand. I'm going to end up collapsed at her feet, begging, humiliated.

Bella reaches out and catches me before I fall, just as a man steps between us and she is pulled away.

A sudden ache shoots up my forearm and I look down to see a hand gripping my elbow. When I look up, I'm rocked, not only because the angry face leering at me belongs to Jake Pease, but because, much to my confusion, seeing him up close, I realize he wasn't the guy on the surfboard. I must have been hallucinating, after all.

"You're coming with me," he says.

I snap out of my daydream and resist. "No, I'm not. Let go!"

He doesn't. Instead, he pulls me toward one end of the tent. The crowd, which has been closing in on us claustrophobically, parts like the Red Sea, gaping as we pass. We exit through a makeshift cedar fence that hides the working end of the tent where the staff is huddled.

Jake is staring straight ahead, clutching me with such iron force that any attempt to wiggle free is futile. We head up a set of blond wooden stairs hidden by the dunes and a waiter carrying a covered tray steps aside to let us by. Now I get it—this is the servants' access constructed simply for this wedding. Talk about no expense spared.

"Are you taking me back to my car? Because it's over there." I incline my head to the far side of the house, but Jake doesn't care. He is pissed and annoyed, his jaw clenched. I wonder why he didn't let the guys in green haul me off, since that's their job.

"Honestly, you can let go. I'm not going to do anything. I said what I came here to say."

He loses it then, jerking my arm so violently my feet slip on the platform. "Listen, you little shit, you've ruined this event. I'm supposed to be toasting my brother and instead I have to deal with you."

"It's not my fault—"

"Didn't we make it clear that if you came anywhere near us, we'd take action?" he shouts. "Well, this is me, taking action."

I don't like the sound of that. "You're not calling the police, are you?"

"Not your stepdad, that's for sure. I'm talking about the Barnstable DA and the state police. *Real* cops with *real* power to lock up disturbed people like you."

He's right. The DA can do what Bob can't—get an emergency order to throw me in the psych ward until Monday. My stomach churns at the idea of being locked in there for seventy-two hours. "Please don't. I'll go. I promise."

"Too fucking late. You should have thought of that before you crashed the party."

"Whoa there, bro."

We both turn to find Dani, hands in pockets, smiling. "Chill out, J.D. She didn't do anything that bad."

"She harassed the bride. That's bad," Jake growls.

"Let security handle it then. You're the best man." Dani waves to the celebration below. "You've got more important things to do than handle her."

"Security is useless. Where the fuck were they an hour ago? How did they let her get in? When this is over, I swear, heads are gonna roll."

Including, I think, *Sheila's.*

"How about I take care of her?" Dani gives me a quick wink. "No one else can toast Will and Bella until you do and this is holding up the dinner. You know how Eve is, everything is perfectly timed to her schedule."

"You can't handle her. She's strong."

Dani makes a fist and flexes a bicep. "You bet I can. Anyway, where's she gonna go? It's an island. The gatehouse is on alert. Come on, J.D., go rejoin the party. Will's counting on you."

Jake wavers slightly, looking torn.

"Didn't you just say the police are on their way?" Dani prods him.

"Yeah, but they're coming from Barnstable. It'll be a while."

She encircles my wrist with her hand. "Don't waste another minute thinking about this," she says to him. "You've done your good deed for the night. Now go have fun."

Reluctantly, Jake drops my arm and I rub the spot where his thumb was digging into my flesh. "I never want to see you ever again," he says, shooting me with a finger. Then he heads down to the party, leaving Dani and me in the dusk.

"Well," she says, pulling me close. "We finally meet."

I have no idea how to respond. Is she friend or foe? She seems nice, different, not cut from the typical Pease thousand-thread-count cloth. But my adrenaline is surging and I'm emotionally spent and probably facing criminal charges so my judgment in this instance is not tip-top.

"Hey, buck up, champ. Everything is going to work out. All you have to do is give me the photo you showed Bella."

I could try feigning ignorance or claim Bella has it, but I'm not in a position to negotiate. Reaching into my pocket, I take out the Polaroid.

Dani doesn't even look at it before stuffing it in her own pants. Then she says, "You tell your dad you were coming out here?"

That throws me for a loop. "My dad?"

"Stepdad, whatever. The cop."

"He was my mother's boyfriend."

"Right. I mean, you didn't give him a heads-up, did you?" she asks, gripping my wrist tighter and it strikes me that maybe she's not so friendly after all.

For a second, I consider lying. I could tell her, yeah, I gave Bob firm instructions that if I didn't return by such and such a time, he should send out his "boys," as he likes to call his officers. But that's a nonstarter. If she knows how much Bob sucks up to the Peases, how much money they give the department, she'll know he'd never have allowed me out here.

"What do you think?" I say, cringing as her glossed lips thin into a smile and she whispers, "Good."

Bob told me time and time again to stay away from Heron's Neck and this wedding. Would I listen? Nope. And what did I get out of this adventure? Not much. A chance to confront Bella. That was fairly satisfying. But I am no closer to finding Kit than I was yesterday.

"Come on," Dani says, leading me up the stairs. "We've got to get you out of here before the DA arrives and makes this even more of a shit show."

I want to stop and ask her to explain, but she's hooked her arm in mine and now we're in a full march.

We turn right, away from the main house toward the bay and climb a knoll. "Last winter, after the Logan thing, I felt sure that you'd be back," Dani says as we make our way down the dune, our feet sliding in the deep sand. "The rest of the family thought I was overreacting, that Arthur's letter would put an end to it. But they know nothing about obsession. I do."

The music and chatter are now far behind us. We are at the remote end of the island where there is no ambient light, no sound other than the lapping waves and the wind through the marsh.

"Okay, but you have to admit I have a valid reason for being here," I say, trying one last time. "None of you will let me anywhere near Bella, but she's the only one who knows what happened to Kit that night. I just need her to tell me. In case you can't see for yourself, I'm beyond desperate."

"Sorry. Can't help you there." Placing her ear against the phone, she says, "How far are you? All right. She's here." Clicking off, Dani points to the bay where a boat has just turned its lights on and is puttering toward us. "Here's your ride."

There is the faint chugging of an outboard engine and a run-of-the-mill Boston Whaler emerges. It drops anchor and the captain jumps out, landing with a splash. As soon as I catch sight of the damn Mets cap, I go numb.

"No. Not him."

"Don't worry," Dani says, keeping tight hold of me as she leads me to the water. "Rick's gonna take care of you."

Rick. So that's the name of my stalker. "Can't you drop me off at my car?" I plead, resisting more as he gets closer.

"You'll never get off the island in that car, not now that Jake's alerted security," Dani says, handing me over to him like I'm a hostage, which I am. "She's all yours. Thanks."

He nods. "By the way, there's a boat coming over from Indigo."

Dani grimaces. "Cobb? What's he up to?"

Yes! Cobb Cooper coming to my rescue. Eleven years too late, but on time tonight.

"Who knows?" Rick says, squinting at the approaching vessel. "You want me to stick around in case he causes trouble?"

Dani bites her lip, mulling the offer. "Nah," she says after a moment of consideration. "More important to get her out of here before he shows up and tries to be a hero."

"You sure?" Rick zips open his jacket to reveal a nasty-looking gun that I recognize from my DHS experience as a Glock 19— lightweight, easy to conceal, and powerful. My blood turns to ice. Certainly, a weapon of that caliber isn't necessary to dissuade a practicing Buddhist.

"Put that away," she says with a slightly curled lip.

"Your call," Rick says, then zips up his jacket, turns, and leads me into the water, my sandals slipping off as we wade deeper.

"Where are we going?" I ask, as if I can't see the boat bobbing a few feet away.

"Shut up," Rick says. "And climb in."

I do as ordered, not seeing any other way out.

"Get down," he barks. "Way down."

I'm about to lower myself into the fishy smelling bottom of the boat when in my peripheral vision I catch sight of a bright orange flash followed by an ominous pop.

Rick and I both turn to see a figure in a dark hooded sweatshirt on the beach starting up the outboard engine on a dingy as the long, graceful form of Dani Pease staggers and tumbles backward into the gentle surf.

THIRTY-FOUR

BELLA

Bella surreptitiously checks her gold Bulgari as Will's college friend Dingo launches into yet another tale about the groom's debauchery, to the polite laughter of their guests. It has been exactly sixty-three minutes since Jake returned without Jane Ellison and there is still no sign of Dani.

She scans the crowd for Cecily, who appears just as concerned as Bella feels, head bent as she discreetly checks her phone a few tables away.

"Excuse me," she murmurs to Will, who's beaming at Dingo, so enthralled is he in the retelling of his youthful misadventures that he hardly notices when she pushes back her rattan chair and stands to leave. "I'll be right back."

She manages to catch Cecily's eye and nods to the bar at the far end of the expansive tent. Serena is already there, surveying not her bustling staff, but the darkened beach beyond. Bella takes heart in this. If Jane had managed to flee or somehow hurt Dani, Serena would have found out from Rick.

Still . . .

"Have you heard from her?" Cecily murmurs as the two women weave in and out of the tables of admiring guests.

Bella stops to shake a few hands. "No," she says, extricating herself from a particularly clingy influencer. "Have you?"

"No." Cecily blinks back tears. "I have a bad feeling."

Bella does, too, but doesn't share that with Cecily as she slides an arm around her shoulders and escorts her to the bar. It is blessedly free of guests for the moment, but that'll change as soon as Dingo's done with his endless, drunken monologue.

"We have a problem," Serena says with a sigh. "I've been trying to call Rick. No answer."

Cecily's face falls. "Dani's phone keeps going straight to voice mail."

"Maybe she can't get any bars . . ." Bella offers, but they all know that while Heron's Neck might be theoretically remote, its 5G cell service is crystal clear end to end.

"I have to find out if she's okay," Cecily says, stepping toward the beach.

But Serena's faster, jerking her back. "If you go down there now, you could fuck everything up. Dani knows what she's doing. Let her handle it."

"Then why isn't she answering her texts?" Cecily is close to hysterics. "I told her not to go alone. Why couldn't Jake go with her? Or Will?"

Serena and Bella don't even bother answering. Bella knows none of them should have let Dani go by herself. It was too dangerous, even if Rick was on his way.

"You don't suppose Durgan got wind of this, do you?" Cecily asks.

Bella locks eyes with Serena. This is exactly what they're worried about. For Bella, the prospect of Bob Durgan butting into the rescue of another Ellison sister is so close to a repeat performance from eleven summers ago she can barely stand it.

"Try Rick again," Bella suggests.

Serena punches a number and holds the phone to her ear, shaking her head.

Fuuuuck! Bella pounds the bar with one fist. They never should have let Dani talk them into giving Jane Sheila's invite. They should have insisted Sheila stay on the Cape and keep Jane in her crosshairs. Too bad that Sheila wasn't as much of a Pease-Phan as they'd thought she was when she accepted Dani's offer months ago to manage Jane Ellison. And at first she'd been doing such a super job, too, going above and beyond the assignment by applying her therapist training to successfully plumb Jane's memories of that night, extracting specifically what she did and didn't remember. She'd been exceeding their expectations—until Provincetown.

That's when Sheila, alone on an unfamiliar street corner, realized her passion for the Pease lifestyle had gotten out of control. She'd actually let a stranger parade her beloved daughter around town until Jane caught sight of her and behaved exactly as they'd hoped, screaming Mabel's name and causing a scene. Jane was supposed to be cornered by Rick, who would summon the police, claiming he had a mentally unstable woman in hand who'd attempted to nab a child. Instead, Sheila freaked out and insisted they pull the plug ASAP. So Rick had to trip Jane in the tower to buy everyone time to reunite mother and daughter.

Bella couldn't blame her, really. Using the little girl as a pawn to set up Jane as an attempted kidnapper was a bridge too far. Even if they'd convinced the child it was all a game, Sheila was so racked with guilt, she had to flee home immediately. Then, in an unexpected twist, the boyfriend left, too, leaving Jane on her own—and vulnerable.

Durgan will waste no time taking her out if we don't get her onto Heron's Neck was Dani's argument and, admittedly, a valid one. That creep had been tracking Jane's every move and would be well aware the others were gone. Serena and Dani were certain he'd attempt to get into the cottage either with or without Jane's permission. No one would have been the wiser when Jane was found days later, dead.

Or, like her sister, never found at all.

So Serena and Dani brainstormed a wild scheme—bring the fox into the henhouse by basically inviting Jane to the rehearsal dinner. Jane wouldn't be able to resist that. This way, they could avoid any unpleasantness at the actual wedding because Rick would already have escorted Jane off Heron's Neck and onto their private plane. She'd be somewhere over the Bermuda Triangle when Bella and Will were taking their vows.

Except now neither Dani nor Rick is answering. And it's not like Serena and Bella can call the local cops. They're screwed.

"Wait. I've got an idea," Bella says, scrolling through her contacts.

Serena squints at Bella's screen, dubious. "Are you serious?"

"It's our last option." Bella puts the phone to her ear and notices, too late, that Cecily is missing. In the night fog rolling off the bay, her faint form disappears into the mist as she heads down the beach.

"I should go after her," Serena says, turning to follow Dani's wife.

"Hello?" a man answers on the other end of the call.

Bella hesitates, searching for the right way to put this. "This is Bella. I think we may have run into a glitch. Rick met up with Dani and Jane, but now Rick and Dani aren't picking up. Maybe you should call your daughter and see if she's okay."

There is a pause and then Jane's father says, "I have a better idea. Just pray, darling, that we're not too late."

THIRTY-FIVE

JANE

I am huddled in the tight lounge of this fancy Boston Whaler, eyeing Rick, my stalker or my savior, I don't know which. He's at the helm, steering me over dark waters to who knows where while I am as unmoored as this boat. I am dizzy with fear, sick with dread, realizing this is my end, despite his assurances.

He claims he's taking me to Provincetown, where Bella has arranged for a private jet to fly me to New York, whereupon I will hop on a different private jet to Bogotá. There, I'll be sequestered and guarded for my own protection.

Protection against, of all people, my mother's boyfriend. Because Bob—the man I trust more than my real father—had, according to Rick, shot up my own sister with an overdose of heroin and left her to die on the beach. Supposedly, he did this to cover up his own, decades-long oversight of, and profit from, the Cape's illegal drug trade.

Bullshit.

None of this seems even remotely plausible. Bob is Mr. Law &

Order. He loved Kit as if she were his own daughter. He literally exhausted himself during the investigation into her disappearance until he had to be hospitalized. He despises the scourge of illegal drugs that destroyed our family and so many others. He's devoted his career to keeping opiates out of Shoreham and raising awareness about the signs of addiction. There is no way he's, what, a *drug kingpin*? Give me a break.

Then again, I never expected to witness Cobb Cooper pull out a gun and pump a bullet into Dani Pease. *Cobb.* I can't get over it. The supposed Buddhist, leader of a peaceful retreat for New Age seekers, the guy who, for a hopeful second there, I thought had come to rescue me actually committed cold-blooded murder like a gangster.

I grip the railing as the boat bounces so high, I actually fly off the seat.

"Sorry about that chop. We've hit the Billingsgate Shoal," Rick says, cutting the engine to a troll. "We'll have to take it slow through here. You doing okay?"

But before I can answer there is a loud *pop* and at the exact same moment Rick flings out both his arms as his body flies backward violently, landing with a thud so hard, the boat rocks. I hear a scream and realize with horror it's coming from me.

"Oh my god!" I cry, going to my knees, shaking this stranger in mad desperation. It's no good. There is no life, just sticky warm blood trickling from the small hole shot through his Mets cap onto my bare, wet skin. I fight back a wave of nausea at the sight of his white eyes rolled back in his skull.

What happened? The question is ridiculous, I think, the *putt-putt-putt* of another boat's engine approaching us stealthily. I am trapped. *I am next.* For a brief second, I consider jumping overboard and taking my chances. But that's too crazy, even for a strong swimmer like me. The shoal will grind my bones to chum, food for the sharks.

"Jane?"

Bob's shout in his familiar Boston accent spikes a fresh burst of adrenaline, sending my mind racing. Maybe he really is here to save me, but what if what Rick said is true? What if he killed Kit and is about to do the same to me?

No matter what, I decide, taking deep breaths, I have to act as if he's my savior. That's the only chance of survival.

"Jane?" he calls again. He kills the engine, the wake of his boat rocking Rick's. All I can hear is the water splashing against the gunnels.

Inhaling a deep breath, I reply with a breathy, "Help!"

Bob pulls up alongside Rick's boat and shines a bright light into my eyes. "Oh, thank god you're safe. Guess I got that suma-bitch before he got you," he says, crossing himself. "You okay, kid?"

"Bob?" I try standing and wobble, clutching the railing for support as I shield my eyes from the light's harshness. "Is that really you?"

"I'm here." *Hee-yah.* "Sorry you had to be part of that, but I'm damn relieved to see my sniper skills are still up to snuff. Had to take a chance and pray you didn't get hit."

The light sweeps across the mess at my feet. It's even worse than I imagined. The blood. There's so much of it everywhere. Suddenly, I burst into tears.

"Hey, hey, hey. You're with me now. I gotcha," Bob says, holding out his hand. "Come on. Just step onto the ladder. You know how."

What choice do I have but to do as he orders? I'm stuck. So I put my foot on the stern and hoist myself off Rick's boat into

Bob's, the phone in my dress pocket vibrating right when I get in. *Shit.*

Bob wraps a blanket around my shoulders. I'm shivering so hard my teeth are chattering. "Jesus, Jane. I told you not to go out there to Heron's Neck. I *told* you. Who knows what he would have done to you if I hadn't shot the bastard? I hate to think."

"How . . . how . . . did . . . you . . . find . . . me?"

"Cobb phoned. Said he saw you on the beach with Dani and this guy in the boat. Said the asshole shot her and took off with you."

This is either Cobb's lie or Bob's. I say nothing.

"Is that what happened?" Bob is peering at me closely, checking for tells to see if I'll answer truthfully. That's when I notice he's not in uniform, not even close. He's in all black. Black jeans, black sweatshirt, and knit watch cap. This could be his version of undercover, but I don't think so.

"Is Dani okay?" I ask, ignoring his question.

Bob hesitates a minute too long. "Cobb called 9–1–1 and is staying with her until the paramedics get there. That's all I know."

And that's when I realize the cold, bleak truth. Rick was right—Bob murdered my sister.

He killed her so she wouldn't reveal that he had the monopoly on the Cape heroin. Nineteen-year-old Kit. He snuffed her out just as she was rebuilding her life. The girl he claimed to love as if she'd been his own daughter.

Which means I don't stand a chance.

"Jane?" he prods. "Tell me. Did that asshole shoot Dani Pease?"

"I . . . I . . . think so," I say, moving slightly so I'm sitting on my phone, which keeps vibrating. Who in the hell is trying to contact me. Erik? "I don't know. I . . . I think I'm in shock. I can't seem to remember anything."

"You? You remember everything." He crouches closer. So close, I can smell the coffee he drinks like water, the oily stench of gasoline on his hands. "Try."

My mouth goes dry as I mentally search for details that'll throw him off scent, wishing my damn phone would stay silent. "Honestly, um, the last I recall was being on the beach with Dani and her saying all kind of threatening things."

"Like what?"

His persistence is a cop thing, grilling me until my voice falters or my tone drops, something that indicates I'm not telling the truth. Girding myself as best I can, I reply levelly, "She said the Peases had ways of taking care of people like me." And then I remember his admonition back when I was in Somerville, when he was trying to talk me out of coming here for my safety when actually he was concerned about his own ass. "Just like you said, Bob. The Peases, they can get away with . . . *anything*."

The loaded word hangs there in the darkness, Bob's boat bobbing on the shoal. Finally, he says, "Let's get you back to the station and have you looked at. We'll take care of that dead dickhead later. Your well-being is my priority right now." He goes back to the helm and restarts the engine.

Instinctively, I sense he's reached a resolution—and it's not in my favor.

I wish I'd had the wherewithal to grab Rick's gun when I had the chance. Not that I'd have been able to use it. I'm dying to check my phone, but I don't dare.

It doesn't take long for the lights of Shoreham to reappear and my spirits lift. Perhaps, I think, I *hope*, he bought my story. After all, I told him I saw Dani shot, but I didn't see who shot her. There's really no reason to kill me, too. *Is there?*

Bob cuts the engine to a wake and we drift into the cove.

Unlike festive Heron's Neck across the inlet, Indigo is pitch-black. I wonder if the devotees have turned in early, then I realize, no, the Peases probably insisted the camp be vacated for the wedding weekend.

"You mind wading in?" Bob asks, lowering the anchor. "I'm gonna radio the Coast Guard and let them know about the scene back there."

Surreptitiously, I remove my phone and hold it to my chest so it doesn't get damaged by the salt water as I trudge to shore. It's high tide and the grass, where the eels and crabs hide out, is mostly hidden. With only a waning moon for illumination, I have to rely on a vague memory of the sandy areas.

When I arrive on dry land at last, I'm surprised to see Bob's still on the boat, deep in conversation on his cell. He's shaking a fist, like he's angry. This is my chance to run.

And then my phone vibrates. I take a peek and my heart sinks as I see it's Stan, probably calling with urgent news about a new lamb. I'm about to decline, when it hits me he could me get out of this. He could call the DA, not the local cops, and make sure someone gets here pronto. Didn't Jake say the DA was on his way to Heron's Neck?

I don't even say hello. "Dad," I hiss, "you have to help me . . ."

"Jane?" a woman says.

There's a splash in the distance that barely registers, all sound being drowned out by this voice of my dreams—and my nightmares. *No, this can't be,* I think, my heart fluttering. This is shock. *This is trauma.*

"This is Kit," she says. And even from thousands of miles away, I can tell she's crying. "Bella called us. Are you all right?"

I can't speak. For eleven years, all I've wanted is to talk to my sister and here I can't say a word. The walls of my vision tunnel.

I need to run, but I can't move. My soul feels separated from my body. "No," I finally manage. "I'm not all right. Bob . . ."

"Don't trust him," Kit interrupts. "If he's there, get the hell away from him as fast as you can."

The splash. It must have been Bob. He's coming for me. "We're at Pekky. Call the DA . . ."

"What's this?"

The phone is ripped from my grasp in one swift move. Bob flings it into the bay with a loud *plop* as he simultaneously reaches out and grabs my neck, pressing down hard on my carotids. I can't breathe, my arms windmilling in a futile effort to fight him off.

Bob, I remember vaguely, has a black belt in karate. I have witnessed him split cinderblocks. So when he kicks my legs out from under me, I go down like a bag of concrete, the back of my skull hitting the beach so hard, my ears ring.

Everything is happening so fast, there is no room for comprehension. He straddles me, his weight pinning me into the sand, his face hidden in the darkness. He is silent aside from a command he directs at someone rushing out from the woods donned in the same black hoodie I saw moments earlier when he shot Dani.

Cobb.

"Now," Bob says, stretching out my bare arm.

This is what they did to Kit, I think, terrified. *Now they're doing it to me.*

"Why?" I croak, thinking of Kit and my father climbing the walls, unable to save me from nine thousand miles away. *"Why?"*

Bob holds up the needle, its sharp tip glinting in the starlight, and says only, "I told you to stay away from them. I told you so many times. This is your own damn fault. Now look what you've gone and made me do."

I try twisting out from under him, but he's too strong and I watch helplessly as Cobb ties a rubber tourniquet around my arm, the rubber digging into my flesh.

"Don't! I won't tell anyone. I promise!" I plead. "Cobb, don't let him."

But Cobb merely steps back as Bob lowers the needle into my bulging vein, aiming the tip toward my heart for maximum dosage. I wince as the sharp point pierces my skin and fire shoots up my vein, the drug speeding through the massive network of veins and arteries and heart until it reaches its destiny, my precious brain.

"Now you and your sister can be together forever. Isn't that what you wanted?" Those are his parting words as he releases the tourniquet, right before a massive crash comes from the under-brush and we are bathed in painfully bright light.

Suddenly, there's the sound of footsteps kicking up sand, fol-lowed by a thud of something or someone hitting the ground. Ra-dios crackle. There are shouts for EMTs. Cobb whimpers. I try sitting up, but already I'm too dizzy.

"NARCAN!" yells an EMT, bending over me so close, her nose is almost touching mine. "What's your name?" she shouts.

I'm fading fast, but I remember enough from my lifesaving that I know I must answer. "Jane."

"Okay, Jane. This is gonna sting a bit." She pushes back my head and the next thing I know, an icy cold chemical is searing the interior of my nostril, making me gag and cough. My cheek smarts and I realize it's from being slapped.

"Stay with me!" the EMT barks before calling for another dose. "Come on, Jane. Fight through it. Come on." *Slap. Slap.*

Another searing inhalation of freezing cold chemical. Again, it scorches my nose and throat, springing hot tears to my eyes. Part of me feels as though I'm being cruelly abused. The other part is being pulled down into a dark, welcoming bliss.

"Don't give up," the EMT shouts, shaking my shoulders so roughly, I'm getting whiplash. "Tell me. Speak. I wanna hear ya talk, Jane. Tell me what you're fighting for. Tell me why you wanna live."

And then, spitting and crying, clutching her sleeve, I manage all my numbed mouth can form before I let the abyss swallow me whole.

"My sister. I want to see my sister."

THIRTY-SIX

JANE

Robert S. Durgan was arrested that night by the Barnstable County DA on a single charge of attempted murder and another of simple assault for sticking a needle in my arm against my will. More charges were to follow, but that was enough to hold my mother's former boyfriend for failure to post a one-million-dollar bond while the DA investigated other serious allegations including attempting to kill my sister and . . . worse.

For fifteen years, at least, Bob oversaw an operation that controlled the distribution of all the heroin, oxy, coke, fentanyl, LSD, Xanax, and other drugs coming into Shoreham. While Shoreham is, granted, a small town, it is also a community frequented by a steady flow of summer tourists and college kids, a ready market for his products. But even worse in my mind is that he had no problem sickening the locals, his neighbors, and their susceptible kids.

Cobb was his boy. It was common knowledge, apparently, that any drug could be had at Indigo, often procured by the very patrons seeking shortcuts to peace and tranquility. By running periodic drug sweeps, Bob was able to eliminate the competition and maintain a hold on his monopoly. That's how he was able to afford the $250,000 SeaVee that, contrary to his claim, he definitely did not pick up for a song at a federal auction.

Which is where Kit came in. She spent the summer before she disappeared tormented by inside information she'd gleaned from Cobb that Bob was his supplier. Sober and determined to stay so, she was furious that the creep responsible for ruining her life was sleeping with our mother and eating at our breakfast table. She decided to confront him in person, a meeting that did not go well. Bob issued various threats while demeaning her as a non-credible junkie no one would believe.

Determined to get justice, Kit asked Bella and Ettie at the bonfire if one of them could drive her to Barnstable the upcoming Monday on the pretense of taking her to college. She'd scheduled an early-morning appointment with the DA. After she told him all she knew, she planned to head straight to Amherst so she wouldn't have to face Bob.

Kit was never able to keep that appointment; Bob got to her first.

Fortunately, Bella left the bonfire and went straight to Chet, who insisted they get Kit and take her to Heron's Neck for her own safety until that Monday. That's how I happened to run into him on the beach and why Chet was trying to shoo me away.

But they were too late. Bob had already injected Kit with heroin and left her to die. When Bella finally found her, she was halfway dead. Luckily, a family friend and superb Boston physician staying in one of the Peases' guest houses that weekend was able to save her life.

Queenie assumed the worst when she saw Bella take the boat out and return smeared with blood. In actuality, Bella was taking the dinghy out so she could plant Kit's Serendipity Seafood T-shirt that she'd stained with bloody fish guts from Jake's chum bucket. But there was no way to explain that to Queenie without divulging the truth about Kit.

In the wee hours of that morning, while Kit slept off the near overdose, Bella, Chet, and Arthur Whitaker plotted the best course of action. Chet insisted Bob be arrested immediately; Arthur noted it wasn't that easy. Kit was a confirmed addict with a criminal history. Bob was a decorated cop. No one witnessed Bob shooting up Kit with heroin, so it would be her word against his. All Bob had to say was that Kit was a rebellious teenager who resented the strict curfews and house rules he'd imposed. With no credible witnesses or evidence, Arthur was certain no charges would be filed.

And then where would we be? Because that was Kit's concern— my mother and me. Having barely survived Bob's attempt to take her life, Kit was convinced he would do the same to anyone else who dared expose him. She refused to return home and live under the same roof as her would-be murderer. There had to be another solution. Chet suggested our father.

Initially, Kit's stay in New Zealand was to be temporary. Having used his impressive connections to secure her a passport, Chet arranged for a private plane to take her to Christchurch, where there was no doubt she'd be safe from Bob's revenge. After three years there, homesick and missing her mother, on a whim Kit called Mom and told her everything.

We're still not entirely sure about the order of events that followed this earth-shattering phone call. According to Kit, Mom was at first overjoyed, then shocked, and then homicidal herself. Ignoring Kit's frantic protests, she vowed to have it out with her boyfriend then and there.

Unfortunately, along the way to the police station, Mom

slipped "by accident" on a sheet of ice, hit her head, and died. The autopsy was performed by a medical examiner who was not only a fishing buddy of Bob's, but also, rumor has it, a frequent customer. Did he cover up a murder? We might never know since the ME died of an overdose a few months later. Whether his death was a homicide, too, is also part of the DA's investigation.

After that, Kit refused to take any chances. If Bob murdered Mom, then I was next on the list. I'd face the same consequences if Kit told me she was alive. As long as Bob was a threat, I must never know what happened that night on the beach of Camp Pequabuck, Kit insisted, despite agonizing over my subsequent mental breakdown due, in large part, to losing her and our mother.

And then I recognized Bella Valencia in Logan and everyone tried to keep me away from the truth. Stan told me not to go to Shoreham. Arthur sent threatening letters. Bella refused to answer my inquiries. Bob claimed he'd already investigated Bella and found she had an alibi. When I rented the cottage anyway, he sent me weird texts about flowers on my mother's grave, having watched me visit the cemetery that night from his own office window, on the hope the mysterious messages would scare me away.

Still, I persisted.

Realizing I was determined to have a showdown, Dani and Serena, Bella's only confidantes, came up with the idea of setting a trap, which I sashayed into readily. The plan was straight from the playbook Chet had used with Kit—get me on a private flight and out of the country. Bella offered her place in Bogotá as a short-term solution I could use while she and Will were on their month-long honeymoon in Greece.

But no one counted on Cobb. After our conversation at Indigo, in which he fabricated the story about Kit being pressured to buy drugs for Jake or Will Pease, he sensed, rightly, my skepticism.

He called Bob, who had me picked up by his two detectives and brought to the police station the following morning. According to Cobb's confession, after our meeting over bad coffee, Bob concluded I was a "liability" and needed to be "removed."

On the evening of the wedding, Cobb's assignment was to serve as lookout. When he saw Dani and me on the bluff, he called Bob, who told him to get over to Heron's Neck ASAP and not let me leave the beach until he arrived. Theoretically, Cobb could have played my savior by offering to take me off Dani's hands. Except Cobb got there after I was already on Rick's boat and Dani, being Dani, couldn't resist making a crack to Cobb about how she looked forward to the day when his white male privilege wouldn't be enough to keep him out of prison.

Cobb flipped out and shot her. Fortunately, he's a crappy shot and the bullet to her knee, while excruciating, was not life-threatening, not that she was about to let him know that. She collapsed into the surf and he, panicked by what he'd done, took off. Cecily was hysterical when she found her wife bleeding on the beach, moaning in agony. So that was pretty much that for the night's festivities.

From a remote feed in the hospital, Dani and Cecily watched Bella and Will exchange vows as scheduled, Eve adamant that not Queenie's apparently natural death nor my near murder nor Dani's surgery would stand in the way of her latest Love & Pease campaign.

Whether Bella and Will stay married is up to them. I do know they've returned to Bogotá and, according to what I've read on Twitter, Eve's daughter, Megan, and one of Will's ushers, a guy who goes by "Dingo," are officially an item. The same article noted Megan had inherited the massive fortune belonging to her godmother, Queenie, so there's that.

Erik and I are no longer. He did as I asked and cleaned out the apartment. So he wasn't there when I got out of the hospital, having spent the night at Bella's insistence. Every once in a while he texts me about getting together for coffee, but I don't have the time. I'm too busy packing and making arrangements for my big move.

EPILOGUE

*P*lease *power down all electronic devices*, the flight attendant informs us as we taxi toward the runway. *Put up your tray tables
and seatbacks in preparation for takeoff.*

This is it. Finally. My pulse dances as the jet pulls away from
the gate. In eighteen hours, give or take, we will be touching down
in Christchurch. Waiting for me there will be Stan and my sister
and her husband, Dylan, and their daughter, Lily, the little minx
who frequently appears in our father's endless sheep photos.

I haven't quite acclimated to the news that Kit is married and
a mother, though I mean, she's in her thirties, so that makes sense.
Or that she has a house and raises chickens, teaches high school
algebra, and has learned to both knit and ride a motorcycle. I can't
believe I have a whole family waiting for me a half a world away,
that they've been there all along. If only I'd accepted my father's
numerous invitations to visit sooner . . .

No. No regrets. The fact of the matter is, we're meeting now
and this wouldn't be happening if I hadn't stuck by my guns that
Bella Valencia was the girl I recognized on the beach with Kit.

Turning off my phone because we're taking off, I text her,
my thumbs shaking as I tap out the letters. If I crash, just know I
love you!

There is the pause of three dots and then an image emerges. It's an old picture of Kit and me, arms around each other, standing on the shoreline of a deserted Nauset Light Beach, the brisk autumn wind whipping our hair in crazy directions.

We're in sweatshirts and jeans rolled up past our ankles. I vaguely remember Mom taking this while we went for a Sunday stroll, just the three of us. It was the last photo taken before Kit broke her leg on the uneven bars and everything went downhill.

I remember, I text.

Natch, Kit replies. It's impossible for you to forget.

ACKNOWLEDGMENTS

A big thank you goes out to my editor, Emily Griffin, whose early enthusiasm, intelligence, keen insight, and gentle recommendations turned an umpteenth draft into a polished product fit for public consumption. I have had many wonderful editors over the years, but your detailed attention—from acquisition to acknowledgments–is unprecedented. I am so fortunate to have you guiding the way.

Along the same lines, I am deeply grateful for my agent, Zoe Sandler at ICM, another bright, enthusiastic light to illuminate the murky world of publishing. Thank you, Zoe, for being such a positive force and for being brilliant. This book never would have had a chance had it not been for your smart recommendations.

As for the idea behind *Do I Know You?*, I must thank the unfailingly polite security detail at Heathrow Airport who introduced me to the concept of super recognizers during my brief detention as a "flagged" passenger in 2003. There are some advantages to being on the terrorist watch list after all, apparently. Patrick Radden Keefe's article on London's use of super recognizers in the August 22, 2016 issue of *The New Yorker* was a font of information, as was Caroline Williams's September 12, 2012 article in *New Scientist* and Alex Moshakis's piece in the November 11, 2018 issue of *The Guardian*. All were so helpful.

Unfortunately, the fictionalized account of Kit Ellison's descent into drug addiction is all too real for so many suffering families. New England has been particularly hard hit by the opioid crisis, with Massachusetts reporting a staggering number of deaths. Though prescriptions for pharmaceutical opioids have decreased in recent years, back when Kit was a teenager, doctors routinely prescribed these highly addictive drugs as postsurgical painkillers. Once the prescriptions expired, accidental addicts, like Kit, were forced to alleviate their withdrawal symptoms with illegal fentanyl, thereby perpetuating a cruel cycle.

As someone who personally has lost a brother to drug addiction, my heart goes out to parents, siblings, friends, and spouses who've spent sleepless nights and restless days wondering if their loved ones were clean, using, or . . . worse. Anyone can fall prey to addiction. *Anyone.* The good news is that as the stigma is lifted and research improves, the chances for full recovery are better than ever. You can find resources for those struggling with addiction and their loved ones on my website: sarahstrohmeyer.com.

A big shout out to the Select Board of Middlesex, Vermont, who proposed the four-day work schedule so I could keep writing. To Dorinda, Maryke, Amy, and fabulous photographer Dave Smith, thank you for putting up with my wacky schedule. Nothing better to keep the demons from gnawing at a writer's confidence than a steady diet of land records, elections, taxes, and dog licenses.

Finally, a warm hug to my supportive family. Thank you, Anna, for reading the early drafts, making suggestions, and just basically feeding my true crime cravings. Thanks, Sam, for making me laugh (and being an awesome role model), and thank you, Charlie, for keeping the ship afloat while the first mate drifted off to the Land of Counterpane, yet again.

ABOUT THE AUTHOR

S arah Strohmeyer is the award-winning, nationally bestselling author of eighteen novels for adults and young adults, including the Bubbles Yablonsky mystery series and *The Cinderella Pact*, which became the Lifetime movie *Lying to Be Perfect*. A former newspaper reporter, she is the elected town clerk of Middlesex, Vermont.